LITTLE SISTERS

OF

WAR

Harvey Tate

This is a work of fiction. Except where noted with historical persons or events, the names, characters, locales, and situations are products of the author's imagination and/or are used fictitiously.

Copyright 2011 Harvey Tate

Dedicated to

Sisters

The Bird and the Bean –

In memory of Sarah Lois

and Mary Jean –

Little Sisters

Present Day

Funny how things turn out, when you're young, you misuse life wondering and fretting about what might be coming. Later you realize 'what might' is rarely worth your time. One day you are looking for fashionable spiked heels and the next, comfortable support hose.

I can't complain. My two boys keep me so busy that time rockets by. The boys have their own world. They see the future as their own. What keeps me grounded is my daughter, Madeline, a five year old red-headed ginger devil. She's full of love and unrestrained energy. Maddie, well she has promise beyond our dreams. I hope someday, if she has need of it, she'll find a special group like I did back in the day, friends who will shape her life.

These days I don't spend a lot of time reflecting on the past. When I do think about the long ago, it's often a recollection of a cliche Coach stuck in my head; a comment made on some long-ago, late-night trip through the Shenandoah. I still hear her voice. *"How long you live is calculated in time; your friends are the measure of your existence."*

I'll never forget her. I can still see her delicately lined face just like I can remember looking at the moon over the Blue Ridge. Those old mountains have an undeniable strength. So did Coach.

In my younger days I kept our history, told the legend. I focused on the unique days, points in life where things are more obvious, more personal, and more fundamental. Still, no one stays young forever.

I can remember when my point of view changed, when I began to see another story. First Zack Junior came into our world, then Andrew, and finally Maddie, they made me into a mother. My universe shifted, but there were still those bygone years of understanding within me. I didn't realize it when I lived it, but in retrospect, I can easily identify that time. It stood as a marker, a beginning; a year which hardened my character, and measured my spirit, the year of the Little Sisters of War.

Why the current interest? Well, soon I am going to see most of those sisters again. When we said our goodbyes I remember thinking I would always be in touch with them. It never occurred to me that even the closest teammates eventually move on, and God has her own plan.

I just wish Taylor would hurry and get here, I'm anxious to get going. It'll be an emotional roller-coaster ride of a trip to old Spotswood College. A journey back in time...I'm ready to re-live the story of the Big Blue Stars.

How did it all come about? Where did it begin? Maybe it began with Catbird and her grandmother's dream.

Catbird

It occurred as a whisper. A modern plea aimed at ancient spirits. "If I can just get by the door without disturbing her, Great Spirit, give me some freaking stealth."

Caitlyn placed her feet carefully, stepping over boards likely to squeak. The biggest challenge would be the rickety hallway table, with her mother's favorite Delft jar on top. It lay in wait, ready to rattle at a careless misstep from a heavy foot. Not that she was big, after all her friends were always telling her she looked like a stick of a thing—tall and thin, although heavier than most people imagined. Her body contained pure muscle from years of hard running and exercise.

She let out a muffled sigh exposing her tension. She almost made had it made. Three more steps. She paused, and then it happened, a slight disturbance of air molecules as old wood compressed and released...creak! She'd been busted by a complaining board. She mumbled to herself, "so much for my Native American guile."

"Hee—Hee—Heeee! Come here, Catbird." A sing-song cackle floated from the recesses of the guest bedroom. An old woman's voice, a honeyed declaration reached out, immobilizing her. The voice belonged to Granny, a force of nature to be reckoned with.

"Come on, Catbird, your little sister summoned a dream, we need to talk."

"Catbird, my ass," suddenly younger, less grown-up, she grumbled silently under her breath, then shrugged; an invitation from Granny led to a good two hour visit.

Great-grandmother reinforced the summons by appearing in the doorway, all five-foot-two, compressed by age into a wrinkled four-foot something. She motioned in a windmill fashion. She seemed always in a hurry, never wasting any precious seconds of her ninety-one years.

Caitlyn loved this irascible old woman, a far cry from their beginning when Mom told her great-grandmother would be coming to live with them. "A clan mother, you will treat her properly."

The image of a doddering old Indian woman stuck in her head. At first, it became too much for her teenage sensibilities. She'd pouted. Their first meeting did not improve her mood.

She saw a shrunken and bespectacled woman, with Rhinestone glasses hanging precariously from her nose.

In no time at all, the old woman won her great-granddaughter's heart. They spent hour after hour together, and she listened intently to Granny's stories. The old woman was gifted at telling tales, and really excelled at gossip. They spent time laughing and talking about the soap operas they both watched. She remembered hurrying home from school on days she wasn't practicing for some sport, just so they could watch TV together.

She could discuss anything with Granny, from boys to politics. The first time she heard her great-grandmother fantasizing about one of the men on her favorite soap opera, she almost choked. "Catbird, that man is juicy; he could put his shoes under my bed anytime."

Catbird became her totem name, one revealed to Granny in a dream. She liked it so much she combined it with her lacrosse uniform number, and used it as her Internet name. They both surfed the net; Caitlyn became "Catbird24;" Great-Grandmother became Oldbird01. In no time at all Oldbird01 logged on Facebook and Twitter.

Every aspect of the young girl's life came under her grandmother's scrutiny.
Today things would have to be put on hold, important things. Last night, she'd made a decision about college. This morning, she awakened with a heightened sense of urgency. She felt older, more mature, needing to get things organized. No time to dillydally...

"Catbird, come sit in council with us, we need another medicine woman to make sense of Little Mouse's vision."

9

Caitlyn acquiesced, smiling weakly as she entered. There sat her little sister, Sarah, at the feet of the clan mother, obviously enchanted. They sat together drinking tea and eating sacred Double Stuff Oreo's.

"Granny, Mom told you Sarah isn't allowed to have any caffeine."

The old woman patted the bed. "Sit, Catbird, join us."

In spite of her teenage angst she found it amusing that the odors and sights she once dreaded in the room overwhelmed and connected her to a long-lost heritage. It gave her a sense of pride and understanding, and mostly it gave her a healthy respect for the old woman.

"Did I tell you that the French watched the Haudenosaunee play your game and called it, La Croix, the cross ... your game, Catbird, you call it, lacrosse."

She sighed, "Many times, Granny."

"Did I tell you that we were a nation of fierce warriors absorbing our enemies into the confederation? We were, and still are a nation controlled by women. A man, when he marries, joins his wife's family. A clan mother controls the governing council."

"That's the way it should be, Granny--women in charge." The old woman held up her hands, beads rattling and spoke firmly. "It is time to get serious. Yes, we believe dreams reveal the soul, contacting the sacred power by gathering in a communal dream sharing. Little Mouse has helped me dream, it tells me you will meet many women on a great meadow. One is a chief who will shape your heart; another eagle warrior will lead you to your destiny. The warrior and the women will teach you the spirit of oneness with the Creator. You must be patient. Your time will come. The path will be revealed."

"Is this like the time you predicted snow on my birthday?"

"Lousy internet weather site, the satellite picture came in fuzzy. I should have listened to the hunk on Channel 13."

Sarah, or Little Mouse, interrupted, obviously bored. "Tell me about the no-face doll, and the legend of The Three Sisters, please?"

"Catbird will tell you. Pass me the plate of the magical cookies"

Caitlyn grimaced. She wrinkled her nose at the old lady's self-satisfied look, hiding behind a smile.

"There were three sisters, Corn, Beans, and Squash...."

Lost in the moment the old medicine woman shut her eyes and revisited the dream she'd seen for her Catbird...

The moonlight shimmered through the branches of The Great Tree of Peace and the tall pines. Below, on the grassy plain, the grasses danced with the wind, creating a picture of the Creator's valley....

Skenandoa-the-deer could not able to keep the feeling of her life force from pounding in her chest. She'd been chosen above the strongest men in her clan to entertain the Creator tomorrow. She looked through the moonlight at the valley. She felt staggered by the bounty below. She asked for the consideration of the Great Spirit. The Medicine people foretold that her clan, The Eagle, would summon the Creator to this valley tomorrow. There, he would watch the Eagle and the Turtle on the plain, and the game would be played for his amusement.

The Haudenosaunee would settle their tribal dispute as they had in this manner for as long as The Great Tree of Peace had been on the earth, playing Tewaarathon, the Creator's game. Her heart pounded with excitement. Tomorrow it might be her. Yesterday, the strength and skill of the men brought the ball to within 1000 steps of the scoring poles.

Tomorrow, she must defy pain or fatigue, and hold the ball while running like the wind, a gift from the Great Spirit. She must endure the striking blows of the Turtle clan and laugh at their futility. All would rejoice when she touched the ball of deer skins over the line of the scoring pole. If the Creator does not see the joy in their faces, He will be bored with the game.

She rested on the netted racquet crafted by her father; The Earth Mother gave the wood her strength. Her mother laced the bent wood with leather strings she had softened with her teeth. She prayed that if she were struck down tomorrow, the Creator would be kind and regard her effort as joyful. If the Creator took her, she knew she would play on with the lost warriors.

A breeze gently shook the tree limbs above her head, and the beauty of the great meadow below. In the trees above, a mockingbird sent a song of joy toward the sky. As he sang, a single feather floated to the earth, a good omen. Tomorrow, at sunrise, she would join with her people and run the last distance until she could no longer run. She hoped for the strength of the bear, the speed of the deer; the ability to take blows like the turtle, and the wisdom of the eagle. Unless life was beaten from her body, she would not fail.

Kate

"Oh God, have mercy!" She rolled over and stretched out her arm, too bleary-eyed to find the high-pitched buzz. "Oh crud, I hate waking up in the dark. I hate clocks." Reluctantly she peeked out from under multi-layers of blankets, laboring to open her left eye and let her right eye get a second more sleep. She found the offending device, blinking and buzzing no more than three feet away. Annoying red numbers flashed, 5:15...blink, 5:15...blink, finally—5:16...blink.

With single-minded malice, she flung away the down comforter, leaned over and hammered the clock with a well-aimed fist, catching it squarely. "Shut up!" Wal-Mart's finest buzzed off in another direction, landing face down. Plastic pieces scattered. With a snarling half-smile she had her first cogent thought. *That'll stop the little blinking bastard.*

She stretched, flailing arms outward, yawning with gusto, anything to clear her fuzzy brain. The clock continued its pathetic buzzing sound. In a daze she mentally talked to the offending appliance. *Stop whining you decrepit piece of junk with your cracked face and dents.*

Kate made her clocks' life miserable and she woke up poorly.

Swinging her long legs out of bed, and holding her toes short of the floor, she knew what waited. "Good God, it is FREEZING...from freaking October to May, this dorm is never warm enough in the morning."

Her bladder sent an urgent message..."Hell with the floor." She yelped, and then bolted toward the door. She danced on a shaggy bathroom throw rug, digging her toes into its pile for warmth. Then she leaned over and shut the door to the other suite. She saw her face in the mirror over the sink. "Ugahhhh! What a bloody mess!"

With indomitable hopes she turned on the shower. Hot, miraculously hot water poured out. She slipped out of her tee-shirt, balled it up, and fired it into her hamper. Without hesitating she stepped into the tub.

When the water cascaded over her it felt like pure bliss. Ten minutes later she stepped out. The cold room became toasty, steamy like an Amazon rain forest. She polished a clear spot on the mirror and scrubbed her teeth and began reciting her wake up calendar. "First, I get this Unity breakfast thing out-of-the-way; forty-five minutes of making nice with my lacrosse buds, then on to classes."

She pointed her toothbrush at the listening image and in her gruffest voice repeated her father's admonition. "School is your first priority, young woman. You are in your senior year and need to focus on what is relevant." Pushing her long red hair back from her temples with both hands, she squinted through the steamy haze into the mirror. This examination started her morning ritual.

"Hmmm..." she noticed her conditioning began to show. Cupping her hands under her breasts and pursing her lips in a mock glamour pose, she eyed herself in the haze of the full-length mirror on the door. "Nice boobs, killer legs, perfect ass, what more could you ask for?"

She grabbed her butt with her left hand and continued the litany. "Round bruises on the outside of each thigh, one on the inside; several bruises on my ankles and calves, and a massive contusion on my right ass cheek resembling a map of—crikeys—it looks like Australia."

She checked her torso. "A gorgeous fading bruise left over from a cracked rib on the first day of practice." No one knew, not even Taylor. Kate worried they'd be all over her to take it easy. She couldn't resist another look.

"Hmmm..." She touched the half-moon scar at the tip of her nose. and a tiny bump on the bridge of her twice-broken nose. It reminded her about Dr. Roberts warning about another concussion.

Kate eyed her other hand. "Then there is the split finger, and too many scrapes on my knuckles and arms to bother counting."

She sucked in her already flat stomach, stuck out her breasts; and put one hand on her hip. Despite the carnage she felt invincible, surly with the arrogance of a true athlete. She flashed an exaggerated smile. "If I knocked out a few teeth, I might be able to make a living waiting tables and turning tricks down at the I-81, Truck 'n Wash diner."

She vigorously toweled her hair dry and brought herself back to reality by thinking about working toothless, smacking gum, and swinging her hips at the local truck stop. She imagined her other self's voice. "*You order the salt cod breakfast, Hon?*"

While Kate finished blow-drying her hair she looked over this year's schedule. It looked exactly like a repeat of their sophomore schedule, uncommonly unbalanced. With nine away games and six home games, they'd be on the highway a lot.

With the hair dryer screaming, Kate glared at April twenty-second, Stone Gap, season over. She lost her focus as she pushed a brush through her hair. The action brought back memories of her grandmother, brushing her hair, talking about the magnificent Shenandoah Valley. Kate acknowledged two people, two voices leading her to Spotswood; Grandma, of course, and a phone call from Coach Von Mater, a routine call to a potential player. She recalled Coach's honeyed southern drawl, its strength and warmth sending an invitation. "We can use a person of your caliber here. I look for players who will grow as human beings as well as athletes."

A sudden blast of feeling, like a tidal wave, rushed through her, an emotion like a flush of heat flowing from her face to a dark chilled pit in her stomach. She fought to hold it back. She'd made promises when she'd come to Spotswood. One to her grandmother that she would graduate, and in a moment of joy in her sophomore year, she blurted out to her coach, Georgia Von Mater, "Coach I guarantee we are going to win a championship."

Grandma was gone and memories of losing her were still fresh. She shivered. Coach left too, only she'd quit. Coach, a reed-thin soft-spoken lady, a true leader, and the epitome of a genteel Southern woman, suddenly announced her retirement, a woman of steel resolve, gone. In all situations, Coach barely raised her voice. Nevertheless, if she asked you, in her well-mannered southern drawl: "Girls would you mind please following me into Hades fire?" Everyone would follow.

Kate took a deep breath and remembered the words that had shaken her to the core. Coach surprised everyone by announcing her intention to leave. Kate's first thought seemed odd to her. *I'm going to miss my chats, and long bus rides through the Shenandoah Valley where I always called shotgun. The miles always passed hypnotically. Coach needed someone to keep her from nodding off. Why did she quit on me?*

Kate always volunteered to ride shotgun because these were times Coach relaxed. On those long boring rides home through the Shenandoah Valley, in the solitary van, pushing on late at night, Kate found it magical. Time both stood still and flew by.

At about the one-hour mark on the ride, Coach relaxed while most slept. Kate smiled, thinking about Coach's humor, quirky, and unexpected. Occasionally, hours after getting out of the van, she would laugh at one of Coach's comments.

She recalled a list of favorites: "When you make a mistake, make amends immediately. It's easier to eat crow while it's still warm...How long a minute is depends on which side of the bathroom door you're on...You only need two tools in your emergency kit, WD-40 and duct tape. If it doesn't move and it should, use WD-40. If it moves and shouldn't, use tape."

One conversation Kate never forgot. Coach approached her during practice, and they talked about what was ahead. Only Kate didn't understand until now. "Katherine, I understand how hard things are for you girls. It isn't easy being a woman athlete; many give up for various reasons, grades, time constraints, personal problems, or a lack of commitment. Taylor, Penelope and you, are my remaining trio. Next year you'll be seniors. You've hung in there through thick and thin. You are a rare bunch, starting players from the beginning."

"It'll turn around next year. Hanging in isn't hard, Coach."

"It's harder than you can imagine, sometimes hanging in costs too much."

Kate's mind returned to thoughts of lacrosse. She exhaled and voiced her thoughts. "I'll do my damnedest anyway. Hell, I can't cry about it. Von Mater's gone."

- ☼ -

Kate had eight minutes to get over to the dining hall. She grabbed her hat, and bolted. A brass bar securing the weathered oak doors of Wilson Hall clanged, rattled and snapped as it opened. A stray gust of ice-cold air stopped Kate in her tracks. She stood motionless, elevated above the campus mall. Crunching metal noises, a door slamming behind her, jarred her into action. She stood alone in the rising half-light.

She inhaled deeply, permitting cool crisp air to stir her senses. A wood stove in the distance—a hint of dampness—food—ubiquitous scents of mountains—the remnants of winter intermingled. She shivered. Bad weather still lurked, dormant and hidden, waiting to be aroused for a final glory ride up

Shenandoah's valley from the southwest. There is always one last storm to announce the arrival of spring.

The breeze moving gently from the north brought a distinctive musk of cow manure. In her four-year stay at Spotswood College, she'd learned to judge wind direction by odor. A wind from the west carried the smell of turkey crap— cow smell came on a north wind. Her senses quickly dulled. "I love this foul-smelling place."

From the top front step, she took a quick look toward the Blue Ridge Mountains, old mountains, worn by the ravages of time, echoing the footsteps of travelers and legends...This hour of the morning they were simply beautiful. She shouted out toward the valley. "Haul ass, Kate Holland, haul ass." She started running.

- ☼ -

With her tri-colored red hair and athletes' body, most people considered her stunning. With her long legs and 5'10" frame, she covered ground effortlessly, settling into a smooth rhythm. To her left and ahead were the lights of Harrisonburg, twenty miles to the south. Of to the right the small town of Crucible nestled between mountain ridges. She ran along Campus Mall. The college sat between the Shenandoah River and the Blue Ridge Mountains.

Her lungs took in cool air like a train took in fuel. She reached full speed when she reached the dining hall's front pavement. A startled sophomore turned toward the sudden intrusion. "Kater; lookin' good," diminutive Daisy Magee stepped nimbly aside with a mocking bow.

Kate's penetrating eyes flashed in Daisy's direction. "Daisy, tell me, do I look fat?"

"Kater, y'all gots four percent fat on your body, the rest fell off y'all when you dumped your redneck boyfriend."

"Daize, let's get some juice and sit over in the alcove, I see Andi and Taylor at the back table."

Last night, her two best friends on the team, Taylor and Andi talked about losing two key players this year. They became animated when Andi mentioned the new head coach, and of course, the three teams in their league that were habitually strong.

Taylor put the season in perspective for them. "Girlfriends, y'all know this is our last year, seniors at last. Just like the years before we all are go-un' to take a beatin from the big'uns, but maybe, just maybe, if we take it a day at a time, we'll make it to tomorrow. That's if y'all can avoid life's cow pies."

Kate and Andi easily understood Taylor's homespun analogies. They'd been together a long time. Taylor's words particularly animated Andi. "Every year we've started playing in the first week of March, we win like crazy until April, and then we get pounded. We barely make it to the playoffs as a fourth seed. We win, or maybe we lose. If we win, we wind up playing...Stone Gap. Season over."

"I hate that team." That caused a giggle. They'd spoken in unison.

Then they talked about what would go wrong this time. Each season started with such promise, and then unraveled just like life, things never going as you intend. For them, it didn't take long to find out how things had changed. Under the new coach, Spotswood's promising field hockey team had a dreadful season. Coach Burke seemed determined to obliterate rather than replace Von Mater. Kate's relationship with Burke could be classified as crap.

Tess Burke, Coach Von Mater's replacement, encouraged an antagonistic attitude, in an attempt to develop a new clique of players. Kate had been the vocal pariah among the captains, hoping to unify the team. A talented field hockey team ended up playing like turkey crap smelled on a westerly wind.

Kate remained determined Coach Burke wouldn't screw up her final lacrosse season. Nothing could dull her appetite for 'the little sister of war.' Every year the grind of long bus trips and studying in the back seat of the van made her evaluate her commitment. *What makes us play?* The question barely formed in her mind when the answer came...*because we have to.*

- ☼ -

Kate glanced to her left. There's Tess Burke, hovering around the freshman table. There they were, Kelly, Brooke, Marisol, Martianne and Caitlyn. Kate figured Coach had her mind set on trying to impress them. *Dyke Bitch*...words she rarely used found the tip of her tongue. There might be something to the vibe she felt from Burke, but judgmental behavior made Kate livid. Her almost spoken remark would make her a hypocrite.

Some familiar voices got her attention, "Kater!" Andi and Taylor yelled as she approached. She answered. The heart and soul of the Spotswood Stars were calling her. She acknowledged them by their nicknames, "Shooter," then Taylor; "T-Bomb."

Andi could barely contain herself. "Kater, Coach Burke told the rookies not to listen to anyone but her, I nearly choked on my low fat yogurt."

21

Taylor leaned close. "Why do y'all think they hired her? Couldn't they have looked for a coach with experience?"

Kate shrugged. "Sure, but you're presupposing they had a clue. What if they were asked to replace one of their seven football coaches? I bet they'd hire one who had football experience."

Andi, never one to linger on one topic, asked, "What do you think about this year's crop? See any good freshman prospects, Kate?"

"Sure did, petite one." Andi stood five feet three in thick socks, and Kate and Taylor rarely missed an opportunity to remind her of her lack of stature.

"Kelly played little league lacrosse in New Jersey, Brooke is a quick learner, Marisol is a gifted athlete and a hard worker, Martianne, believe it or not, played high school lax in California. She went to a lax camp this summer converting from field player to goalie."

Taylor sighed, seemingly disinterested. "Kater, all y'all know y'alls new coach is going to screw them up."

Kate admired Taylor's ability to get more than one y'all in a sentence. She believed three y'alls stood as her record. Her answer made it plain how she felt. "She's not my coach."

Taylor smiled. "You were the one who played field hockey. I played Basketball. So she's yours."

Andi interjected. "I heard some good news. For sure we are getting Ariel Altman as an assistant. She teaches a couple of courses here, and played lacrosse in college."

Kate brightened, suddenly interested. "No shit, that's our second break."

Andi bristled. "Your language—will you ever get it under control?"

Taylor, who didn't care a nickel about Kate's propensity toward profanity, patted Andi on the head. "Ease up miniature one, what's the first break, Kater?"

"Another freshman, Caitlyn, I worked with her yesterday on left-hand moves, when she showed me a switch move, right to left, it looked as sweet as honey. I almost wet my pants. Turns out, she comes from Maryland, and played four years on her high school team and claims to be a direct descent of the Indians who played the game."

"In the immortal words of the Bard..."

Andi interrupted. "Taylor, could we please get through one meal without hearing you quote something from Shakespeare?"

"As you like it, mini one."

"I'm also tired of short jokes."

Kate smiled. They were a formidable trio on and off the field. It occurred to her that next year Andi would be alone. Where would the future leaders come from? She glanced over at the freshmen and mumbled, "Rookies with lots to learn, miles to travel."

Across the dining room, Caitlyn noticed Kate looking in her direction, She nodded, slightly embarrassed by any attention. She thought; *I hope I didn't do anything wrong. Those three are so good they scare the poo out of me, especially Kate...maybe not scare, just make me nervous.*

She and Marisol had made a pact to be just like Kate. Caitlyn remembered the exact moment she decided Kate would be her hero.

During the first week of practice things were hectic. Marisol, Brooke and Kelly kept running into each other. During a break they started arguing. Kate spotted them and plopped down next to them. "What are you four gabbing about?"

Marisol tried to come up with an explanation. "We were thinking about asking our athletic director for new warm-ups if we make the team."

Kate surprised them by popping open a mini box of raisins, stuffing a handful into her mouth, and started talking in a larger-than-life southern drawl. "Nuu worm-ups? Eye don' know? We—all must provide for the revenue producin' teams first, ladies."

She began imitating Tom Lee Skocul, Spotswood's athletic director. Kate's caricature of a snuff-chewing, juice-dribbling redneck made them all laugh. Kate had his mannerisms down pat.

- ☼ -

The dining room reached a noise level near the threshold of pain. Andi, sitting unaffected, carefully and solemnly diagramed a new play that would result in an undefeated season. Of course she drew it in a bowl of grits. Kate, still not adjusted to getting up early, began to slip into a rocking nod of dozing attentiveness. A condition all college students learn. A howl from the front made her bolt upright.

Taylor punched her. "Oh no, Coach Malone makin' his freshmen baseball players sing to the lacrosse girls again, it's...it's...no, it's Stand by Your Man. It's so darn annoying I love it."

History

March 05

Since her freshman year, Kate had been an avid amateur prognosticator of valley weather. In her mind, today would not be a good day to begin a van ride down I-81. A dismal sky and a slight twinge in her left knee helped her decide. Robert E. Lee University was the team's destination. It didn't take long to get there, but when they played this team it usually turned into something memorable.

With an outside temperature hovering above freezing, they threw their belongings into the vans, Kate and Taylor on one, and Andi on the other. When they pulled out the clouds looked ominous. It began to rain lightly. Like a small caravan, two blue and gray Ford vans followed the mountain ridge of the Shenandoah. A trip to Lee took an hour. For the last three years, Spotswood's Stars began with an old-fashioned tail whipping from Robert E. Lee.

Over the North Fork of the Shenandoah River, Kate's mind began to drift. She gazed at the shadowy Appalachians looming over a caravan of Kenworths, Freightliners, Fords, Toyotas, and sundry minivans, all riding a current on a concrete river. Year after year she'd taken road trips to lacrosse and field hockey games. Game after game, college after college, destinations changed, but uniformity in the journey seemed comforting. She leaned her cheek on the cool windowpane and thought about other seasons and other times.

Kate's mind wandered again. *For three years, I could count on looking left up field, and seeing Maggie Maines at attack wing. This semester Maggie is in Africa on a teaching outreach program. I miss her...I guess.*

Maggie, a field hockey captain and friend who'd turned her back on Kate. Life's expectations could change direction in a heartbeat. Later she would realize distance is measured by time, rather than by miles. This moment in her life came when changes occurred most rapidly, ideas, politics, even sexuality. Maggie could always be counted on for a good for a laugh.

She muttered. "Focus on this season and your responsibility. I'm a captain again. I must get it right."

In the team's second gathering, Kate, Taylor and Andi, had been overwhelmingly elected as the leaders. A terse phone call from Coach Burke announced the news. It didn't take them long to organize a meeting at the coffee bar.

The conversation stayed fresh in her mind. "I'm not going to do this, Taylor. I'm going to turn it down, especially after field hockey season. I can't knock heads with Tess again."

"Do it, Kater, how hard could it be? We'll make decisions about what colors to paint our fingernails, or what color headband to wear for each game, or whether we should wear long compression pants or short? When Coach Burke shows her true colors we'll have your back. It won't be like hockey."

Kate sighed. *It's wonderful to have Andi and Taylor as friends.*

- ☼ -

As the van traveled south, Kate tried to fight sleep. She knew this opportunity to study should be grabbed, especially while there remained enough light to read. Tired bodies and aching muscles would hamper any study plans on the way home. The girls had naturally tried to come up with a suitable nickname for the two blue and white vehicles. With much arguing, they finally settled on Vanuno and Vandos. Last year someone, in competitive compulsiveness, taped the names on the side. A few weeks of weathering had created a permanent decal.

Vanuno hummed with muted excitement. Taylor took the opportunity to talk about the selection of long compression pants worn beneath their kilts. "Ladies, long compression pants not only prevent muscle pulls, they also keep you warm. They also prevent those unsightly glimpses of your cellulite as you get knocked ass over tits, and y'alls kilt goes flying up."

Freshmen in the middle rows talked about the game ahead. They'd heard some wild stories and their chatter reached full volume.

The noise finally broke through Kate's trance. "All right ladies, let me tell you about my experiences with Lee University. The Patriots think we are coming for our annual spanking. For the past three years they've been right. As a freshman, I listened to horror stories told by Piper Bonesteel and Emily, the fat goalie. Emily McKean wasn't fat by the way. Taylor and I gave her another label, Emily McEvil, an appropriate name I might add."

Kate saw the younger players lean closer, interested in the story. "Every year something ominous happened at Lee. My freshman year, Piper, the Star's all-time leading scorer, got ejected in the first five minutes for a slash to the neck of her defender.

"I'm sure she did it deliberately, because Piper was hung over and did not feel like playing that day, Bonehead, walked off right by me. She blew her stinky beer breath in my face. 'Okay bitch,' she said to me, 'let's see you score now.' She really knew how to psyche-up a freshman. We lost 20 to 3, and yours truly scored two goals."

"My sophomore game against Lee created another disaster. I had one of those particularly painful menstrual periods—horrific cramps. Like most fem-athletes, I knew the best thing to ease the cramping, play the game."

She nodded her head toward the freshmen. Marisol nudged Brooke and then elbowed Caitlyn. They all nodded in unison and reminded Kate of bobble head dolls...Kate had their full attention.

"In this particular game, a defender guarding me believed in, 'the closer the better,' theory of defense. Her face-to-face tactic annoyed me and I could swear she exhibited a two-day growth of beard. I kept trying to annoy her by yelling comments to Gabrielle, like 'could we get a chromosome check on this babe?' I said some other nasty things. After our beating, we lined up for the traditional team line-up and slap hands, our mock show of good sportsmanship.

"'Goodgame-goodgame-goodgame...' When I got to number 23, my furry defender, I saw tears in her eyes. I experienced a feeling of embarrassment and shame. The ride home seemed pretty gloomy, especially when you lose 19 to 6, and you know you've behaved like a jackass. Oh, on a positive note, Andi arrived, and began her assault on Piper Bonesteel's records. Our Pea Shooter scored half our goals."

Kate stayed on a roll. "Last year, Deanna Delong, one of my good friends from home, transferred to Lee. I felt good about the prospect of chatting about home, about guys, summer league, and past little league games. During team warm-ups, Dee and I bet a buck for each goal scored. I wondered if I would have enough money to pay up. The game started, and on the draw, the ball flipped up and back towards Dee. Courtney Zuck, a freshman then, stepped on Dee's cleats. Dee tripped, regained her balance, stepped in a rut and snapped her ankle.

"Both teams huddled together at midfield, waiting for paramedics, no one on either team looked at Dee. I guess we thought it could have been one of us. It's hard to admit your own vulnerability. Everyone is one bone break away from ever playing again.

"Courtney looked upset. I told her to forget it; it's our team against theirs. We lost 15 to 9. Shooter scored five."

The tale ended as they pulled into Lee University's Field House parking lot. Rain came down at a steady pace. Kate had a positive thought; they'll never play a game in this kind of weather.

- ☼ -

The score was five to one in Lee's favor when a wind created a horizontal slant in the driving rain. When players faced the wind, the rain hit their faces like tiny chilled slaps. Players on the sidelines and remaining fans were huddling under a makeshift tent of umbrellas.

Lee's coach took the full brunt of the storm. She walked the sideline as if strolling along on a sunny day, determined to dismiss any thought of postponing. There couldn't be a weather problem if you ignored it. Obviously she wanted to finish the game.

Kate's uniform was completely soaked. Her gloves were saturated and provided little grip on her stick, but she couldn't remove her gloves because her fingers were beyond numb. Halftime approached and a girl with a clock walked out on the field to count down the last-minute. Lee attacked to the right, trying to put one more in.

Taylor anticipated a pass, cut in front of her girl, and picked it off. Kate ran up field, but she knew Taylor would take a peek. Her mind whirred with possibilities.

Into the teeth of the storm, Taylor threw a bullet to Kate. Kate picked it clean and switched to her left hand. The net rippled; score! The fans peeking beneath the mass of umbrellas were shocked. The halftime score became a respectable 5 to 2.

- ☼ -

Rain changed to sleet, and in time, sleet eventually changed to a kinder snow; it felt less penetrating. There comes a time in discomfort when it no longer matters what comes next as long as it's not death. Two things stood out in Kate's mind later. Coming to the sideline to be relieved by Black Jack, and finding Zack Tyler, who offered his body under his shirt to warm her hands. It brought back some feeling, and my—oh my, he felt ripped.

Then, in the final minutes, she suffered through muffled sobs from the Lee defender. Tears were proof of the insanity of the moment. The game ended as expected, 10 to 5, and Kate couldn't decide what concerned her most, a lack of feeling in her toes, or the pain in her warming fingers. On the way to the field house she put her arm around Caitlyn. "You played well, Kitty Cat. Add this one to your history book."

- ☼ -

Inside Lee University's locker room, Kate stood naked among her peers, wishing she'd remembered her mother's advice to always take extra underwear. The locker room sounded unusually quiet until Kate's friend, Deanna, breezed in shouting "howdy." The Stars looked up. Most looked annoyed. Deanna smiled at Kate, and ignored any glares.

"Kate Holland, your semi-perfect ass is soaked."

"Dee, you noticed, probably because it has been a long time between boyfriends." They'd been picking at each other since their elementary school days.

"You're soaked. I have a dry sports bra, and a pair of shorts. My bra will be too big of course."

"Thanks, Dee, I'll just pluck out any Kleenex, like I did at the junior prom."

Deanna rummaged through her bag, smiling, probably remembering the junior prom. "Kate, we are going to get together some time this season; if I can find the time."

Kate promised they would keep in touch, but knew it would be difficult at best. They left it with a common refrain. "I'll see you at Easter, dawg."

Later, in Lee University's dining hall, another Spotswood legend emerged. It began in the serving line as you approached the cashier, a wizened serving lady, who snapped out a practiced statement. "White or wheat?"

Her job seemed to be handing out slices of bread. The woman fingered a stack of sliced bread with the jaded detachment of a Las Vegas blackjack dealer. The latex glove yellowed by age gave a clue to her know-how.

Gabby, first in line, made her choice. "White."

The utterly bored woman flipped two slices of white bread on Gabby's plate. "White or wheat?"

Next, Andi answered. "Wheat."

"I'm sorry, we're out of wheat." Andi frowned but obediently accepted her slice of white bread.

"White or wheat?"

Marisol stood right behind Andi, momentarily confused she still knew the right answer, "White."

And so it went through the Spotswood team. Each subsequent order of wheat wearily but politely turned down. The next several players would overhear the exchange and give a correct reply. The last three in line, Martianne, Taylor and Kate, were aware of the fate that awaited them. "White or wheat?"

Martianne stuttered out "white" as her choice. Taylor, of course, cut to the chase. "Y'all can give me y'all's white." The bread slice spun out the cafeteria worker's hand like an ace from a croupier in Las Vegas.

Behind Taylor, Kate, the final person in line, stood patiently. The girls chuckled at this comedic server and her ridiculous inquiry. However, something in Kate's studied approach caught everyone's attention.

"White or wheat?"

Kate's voice sounded emphatic. "Wheat!"

The girls exploded in laughter.

Resolute Taylor

Spotswood trudged their way through the snow-covered parking lot of Lee University. Running shoes compressing snow sounded unnerving in the darkness. In the time it took for the girls to eat a half-inch of fine powder fell on the ground. The howling storm, which had soaked them during the game, became a gentle hissing snowfall. It looked like a winter wonderland in March. If the girls weren't so tired and damp, they might have enjoyed it.

They piled inside the vans, seeking comfort from the elements. Taylor slipped into the driver's seat. She turned toward Coach Altman. "I'll drive. I'm used to this weather."

She tipped the rearview mirror. Kate, always the last person on the bus, took her seat. Kate started talking to the rookie, Caitlyn. It felt comfortable the moment Taylor slid in behind the steering wheel. She never felt more relaxed than when she knew things were in her hands. Like most good athletes she found comfort in repetitive activity, this routine allowed her to maintain her confidence. To her, control guided the way to victory, and success meant everything. She'd been All Conference in basketball and lacrosse for each of the last two years.

To Taylor, a game could be won with her willingness to commit her body to its full force, every second she played. She relied on a combination of physical strength and agility to position her body correctly. Her statistics were a bible of her determination. She led the team in interceptions and forced errors. Coach Von Mater called her an intimidating presence on and off the field. On the field, these things defined Taylor, especially to the people who knew her casually.

To the few, the very few, who knew her well she became a staunch friend and ally. People often presumed she was a naïve farm girl, not very sophisticated. None of these things measured the depth of her character.

In the mirror she noticed Caitlyn turning to Kate, probably for some reassurance about her driving ability. She could hear Caitlyn's hushed voice. "Should Taylor be driving?"

Kate's words drifted to her in a moment of stillness. "My obsessive-compulsive control freak is at the wheel, now we can sleep."

In the darkness, Caitlyn must have felt comfortable asking questions. "Why do you and Taylor get along so well? Do other people like her?"

Taylor smiled when Kate answered. "Men on campus sure like her. They admire her tall perfectly proportioned body, and auburn hair. Normally she wears it bound closely to her head in a single braid. When she lets it down a cascade of dark copper-colored elegance makes the boys go nuts. She is simply stunning, but complex, more complex as you get to know her."

As she focused on the road ahead, Taylor gladly put Kate and Andi on her short list of friends. They were willing to put up with her contradictory mix of emotion and intellect. She checked the mirror again. Kate slept. There could be little contradiction in Taylor's allegiance. She remained a paradigm of loyalty.

Taylor turned the ignition key and shouted, "Time to drive, y'all. Nervous chatter filtered forward, exactly what Taylor needed. The more noise, the more she focused.

March 08

Exit 26B of Baltimore's Beltway takes you to Timonium University. As they turned right at the strip mall, and encountered traffic on York Road, the Maryland girls began to point out familiar things.

Taylor turned her attention to Penelope, another Marylander coming home. "Penelope, are your parents bringing cupcakes?"

"I hope so T; they know how you enjoy them."

Taylor thought it might be a good time to school the rookies. "One more right turn, and in an instant y'all will see what yawl's thinks is a pastoral setting. You rookies notice the charm of an area tucked away in a densely populated area. Timonium's campus is classic, and a painted white fence surrounding it makes y'all think of a horse farm, ergo the Racers nickname. Timonium is division II. We will be going against scholarship players. It doesn't mean jack squat. We can beat these crab-cake eating bee-aitches. Sorry, Kate, Andi, Penelope, Traci, Caitlyn, and Gabby, apologies to your Maryland heritage."

Last year Timonium's Racers had been outstanding. They were a senior dominated team and moved the ball with sharp passing and skilled stick work. If the Racers were as talented as usual, today's game could be a blowout in their favor.

Taylor began her warm-up. She played catch with Marisol and had to dodge a little girl in diapers running nearby. "Dang, that child has a lacrosse stick. No wonder these 'crab-cakers' are so good, they live this stuff. I guess I'm glad we have our own Marylanders."

During warm-up's, Taylor watched the opposing goalie as the coach took practice shots. All of the concentration seemed to be on high shots. Her palms began to itch, could it be an omen? A short goalie; maybe about five two, struggling in that particular area, this could be interesting. "I need to talk to Andi and Kate."

As the speaking captain today, so she goosed Andi and Kate out toward the center of the field. Kate grimaced. "Damn, Taylor, I recognize those umps from last year's game."

Taylor shouldered her way in front. "Y'all hide behind me, Kater."
It looked somewhat ridiculous to see Kate, hiding her five-foot-ten inch frame behind Taylor's five-ten and one half.

"Oh, for crying out loud, Taylor, I hope she doesn't remember me. In all of my games, high school or college, she gave me my only red card."

Andi, who had been silent, made a pronouncement. "Maryland umpires, good for two things, their notorious home bias and good for nothing. Remember two years ago, this umpire called back one of Kate's goals for a phantom violation."

"I remember." Taylor and Andi talked as if Kate were truly hidden behind them.

"Remember how she got so frustrated, she screamed, 'I'm a Maryland girl, too, give me some calls.' Then this umpire waved her red card over her head, announcing to all assembled Kate's wicked behavior."

Both umpires approached to shake hands. The older ump stared at Kate and said, "Hey, Maryland girl."

Taylor responded quickly, in her best southern drawl. "Ump she's, uh, not with us."

There was no response, no smile. They knew they were screwed.

After the mid-field meeting, Taylor separated herself to put her game face. She walked quietly away. She would need a stretch, and she always stretched alone. This day things seemed different, final, a last trip to Timonium. She enjoyed coming north. She loved to tease Kate about being in Yankee land. For years Kate argued Maryland sat below the Mason-Dixon Line, but to no avail. Taylor had her own sense of geography. Besides, what could be more fun than annoying Kate?

Three years ago, as a freshman, Taylor remembered how resistant she'd been about playing lacrosse. Coach Von Mater had talked her into playing, convincing her she needed conditioning, and that basketball and lacrosse had similar strategies. She remembered being agitated by wearing a kilt as a uniform. Who played in a skirt? She quickly found out real women did play this game, and they wore a 'kilt.'

Her first day of practice, Piper Bonesteel blew by her at full speed, and used her stick and hip to knock Taylor on her butt. Taylor dusted herself off. Piper jogged by. "Get ready, hayseed, or I'll do it again." That lesson became firmly planted in her mind. She wouldn't have it any other way. Coach was right about lacrosse and basketball being similar. The stick work however, made a big difference. Something Coach failed to mention.

Piper taught her to be ruthless but she chose to study Kate's game. It seemed effortless and amazingly unselfish. In little time she had to admit the Yankees could flat-out play this game with a net.

Taylor glanced over at Kate performing a pre-game ritual with Penelope, poking her stick at Penelope's shoulders and head, and taking several good whacks. Marisol, one of the freshmen, noticed and turned to Taylor. "What are they doing?"

"They've been doing this for four years. Penelope is one of the special people, maybe the quirkiest of goalies. Her icy blues can send shivers through you. Kate is the only one who can lock eyes with Penelope."

Taylor nudged Marisol. "I swear Penelope's eyes just flickered. Thank God you're on the other end of the field...oh, sorry I forgot y'all are playing defense today. If her head starts to spin and her pupils go vertical, let's both get the hell out of here." Taylor loved to tease freshmen.

- ☼ -

A voice from the field speakers crackled. "Ladies and gentlemen, we would like to remind you any derogatory comments directed toward the officials, players or coaches will not be tolerated. Alcoholic beverages and smoking are prohibited. Here is the line-up for your visiting Lady Stars, from Spotswood College." Timonium University played their lacrosse games on an artificial turf field. Taylor loved the true bounces and ease with which she could pick up ground balls. However, as a purist, she preferred the smell of grass and the ruts she knew so well, of Spotswood's field. The announcer began the introduction of the teams; "Starting in the goal, number 33, from Lutherville, Md. Penelope Preston." Penelope sprinted under an arch of lacrosse sticks toward the opposing coach and shook her hand. As they were announced, each remaining player repeated the action. Taylor could feel her hot blood rising. When play began she turned to cold calculating ice.

The Stars fought and dug for every ball touching the ground. Spotswood's team contested every step and every inch on the field. Timonium's Racers still possessed skill and stick work, but this game wasn't being won by finesse. Both teams were skilled. This game turned on the intangibles. A loose ball, a bobbled pass, any hesitation brought a crowd of defenders. It had become a test of character.

Crowd noise sounded evenly divided. Many Spotswood parents lived nearby and were there to cheer on their daughters. Along one hillside were the Hollands, the Prestons, and the Birdsongs.

Mrs. Birdsong explained the game to an old woman, sitting comfortably on a folding chair. "Gram, this is supposed to be a graceful and ladylike sport."

"It's the Creators game, Cindy, but this looks like a bloody dogfight to me." The old woman seemed to be enjoying herself.

"Technically, Grandmother, lacrosse is a non-contact sport."

"Stop blowing smoke up Granny's—Oh! That girl just got hit in the face."

There was good news and bad news in the first fifteen minutes of the game. The bad news was Ginni's broken nose. The good news...the Spotswood players were faster than the

Racers. The recipe for defeat cooked right there on the artificial turf. In the first half, Andi, Gabrielle, and Kate all ripped the nets for two goals. Traci and Caitlyn chipped in with a goal each. On the defensive end Taylor began to plan. *We can win this one.*

Ten minutes before halftime, an all too familiar sound echoed on the field; the umpire's whistle began to blow, dictating the tempo of the game; a snail's pace favored the Racers.

Limping bodies littered the field. Ginni came back for the second half, broken nose and all. She had something that appeared to be a tampon stuffed up her nose.

Courtney and Gabrielle took checks to the head from the Racer defenders, and the umpires failed to call a penalty either time. With eleven minutes to play, the scoreboard displayed 11 to 11. Taylor looked up at the scoreboard and noticed the symmetry of the numbers.

The draw became vital, and Andi would concentrate on getting the ball elevated. Taylor and Kate were both tall, a distinct advantage over their defenders. The whistle blew and Kate snatched the ball in the air away from her defender. She passed it back to Andi and she took off. Andi drew a double team at the eight-meter mark and avoided it by going behind the goal and passing to Kate.

Andi threw the ball in a high arc and Kate broke toward the goal, she elevated over her defender and caught it, shooting the ball in one motion. The ball went into the net, a beautifully executed quick stick. Taylor went wild.

Tweeeet! The umpire waved her arms; "In the crease, no goal, ball back to the Racers."

Taylor could see the anger rising like a red tide on Kate's red head. She called out. "Damn it, don't argue with the umpire."

Coach Von Mater had drilled them continuously. "Arguing is repulsive. Stay cool." Taylor clamped down hard on her mouth guard and concentrated on defense. The Racers brought the ball up the field, attacking the Spotswood goal. The fortunes of this game were reversed in a few seconds. Taylor felt a bump from behind, hard enough to knock her of balance. She stuck out her hand, grabbed a clump of fake grass, and recovered. By the time she looked up, the Racers had scored. "Shit! Shit! Shit!"

Taylor steamed. She heard a voice coming from the other end of the field. "Stay cool." Kate smiled. Her black mouth guard gave her a wicked toothless grin.

The next six minutes played out evenly with frequent calls for rough play. The Racers scored the final goal when Taylor gambled on an interception. She missed — they scored. The score ended 13 to 11 for Timonium. The Spotswood team won a sizeable number of bruises and lumps, but the bruises to their egos were the ones that hurt the most.

Taylor walked over to Kate and Caitlyn. "I don't care how good the steamed crabs are, I just want to get out of this state. I need to see the hills of Old Virginia."

"Me too, girlfriend," Kate replied

Caitlyn and Marisol

"What crime did I commit?" Marisol yelled at her phone, trying to get some sympathy from Caitlyn.

"I don't know, but before you get all bent, she wants to see me too. So, maybe it's a white or wheat thing. Maybe we did something in Maryland? I'm coming over. I'll be there in ten minutes."

Things went south for Marisol this morning at breakfast. She felt an unexpected tap on her shoulder. She spun around to face Kate, even more surprising, since Kate rarely visited the dining hall for breakfast. Everyone knew how she felt about early mornings.

"I want to talk to you before practice today. After classes I'll meet you in the training room, about a half hour before practice."

Marisol's jaw dropped, dumbfounded, as Kate turned and walked away... it seemed obvious Kate deliberately sought her out. Her first thought had been what did I do wrong?

On her walk over to Caitlyn's room Marisol tried to sort out the implications, Kate seemed serious and that disturbed her. Kate had become their favorite. Andi with her lacrosse skills awed them. Taylor, well Taylor scared the 'bejezzus' out of them, but Kate, they all wanted to be like Kate. She could play the beans out of lacrosse, and she looked like a model. So one look, one glance from her scary green eyes, and they would all spend hours discussing what it actually meant.

Caitlyn was brushing her teeth when Marisol burst through the door. "Let's go over to see Kate together. So, what did you do?"

She spit her foamy suds out as an expletive, spraying her reply. "Bull stuff, I'm pretty sure it couldn't be me. It must have been you."

They took their practice bags, and they started walking and arguing toward the locker room. Marisol started getting hyper. "Let me ask you again, why did you, make Kate mad?"

"Me? I know it was you."

"You don't think Taylor's pissed too?"

"Mother Bear, I hope not."

"Maybe it's something good?"

"Marisol, I trust my Native American instincts. My great-grandmother probably is having a dream about this, and I can tell you it's not a good one."

They were waiting on a bench when Kate came in the room. Her familiar smile no longer announced her. "Hello ladies, I want to talk to you about something serious, so pay attention. Marisol, how much do you weigh?"

Marisol got caught off guard, *what is this all about*? She saw the look in Kate's eyes that meant she wasn't playing, so she answered. "I think, one ten."

Kate pointed at Caitlyn. "And you?"

Caitlyn shrugged, "One hundred twelve and a half."

Kate smiled a knowing superior look. "Listen, I want you to know I like you. I respect you, and I am glad we are teammates—so far--now, this being said, listen up. Just a couple of things, and I want the truth, understand? Marisol, tell me exactly what you ate for breakfast."

"What? What's this all about?"

"Just answer, I'll get to the point in a minute."

"Okay, I ate a banana, a muffin, and drank some water."

Kate glared at Marisol. "You ate the whole muffin?"

"No, I don't think I ate all of it."

"Now let's get to you, Caitlyn, what did you eat?"

"I'm never hungry in the morning, I just drank some juice."

Kate paused... "When did you have your last menstrual period?"

Caitlyn's face reddened. "That's not something I discuss in public."

Kate interrupted her. "This isn't public. We're on a team, anyway you told Brooke, who told Paige, who told Jen you haven't had a period for six months; don't start acting petulant, this is important. Marisol, how long has it been since your last period?

"Two months, but that's not unusual."

Kate frowned. She looked serious. "Last year when I needed an x-ray on my ankle, I struck up a conversation with a doctor at the Hospital. She seemed interested in athletics and asked me if I would help her with her research. She asked if I'd let her give me a bone scan, at no cost. I did it. Later, she told me everything looked fine, but added that I happened to be a prime candidate for Female Athletic Triad, it's a syndrome many women are unaware of."

They were listening very carefully now. "The doctor showed me scans of thirty year old women with bone densities of seventy-year olds. When those women reach forty, they risk breaking their bones just by getting out of bed in the morning."

When Kate mentioned broken bones, Caitlyn interrupted. "I know what you are talking about, a girl from my high school ran track in college and she had to quit in her senior season because she kept breaking the bones in her shins, one time she broke nine in one meet. I didn't know this kind of syndrome existed."

Marisol spoke. "What are the signs Kate?"

"First, it usually occurs in women driven to compete, and at the highest levels, sports, grades, life, or whatever. You do not have to be an anorexic. By the way, you all know your weight within ounces. Sounds like you might be obsessing. I bet you weigh yourselves morning and night. Three things have to happen; one, you start a disordered eating pattern to make you faster, or whatever. Second, missing your menstrual cycle for more than three cycles, or amenorrhea, interferes with your estrogen level, which promotes calcium accumulation in the bones. The third event is the premature onset of osteoporosis. Once this happens after the age of twenty-five, it's too late. You can never recover, it just gets progressively worse."

It was a small moment in their lives, but a life-altering one. Kate told them they had to eat breakfast with each other, and to include Brooke. "I want the two of you eating plenty of calories in the morning. Drink milk, if Brooke tells me you're skipping, I'm going to have the head trainer certify you as unfit to play, by the way, thank Jen King, she's the one who 'ratted you out.' Just in case you are wondering, yes, I am potentially one of you."

She paused. Her words gained their full attention. "Although it's hard to believe, we are not immortal. Nothing lasts forever. See you later. Wait, Caitlyn, let me talk to you."

A shiver swept down Caitlyn's spine.

When Marisol left Kate finally smiled. "After the game in Timonium, an old woman stopped me. She looked frail but her grip on my arm seemed pretty strong. She told me she liked my game and that she'd seen me play before...in a dream."

Caitlyn groaned, "My great grandmother."

"Yes, she told me to call her Granny. She also told me to tell you I was the eagle warrior and you'd better listen to whatever I said. At first I thought Granny had been smoking weed for glaucoma, but I figured out quickly she was sharp as a tack. She told me your totem is a catbird. So I promised we'd call you Catbird or Cat."

Caitlyn grimaced. "She's a little wonky at times."

"I liked her, Catbird. So get used to the name. We all wind up with nicknames. I'm Kater, Taylor is T-bomb, Andi is Shooter, and you'll hear the rest. Just be thankful she didn't call you something embarrassing."

Paradoxes

Lacrosse is often referred to as the fastest game on two feet. It requires enough stamina to run a marathon, with the sprinting ability needed in a four hundred-meter dash. A good team needs help from the bench, and today the subs were going to get some game experience. Spotswood usually dominated against Sweet Water or 'Watermelons'.

They weren't really called...Watermelons, but their uniform colors of pink and green, and their name, led to some understandable teasing.

The clock showed twenty minutes left, Kate, Andi, and Taylor stood on the sidelines cheering on the girls who normally were on the bench. Kate appeared especially pumped up; her freshmen were showing they'd learned their lessons well. "Kelly and Brooke are getting in some good time."

Taylor nodded. "Look at Kelly, she just dodged between those two defenders and used her hip to move them. Did you see that? I taught her the move."

Kate didn't listen. She'd instantly spotted a potential disaster. The two defenders were not so skilled, and they didn't react well to the fake. She almost had time to shout out a warning.

"Oh no..." Kelly went down quickly and hard. Coach Burke sprinted on to the field with both trainers in tow. Kelly's knee became the focus of the trainers' attention. The game stopped, and both teams huddled separately in the center of the field, gathering their thoughts and trying to refocus. Kelly sobbed as she lay near the Sweet Water goal. The players on both teams were making a conscious effort not to look in the direction of those sobs.

Doctor Waugh, on call for all the home games, arrived within five minutes. The doctor quickly assessed Kelly's leg and dialed his cell phone. Crucible's Volunteer Emergency Team hurried to the field. A few Spotswood teammates peeked in Kelly's direction when she was assisted from the field. A final score of 22 to 3 in Spotswood's favor seemed little consolation. Losing a teammate made them feel like they'd lost something.

- ☼ -

The sun warmed Kate's neck as she struggled to keep her attention on the professor. It reminded her of something her father said. Dad always maintained God was a prankster. "I think any Supreme Being which has to endure the slow passage of time watching over people would be bored out of his mind, and certainly would not be opposed to throwing in a few jokes."

Thus Kate's explanation for Professor Kasich, God was a comedian. Every Tuesday and Thursday she endured J.E.B. Kasich and his annoying voice. His passions in life were football, the "War of Northern Aggression," and bashing women as a species. She scanned through her reading for Kasich's class tomorrow—maybe this time God's joke had gone too far.

March 11

The descent into hell began Tuesday within ten minutes of the Kasich's class, a level of Hell surely designed by Dante. Zack, one of the athletic trainers often assigned to lacrosse, sat next to her, he made eye contact and nodded toward the clock, a sign the topic was going to change. Professor Kasich was rambling on about the real outcome of the Civil War. As he often did, he changed his topic in mid breath. The hellish clock began to tick.

"I have previously commented as how some northern boys are almost as tough as southern boys on the football field, and of course any male athlete is tougher than female athletes."

Kate blinked. She sensed trouble brewing. Another circle of Hell loomed in sight. Then, without warning, Kasich shot his verbal arrow straight toward its intended target; "Take the phrase, 'women athletes,' a contradiction in terms, or an oxymoron. That's the way I see it."

Kate sucked in her breath, a prelude to a volcanic eruption, just as Zack strategically placed his hand over her mouth. In the pantheon of Spotswood lore it became a heroic maneuver. He silenced her just in time. Kasich's atomic statement, dissipated, the fallout now negligible. Kate, silenced, turned slowly, realizing what'd just happened.

She whispered. "Thanks, Zack. If I keep my mouth shut I will get an A…"

"…If I keep my mouth shut I'll keep my A."

He nodded. Kate repeated the mantra. "If I keep my mouth shut I'll get an A."

She winked. "I owe you, Zachary Tyler." Kate saw his smile and thought how attractive he looked. Tall and muscular with a slow athletic way of moving, he turned a lot of girls head's on campus. Kate loved his dark hair and light blue eyes. They took several classes together, and had established an easy relationship with an ability to quickly fall into a meaningful discussion or argument. They could joke openly, and he often identified her as one of the boys.

Lately, Kate felt more than a passing interest when near him. She hoped he hadn't noticed. Zack and Traci's were together, and Traci was her teammate. Traci recently joked about Zack spending so much time stretching Kate's hamstrings in warm-ups, that Kate had developed the strongest 'hams' on the team. Kate unconsciously licked her lips, savoring the soft touch and a lingering taste of Zack's hand across her mouth. She whispered. "Ignore it Kate."

March 12

Before going to the training room on Wednesday, Kate called to make sure a trainer would be available to give her hamstring some electrical therapy. Amber said she would be there. Kate became accustomed to squeezing the maximum from a minimum amount of time. The professors were generally very helpful about rescheduling things, but athletes pursued their degree just like other students, except they practiced, traveled, and trained in addition. It could be draining being involved in two intercollegiate sports, and impossible to do all of these things and still find the time to eat.

Time in the training room allowed Kate to catch up on any local gossip. When Amber turned off the electricity, Kate relaxed. Electric stimulation required a period of heat to draw blood to the area as a healing technique. While wrapped in heated towels, she used the time to chat. The room filled with an eclectic group of athletes. Mooner, the gigantic tackle on the football team ranted about last weekend's party. In an unlikely confluence of events, Mooner, or Morris Mooney to a very few people, became her study partner three years ago.

He droned on. "I was so, like faded this weekend..."

Kate smirked. Knowing everything Mooner said had to be a lie. "Yep, Mooner, you put on aftershave and the whiff of alcohol made you high."

"Shut up, Kater."

Serious students and serious student-athletes avoided alcohol, yet alcohol consumption could be staggering at times. After drinking stories, the next topic became predictable, something deeply rooted in every student's mind, conversations about sex. The chatter would be impossible to recall, mindless drivel created nothing of substance.

Kate turned her attention to Mooner. "Mooner, I talked to your ex-girlfriend last week. She said you were a virgin, and after you two had sex, she decided to become one too."

"Shut up, Kater."

"Wow, another intellectual rejoinder from my giant friend."

Mooner knew better than to take on Kate in a locker room quip session. Even with this knowledge he couldn't resist a parting shot. "I hear your team is going to finish fourth again this year."

"You big donkey, if we finish fourth, I'll let you lose your virginity with me."

The locker room exploded in laughter. Mooner understood he had to save his reputation. "What do I get if I win?"

- ☼ -

At practice, Coach Ariel Altman, the young assistant, described their workout routine to a coach from a nearby high school. Coach Altman looked young enough to still be out on the field. She'd played her college lacrosse at Cornell. The defensive players enjoyed her intensity and would playfully mimic her. They butchered her New England accent; "put yah stick on her bod-day—don't push, just "guy-dah" away from the goal; Guy-dah—guy-dah—gosh dahn it, guy-dah big ass inta the bleachers."

When Altman heard they were going to provide some help to this new high school coach, she graciously volunteered her help. The young girl showed up bright and early and was by anyone's account drop dead gorgeous. After ten minutes with Ariel, Coach Burke must have decided talking to this woman looked like fun. "Coach Altman, I'll take over."

Coach Burke sounded particularly arrogant today. "You go see if the goals are padded correctly." She turned with a patented smile to her new task. "We begin with warm up exercises to stretch muscles. During each practice, we run a light two-mile run, on days after a game, five miles. On the field, we work in lines and practice shuttle passes. While the passes are going on, the goalies are blocking shots by whoever is not needed elsewhere, that's usually Coach Altman.

"We then take shots on the goal, with the goalies in the cage. We move into the eight-meter mark and fire at the goalies. This quickens their reflexes. The offense works on quick sticks, trying to catch and shoot in one motion in front of the goal, also rolling the crease. The goalies use this time to work on clears, or passing a saved shot up the field."

Coach Burke must have noticed Kate relaxing near the goal and waved her over. Kate became immediately suspicious. Coach Burke kept on talking. "We follow up with footwork drills and ankle and hamstring exercises. The defense works on double-teaming, and we use a zigzag passing drill up the field. We end with three versus three drills, with a goalie in the cage."

When Kate jogged over, Tess Burke introduced her, an introduction laced with sarcasm. Kate got the message. "Kate's our resident lacrosse historian, she claims a background second to none, and she tells me she's been playing for twelve years. Isn't that right, Kate?"

Kate nodded hello. Coach Burke continued, "Kate will tell you some of her fabulous background."

Kate smiled and thought; this chick is putting me on the spot. She wants to see what I've got. She took a deep breath and launched into Lacrosse 101. "Native Americans called lacrosse 'the creator's game' or 'little brother of war'. We women players like to call it 'little sister of war.' If the Native Americans from the seventeenth century were to time travel to a lacrosse game today, they would easily recognize the women's game—men's—not so much. Recently, women's lacrosse has exploded in popularity.

"Title IX, a relatively obscure federal law from the 70's became the women's rule ignored by the Athletic Directors and sports administrators, because sports were for boys and men to pursue. When the girls asked for equal consideration, the men in charge used the same rhetoric the good old boys always use when faced with an inevitable change in events. 'You are not as strong, you are incapable, and we are protecting you.' It took some good lawyers to get their attention."

Kate took a breath and continued. "A few court cases later, and a push to comply with Title IX led to new teams popping up everywhere, even in the heartland of chauvinism. Every time the chauvinists complied they blamed women's sports.

Whatever they cut, they blamed the women and damned Title IX. And, by the way, would the good old boys have less than seventy players on a football team? I think not."

Kate didn't pause. "The county league I played in during high school is as 'cutthroat' as any in the United States. The competition is intense, fueled by a need to succeed in order to get accolades and scholarships. The coaches were usually men who'd once played lacrosse. They turned up the intensity, and increased the likelihood of contact. Greater intensity led to some vicious checking and high-speed collisions. After all, daughters always try to please their daddies.

"Lacrosse is the type of sport athlete's love. We love the competitive flow of the game, the thrill of running almost non-stop for over an hour. I especially love the feel of a powerful stick in my hands, the smooth ball. Every time I step on the field I get a warm tingly feeling. What about you, Coach?" Kate looked directly into Coach Burke's eyes.

The fixed stare and a lightning flash of green caused Coach Burke to blink. Tess Burke could barely conceal the look of disgust on her face.

- ☼ -

In the locker room, Burke called the team together. She must've thought she needed to establish some dominance. "I know we have a long-standing tradition of meeting in the center of the field during warm-ups for a silent prayer. I think this might be offensive to the other team, so I want us to pray out of sight before we go on to the field."

No one reacted. A lack of response was taken as accord by the coach. She clapped her hands in encouragement, and shouted, "Let's sweep out the old and bring in the new. We'll start a new tradition."

They began their prep for the game. Standing in shorts and sport bras, they thought about what Coach had said, however, tradition is sacrosanct to athletes. The room returned to a low hum, at this moment they could only focus on the upcoming game.

March 13

Thursday morning's weather presented a hint of spring, a harbinger of good things to come. The temperature turned cool and the air carried a touch of humidity. Each deep breath taken felt like drinking from a country well, sharp, clean and invigorating. Kate's itinerary included Professor Kasich's class and some research at the library for a paper.

The game against Mount Shiloh started at 4:30 P.M. Mount Shiloh College happened to be a close fifteen minute drive southwest of Spotswood's campus. Kate liked the people she'd met there. No matter how things turned out, good sportsmanship abounded. Mount Shiloh had a tradition of religious principle's promoting harmony.

- ☼ -

At 4:00 P.M., the players from Spotswood gathered in the center of the field. They formed a defiant circle and knelt in silent prayer. The Mount Shiloh players stopped what they were doing and joined them. The captains of both teams were very good friends, and although they would never admit it, they'd agreed over coffee last night at Brannigan's Pub on the joint ceremony. When the team finished the prayer, Taylor shouted. "Amen all y'all, let's kick some ass for God."

Both teams responded in unison, "Sisterhood!

The game turned out to be tougher than Kate anticipated. The Eagles were sure God had their backs, and were hell-bent on proving they deserved this preferential treatment. Mt. Shiloh had obviously done their homework. They concentrated on Andi.

The half ended with the Eagles on top, 3 to 2; Spotswood's team walked off, and gathered in a huddle near their bench. Kate stood motionless, not leaving the field, and then after a minute of inactivity she started walking toward the goal. Her move caught a few players attention.

"I'm invisible." she said to the surrounding mountains.

Coach Burke happily ignored her and everyone else seemed unsure of Kate's intent. No one wanted to call Kate over. Most of their eyes shifted toward Taylor, expecting the answer to come from her. Taylor shrugged. "She'll come over when she's good and ready. So y'all leave her be."

When the clock indicated zero, the second half began. Both teams took the field. Kate noticed Gabrielle coming toward her.

"Um, Kater, they elected me to come over here and talk to you, are you all right?"

Kate stood motionless.

"Kater are you all right?"

"Gabby, can you see me?"

"Of course I can see you, are you nuts?"

"You can see me? Could you see me earlier?"

Gabrielle paused, "Yes I saw you."

"During the whole first half—you could see me?"

"Yes, Kate."

"Well then—PASS ME THE F***ING BALL!" The profanity echoed along the shimmering ridges surrounding the college of Mount Shiloh. Most people would have thought it impossible to silence mountains, but the fans, players, and passersby's all knew it could happen.

- ☼ -

The second half became a Star's game. The passes started coming Kate's way. She became 'un-stealth.' When Kate scored three quick goals, the defense shifted away from their triple team on Andi, now open she poured it on. The final score was Spotswood 12 and Mount Shiloh 4. Andi scored seven goals. Coach Burke commended Andi for her great game and told everyone she'd nominate her for Player of the Week.

On the way back to the van, Kate and Taylor started laughing.

"Mother bear, Kate, I think you're crazy."

"Maybe, but obviously I'm now visible."

As they continued toward the parking lot, Kate saw Coach Von Mater sitting near the tennis courts overlooking the lacrosse field. Kate elbowed Taylor. "How long has she been here? Did she watch?"

Kate spoke as Coach Von Mater walked by. "How'd you like the game, Coach?"

Coach could be a woman of few words. "Genius, Katherine, genius, even though your intellect is slightly evil."

Kate felt a glow begin in the center of her body. "I miss that old woman. She looks tired though."

Then Kate's face turned bright red. She spun and faced Taylor, "Oh my God. Coach heard what I said on the field?"

"They heard you thirty miles away."

College Life

March 14

Wilson dormitory had been Kate's home since her freshman year. Built in a Georgian style, it occupied the campus like an island, surrounded by a sea of flowers, bushes, and stately oaks. The landscaping isolated Wilson, making it a pocket of green in a verdant countryside. However, large and majestic oaks surrounding the building gave the place real character.

Air-conditioned for those sweltering summers, and somewhat warm and toasty during winter's worst, Wilson became a part of her.

When the weather felt right and the windows were opened to catch the evening breeze, the trees whispered and creaked; voicing imaginary stories in long forgotten tongues.

The third floor, where Kate lived, had the largest suite in the building. Room 301 consisted of two large sections connected by a bathroom. At the beginning of each year, the college assigned rooms—unless one put in a bid at the right time. Kate took advantage of friends' advice during her freshman year. She arranged with Casey, her freshman roommate, and two others, Frances and Candace, to put in an early bid for this particular suite. Casey and Candy took one room, and Frances roomed with Kate.

During their sophomore year, Franny dropped out of college. No one ever bothered to request rooming with Kate after Franny left. Her reputation of being nearly intolerable to live with spread like peanut butter on toast. Mostly, people talked about her vacuuming and cleaning at midnight.

Room 301 became a central meeting place for all sorts of groups. One Friday night after dinner, a group of friends relaxed in Kate's room, making small talk.

With the TV on and popcorn popping, they chatted. Out of the blue, Daisy asked, "Who do you think is the best looking guy on campus? Jen, you and Jackie Blue, gay or not, have to answer; no exceptions, and guy means male, got it?"

The group in Kate's room posed an interesting dynamic, Jen and Jackie Blue because of their sexual orientation, and the others with random quirks and eccentricities, all added energy. Casey, brought shyness, and naiveté. She languished in platonic relationships with men. Daisy's vibe came from being a flaming extrovert who dated everyone. Black Jack was engaged and semi-serious.

It made an affable mix. Both Jackie's, by coincidence, bore surnames of Patton. On any campus, it was not unusual to have two people with the identical last names. However, since they were often in the same circle of friends, they were identified by color. Jackie Blue, had piercing blue eyes, and Black Jack—African American.

Jen, in an uncharacteristic response said, "Let me go first, I have my ideal man all picked out". This caused the group to move their heads simultaneously toward her in disbelief...it looked rehearsed. "Well, I mean—you know. It's not impossible I'd think about some man in a certain way—and uh.... If I weren't gay I'd pick Kate's ex, Boomer."

Kate jumped up. "That's it, you and me, outside, now."

"Ah, Kate, blow me. You'd lose that battle."

"That's physically impossible, oh conflicted one."

They both laughed.

Black Jack literally rubbed her hands together in a lame caricature. "My turn ladies; let's get down to bare facts. I want a turn with the guy I see hanging around Kate all the time. What's his name, Daisy? You know all the men on campus. Is it Zack?"

No one spoke and Kate felt a flush of embarrassment creep into her cheeks. She did what you should not do; she answered defensively, and said, "I don't hang around him all the time."

Just then, a loud noise broke the tension. A poster fell from the wall. It hit Casey on the head. A simultaneous screech of... 'Matilda', rocked the room. The noise echoed down the corridor. Matilda, a ghost legend in Wilson Hall, came from the early fifties to haunt the building. The story, passed on by generations of college students, grew larger. A falling picture could scatter any group.

March 17

Team photos were being taken this Monday. Individual shots were taken of each player for the lacrosse brochure. They dressed in their home whites.

Spotswood's were white with a zigzag royal blue stripe running diagonally across a big blue star in the front. The number, also royal blue, and edged in gray, showed on the front and back. They all wore a blue and gray plaid kilt. They also wore short black compression pants under the kilt. They widely agreed they had the best uniforms in the league.

Picture day became a fun day. Joking and relaxing as they waited for their pictures to be taken, became the order of the day. Practice got cut short, with girls spending more time on their hair than in preparation for tomorrow's game. After four hard fought games the team seemed pleased to unwind.

The fact that this next team traveled to Spotswood was also a bonus. The vans would be in the garage. The new players felt lucky for the break. The veteran players knew this plan had been put in place by Coach Von Mater. She always had picture day at the beginning third of the season. A day of rest felt golden when legs began to feel the effects of competition. Tomorrow they'd be back in the thick of it. And, the remainder of the season loomed ahead.

March 18

Today's game against the Colonials of Jefferson and Henry, pitted two teams in turmoil. The scouting report mentioned a team riddled with injuries, and loaded with new players. Last year J & H narrowly defeated Spotswood, playing on their home field, this year Big Blue stood ready to return the favor. The Stars were always tough at home, partly because of their field, a small pristine green gem.

From the main campus you walked toward the football stadium and cut behind the chain link fence or walked through the gymnasium to find the lacrosse field, 50 by 110 yards of green brilliance. The area was limited, with barely enough space for a scoreboard, let alone amenities. Maybe it wasn't the best stadium, but like the owners of a one-eyed, three-legged, one-eared dog called Lucky, the girls loved it.

Kate held a special affinity for this field. One particular morning she'd stretched out on her back, cradling her head behind her folded arms, and smelled the odor of the grass as if it were a bouquet of flowers. She stayed there for an hour, letting the rising sun warm her. On many other occasions she'd spent hours walking its green boundaries. Kate wanted to capture every memory of her days as an athlete. She could close her eyes and recall every inch. A cozy combination of sun and grass gave comfort to Kate. In times of turmoil it brought her peace.

Jefferson and Henry's lack of focus showed on the first play of the game. They watched as Catbird picked up the ball from her position and ran away from her girl, straight toward the goal. The inexperienced Colonials pulled back to cover man-to-man. Cat saw an opening and took it. She went untouched and scored. She jumped up and down, ecstatic. High fives and a mini celebration ensued. Things began to look easy.

Everything worked well but Kate, ever the realist, began to worry about injuries. She remembered Coach Von Mater's rule number one. A negative thought in your head is a blueprint of things to come.

When the score reached 10 to 1, Kate took over. With fifteen minutes to go she decided to slow down this disaster. Rule number two. Never humiliate a team. Coaches have long memories. She circled behind the goal, attempting to use some plays to slow things down.

The score ended at 12 to 2.

When the teams walked off the field, Kate walked near the fans at the end gate, most of the football players were hanging around.

"Way to go, Kater. Good game. We'll all show for y'alls next home game." As she passed through the gate, she overheard Zack Tyler talking to a couple of his football buddies.

"...these girls are athletes, and they're tougher than you think. I've seen them play hurt and they could outrun most of the guys on our team... Oh! Hi Kater, good game." he seemed surprised and embarrassed.

"Thanks, Traci really played well too." She felt like a goober. *Actually, Traci sucked today. Why did I mention his girlfriend?*

March 19 - Mocking Bird

The 'dead' Mocking Bird outside of Kate's window kept trying to interfere with her sleep. His cry changed from an elegant chirp to a sound like a creaking pump handle, imitating the clamor of a blue jay. SKREE! SKREE!

She moaned as he began to mimic a crow. "Jesus, Mary, and Joe Fish, someone kill the fudge-nut mockingbird again." Kate had vowed to limit her profanity. She decided her vocabulary was becoming too—too earthy. Andi and Coach Von Mater complained all the time. With just Andi remaining it fell on Kate to show self-control.

Dead Mockingbird's voice seemed to subside. She drifted back into tranquility. Silence felt heavenly. CHACK! CHACK! CAW!

"Shut the...fu! Oh no! Damn bird," another slip in her vow.

She screamed. "What time is it?" The red glare of her alarm clock winked through its chipped and cracked face, it answered her with 6:39 in the morning; she readied a punch, but stopped when she remembered the alarm didn't awaken her. Kate sat up anyway. Her mind whirred incoherently. *How can I kill that bird again?* She knew this day would start with a headache, "Blasted bird."

Several weeks ago, Kate had thrown a book out of her window and into the tree, aiming at the offending bird. When Kate retrieved her book, she saw a campus cat with something gray in its mouth. Kate knew she'd knocked the big-mouth creature into the clutches of said cat. Kate killed the bird.

Kate experienced momentarily happiness, and then disturbed, her grandmother always displayed a fondness for mockingbirds and she guessed killing one brought bad luck. She felt so badly about her ripple in the cosmic karma she had wandered the halls confessing to all she'd killed a mockingbird. "I killed the bastard."

The bird was legendary, and Kate didn't have to elaborate on who she meant by 'the bastard'. Everyone congratulated her.

He remarkably and vigorously resurrected the following morning.
The people in the dorm gave the bird a new name; The Dead Mockingbird of Wilson. With his resurrection came a renewed vocal exuberance. He learned to imitate Shelly's car, especially the grinding noise and the tapping of her valves. Errrr-raw-raw-rahhh-tick-tick-clack.

Mornings like today were a harsh reminder. Never try to kill a mockingbird—especially with a book.

- ☼ -

Today's lacrosse practice involved a conditioning swim in the evening. Accumulated damage to your body after two weeks and five games has to be dealt with. A player cannot continue accumulating bruises and knocks without some kind of a break. Unfortunately, there wasn't any real-time off until Easter.

Athletes who put themselves in the way of pain have to deal with the consequences. The pressure to win is usually self-inflicted, but the pressure to play with injuries comes from coaches and peers. The pressure is subtle. The injured athlete almost becomes a non-person, relegated to the fringes of the group. The only way to be welcomed back into the camaraderie of the team is to participate and contribute. In sport, there is little patience for the wounded.

The team, in this regard, is not unlike a pack of wild animals; the weak are not tolerated.

The day improved. She stopped by the Athletic Center and saw Blake as replenishing the medical kit. Blake was the most senior of the trainers. A couple of Tylenol from Blake and she would feel better by her first class. "Blake, how's the team holding up, any problems from last game?"

He looked up from counting rolls of tape and ice packs. "Kater, your team is like a combat unit. Half of the girls are hurt and half will be. Thank goodness, you and Taylor and Andi have avoided anything big. Let's see, I can't remember anything ever too serious for you guys."

He paused and appeared to think over the four years he'd worked with the women's lacrosse team. "Well, I forgot a concussion you got in Stone Gap. Remember? A girl clocked you in the head with a stick just as the whistle blew. Your head developed a knot on it about grapefruit size. I kept asking you where you were at. You yelled at me. 'Don't use bad grammar. I'm at Shiloh and you know it.'"

Blake continued, on a roll, literally, and started cataloging injuries. "I think you broke your toe when you were a sophomore. We taped you and you finished the season, never missed a game."

He continued to ramble. "Dislocated your shoulder last year when you were knocked into a goal cage at Alamance Creek. We used X-rays and ice, and darned if you didn't play the last two games."

He paused briefly, "Of course your chronic hamstring problem and ankle problems you brought with you from high school are always there. You've got the greatest knees on the team, strong and...wait. I forgot the time you took a stick in the face at Appomattox. You cried like a baby, what a wimp."

She interrupted. "Blake, can you stick a cork in it? I've got a class in forty minutes and I need to get some food in me. Can you put some hot balm on my hammy and wrap it? I love to stink up Professor Paciarelli's class. Anyway, that time in Appomattox I cried because of my black eye and the fact I was nominated for Spring Court...you asshole."

She rolled her eyes. "Oh no, I did it again."

Blake seemed unaffected. "Well I seem to remember you getting chicken pox or something." He mechanically slathered Kate's thigh and put a wrap around it, without a thought to any intimacy in his action.

"Blake I'll see you later," she said.

"Yep, you and Andi and Taylor have gotten by pretty easy."

"Bite a big one Blake, and Taylor had chicken pox."

She left in a much brighter humor. The odor of the balm permeated the Ace Bandage wrapped about her thigh, it smelled like the locker room. Its warmth felt comforting on her sore hamstring.

Kate's mind began rapidly spinning in all directions. I wonder if I could market the odor of a locker room. I'll bet I'd make millions selling this stink to old jocks who want to recapture their youth. She wondered how to go about collecting 'odeur de jock.' She could sub-contract to clean locker rooms, distilling malodorous gold from old socks. She also wondered why everyone referred to female athletes as jocks. Did she not see the bigger picture?

Outside, she could tell spring was coming. A warm front from the south boosted her spirit. The walk to class took her past Massanutten Hall and the campus center. *Mmmm...I smell baked goods.*

Kate reacted, drawn to the snack bar and an odor of hot cinnamon buns. This had been a student favorite for over forty years. They were initially called muffins from the Massanutten. Through the years, they were identified by endless students as Massanuttenmuffins. Spoken as one word and with a southern drawl, it could be a mouthful to say as well as to eat. To the rest of the world, these muffins looked like an enormous breakfast roll. Their renown came from grilling in unlimited pats of butter. Kate craved them like an alcoholic yearns for a drink.

She settled into a booth and stared at the clock on the wall. *They taste so good; one per month, usually to fight the mood altering effects of PMS, and only as a favor to the rest of humanity.*

She wondered if there would be time to eat the whole thing or if she should she wrap half in a napkin, her class started in fifteen minutes. Then it would be time to face her favorite nemesis, Alicia. This class was evolving into an ongoing battle between the two of them. *I'll wrap it and get moving.*

The classroom had been set up in a semicircle. Kate took her seat in the far-left front row. Classmates wandered in and chatted casually with each other. She engaged in small talk and laughing banter with the group nearest to her, typical of students preparing for class. The room's atmosphere changed noticeably when Alicia entered.

She was a cute brown-haired, petite girl who exuded an aura of self-importance, a skillful and refined egotist. She selected a seat at row's end, a polar opposite from Kate. No one understood why, but whenever Kate discussed a subject, Alicia always took a contrary position. Other students channeled their energies toward finding a way to get Kate to cast some verbal bait on the conversational waters. They all expected Alicia to rise to this bait. Then the hour would be entertaining, informative, and stress free for them.

Dr. Paciarelli threw out her first inquiry. Answers were sparse and she began to look around the room.

"I think we'd all like to hear Kate's opinion, Professor." Ryan Malone made an unsubtle and desperate attempt to start fireworks. He still carried effects from last night's hangover. The class held its collective breath, hoping. Dr. Paciarelli played the role of innocent adjudicator, but she secretly relished the prospect of another verbal set-to.

"Okay, what is your response, Miss Holland?"

The battle began. Twenty minutes later they drifted off topic into a discussion about early man and a possibility of missing links. Alicia and Kate were going at it. Paciarelli hadn't gotten this much fun from a discussion group in ten years.

Dr. Browne

After dinner, Kate led a group of young players to the pool for their team swim. They just sort of fell in behind her, like ducklings. When they reached the natatorium, Kate threw down her gym bag and sat unceremoniously on a bench outside. A group from the local elderly center still paddled around. It could be awhile before they could use the pool.

The freshman gravitated to a now silent Kate. They sat next to her on the long concrete bench. She felt a responsibility to offer an explanation. "Early, for the first time, girls, we might have an hour before we begin our exercise swim, anyone care to lift in the weight room?" There were no volunteers, so they lounged, taking advantage of an unusually mild evening. The conversation turned to parents and how they could drive you crazy.

This collection of younger players had begun developing a unique relationship with each of the captains. When Kate spoke, they listened right away, determining how serious she seemed. If they thought Kate wasn't sermonizing, they talked and chatted with her, waiting for the joke. They often kidded her and teased her. They poked and prodded, trying to agitate her. One look, one gesture and they stopped.

Taylor, however, engendered fear. They tried to avoid doing anything stupid or making any wrong moves on the field, which would draw Taylor's wrath. She simply scared the be-jezzus out of them. In a moment of clarity, when the younger players were talking about the rest of the team, Paige summed up

Taylor best. "Do not approach Taylor first. If she speaks to you, then you may answer. Do what she says. She will tell you when it is okay to be friendly. Do not look directly into her eyes. Go where she points you."

They had a different take on Andi. They emulated and admired her, trying to mimic her athletic mannerisms, but they rarely listened to her. Mostly, the younger players knew to get out of her way. Andi was a whirlwind. Her intensity made it hard for others to get close or keep up. When Andi stepped on the field, she had one thing on her mind, scoring.

Each group held their own memories, their own bonds. It wasn't unusual for freshman to link with seniors, or the captains. They weren't coming back. Although the new players wanted acceptance, they isolated themselves. Brooke, Marisol, Caitlyn, and Martianne would frequently gather in isolation. Paige and Stacey, just one year removed from the memory of their first season, rarely joined them. They were forming a bond to deal with the stress of college, and from pressure to succeed in athletics. They would eventually find their role, and form the nucleus of the future.

Kate figured they thought of her as an older sister. She knew the future of this team belonged to them, and she simply existed as a symbol of the present, and soon the past. She wasn't mentally ready for icon status. While they spoke, Kate noticed how freely they communicated, and how unconcerned they were about blurting out their most intimate thoughts.

"Gary's ass is so tight. I wish I had the cojones to ask him out."

"Anyone hear about one of the soccer players and a trainer going ghetto?"

"Anyone hear the rumor about one of the women's coaches being a lesbian?"

The most embarrassing thing was their Kate-ism's; Marisol always quoted Kate. "Nothing lasts forever," as her inducement to play hard now.

Cat would answer; "We are not immortal," Brooke often eloquently offered her portrayal. "Will it matter one month from now, or in a year? We have nothing but the present and only expectations for tomorrow." Kate usually hid her face.

Occasionally they shared too much. Each one could mimic Kate's profanity-spiced declaration to, "pass me the f***ing ball," and of course they all were capable of yelling; "white or wheat...wheat or white, give me wheat."

- ☼ -

"Hello young ladies, are you enjoying this fine evening?" Dr. Browne, the President of the college, approached them, obviously out for an evening stroll. The freshmen knew Dr. Browne from several functions and were slightly awed by his demeanor and presence. He was a large, soft-spoken man who presented thunder in his voice. His slight southern drawl imbued his speeches with charm, and he could work a crowd like a preacher at a revival meeting.

His deep voice snapped the group to attention. His voice rang through the evening, sounding like Professor Howard Hill in the Music Man, selling his musical instruments.

He paused for a fraction of a second and peered at the girls under the fading light. "Why Kate, I didn't see you there. How have you been? It has been a long time since we've chatted. Is this your team?"

"Well, President Browne, I'm just fine and dandy, how are you?" Kate seemed relaxed and casual while the freshman looked at her wide-eyed.

"Fine just fine, it has been a while since we drank coffee and you gave me your opinion about how to run the school. Y'all mind if I join you?"

"My bad, Dr. Browne, join in."

Dr. Browne eased on the bench next to Kate. "I always enjoy your company."

He turned toward the others and said, "You ladies won't tell Kate's boyfriend will you?"

The group nodded and mumbled a "No sir" in unison. Brooke nudged Martianne into silence. She'd anticipated Martianne blurting out that Kate no longer had a boyfriend.

Kate and Dr. Browne discussed the team's prospects. She finally remembered the others, and turned in their direction. "Let me introduce you to the team; these are our freshmen, Brooke Gipson, Martianne Bourialis, Marisol Flores, and Caitlyn Birdsong. We occasionally call them a variety of nicknames. None are firmed up, yet. Ladies, this is our President, Dr. Browne. I want you to say hello to him whenever you see him, do you understand?"

The group nodded in unison.

"Dr. Browne is our best fan. You may have seen him at our home games. He comes to as many games as he can, right Dr. Browne?

"I sure do Kater" he replied.

The girls were shocked to hear President Browne use Kate's nickname.

"Let me tell you girls something about Kate. When I came here as a new appointee, I looked for a way to get to know the students better, in an informal and personal way. The first few weeks were frustrating. Indeed, nothing worked. I used the ideas my social committee suggested, and tried teas and socials to meet the students. It didn't seem to work. One day I thought I would eat in the dining hall with the students. Maybe I could stir up some conversation. I wound up sitting alone and ignored, as if I carried the plague.

"Just at my lowest point, Kate walked in and plopped down next to me. She started talking about the weather, asked how I enjoyed Spotswood, and the next thing I knew, she took me from table to table, introducing me to other students. It became an ice breaking moment. We wound up sitting at center table, surrounded by people asking questions. She gave me that opportunity. Correct, Kate?"

"Dr. Browne, I needed the company, and the idea of you needing my help to draw a crowd is laughable."

He continued, "She invited me to a game, and I have been following field hockey and lacrosse ever since. Now, you women promise not to tell the football team or baseball team about my being a fan, will you?"

There was a chorus of exuberant no sirs, and never, from the girls. Kate interrupted to remind President Browne of tomorrow's scheduled game against Skyline University. "We hope to see you at the game.

"I'll try to adjust my calendar. Let's see, I can always ditch...ummm...finance meeting."

He waved goodnight and continued his stroll. The freshmen were almost slack-jawed as they looked at Kate.

March 20

Game day, captains from both teams led warm ups. Spotswood's team sat in a circle at mid-field, enjoying each other's company and getting loose. The soft grass and the smell of the surrounding trees seemed to be a natural tranquilizer. The field was in good condition, cut low, and looking like Jose had trimmed it with a level. Kate and Gabrielle started talking strategy—what to do to agitate any opposing goalie.

The sun warmed their backs and the clear sky energized them. Kate moved into the center with Andi and Taylor. They began to perform a series of exercises, which pulled and lengthened their muscles. These were designed to eliminate pulls or strains in the all-important legs. They were together as a team, but each utilized her own routine to minimize injuries. Some of the girls had to take care of game time superstitions.

Taylor always left the circle and took a place at the sideline to stretch on the bench. Traci and Gabrielle stretched each other's legs, alternating positions. Jen and Ginni worked together while standing up. Coach Altman walked around the circle touching everyone's head. If you were an observant person you could see some of the freshmen developing their routines, routines made things less stressful.

Zach performed as todays on field trainer. He jogged over to help stretch Kate, as he normally did, a predictable routine. Unavoidably, stretching is an intimate moment. Kate stretched out, lying on her back with one leg straight up in the air. She held the leg as stiff as possible. He stood with his legs straddling her one leg and took her foot in his hands, bending the toes backward toward her face. Then he slowly pushed Kate's leg in an unnatural direction, backward, using the inner part of his thigh. The trainer has to lean into a leg while grabbing the hamstring to apply pressure.

The more steadily and slowly pressure is applied, the farther a leg goes back. Muscles stretch like a rubber band. It looks extremely painful and it is. Kate inevitably said to whoever stretched her: "A little farther and you can make a wish," or sometimes, "six more inches and you'll kiss me." An expression she used to jokingly let them know she couldn't take any more pain.

Today Zack responded by saying, "I'd take your kiss." Shocked, she looked to her left. Traci had her eyes focused on them. Besides Zack's massaging touch, Kate thought of another thing. *Damn, if she overheard I'm betting I won't get any passes from her today.*

The draw went to Skyline University, and they shot immediately. Penelope stepped forward to cut off the shooter's angle. She stopped the shot; then she walked behind the crease with the ball. She confidently looked left then right to see who covered whom. Jen used her speed to come back toward Penelope and took the clearing pass. Women's lacrosse is attack, attack, and attack, as opposed to the defensive and slow-moving men's game.

Jen passed to Andi, who ran the ball toward the center. She drew quick attention, and an immediate double team. Cut off, Andi threw the ball to Kate behind the goal and Kate passed it to Gabrielle, who shot into the goal. On average the transition took 45 seconds, and covered a distance of nearly two hundred yards. This occurred at least one hundred times a game. Lacrosse could be a blur within a marathon.

Penelope stopped shot after shot, her body took a beating. A goalie's life is a hard one, stopping a shot is instinctive and often lucky. A ball shot hard and at a short distance goes right by a goalie before she can react. It becomes mind altering. Most shots are stopped by their stick, which has a larger net area or 'crosse' than the field stick. A significant number of balls strike the body. A ball can actually numb your body with pain. Goalies have the ugliest bruises, especially on their legs. Everyone agreed there is nothing nastier looking than a naked goalie.

The ebb and flow of the game played out evenly for fifteen minutes. Then Coach Altman whistled out to Taylor, she held up two fingers. This indicated a call for a modified hidden zone defense. Within minutes, the Hornet offense ground to a halt. Taylor stood out as the heart of the zone; she disrupted any pass and any player attempting to penetrate. Marisol and Jen used their speed to slide along in front, closing off all open passing lanes, making it hard for the Hornets to attack...The Hornet coach screamed; "Time out!"

Players dropped their sticks where they stood and walked toward the benches. Spotswood led Skyline by four goals. When play resumed they would pick up their crosses and begin play, a holdover routine from the ancient game. Sticks symbolically placed, represented constant motion.

Spotswood welcomed the timeout. They gulped water and tended to various bumps and scrapes. Coach Burke encouraged them to "score more goals." Coach Burke was still not comfortable giving instructions to players who knew more about lacrosse than she did.

Most of the girls absorbed her comment with indifference. As they stood together in a huddle on the sideline, the steaming mass of sweating females stood at its closest to the fans. The men on campus generally regarded the lacrosse team as 'hot looking', which received validation from an annual poll by the Shooting Star Times, the school newspaper which choose them the most attractive group of women on campus. This game, however, did not involve a beauty contest.

The women on the field displayed little concern about appearance. The huddled players were hardly an advertisement found in the Southern Lady magazine. They spit and choked dust from their throats as disgustingly as any athletic team, male or female. They also adjusted their clothing, often pulling their shirts off to towel away the sweat. The male fans really loved time outs.

Then, in one of those situations guys wait and prayed for, Marisol pulled her jersey over her head. She stood there in her gray sports bra, soaked with sweat and revealing what her loose jersey covered. Marisol was endowed with physical assets that could make a grown man whimper. As she put an ice pack on her shoulder, and listened intently to the coach, the right half of the football team's offensive line nearly fell out of the bleachers trying to get a better look.

Big Blue returned from the timeout with a vengeance. Kate started out open near the goal. Traci caught the ball. She looked at Kate, and then turned away. Kate felt sure Traci froze her out. She figured Traci ignored her, and would later claim Kate didn't get open. Kate felt generous today or possibly paranoid. She'd let Traci live.

The whistle blew for halftime. The score said 12 to 3 in favor of Spotswood. Generally, Kate would remain with the group, first gulping down large quantities of water and repairing any damage that needed it. When the team came off the field, Kate noticed Dr. Browne sitting on the sideline bleachers.

She walked straight toward him. He stood as he saw her coming. "Good game Kate, the team looks excellent today."

"Thanks for taking the time to come to the game. We appreciate it when the President comes to watch us play."

When Kate returned to the team, several people in the crowd approached Dr. Browne, thanking him for attending the game and for doing an outstanding job. Dr. Browne smiled at Kate's political and effective greeting.

Martianne, the rookie goalie took over in the second half, an opportune time to test her developing goalie skills. She was a quirky character off the field, now they would see what she could do on the field. The Stars continued to shoot at will and the score rose to 18 to 5 before fifteen minutes passed in the second half.

Wholesale substitutions began. Andi had broken the single game scoring record with 11 goals. Martianne played well, and Penelope congratulated her on a job well done. Goalies developed a small sisterhood within the team.

When the game ended, the Hornets sullenly lined up for the final congratulatory handshake and Kate led Spotswood through the line. Midway through the lineup, Kate saw Boomer, her old boyfriend at the fence; it looked like he was talking to Missy Gray, his old high school girl friend. "Well, he's moved on with his life—Good for him—Asshole."

Battle at Tidewater

March 24

Getting to Tappahannock University took over three hours. Somewhere near Charlottesville they stopped for a break and started their slow descent toward sea level. The last half-hour on Mechanicsville Turnpike seemed like the longest part of the trip. As they neared campus, Marisol and Caitlyn noticed some veteran players seemed restless. The beautiful surroundings obviously did not calm their anticipation of the game awaiting them. Tappahannock's Clippers were always tough. They were located 90 minutes away from and Baltimore, less from Washington, making it easier to get experienced people for their programs. They were usually loaded with top lacrosse players.

Marisol whispered. "I wonder what kind of game we're in for today."

"Don't know, but it is sure pretty here."

TU's campus sat near the Rappahannock River on a rise of ground elevated above its green, lush, tidewater site. The college had a postcard look.

In their last three games against the Clippers, Big Blue had lost three times, with a combined difference in score of four goals. Two of the games were played in overtime.

As they walked toward Clipper Field, Kate and Taylor began drilling the freshmen about today's game. Taylor made a proclamation. "Pay attention, freshmen. This is not going to be easy. The Clippers have beaten us three times in a row. I've never had a victory against them, that streak is ending today."

Cat nudged Marisol. "Check out the captains. They look serious."

Today, Spotswood's Stars were wearing their blue tops with a lightning bolt of white across their chests. The white stars running the length of the right sleeve revealed their nickname. The kilts were gray, and they wore short black compression pants underneath. As they were warming up, Kate measured her team. We look so cool. Everyone is sharp in these uniforms. All we have to do is handle this Clipper team.

Then, when she finished her appraisal, Kate studied the Clippers. She recognized six players from home. Everyone else seemed new to her. She began reciting a roll call to anyone who would listen. "Number, 1 is Michelle Delaney from my old high school, Friendship. She was one of our leading scorers her senior year. Jewell Brett, number 3, from Magothy Park, she's on attack. Donna Hilburn, number 10, from St. Anne's, is Andi's best friend from high school. Number 8, is Lois McComb. She is the meanest, 'bee-aitch' you will ever find on defense. Brenda Lerczak, number 9, is Lois's pit bull of a buddy. They can crack pecans between any spaces they leave for you on attack. Then there is number 77, my all-time favorite player, Dixie Phiffer, also from Friendship. She got drunk at our high school prom and 'yakked' all over my shoes. Of course, she is the leading goalkeeper in our league."

As usual, Captains met to go over ground rules. Kate served as speaking captain today. Andi and Taylor chatted with the captains from Tappahannock until the umpires wandered over to greet them. "Hello ladies, I see you all know each other. This is my first MVVC league game and I am looking forward to it. My name is Susan and this is Grace," she indicated the other umpire who immediately perked up. "I know these criminals. I've done lots of their games before. Who's speaking today?"

Kate replied tersely. The game had begun. "I am, Grace."

"Me." Lois McComb spoke, and then extended her hand toward Kate. "Good luck today, Kater." The looks on Lois's face told her don't come my way. Her smile seemed as cold as her intentions.

"Call it in the air, Spotswood." A spinning silver coin thudded on the turf.

Kate shouted, "Heads."

"Clippers get the ball. Stars get to pick the goal you want to defend." Kate took the end that had the most sun. The second half it would be slightly harder to see.

The umpire continued her rules interpretation. "Captains, have your teams ready for stick check, any additional sticks must be checked now. Everyone get a mouth guard in their mouth when they step on the field. Make sure your players get four meters away when I call a foul. I do not want to keep repeating myself. Any player or ball near any benches will be whistled and brought back on to a safer area of the field. Watch the checks around the head; I will card you if you violate the bubble."

Kate had heard this before; she half-heartedly listened while she looked out toward the Rappahannock, and thought about this being her last game on this field. It was a beautiful place to play.

Grace inspected every stick to make sure it they were legal. The newest sticks were curved slightly to circumvent the rules, and added five miles per hour to a shot. Kate owned one of these new sticks.

Every nerve ending in her body twitched. A cloudless sky and waning sun added to the tidewater surroundings. Odors drifting across the field were oppressively sweet with a salt-marsh smell. She felt she had been given a gift today. The noise and the fans on the sideline disappeared in her mind. The odor vanished. Kate recognized the feeling. She was in the zone.

~ ☼ ~

This game wasn't for the faint hearted. From its start, checking became fierce. Tappahannock settled in defensively on Andi and Kate. They were playing a tough sliding zone and helping each other when Kate or Andi got a ball. Michelle, on attack for the Clippers, found Big Blue's zone equally impossible to penetrate. Taylor contested every pass and immediately made several interceptions. Whoever wanted the ball, most, would prevail.

Andi broke free and ran into a triple team in front of the goal. She shot a rocket past a triple team, and it somehow found a minute space between sticks. The score registered one to zip, Spotswood.

Lois and Brenda, numbers 8 and 9 for the Clippers, were playing better than they'd ever played before. The Clippers got a penalty shot for an obstruction call. They converted their shot and tied it, one to one. Kate began to notice a weakness in the Clipper defense. It looked like a small spot, but it became clear what needed to be done. Kate's skill relied on her catching in a crowd. She could snag a ball thrown in a group of players as if she were alone. She seemed able to focus only on the ball. She could help win this game.

Do something different, popped into Kate's mind as she sprinted down into the defensive end when the Clippers got the ball. Number 10, on attack for the Clippers ran down the right sideline, cradling the ball and looking for someone to get open. Kate approached behind her, from the right, and checked the ball loose before crossing the thirty-yard restraining line. Number 10 was shocked to see the ball bouncing forward into Courtney Zuck's stick—turnover. Big Blue came back on attack.

Transitions were difficult. Paige, suddenly had trouble when double-teamed, and often lost control. Traci and Gabrielle kept inching forward to help her. In this instance, Paige passed to Gabrielle. Gabrielle had to have been Big Blue's slowest player. Her strength lay in her bullet-like shot and fearlessness. She sprinted forward and noticed Kate, in the middle and double-teamed. There looked to be six inches of open space in front of Kate's stick. Gabrielle threw a laser pass.

Kate didn't flinch. Both defenders lunged where the ball should have been. Kate and the ball disappeared, headed one-on-one with Dixie Phiffer, the best ranked goalie in their league. Kate held one advantage. She knew what bothered Dixie the most. She ran straight at her. Dixie stood frozen. Kate picked a spot and fired the ball in the back of the net. Dixie hated when a ball came directly at her out of a cradle without warning. If Dixie stayed still, she got nervous. She played best moving around.

Players like Gabrielle and Traci knew they were in a supporting role today. Kate and Andi were Spotswood's main

85

attraction. The Clippers answered Kate's score with a quick goal over the top of Penelope's stick. On the ensuing draw, Kate sprinted in and picked off the ball mid-air. She turned and immediately bumped into a triple team. With no hesitation, she passed to Catbird, who looked open on the left side. Cat ran toward the goal and passed to Andi just as she reached the arc. Andi hit the nets for another goal. Big Blue forged ahead three to two.

The next draw headed toward Kate again. She used her hips and speed to get it again. This time, instead of driving toward the middle she switched hands, and turned down the right sideline. She was open except for Lois and Brenda standing firm in front of Dixie. At first, Kate thought of going behind the goal to set up a play, but as she switched hands, Brenda flinched and started to go right to cut her off. Kate put on a burst of speed and drove by Lois. Lois swung her stick past Kate's ear; she could hear the 'whoosh' as it went by. Kate brought her crosse into her body and fired a left-handed shot in the upper corner of the goal. The Spotswood bench exploded in a cheer, they were ahead four to two.

As Kate lined up at the circle for the next draw, she realized four other Clipper players were standing next to her. Her success made it crowded in her neighborhood.

She began to feel the adrenaline of lacrosse. It made her talkative. "Lois, I'm surprised you think you need help." Kate looked for a way into Lois's head. She heard Dixie Phiffer yelling from the Clipper goal, "Shut 28 down."

Kate wondered if she could goad Lois into an unsportsmanlike yellow card. Grace, the umpire, did not tolerate profanity, especially anything loud enough to be heard by the fans. Kate had an idea. "Just think, Lois, Dixie and I were best friends in high school. Do you think you could like me?"

Lois broke her silence. "Shut your arrogant mouth, you asshole! No one likes you."

Kate turned to smile at Lois just as the ball flipped into the air. She followed the ball's flight, judging its arc. *Focus, Kate*, she reminded herself. This game heated up to thermonuclear temperatures. Just before halftime, Penelope withstood a barrage of penalty shots taken by Tappahannock. She stopped all but one of five attempts. The halftime score was four to three in favor of Big Blue.

- ☼ -

Kate downed her last bit of water as their five-minute rest period ended. Kate wished more fans were there. A very small crowd witnessed the game, an excellent game. She spied her father. *Good old Pops*. The rest of the world is missing this.

Coach Burke shouted out her last instruction. "Same group ending the first half will start the second half. Let's huddle for a cheer."

The team chanted: "Go Big Blue, fight, fight, fight...Spotswood Stars... INTENSITY!"

Kate had her mind in this game when the whistle blew. She stayed minutes ahead of everyone else.

Both goalies were still hot. Dixie, in particular, became a whirlwind in the goal, turning away all of Big Blue's shots. Each team had only scored two goals since the half began. With twelve minutes remaining, the Clippers got a big break. Taylor got knocked flat on her face by someone behind her. When she got up, blood poured from her nose. She had to be taken out. It would take several minutes to stop the flow of blood and then

87

Taylor would have to change her uniform shirt. Spotswood called time-out.

Taylor called for the trainer and for an extra jersey. She found a likely victim. "Take off your shirt, Brooke."

At the whistle both teams trotted back out. Twelve minutes to go, and Spotswood led by one. *We can do this*, Kate thought; especially if Taylor gets back in the game. The next ten minutes seemed like a nightmare for Big Blue. The balance of power shifted. A tide rolled in for Tappahannock, and they were riding high. With eight minutes remaining, Stacey failed to double number 3, and the Clippers slipped in a goal. The game was tied.

The clock continued ticking. Kate tried moving down to mid-field, but couldn't get the ball past the twelve-meter mark without being triple teamed. Traci and Gabrielle ran out of energy and were replaced by Brooke and Allison. Coach misjudged her substitutions, leaving Traci and Gabrielle in the game too long. At a critical time two inexperienced players were expected to hold off this veteran Tappahannock team.

With four minutes left, a Clipper intercepted a pass, and broke toward the goal. Spotswood's defense converged on her, and with a smooth move, the Clipper player maneuvered Stacey into an obstruction call. Tappahannock drew a penalty shot. The crowd became silent, waiting. All twenty-four Clipper fans roared when she scored. Tappahannock jumped ahead seven to six.

The remaining four minutes seemed like a blur to Kate, every ground ball created a scuffle. One grounder rolled between two opponents. Both raced toward the ball. Someone would have to move aside. Rather than give in, they collided face first with a splat. The ball stopped dead between them as they both fell backwards to the ground. Andi swept in and scooped up the ball while the two players struggled to get up. Andi dashed straight toward the goal, the dazed players forgotten. She quickly picked up a triple team, and passed to Kate. Kate rolled around the crease. Her defender followed. It didn't take long for another girl to join in on the chase. Kate had their full attention.

Voices screamed from everywhere. "Twenty-two is breaking. Here comes twenty-two."

"Check her! Watch twenty-one!"

The frenzied movement disrupted the carefully planned defensive scheme. A Tappahannock player drew back, filling a hole in the now empty center. Andi stood open at the eight-meter mark, alone. Her legs began shaking with excitement. No one guarded her. Quietly she kept repeating. "See me Kate...see me Kate...SEE ME!

Kate jumped in the air. This elevated her over the sticks of the double team. In a fraction of a second she saw Andi, and while still in the air, dropped a pass to her. Andi fired it in. With one minute to go the game was tied at seven.

Taylor arrived back on the field wearing Brooke's number 4. The ball went to the Clippers on the draw. Everyone on Big Blue's offense followed, all except Kate. She stood sandwiched between Lois and Brenda, at the twelve-meter line. The ball rolled loose. Taylor cut through a crowd, running full tilt she scooped it up. The seconds were ticking down. She stood fifty yards away from victory.

Ten! (Tick) Taylor drew a triple team and no one looked open. Eight! (Tick) Taylor turned toward her own goal and saw

Penelope come out to the twelve-meter mark. She passed backwards to her goalie. Now they were ninety yards away from the Clipper goal.

Seven! (Tick) Penelope stepped forward, and with the oversized goalie crosse, heaved the ball the length of the field. Everyone turned their eyes downfield to see Kate, surrounded by Brenda and Lois; they were marking her perfectly. Only luck could intervene.

Dixie Phiffer's inability to stay still became the instrument of that fortune.

Six! (Tick) As the ball arched down, Kate narrowed her focus. "Stay, Kate... stay, Kate."

Just as the ball reached the group, Dixie bolted out from the goal trying to help intercept it. Five! (Tick) She bumped into the back of Brenda and knocked her forward. They both sprawled. Kate snatched the ball inches over Lois's extended stick.

Four! (Tick) Kate whirled, stepped carefully over the bodies on the ground, and fired her shot at an empty goal.

Later, Kate thought about how she did not join in the celebration at mid-field. The freshmen jumped into each other's arms, and ran out on the field at game's end. She remembered helping Dixie up and telling her how sorry she felt. She remembered apologizing for the way things happened as they hugged each other.

"Kate, when I saw you waiting for the ball, well, I knew you'd get it somehow. I panicked, and moved out too far. I guess this time I should have stayed still."

Kate recalled a tap on the shoulder and standing face to face with Lois McComb. Lois wore streaks of dirt on her face, earned by sweat, dust, and... tears? She graciously stuck out her hand. She tried to say something, but Kate interrupted. "Lois, I respect you and the way you play. I admire your game. You made me tougher. I needed to be, to survive against you."

There was no physical hug exchanged between the two players, just a nod and a final "good luck" between them. Kate knew she couldn't celebrate in the face of such a tough opponent.

While the team gathered and packed the van, Kate turned east toward the water. The heavy scent of salt-water marshes along the Rappahannock smelled delicious. The marsh grass at the edge of the river's bank captured the amber from the light of the setting sun. She watched the reddish-gold hue of the sky empty from the horizon. This area, the Northern Neck of Virginia, looked like a postcard of Southern charm.

The long trip home was enjoyable. The team stopped at a burger place and created an event with the quantity of food they'd consumed. Paige, Marisol and Brooke were still chattering about the game, going over the highlights. "Coach said she is going to nominate Penelope for player of the week for the way she played in this game. What do you think, Kater?"

Kate slid in next to them and said, "Sounds right to me, she played outstanding ball."

Paige kept repeating, "I can't wait until I'm a senior so I can tell all the freshmen about this game."

Kate leaned back and thought about the field at Tappahannock, and the sweat and tears left by the girls from Spotswood. We are part of their field. I only wish more people could have been there.

- ☼ -

After a long drive from the east, the welcoming mountain night made them feel better. Moon and stars sparkled in the sky as a reminder beauty could be found in the Blue Ridge as well as Virginia's tidewater. Kate felt too tired to stop at her sports locker to drop off her laundry and stick bag. The tower clock struck at midnight and she had to get up early for class. She searched for something to give her a spark of energy. At least my paper on adolescent behavior isn't due until Friday. Thank goodness Easter break is coming up, too bad I won't be able to spend much time at home, only one glorious week.

Athletes often cut their free time short in order to maintain top shape. One week of inactivity could dull the muscles and take away your edge. Tonight, as she hauled her bags up the steps toward her room, she thought about the edge—the edge of her head hitting her pillow.

March 25

Kate's nose tickled. She brushed at it as if a bothersome insect flitted nearby. It was the sun. The light beamed through the window glass. She extended her legs, full length, and touched her toes on the bottom bed rail. She pressed harder, concentrating on enjoying the feeling of her muscles stretching. She forced her eyes open and looked about. The familiarity reassured her. If her room were an odor it would be the smell of grilled muffins.

She gave herself the luxury of looking like a slob this morning. A quick shower and dusting with baby powder became her only concession to vanity. Her mind shifted to a

Massanuttenmuffin. Somehow, the thought of a butter-fried muffin did not seem to be the answer in Kate's mind to the breakfast quandary. Kate thought it would be a good time not to spend her money on a muffin, when her breakfast is included in her dormitory fee. Why not use what her parents paid for? These moments of clarity were all parents hoped for.

The jog to Howard Hall just increased her appetite. When Kate checked in at the entrance, she showed her dining pass to Olive, a permanent fixture at Spotswood for twenty years. "Good morning, Miss Olive," Kate mumbled.

"Good morning, Kate, you don't usually show up until dinner. What's the occasion?"

Olive acknowledged her and knew her name. This caught her off-guard. Kate thought she normally spoke gruffly with students. Olive took on a preeminent status as Spotswood's meanest woman. "I'm here for some of your delicious scrambled eggs, Miss Olive, lots of them. Although...I really wish you were making those western omelets you make at Christmas. I'd get up early for one of those."

"Kate, you get whatever else you are going to eat, but wait a few minutes for your eggs and I'll send out your omelet."

Kate was astonished. Special orders were rare and only for unique dietary reasons. Ordering a special item had to be done in advance—way in advance.

"Thanks, Miss Olive, I don't want to be a bother."

Olive smiled, an expression verifying her genuine humanity. "Kate you have been coming in here for years and you always say hello or have a pleasant greeting for the servers. You chat with them and try to engage them in conversation. We talk amongst ourselves, you know. You wouldn't believe how we complain about the lazy arrogant students. Did you know you are the staff's favorite?"

Kate walked away feeling even better about the day. It did not take much to make someone feel special. Kate was given an unasked-for gift. Olive's words were an omelet hug.

- ☼ -

After practice, Kate and Taylor relaxed, sitting on the edge of the low wall in front of the gymnasium. They leaned back, admiring the boxwoods and colorful geraniums placed meticulously in a solid layer of cedar chips. This delicate landscaping contrasted with the austere brick façade of the gym. They were talking shop, discussing the roles and the prospects of some of their teammates. Kate thought about injuries. "If we lost Andi, we'd be done, T."

"She sure is a windup toy, Kater, crank her up, put her out on the field and get out-of-the-way."

"She's the shooter, the go-to-girl. What bites me is her boundless optimism, and heart." While Kate and Taylor chatted, Black Jack and Paige joined them.

Jackie seemed eager to join the conversation. "What's up? And, who are we talking about?

"Andi, of course"

Never shy, Black Jack jumped into the conversation. "Right, Andi is the heart of the team, so that makes Taylor our muscle."

A few late-comers caught the tail end. "What about Kater?" All eyes turned expectantly toward Black Jack.

"Well if I am permitted to give an easy answer, I would say Kate is the brains of this outfit...old school."

They laughed spontaneously. Marisol yelled over the hooting. "I want to be like Kate when I grow up." This caused more cackling, since everyone knew Marisol's seriousness.

Jackie called the group to order. "I propose we pick the best and be done with it. I will announce the category and the winner as determined by the group. OK. The first category is..."

"Best shot?" They conferred, and Jackie announced..."Andi."

"Best defense?" This required more conferencing..."Taylor."

"Fastest?" This took longer, with some arguing..."Jen."

"Best looking?" Categories suddenly got eclectic—"Marisol."

"Most Stamina? Andi."

"Best at intercepting passes? Taylor."

"Best passer? Gabrielle."

"Biggest mouth? Paige."

"Best tan? Black Jackie."

They were on a roll, amusing themselves with their selections.

"Biggest feet? Ginni." This got announced as Ginni joined the group.

"Best hair—no contest, Traci. Okay, last category."

Jackie paused for dramatic effect. "This will probably answer all questions. Who would be your first pick if you were going to start a team?"

"Kate!" The freshmen shouted in unison.

Jackie continued, "Thus my choice of Kate as our brains. We have heart, muscles, brains, making the trinity of our team. Alright, whom would you pick next?"

Marisol shouted from the back. "God, she goes to her left better."

"Also, God rolls the crease better."

The group broke up, still discussing their choices.

As they separated, Taylor grabbed Kate from behind. "Kater, I'm staying with you tonight, Okay?"

Kate knew Taylor wanted to get away from her roommate tonight and needed a place to stay. Kate didn't mind the company. The only thing she missed about ex, Boomer was late night conversations. She often liked to unwind in the evenings with someone to talk to. Boomer filled the role for two years. Their breakup became inevitable. Their conversations were often one-sided. She'd just gotten bored with NASCAR and who had the hottest Buffalo wings.

Kate knew she would adjust and find someone else to talk to. She liked the company of men.

Kate hunched over her computer, working on a research paper. The spelling and grammar checker kept insisting she fix a sentence fragment. The persistence of the computer drove her crazy. She clicked ignore.

In the meantime Taylor took a long hot shower. Kate started wondering if college students took longer showers than any other group in the world. If they did, someone should find a way to make a profit from this eternity in the tub. If a profit could be made then Kate must find a way.

Her imagination spun. If I invented a steam oven using a shower's hot water supply, you could cook your breakfast or lunch while you washed. I would need some good telemarketing scheme.

Kate became deeply involved in her latest get rich quick idea. She envisioned the TV ad…And would you be interested in a free sponge/spatula to go along with your cooking and showering needs?

Taylor turned off the water.

Kate mused. *She probably wasn't in there long enough to finish cooking the turkey.*

Kate was notorious for monumental leaps in imagination.

Taylor padded in, water dripping from her like a mini-rain; she towel dried her hair and stood there totally naked. Taylor had to be the most uninhibited person Kate knew. She brimmed with a sense of confidence about her body, and rightly so. Kate had never been called prudish, but she felt awkward, only because she sat in the presence of legendary confidence.

"Taylor, I have to agree that you have the best woman's body I have ever seen, and sad to say after years of showering with athletic women, the number I have seen is considerably high. If I were getting cosmetic surgery I would take in a digital photo of you to work from."

Taylor didn't bother to answer. As usual, she disregarded compliments, as well as criticism. "Kate, did I tell you Sam McIntire asked me if y'all might be interested in dating? Sam is really a great guy and good-looking. I told him I would ask, but if you are not ready I will tell him to forget it."

Taylor's subtle attempt to make sure Kate had male companionship was sweet. Kate knew Taylor really worried about her, and she would do whatever she could to make sure her friend stayed happy.

"Taylor, I love you dearly, but I am not like you when it comes to men. You have not been without a boyfriend for more than two weeks. Is that a good guess?"

"Not true, Kater, y'all recall I did not have a boyfriend for a long while during the beginning of second semester, our sophomore year. The year I broke up with Jimmy Chantey because he got too possessive. Five weeks later I dated Eric."

Kate looked into Taylor's eyes, a good place to look since she still stood there without clothes on, and said, "Taylor you were infected with chicken pox and were quarantined for four weeks. You started dating Eric while you were full of purple welts. Don't you remember?"

"I remember this." Taylor grumbled, "It is absolutely impossible to argue with you. With you the answer to white or wheat is always going to be wheat. I do not ever recollect losing an argument in my life, because I learned early on when we became friends to shut up when y'all started talkin'. I'll tell Sam to get in line."

Kate displayed a puzzled look. "Wait, line, you said line, what line? Name me some names."

"Kater, y'all are such a big dork. I told my Eric if I see him hangin' around you, he'll be minus parts he dearly admires, and I'll be playing lacrosse with them.

"You want names, I'll give you names; Bubba, Billy Bob, Boots, Cooter, Scooter, and Junior."

"Good grief, T, you listed the entire Crucible Volunteer Fire Brigade."

"I rest my case, connoisseurs of womanhood, all. Goodnight girlfriend." Taylor slipped into bed and fell asleep in two minutes.

Kate, unfortunately, would let her mind spin for another hour before she rested, thinking about everything, and nothing.

She thought about her friend snoring lightly in the other bed, Kate and Taylor, a strange pair, but irrevocably friends.

March 26

The Appomattox team warming up on their field recently became a division two team. Theoretically, the schools giving scholarships outclassed them. Lately, there were moments when Kate wondered if Coach Von Mater had a plan when she'd scheduled this game two years ago. The Coach had mysterious ways, and she confided in no one.

Andi agreed. "She brought this team to the brink, and she abandoned us."

"Yep, true mini-you, but then at other times...I know Coach would not leave a job unfinished. What happened, and why? I wish I could take one more ride down I-81 with the old lady...to get an answer."

Andi, as usual, brimmed with confidence about the game. Timonium's game early in the season boosted her expectations, and buoyed her confidence.

"This team lost to Timonium by seven goals. We can beat them."

Spotswood set up three lines for a passing drill. Black Jack agitated the troops by mocking Andi. "Andi said give 110%. Will we be down to 90% for the next game? I mean, after all how can you give more than 100% of anything?"

Traci joined in with her analogy. "100% of a pie would be all of it, 110% must include the pie plate, except adding a plate would bring us to 200%, right?"

Black Jack called on Stacey for the definitive answer. "Stacey, you're a math major aren't you?"

Stacey didn't seem interested; she turned toward Andi's line for her passing drill. "Leave me out of this, Jack. I am not going to piss-off Andi and find her running up my back later."

Stacey normally had an easygoing attitude, things had changed recently. Everyone noticed, but no one could get her to talk. Stacey kept her teammates at a distance. It even affected her performance on the field.

The Appomattox Cannons were under a lot of pressure to win this game. Rumors circulated that their coach expressed disappointment about their season. This put them in a somewhat untenable position. They were expected to beat a smaller school, but Spotswood occasionally became a proverbial tiger held by the tail.

Appomattox's coach looked worried about the Cannon's prospects today. Unless Appomattox knocked off Spotswood, her team would have more losses than wins, and an additional shame of being beaten by a division III team. This turn of events would make for a long ride home.

Team captains met and shook hands. Kate noticed the Appomattox captains seemed tense and were not in a joking mood. No pleasantries or chit-chat were exchanged, even when an umpire inquired about their trip. Their meeting ended quickly, both teams intent on going through their pre-game rituals. Taylor went toward the sideline to stretch on her own. Zack stretched Kate in mid-field, and Traci and Gabrielle stretched each other. They were ready to roll.

Keys to winning this game were ball control and minimizing the number of turnovers. Today, Gabrielle seemed to be able to find an open spot as she cut in front of the crease. Kate noticed the mismatch and began taking advantage of her height to pass to Gabrielle and Traci as they cut diagonally in front of the goal. Gabrielle and Traci each scored, and Andi scored three more times to make it 6 to 2. Kate reasoned Big Blue's offense could control this game with sharp passing and taking high percentage shots.

With 10 minutes left in the half, Kate flipped a pass to Taylor who'd crossed over from the defensive side. She ran directly toward the goalie. Running at full speed, Taylor fired a shot. Appomattox's goalie caught it in her crosse, but then dropped it. She turned to locate it, and kicked the ball backward with her heel. Taylor scored.

"Woo hoo, give me five, Kater." They extended their arms straight up and slapped their hands together. Kate really disliked celebrating in front of another team's defense...but, T-bomb had just scored.

Coach Von Mater used to warn then about celebrating prematurely. It could be like pouring gasoline on a smoldering fire.

This is exactly what happened. At halftime Appomattox closed the gap. The whistle blew and the score read 7 to 5 in favor of Spotswood. The Big Blue defense came off the field arguing, they sensed Appomattox gaining confidence. The water jug became the eye of the storm. The offense squabbled, confused, and the defense sounded annoyed. All of them were gulping water and spitting clots of dust, looking for a way to clear their heads and figure out what had gone wrong.

The Spotswood team needed all of their halftime minutes to re-group, and look for ways to put more points up. Coach Burke gathered everyone together. She raised her hand for quiet and addressed them. She paused for dramatic effect. "We must get the draw more often. Get out there and fight."

The team seemed to process the words, and then dismissed her. They began to talk among themselves. This indicated a team still out of sync. They formed for their cheer. Kate stopped them with a sharply spoken word. "Listen!"

All paused as Kate explained herself. "The other team is laughing it up, having a good time. What happens in the first five minutes of this second half is critical, we need to break their spirit. Crush them, and grind them into the dirt." This seemed to motivate them.

Spotswood won the draw. Taylor broke free, picked the ball out of the air and passed to Kate. The Spotswood offense moved into position. Kate stood virtually still with her defender waiting patiently in front of her, waiting for a move. The other defenders spread out, each marking their player. Kate cradled the ball and kept switching from her right hand to her left hand and back, almost hypnotically, rocking.

Coach Burke turned to Coach Altman and asked, "What the hell is she doing?"

Kate called out a play—"Blue cat!" The Spotswood offense moved quickly. The move left Kate isolated one-on-one with her defender, and Appomattox's goalie. She switched to her left hand and smiled, the goalie yelped. Kate faked a step to the left and spun right, shot, and scored. It would be Kate's best goal of the day and it happened without celebrating. The Cannons' young goalie muffled a sob.

The final score was 14 to 8. Andi scored eight times and looked like the old Andi, ready to take over the league lead in goals. The Appomattox coach congratulated Andi and Taylor.

She asked them about number 28. Taylor answered, "Ma'am, she's not done yet." The Appomattox coach looked puzzled. "She's over there, with your team." Andi pointed. "She told us she wanted to talk to your goalie."

Kate stood in the middle of the Cannons talking very seriously to their goalie. When she returned, Andi couldn't contain her curiosity. "What's up, Kater?"

"I told her by losing control of your emotions you lose control of yourself, and self is all a goalie has, the more self, the better goalie performs. I also apologized for our behavior after she accidentally kicked in a goal."

Kate muttered something about gaining 'self' and walked toward the locker room.

Andi had a puzzled look. Taylor knew what was coming. "Taylor you know Kate as well as anyone, do you ever get the feeling she is...well, different?"

Taylor stopped packing her bag, turned her attention toward Andi, and thought for a moment before she spoke. "Kate is as normal as all y'all. If y'all's cat dropped a litter of kittens in an oven, would you call them biscuits? No? Well, Kate's no biscuit."

Taylor's boyfriend Eric walked out on the field to greet her. She jumped in his arms, locking her legs around his waist. He staggered but held on. Taylor gushed, "Did you see me score, honey?"

Eric lugged Taylor up the hill toward the lockers. Fortunately he lifted free weights every day.

Annapolis

March 28

Kate was packing her suitcase when Jen stuck her head into her room. "Easter break." Kate answered Jen's unasked question.

"That's all you are taking home?"

"I packed last night. I want to get out of here after my one o'clock. I am so ready to get away from this place for a while."

"I know what you mean. This break is too short—too short to get in trouble."

"What about you, Jen, are you going home?"

"No, I'm staying here. I have a campus job; it will keep me away from my family and the inevitable arguments."

A close bond formed between Kate and Jen that they'd never discussed. It began when they first met three years ago. A three by five card, posted in her dorm had caught Jen's attention while she suffered an emotional low point.

Want to play LACROSSE? Contact Katherine Holland, room 301.
Can't play? I will teach you. Need a stick? I've got one.
Call 5551.

Kate left at noon. The trip home took three hours, and the traffic around D.C. stayed remarkably light, except for a twenty-minute delay for a burning truck on I-495. After she arrived, it did not take long for her to settle in. She fell into her bed, sound asleep until the phone rang.

Kate's mom yelled out to her. "It's for you, Kiwi. Kiwi, her Mom's pet nickname for her, a secret Kate doggedly tried to keep from everyone. It came from a combination of Kate and Peewee. It made her cringe.

"Hi, Kiwi." Kate recognized Deanna Delong's voice immediately. She knew about her damn nickname.

"Dee, I wondered when you would get around to calling me."

"Kiwi, you and I must hit 'Naptown' tonight. I hear the Mid-Shipmen are out in force, and you know I am looking for a connection since Brad dumped me."

"I believe you dumped him."

"Whatever, Kate...I haven't been to Annapolis in a while, and you know how well we work together as a team—so, are you going to be my wingman, or what?"

They had not spoken since the Lee game. They were the kind of friends who picked up in the middle of things, barely missing a beat. Kate didn't hesitate. "Okay, pick me up at nine. Let's go to the docks, and start at McMarley's, and try not to dress like a whore."

Kate hung up before Dee could answer. She knew her last comment would agitate Dee for at least two hours. Kate knew how to get under her skin.

- ☼ -

It seemed unusually warm for the end of March, but still typical Maryland weather. They'd enjoyed sightseeing. Several men looked them over and Dee ignored them. Dee had a problem finding a guy when she put her mind to it. During high school, Kate loved going out with her because Dee was a certified guy-magnet. Kate always assumed there would be leftovers.

Later in the evening they were sitting at an outdoor table at O'Boyle's. Kate leaned back and looked up at Francis Street. She peered at the lighted dome of the Maryland State House. It presented a perfect image, along with the smell of the water from the Severn, and the uniformed Middies walking along the dock. They were hurrying back toward the Naval Academy. The long line of boats extended out along the pier, rocking in the chilly water of the Severn River, creating an atmosphere, which lured people to this place. A breeze started a few boat bells ringing, which added ambiance.

Annapolis had a therapeutic effect if you stayed away from the night life.

Without any predetermined accord, both Kate and Dee declined several drinks proffered by young Romeos hoping to get their attention, among other things. They were content to take pleasure in the night, observing people and enjoying each other's company, two old friends who had recently faced each other as opponents.

The temperature began to lower as the evening wore on, and they both drank coffee. Alcohol would have been out-of-place for two athletes hanging on to the vestiges of a training regimen.

"You know, Dee; just sitting here is absolutely marvelous. It made me think about something my dad said, something which finally made sense."

"Easy, Kiwi, I love your dad."

"Yes, yes. We all love him, especially my friends."

Kate affected a pout. "He said the first quarter of your existence, it's important to be from someplace. It helps define who you are and makes it easier to move on with the rest of your life."

"I understand, Kate, if we are going to be from someplace, this is the best. We're just two 'Naptown' girls." They sat back, taking in the air and sounds of the times of their young lives. Deanna's mind drifted to their shared passion. She smiled, remembering their game this season.

Dee broke the silence about their game. "Kate, have you ever played in a more miserable game?"

Kate thought about a field hockey game played in the rain and sleet at Frostburg University. It came close but not quite as bad as Lee. "Nothing compares. It sucked big time. Did my Mom get your clothes back to your Mom?"

"Yep, and she asked about all of the Kleenex—you know— in my sports bra?"

Kate glared at Dee. "Careful where you are going, girlfriend, I know where all your dead boyfriends are buried." In an instant their laughter echoed along with the boat bells.

"You know what I'd like, Kiwi?"

"Mmmm—let me guess, a man with stamina?"

"Better, I'd like us to meet one more time on the field. I know this sounds gay, but I love playing against you."

"Me too, Dee, I know when we play, good shit is going to happen."

"You have a way with words, girlfriend."

- ☼ -

Finally, the time came to return to school and take the trip around hell highway. When Kate passed Manassas, she began to breathe easier. Spotswood and her friends were gathering.

Except for a Medi-Vac helicopter landing on I-66, nothing significant happened. Just past Haymarket she saw a large herd of cows grazing contentedly in a pasture. Her father told her when you see cows rather than houses or shopping malls; you are in a place, which is more hospitable to human beings.

As the highway opened up she replayed a cryptic text message she'd received from Jen before leaving home. Jen's message played around in the back of her mind while she drove. Chief Star makes a rainbow connection. Talk to you when you get here, Love Jen.

Obviously, there had to be a problem involving someone gay, but who could it be? The Chief Star reference made her think about the team. Kate knew a few gay women, but only two played for the Stars, Jen and Stacey. Jen wouldn't relay a message over the Internet concerning her love life, and any reference to Stacey would be indiscreet since she stayed very secretive about her sexual orientation.

Kate might have been the only one who knew about Jen and Stacey. It seemed odd how it all came out. She and Stacey were soaking in whirlpool tubs in the locker room. Stacey seemed to be distracted and Kate asked her what troubled her. Kate realized later it's sometimes better not to ask.

"I've never said this to anyone else—I'm gay.'

"Okay and I need to know this... why?"

"You don't judge me, you never have, and I guessed you knew, and you never avoided me. I knew you wouldn't."

"Okay, thanks for sharing. Hey, don't squeeze my butt anymore when you hug me."

"Dude, I never squeezed your butt—in your dreams maybe." Kate never repeated the conversation.

When Kate casually dismissed Jen's fear and acted as if her declaration meant nothing. Jen responded by doing something she said she hadn't done since her twelfth birthday, when, during a game of spin the bottle, she wished for it to point toward Jane, and figured out the cruel joke life had played on her. She began to cry. She covered her face, and cried quietly. Afterward Kate decided these were tears repressed for many years, tears, which only flowed in the darkness of her room when Jen couldn't take the absurdity of life.

The dorm bustled, a hive of activity with people returning from vacation. Everyone exchanged news and gossip. A week's break from one another created a void of information. A small school like Spotswood produced intimacy larger schools could only duplicate in microcosm. There were no strangers on this campus, and just like a family, anyone strange, anyone unusual and different were tolerated as family.

A southern and mountain perspective made for a friendly aloofness. Secrets were kept for decades on this campus. Secrets everyone knew about, but never discussed. If you were part of the society, nothing mattered from mayhem to madness. If you were not in this society, you of course would be a candidate for punishment. 'He needed killin,' often came up as a legal defense. Kate knew if she waited, Jen would bring her news or a name of who needed killin.

A screeching vacuum signaled Kate's return and effort to organize the process of returning to the college life.

Every 10 minutes or so someone would stick their head in and call out a "hi!" The conversation would begin all over and people would fill each other in on any interesting news. The oral history of a college is spoken in the trivia of day-to-day conversation. These times would be remembered and cherished in later years. Things said, would be forgotten.

Finally, Jen arrived. She breezed in, nodding her hello. Kate saw her agitation. "What has you buggin?"

Words spilled out in a torrent from Jen's lips. "Kater, I've got some news I think you ought to know."

"Would it have anything to do with double coupon day at IGA?"

Jen hesitated for a second, took a breath, chose to ignore any remark and continued. "It concerns our team and one of the players."

Kate ran several scenarios through her mind. She waited patiently.

"Last Wednesday when y'all went home, I stayed on campus to work in the weight room. I used the weights and got paid to maintain the room for a senior program in the evenings. One night I ran into Stacey and found out she stayed on campus too. She worked in the athletic office. I talked to her about being alone, and asked if she wanted to get together for dinner some evening. She seemed agitated and almost annoyed."

Jen paused for effect. "Then Stacey made it clear she'd made other plans, and would not be on campus very often. I got knocked back by her next comment, 'So don't bother calling me.'"

Kate shrugged. "Maybe Stacey thought you were hitting on her, and she acted defensively, because, you're not her type."

"Kater, you know I am very particular about my sex life. Stacey sleeps around, and is not very moral. I call her a friend, but not that kind of friend. I am confiding in you because you're my boo, and a captain of the team."

Jen emphasized the word captain as she continued. "Well, Captain, Thursday night I met with our senior citizens and worked out. I shut down the weight room and went to the front office to drop off my key. On the way to the Athletic Director's office, I passed Coach Burke's office. The halls were dark so I was surprised to see a lit office. I figured I would drop in to see if Coach might be working late. The door eased open about an inch or two, so I went in. Well she had been working late all right. She worked over Stacey. Coach, the ugly bitch, stripped to her panties over Stacey—both of them butt-naked. They were tangled around each other on top of the desk. For crying out loud, lips—body parts, ugh! It looked wrong, Kater, I thought my eyes would catch on fire. Give me some water, I need a drink."

Jen seemed genuinely shaken.

Kate acted appalled, but felt somewhat amused by Jen's reaction. "Here, drink this." She handed Jen the water and took a swig herself. The image of Coach and Stacey ran through her mind, making her queasy. Truly upset, Jen really wanted to relinquish her responsibility. Kate saw irony in Jen's position. As a gay woman who considered what two women did together their own concern, she shouldn't be shocked to see two women making love, but her anguish came from who the participants were.

Stacey and Coach broke an ethical barrier with their romance.

Kate knew the next words Jen would utter would be the words, which would entangle her in this problem.

"Kater, what should we do? I haven't said a word to anyone. I slipped out before they saw me and I've been thinking about what I saw ever since. Nasty bitches, they could have at least locked the door."

Kate took a deep breath, looking for her center. This kind of situation put Kate in the middle again. Kate's mind, however, became icy calm and she visualized herself as the eye of a hurricane. Kate admitted fearing the commotion, but too stubborn and self-assured to turn away.

"Start with the obvious." Kate talked to herself as well as to Jen. "We could confront the situation by bringing it to the attention of the Athletic Director. This would undoubtedly turn into a game of 'she said she said.' We could confront the coach, but I don't think any of us trusts her. We could deal with Stacey, but I think she has issues, which cannot be worked out by you and me. Answering the matter of, 'what do we do,' is more like, 'what do we want?' The result either way would be divisive."

Kate took a deep breath. "Jen, I think I'm going to meditate for an answer. When I need to make an important decision, reciting a few Zen thoughts helps. I need to chant my Mantra of Great Compassion. Once I abandon logic and conceptualization, I will be able to answer your uncertainty."

She paused for effect. "The answer is—to have no question." She sighed with relief and smiled at Jen. "I need a beer."

"Kate you are so full of crap. Christian Buddhist, or a bullshit artist; one will do as well as the other. We need your help."

Kate looked indignant, but she mustered a small smile. "Jen, we can't do anything. You don't have photos, so it's your word against theirs. I think I'll talk to Taylor and Andi and make them aware of what happened. You can put it to bed, metaphorically speaking. What Coach did was wrong but considering Stacey's age, not a crime. She also upset the Karma of our team. If I'm not mistaken, she'll ultimately pay for her behavior."

They agreed to not say anything now and to focus on the upcoming game and their classes. As Jen left Kate's room, Kate wondered if she'd taken the wrong stand ethically. *I think I just wimped out.*

- ☼ -

Later in the evening, Kate, agitated and on the toilet, casually read Q and R in her dictionary. All travelers were checked in and ready for whatever life held in store for them. Jen's tale would be played out later. She hoped for a positive result. Kate just wanted to enjoy the calm before the storm, except the phone rang, intruding on her serenity. Mid-grunt, Kate felt grateful to Alexander Graham Bell for inventing cell phones.

Zack Tyler's smooth southern drawl spoke on the other end. He wondered if she would mind if he stopped by. For a split second she searched her mind for a way out. *He has a girlfriend.* Then, in another instant, her objection seemed childish. *He obviously wants to ask me about something, although he is a darn good-looking guy.*

Aloud, she said, "Love the company. See you when you get here. Later." Somehow it felt good to Kate. It revitalized a part of her she'd tried to ignore.

April 01

Andi and Taylor met Kate at a Pub on Tuesday night. Brannigan's strictly adhered to laws about serving alcohol to minors and this insured they would probably not run into any of their teammates. Besides, Kate, Taylor, Penelope and Jen were the only players who were twenty-one.

The waitress brought their pepperoni pizza and tiredly plopped it on the tabletop. Kate picked up a slice and folded it. She told Taylor and Andi what Jen had seen. She took the folded slice of pizza and stuffed it in her mouth. Andi and Taylor glued their eyes on her, they looked horrified as Kate said, "... and Coach licked ..." Kate used the pizza to demonstrate.

The resulting sounds from Taylor and Andi resembled kittens calling for milk, "Eeeyew! How gross."

Taylor called for a lynch mob and Andi wanted to know if this wasn't an April fool's joke. Kate nibbled at the crust and pretended to pick a hair from her pizza. Kate's gesture made Andi turn green around the gills. "Stop, Kater, we get it."

Finally, they worked their way from anger to reason. In about the time it would take to eat a slice of pizza, they were making rational comments about the situation. They were the best of the best and Kate felt honored to be among them.

"Kater, I don't think you should talk to the Athletic Director about this." Taylor assumed command at the table, as if it were a lacrosse field. "I think Andi should talk to him and present the situation as we see it. Now Kater, exactly how do we see it?"

Kate reiterated their position. "We feel what the coach did was ethically wrong, but we assume since they both are over the age of consent, they are entitled to privacy."

"Hell, Kater, a few more miles to the west of here is West Virginia, and 14 is the age of consent. We want the AD to be aware and make sure Coach is thinking about our team—all of the team."

All three agreed to continue this season without any distraction. They wanted to put this situation behind them, now. But, right is right, so Andi would make an appointment with the Athletic Director after tomorrow's game.

Kate belched. "Excuse me, girls, but I need to relieve myself."

"Lovely, Kate, you are so refined."

Kate left the table satisfied she had grossed out her friends.

"You know, Taylor, if Kate talked to the AD, she would probably tell him off if he didn't react the way she wanted."

"I agree, Andi, you are the most diplomatic one, in a teeny-tiny kind of way."

"Taylor, no short jokes, and no offense, but it appears we're surrounded by lesbians. They seem to be everywhere." She leaned in and whispered in a conspiratorial manner. "I am not even sure about Kate."

Taylor looked grim. After she deliberated for a second, Taylor made her judgment. "All right, let's look at the facts, she's good looking, she can run fast, and is athletic. She has tremendous stamina, she plays lacrosse better than most, and she is as smart as a whip. She's very aggressive, and have you ever noticed her legs are a little hairy? It's also a fact she doesn't have a boyfriend, does she?"

Taylor pronounced a verdict: "Thus it is so, as the day turns into night. She must also be on the gay team."

Andi, not known for her quips, paused thoughtfully. "Well, given the facts as you've outlined them, she's starting to sound pretty good to me. I'll have to drop my boyfriend first, but I will date her. The longer I play on this team, the more inclined I am to—Yeah, I'd date her."

They were still laughing when Kate returned. "What's funny?"

Taylor and Andi were caught in an uncontrollable case of giggles. Laughing until their faces turned blue. Kate felt out of the loop. If she wasn't in on the joke then she decided to leave. "Time to go, ladies, but before we leave I want to state that there are no more or less gays on an athletic team than on the chess team. We have twenty-five players on our squad. Only two of them appear to be less than straight. People are people, so let's be good Christians and forgive and forget."

"Good idea, Kater, after all, what more could go wrong?"

Before they left Brannigan's, they encountered a situation made more complicated by the situation between Coach and Stacey, something else to add to the list of sins. They spotted Marisol, Brooke, Cat, and Kelly in the Pub. The team rules were plain, no alcohol unless you were twenty-one. If you were caught drinking you were turned in, and you could be suspended.

Taylor swore. "Damn, I thought this place didn't serve minors."

Kate rationalized. "They were sitting with an older crowd."

Andi went bananas. "This is a royal pain. If we report these poop heads, we are going to go face-to-face with Coach Burke. I'm not sure I feel comfortable about reporting them for violating our code of conduct to someone who violates the code of ethics. It makes me feel freaky."

Kate suggested she'd handle the players, since she worked with them from the beginning. Taylor presented another suggestion. "I will take responsibility for puttin' them straight."

Taylor headed back into Brannigan's. While they waited, Andi asked Kate if she'd like to confess her sins.

"What sins, Shooter?"

"I heard Zack Tyler called you."

"How did you hear about him calling?"

"Blake is his buddy and he overheard the conversation."

"Well, he called me last night and came over for a visit."

Andi could not be subtle. "So, Kater, how did it go? What about Traci?"

Kate paused to find the right words. "He gave me a gift he brought from home. He loves to hunt and barbecue, so he brought me some barbecued venison. I tell you, how can a woman turn down a handsome man who brings her meat? I don't think Traci is worried. Although he did say they were arguing a lot lately."

Taylor appeared from Brannigan's, waving them on. She piled in the car. Taylor could barely contain herself. She told Kate and Andi she'd walked in just as the girls were getting ready to drink a pitcher of beer. She said the girls nearly fainted when she slipped into their booth.

Kate laughed. "It's good to see they're not counting calories."

Taylor frowned. This wasn't time for jokes just yet. "They started stammering about the guys who brought them, insisting they drink some beer, and they were soooo sorry and...please forgive us, etcetera. Brooke started to blubber and promised she would not come to Brannigan's again. Marisol wanted to know if I was going to tell anyone else. I told her I was going to handle this myself. I told them I did not believe their stupid story, to stop lying, and learn a lesson from their mistakes. I also told them Andi witnessed them violating the rules."

Kate and Andi were impressed with Taylor's tactics. They applauded politely, a mocking gesture simulating old women applauding at the opera.

Taylor forged ahead. "I told them we would be hiding in the parking lot to see if they left immediately. They were all over me, thanking me and apologizing. I could hardly keep from laughing. I left as they were getting their jackets and calling for a ride."

Taylor shook her head and sighed. "Y'all, I am tired of lesbians and freshmen. I'm feelin' like a momma coonhound with too many pups and not enough teats. I would like to concentrate on lacrosse for a while."

They rode home and avoided any conversation pertaining to the team. Andi turned toward Taylor. "Zack Tyler brought Kater meat. This sounds like a love triangle in the making to me."

No Cheating

April 02

The Bulldogs of Clifton Forge were traditionally Spotswood's least favorite team, not because of any particular players or the dingy industrial look of their campus, but because of a long-standing tradition of animosity and abrasiveness by their fans and their coach. It didn't help that Coach Von Mater had mentioned she felt that CFU lacked class. They also had an ugly, heavy breathing bulldog as a mascot. He came to all of the lacrosse games and always urinated on someone's shoes.

Thankfully, fate had been kind and this year's Clifton Forge lacrosse team was in a serious world of hurt. Their obnoxious coach, Betty Borland, had finally driven away some of her seniors and seriously weakened a mediocre team. They played an aggressive and dangerous style of lacrosse, something their coach demanded.

When the Stars were warming up, Taylor echoed everyone's sentiments. "Games with these Bulldogs remind me of a bar fight."

"When and where did you come up with such a comparison?"

"It's rough out there on the farm, Kater. You'd think it was all cow's teats and kittens—but it isn't."

Andi poked Taylor. "Look, the coach is walking up and down the sideline yelling at the officials and her own players, and the game hasn't started."

No player on the team for more than two years would consider taking it easy on a hurting Bulldog team. They had learned their lesson the hard way. It gave the team a singular mind-set. Almost everyone thought of ways to harm or humiliate this team at the opposite end. When the umpires started a stick check, Kate always watched the opposing team check their sticks. She liked to see if anyone tried to hide any problems. After all she knew every trick in the book. She saw something. *Okay, number 8 is pulling her strings tight after using pliers to tighten her pocket.* She filed this information away.

The game started. Clearly Big Blue could easily penetrate a weakened Bulldog defense. It didn't take Andi long to live up to her nickname—Shooter. She fired the ball at the Bulldog goalie at every opportunity, and more. At the other end, the Bulldog offense got stopped early and often. When the scoreboard clock read ten minutes remaining in the half, Coach Burke called time out.

The scoreboard showed eight to one in favor of Big Blue. "Black Jack, replace Kate." Coach Burke started her substitution routine. After eight games, everyone knew the pattern. Kate, Andi, and Taylor would rest but not at the same time. Brooke would replace Taylor, Jackie replaced Kate, and Allison would play a few substitute minutes for Andi, often switching between defense and offense.

This kept players fresh enough to play at their peak for sixty minutes. In a tight game, Kate, Taylor, Andi, and Jen might play the entire sixty minutes. Of course if it stayed close Penelope remained in-goal. This was the evolution of team. Everyone knew their role and expected to fill a specific job. They may not like their role, but in most cases, they were willing to contribute.

Of course athletes were never satisfied with second best. Black Jack often said she wished Kate were enrolled in an accelerated program so she could graduate early. Kate didn't feel offended. Black Jack wanted her starting job.

Today, some new wrinkle in their dynamic changed; an adjustment in routine occurred. Stacey replaced Jen and when Jen returned, Stacey stayed in and subbed for Courtney. Kate and Taylor noticed immediately. When second half began Stacey stayed in the lineup, this time for Ginni. Andi finally noticed and nodded toward Taylor, then motioned with her palms turned up as if to ask a question.
Taylor shrugged and shook her head.

Clifton Forge turned to their tried and true tactics. On the Star's offensive end, fouling and rough play were in order. Betty Borland screamed for more of this action. She obviously wanted Spotswood to be content with scoring on penalty shots.

On one play, Jen got pounded. She wound up tripped, knocked flat, and then stepped on. The officials were so used to the tenor of this game no whistle sounded. Kate narrowly avoided Jen's stretched out body. She scooped up the ball and turned her eyes toward the goal. From the sideline a shrill voice bellowed. Coach Borland trumpeted. "Knock them all down."

With Jen's treatment in mind, Kate made a plan. She fired a shot, using the full length of her stick to crank it as hard as she could. At fifty miles an hour her ball struck the goalie squarely on her mask and ricocheted twenty yards back up field. It appeared to most people Kate had shot wildly. The goalie was stunned, more disoriented than hurt. She rocked back, and in a parody of slow motion, dropped to the seat of her pants. The umpire had no choice. "Yellow card, warning for a dangerous shot, number 28, go to the sidelines."

As Kate trotted toward Spotswood's bench, she passed by the Bulldog's coach she turned her head toward the coach. "How many goalies did you bring with you today, Coach?"

Betty stopped yelling, shocked into silence. She immediately called time out.

The last twenty minutes were played at a less chaotic tempo, and very little fouling. The Stars shut their offense down when it reached eighteen to three. No matter what, the Clifton Forge coach continued to yell from the sidelines, her voice an irritant in an otherwise beautiful day.

Then something happened which surprised everyone. With two minutes to play, number 8 for Clifton Forge scored her team's second goal of the day. That's when the surprise happened. Kate, the speaking captain, approached the official. "Ump, we'd like a stick check on number 8, the girl who just scored."

The umpire looked amused. She summoned number eight over. She checked the pocket and the ball disappeared below the top of the crosse. "Illegal stick," she called, "no goal."

Today's victory cost the Lady Stars some contusions and some abrasions but they had sent a message to the Bulldogs. Another message went almost unnoticed. Stacey had played the entire second half and Allison sat sulking on the sideline. Allison looked genuinely upset. She'd played less than a minute.

When the teams lined up for the game-ending handshake, Allison stayed on the sideline, talking to her parents. Kate had a bad feeling about their conversation. She shook it off and gathered her stick bag and mouth guard.

Almost unnoticed, Coach Borland approached her. "Kate, I want to congratulate you on four good years. I will not be sorry to see you graduate, but I loved coaching when you were in the game. Is there anything you wouldn't do to win?"

"Yep," Kate replied, "Cheat."

Betty smiled and turned away, then spun around quickly, almost as an afterthought. "If you ever think about coaching, I would love to have you. Give me a call if you are interested."

Kate's mouth opened in surprise. She flinched in surprise when she heard Taylor whispering. "Y'all notice she played Stacey more than Allison, this is going to cause problems for us, any suggestions, y'all?"

Kate shrugged and said, "I wish I could wash my hands of this situation."

Andi looked perplexed and said, "Who said that, Pontius Pilate?"

Taylor grunted. "Y'all, Shakespeare said, 'Our remedies oft in ourselves do lie, which we ascribe to heaven.'"

- ☼ -

While they showered, they talked about the game. Andi, Taylor, and Kate, three stalwarts stood shoulder to shoulder in a healing mist. Andi asked Kate about knocking down the goalie. "You did that on purpose. I think I would have just scored the goal."

Kate rinsed off and grabbed a towel. "Where's the fun, Andi? The Bulldog coach needed to see a consequence for hurting one of our players."

Andi seemed befuddled. "I don't get the way you think."

Taylor poked her face from under the shower, blowing a geyser of water. "She doesn't think Infinitesimal One. Our Kater is a natural Samurai Warrior. There's nary a thought in her fluffy red-head."

Kate had an answer. "I have better things to do than stand around with soapy naked women. This is not something I enjoy." Kate toweled off, and left them alone.

Andi's sense of humor caught Taylor off guard. "I guess we can put away any rumors about Kate's sexuality."

She started to giggle. "Andi, y'all should never doubt it. Keep y'alls boyfriend on a tight tether. I have mine on lockdown."

Kate returned to her dorm and immediately started to grind out some work on a paper due next week. She sat down at her computer looking at Internet articles. The Internet took forever to download. While she waited, Kate thought about the lacrosse team, and the bond of sisterhood forming between them.

With one or two exceptions, everyone seemed to enjoy being together. The stability of any athletic team hangs precariously, like a spider in a finely woven web. A team can be effective only if all the strands remain connected. The team's core is a gathering of all their natural forces, and at the confluence of those forces, is one's heart. The nucleus differs from year to year and from team to team. What was it she'd said to Marisol and Catbird? Nothing lasts forever. Kate hoped she wasn't a prophet. She intended to finish this battle with her Little Sisters of War.

The article she waited for printed out nicely. She had one more thing to do. Kate picked up her phone and dialed, talked to the receiver. "I am punching buttons, why do they say dialing..."

She heard a familiar voice on the other end. "Zack, I have some studying to do tonight, and I'll be in the library until nine. Afterwards, would you be interested in a coffee? I just love mocha lattes with extra sugar. Can I interest you in one, or a frappe, how about a Pepsi and a Moon Pie?" Kate knew the way to a southern boy's heart, and that she stepped on dangerous grounds.

He answered; "My pleasure, Kate, what's up?"

"I'm not a big fan of peanut butter, but occasionally I need some. Tonight I need male companionship."

She heard him laugh.

Stories

April 03

Three times a year Spotswood's campus newspaper sponsored an outdoor art festival and dance, The Spring Fling. In addition, the Galaxy gave awards for the best-dressed, best looking, and most talented group performance. For the past three years, the lacrosse team won the coveted award for best-looking. Results were announced and editorials were written. This year, the lacrosse captains decreed they were going to try to win at least two awards, if not all three.

Due to their competitive nature, the captains made their team take an unambiguous vow. No one could physically harm any member of the Jazz Band—last year's winner of the Talent Award; In addition, no intimidating the drama club, the winner of Best Dressed.

Andi created a mini-quandary. She wanted to act out bible verses. A short argument later, and they decided to perform a Broadway song and dance routine. Taylor sent Gabrielle to Dove's bait store and grocery to rent the video of West Side Story. Dove's still rented old videos, one of a dying breed. She tapped her finger on her head. "I forgot to remind her not to get anything to buy anything to eat at Dove's. Coach Von Mater's rule five, never buy food in a store that rents videos and sells bait." Taylor knew the rules governing the Valley.

Kate responded with, "Never buy groceries where they sell handguns and ammo."

"Heck, Kater," Taylor answered, "y'all wouldn't be able to buy groceries around here then."

The team gathered dutifully after dinner. Taylor started by telling them they were obligated to win all the prizes this year. Taylor also reminded the group of a $100 award they'd donate to The American Cancer Society, and, if anyone had any suggestions, she would consider them.

Kate stood up. "I will be wearing a simple black sun dress to the Fling, very short and low-cut, possibly illegal in Virginia. In West Virginia I'd be considered a hot 'Hootchie Mama.' I would hope everyone else dresses in something similar. Show some skin."

Taylor turned to Andi and remarked, "I hope Wal-Mart is ready for the invasion of freshmen looking for a short black dress for tomorrow's dance."

Once the meeting ended they walked off in different directions. Kate watched them slowly dissolve into small groups. She experienced a strange emotion, a desire to hold on to this evening. The companionship of teammates was a wonderful thing, a bond of sisters. They were a dissimilar group of people forging a history together. She saw them injured and bloody, holding on with their last ounce of energy. She heard them cry and laugh. She listened to their stories and truly loved them. Many times during the heat of a game, she heard someone call, "I've got your back."

These were her little sisters. They fought a common enemy, and refused to break. They may lose, but they could not be defeated. Every victory and loss fashioned the character of this team. Someday, Kate would only have a recollection of her teammates and their spirit. Tonight she needed to collect more memories. Kate yelled out...her voice nearly a screech. "I've got popcorn and Pepsi in my room, anyone interested in swapping stories?"

When Kate returned to her room, she rummaged through her closet and found a case of popcorn her family had given her, part of the proverbial parent's 'Care' package. She used her microwave and began filling a large tin with popcorn. In less than ten minutes her room filled with chattering females.

Half way into a full tin, Taylor and Jen arrived with Jackie and Gabrielle. Claiming their rights, they chose the best seats, and begin dipping their hands into the warm popcorn. Brooke, Marisol, and Catbird were the next to arrive. They drew up some large cushions and sat close to the food. Lively conversation overflowed.

They began swapping stories.

"We were driving down the highway when Taylor screamed, 'Stop the van!'" Kate paused for effect and to grab another handful of popcorn.

"Two years ago year Taylor lost her pants in a fire in the van. We were traveling back from Stone Gap when smoke started pouring in through the back of the van. Coach Von Mater stopped the van and everyone piled out. We called a service station and they towed us to a repair shop. We waited two hours while they fixed it. Later, Taylor checked her team bag— her favorite slacks were missing. She figured she'd knocked them out when she jumped out of the back of the van. Well, I can tell you Taylor had a fit."

"Those pants cost me a lot of money," Taylor said. Kate proceeded. "The next year, when we traveled to Clifton Forge, Taylor recognized the spot where she lost her pants. 'STOP!'

Taylor yells in Coach's ear... Coach slams on the brakes, and before we stop, Taylor has hopped out of the van. She began hunting around on the roadside through the weeds and the rubble. Lo- and-behold, she pulls out these ratty looking, dirty smelly pants. Damn if she didn't find them, bugs and all."

Taylor took her turn and described how wildly Kate played defense. Murmurs of assent abounded. Evidently the rest of the team had witnessed her aggressiveness. They all added to Taylor's story. They turned on Kate like a pack of dogs on a cat.

At the height of Kate's embarrassment, Andi took pity on her friend and interrupted. She described her only reprimand from Coach Von Mater.

"We were playing Catholic College at home. They were ahead by one goal with one minute to play, and they had the ball. Coach Von Mater whistled and swung her hand in an arc while holding up one finger. We knew this meant that everyone, including the offense, would come down to help at the restraining line. The one finger indicated one player stayed at home on offense. Gabby stayed home. We were double-teaming everyone, including the umpire.

"With fifteen seconds left and the game about over, the ball popped loose. We were near our goal, one hundred yards away. Maggie passed to me out on the left, and I saw no one in front of me down the field. With ten seconds on the clock, I bolted up the field. Half-way to the twelve-meter mark the whistle blew and the game ended. We lost by one.

"After the game, Coach took me aside and said, 'Andi, did you see Gabrielle standing at the eight-meter mark at the end of the game?'

132

"I said yes. I saw her when I got to mid-field, but she looked double-teamed by Catholic defenders. Coach asked if I knew how much time remained on the clock. I told her five seconds.

"Then she got this steely look in her eyes. 'How far away were you?' I guessed fifty yards.

"I knew after I said what I'd done wrong. She said what I should have known. 'What is the world's record for running fifty yards?' I felt crushed. I knew if I'd thrown the ball, anything could have happened. We might have gotten a shot off. Coach turned her back and said, 'I'm disappointed.'"

Marisol sat slack-jawed, popcorn on the floor, looking puzzled; "Angry—that's angry? Heck, did she curse you or rip off your head then spit in the bloody stump?"

Andi mumbled. "I wish she had. What she said seemed worse. Next to God, I never wanted to let someone like her down."

Gabrielle talked about last year's trip to the Boar's Inn. "You freshmen don't know this, but every year we made it to the MVVC tournament, Coach Von Mater took us to dinner, at her own expense mind you. We all dressed in our best outfits because this place was impressive. The Boar's Inn is near Charlottesville. It's this picturesque resort on a big estate. There are shops, spas, and even a waterfall. The grounds are gorgeous, lots of paths and a lake to walk around. Of course, we all looked out-of-place being the youngest and best looking people there."

"You have to understand, this is four-star dining. We sat down and the Wine Steward started speaking French to Jackie. Of course she answered him and almost ordered drinks for all of us, until Coach came over and shooed him away.

During the laughter the normally quiet Ginni began to speak. "I think ringing the Chapel bell last year, after the Clifton Forge game..." Her voice broke, catching some people by surprise. "The saddest thing I have ever done." What she said quieted the room.

She continued, talking almost to herself. "Every year there is a victory which justifies the ringing of the Chapel bell. Usually the captains do it, but sometimes, anyone can. Last April we played Clifton Forge, away. When we beat them, we clinched a bracket in the tournament, so we were excited about it as we headed home. We got back on campus about ten thirty, just about the limit Dr. Browne put on how late the bell could be rung.

"When we unloaded the van, I asked if anyone wanted to do the honors. We were exhausted. It looked like we were going to pass on bell ringing. For some reason though, I took it as an insult. I'd played my butt off in a well-deserved victory. So, I climbed the tower and rang the victory bell. I rang the bell repeatedly just to emphasize our victory—over, and over."

Ginni's voice weakened, the room grew even quieter, waiting for the end of a story most of them knew. "I could have waited, but I rang the damn bell. When I came out of the chapel, I saw Gabby jogging over toward me. I could see she looked upset. She told me Lisa, my roommate had been killed earlier in the evening. Hit by a car while walking along the River Road. She never knew what hit her. Then I realized—I just rang the victory bell. She flew fifty feet in the air—I rang the damn bell."

A hush fell over the group. In the silence, Andi whispered Ginni's nickname..."Bigfoot, the bell wasn't for victory, the bell rang for Lisa, and God's destiny made you ring it. In my religion class I learned Himalayan priests ring a bell to announce the arrival of a soul in Heaven. You were ringing the bell to honor your friend."

The group sat silently for several seconds, then like young people everywhere who reflect on their own mortality, a few coughed to cover their embarrassment, and then they moved on.

"Can anyone tell me why Coach Altman pulls a hair from everyone's head before the start of a game?" Allison sported a puzzled look on her face.

Traci blurted out. "No shit, do you mean when Coach Altman comes around the warm-up circle she's pulling out hair? I always thought she tapped every player on the head. I've seen her chase after someone who got out of the circle before she could touch her head."

Paige confirmed Coach Altman's strange habit of pulling a strand of hair from every player's head. "I have seen her standing on the sideline twisting the hair into something. I thought you guys knew about her good luck ritual?"

As they sat there contemplating the mystery, Marisol and Brooke put their heads together. Marisol sat a little more upright. "We have a story. I want to tell this, but you all must promise to keep it among ourselves. It concerns one of our teammates."

"Have any of you noticed anything weird about Martianne?" A simultaneous sigh from Taylor, Kate, and Andi made an audible whoosh, which turned heads. It caused another laugh.

"I'm serious." Marisol misinterpreted the laughter.

"She's from California." Jackie always had an answer.

Andi nodded knowingly. "Jack that explains almost everything...Martianne is from the left-coast."

Traci shook her head. "It must be AC-DC."

Jackie snorted. "Try OCD."

Marisol opened the floodgates. Almost everyone noticed how she always walked with some part of her body against a wall or touching someone. It was a strange sight to see, her shoulder on the wall, dragging down the corridor. When she reached a doorway, she would reach her arm across the gap and pull herself past the gap. They all nodded in agreement when Jackie said, "The skies are not blue in Martianne's world."

Brooke chimed in. "I know y'all remember the day we swam together as a team, for exercise. We all undressed together in the team room and put on our swimsuits. Some of us wore our swimsuits under our clothes, so when we undressed we were already wearing our gear. All of us were wearing some kind of casual clothes, or we were wearing sweats. Martianne came dressed in a pink party dress with lace around the hem, and the neck....

"Her locker is next to mine so I noticed her as she undressed. Martianne wore her swimsuit under her dress, not a big deal, right? Well, after we swam together, we showered. I remembered thinking about my high school days and the embarrassment we suffered when we undressed, you know, comparing stuff, feeling inadequate. Doesn't every high school have a Toni Anzalone, with tits as big as watermelons?

"Anyway, there was no awkwardness here. We all peeled off our clothes, and showered as a group. No one seemed to be self-consciousness. Kate, Taylor, and Andi stood around at the shower in the middle, chatting and laughing while they lathered up. Then I noticed Martianne showering in the far corner. She lathered up with her suit still on. Then when we got back in the locker, she put her party dress on over her wet outfit. She dripped like a leaky faucet from under the hem of her dress, water poured out. It looked freaking weird."

April 04

The following day, the team had a spirited practice. Afterward they spent very little time hanging around. The girls took off, getting ready for the dance, agreeing that they would meet at Wilson exactly at 7:30. The dance was held on the campus mall, and the decorations surrounding the band platform gave the grounds a cheerful look. The weather cooperated and lent a flush of warmth to the festivities.

Andi had orchestrated a full assault on the judges. The lacrosse team would enter the grounds as a group. The sight of sixteen nubile, attractive women promenading together presented a certain effect on the libido of the judges. The short dark dresses were a hit.

For short time the students were lost in a world without books, exams, or pressure. At the end of the hour the category winners were announced and applauded. Women's lacrosse won the trophy for best-looking, and one hundred-dollars. They also won best dressed, which meant they'd be able to donate two hundred dollars to charity. The lacrosse girls were denied in their quest for a sweep. During their musical routine, Marisol who volunteered to sing Maria's part lost her place. The whole routine fell apart. Later Marisol apologized, but in true Spotswood style reminded everyone you can't win 'em all.

With the merriment in full swing the lacrosse team made their exit. They had to leave the dance early because of their long trip to Calvert College in the morning. It meant they would have to be on the road by six thirty.

Hurley-Burley

April 05

Early morning damp sent shivers through Kate and her assembling teammates. A cold front had moved in late in the evening. They dawdled in, two or three at a time, still rubbing the sleep from their faces. If only the others could see their vulnerable morning faces. They seemed so little-girl-like. In a few hours, they would be fierce warriors on the lacrosse field. Warrior women filled with the juices of competition and straining muscles.

Kate looked south toward the river and the receding mist; it conjured up thoughts of inhabitants from the past, hanging on to their existence in this beautiful and merciless valley. The people who survived here were sturdy. They were all substance and sweat, their daily existence the stuff of heroes, hardy pioneer women producing meager morning rations, lugging cast iron pots which would tax the strength of today's men. Today's women stood tall on the shoulders of their predecessors.

A Whippoorwill intruded on her thoughts, repeating its name over and over, as it prepared to declare the morning. This singing bird announced the end of night, and prospects of better things to come. Its song seemed to be created to drive the ghosts from Kate's mind.

Girls grudgingly picked through a box packed with breakfast items; bagels, pop-tarts, and several kinds of juice put out by the dining hall staff. You could see them through the mist, behind yellowed window lights, preparing breakfast for the rest of the college. While they stuffed equipment and extra clothing into the van, Kate looked up to see Zack Tyler's jeep come rumbling into the parking lot.

The lights burned through the morning glow, the Jeep sat there like a twenty-first-century cavalier's steed, snorting and rumbling. Zack stepped effortlessly from his jeep, in an athletic manner he'd probably rehearsed. He approached Traci and in the still air of the mountain morning you could hear them arguing. Most people were too groggy to pay attention. Kate however, became very alert.

He shook his head and walked back to his jeep. Then something happened that caught Kate totally by surprise. Zack turned toward her. He handed her a white sandwich bag.

"Kate I thought you might like something warm to eat. I know you like these cinnamon buns. To be honest I brought them for Traci but she said she doesn't want anything from me. Do you mind?"

"Thanks, I can use these. Carbs can keep me warm."

He handed Kate the bag and put his arm around her; "How about a hug for a little heat?"

"That's better than carbohydrates, Zack."

Later Kate thought about her reaction. It might have been a response that had been germinating for over a year. She'd leaned her head on his arm, looking for more warmth. It seemed natural. He'd taken care of her dozens of times. Then, without thinking she lifted her head and kissed him.

A shock wave passed through her. He kissed her back. They said nothing, but something changed between them. She took a deep breath. A spark had been ignited between them. She stepped back and dampened the moment. "Thanks, Zack. I've got to go."

She turned her back on him and stepped into the van.

The van seemed cool as they started north. The drive along I-81 gave Kate time to salvage some sleep. She stretched out, lying across Jen's lap with a pillow under her head, sandwiched between Daisy and the window with her feet still on the floor, looking for the gift of early morning catch-up sleep. She nodded off.

The sun warmed the interior of the van, and an hour later Kate began to stir. She startled awake, but Jen gently pressed her down like a mother did to a child awakening from a bad dream. Jen lightly stroked Kate's hair, a comforting gesture between friends. In the twilight sleep she mumbled, "Zack, you smell good."

Jen whispered. "That's me and the smell is muscle balm. I think your mind is on something other than the upcoming game. So sit up—remember Traci is sitting two seats in front of us."

Kate slowly stretched her muscles by extending her legs all the way to her toes. She compressed Daisy into the wall of the van. "Where are we?" Kate looked out the side windows as she checked the passing road, trying to determine their location.

Daisy was reading a textbook when Kate's muscular legs crushed her. She answered quickly. "We are coming up on the junction of I-70, just outside of Hagerstown. Could y'all let me breathe now?"

- ☼ -

Calvert College sat on a beautiful campus in the Catoctin Mountains of Maryland. It was full of rustic inviting charm. The vans made their way along winding roads until they were at Calvert's Cardinal Sports Complex. The lacrosse fields were in a natural bowl in the side of a hill. The surrounding hills were smothered by natural forest and the site looked like an Andrew Wyeth painting. Unfortunately, the Calvert Women's Lacrosse team played their games on this field, and they played as if they were a horde from the Gobi desert.

This would be a difficult game for the Stars as long as Francesca Falconer played on the Cardinal team.

Francesca carried herself with an aristocratic air, which, in fact, encouraged the manner in which she tilted her head, literally putting her nose in the air. Every move looked graceful and her habit of flipping her hair made her seem arrogant. She was a hell of a player and the fastest lacrosse player Kate and Taylor had ever encountered. God spent extra time in bestowing gifts on this girl, good looks and graceful mannerisms, and as a parting favor he gave her speed. The rest of the Calvert team played like lumberjacks, chopping down players like trees. Sticks were wielded like axes. Kate loved the challenge of playing this team.

The warm up exercises were a necessity today. The long ride stiffened the pre-arthritic joints of some of the players so they paid particular attention to their drills. Taylor and Kate began a mocking banter while they were leading drills. They started mocking Francesca four years ago. It started as a little game-within-a-game to lessen their reaction to this intimidating Cardinal. "'Fron-cheska' darling, do you mind if I bend your leg until it touches your butt?"

"Why 'Fron-cheska,' I would love to have you bend my leg, just make sure you avoid the silver spoon that's up my ass."

Their unexpected teasing kept the entire team in stitches. The girls all seemed to relax. The freshmen began to chatter. Cat barked out her bravado. "Francesca looks like she would faint if you came close to her. I'd like to take a crack at her."

Taylor overheard her and smiled. She turned toward Ginni and Jackie, "Big Foot, do you want to tell her, or shall I?"

Ginni shook her head, "Let her find out for herself."

The umpire blew the whistle to call out the captains. Taylor spoke today. Kate and Andi joined her while they waited for Calvert to come forward. Taylor turned to Kate, "It looks like we are finally going to talk to Fron-cheska. She's the speaking captain."

The introductions and handshakes were accomplished and the players exchanged chitchat while they waited for the umpire to check the scoreboard time. Francesca spoke directly to Kate and Taylor. "I'm sorry this will be our last meeting. You two have been tough on us for four years and on me in particular. I sent you both an email. Look for it when you get home."

Kate grimaced. She hoped Francesca hadn't heard their warm up conversation.

They again shook hands and left for their team's huddle. Two minutes later the game began.

Spotswood controlled the draw and Andi took off, flying toward the goal. Andi remembered this team and she anticipated the crunch as two Calvert defenders tried to separate her from the ball. Before they could sandwich her she passed to Cat, who spun quickly and passed to Kate at the eight-meter mark. Kate lowered her shoulder and braced for the impact as she shot the ball into the upper right corner—Goal! One score, three bruises, the game was on.

The ebb and flow of the first half was typical of the games played between these two schools. The quick accurate passes of Big Blue kept their team ahead. The physical style of Calvert created turnovers. Every once in a while, a lightning strike from Francesca would give Calvert a goal. Cat finally had her opportunity to cover Francesca. She scored with Cat lagging far behind.

Black Jack subbed in after Kate scored her third goal. The sideline welcomed her, she felt pain. Kate immediately asked for a bag of ice. Number 20 had chopped her hard with her stick. Even with gloves on the pain coursed up her arms. The hurt eventually subsided and barely registered in Kate's mind, but the ugly red puffiness grew. As she settled in on the bench, Kate looked left and right, she noticed ice bags everywhere. Ginni held a bag on her head, Traci iced her knee, Cat put ice on the back of her neck, and Jen, out on the field, looked like she had gauze stuffed up her nose. Brooke took a check to her head and sat out as a precaution

Kate got lost in the moment and leaned back, staring at the beauty of the hills and the well-manicured field. If she could only block out the noise of Brooke sobbing on the end of the bench, she could really enjoy the ambiance of Calvert College.

Kate became emotional as she thought about this being her last game against the Cardinal. Somewhere in the back of her mind, she heard the whistle for the end of the half. Kate thought this must be how the Native Americans played the game—no boundaries, and no quarter given until the game ended. Today's game would not settle a dispute between tribes, but it would settle the test of skill between two different philosophies. The victor could claim they were the superior team—for the moment.

- ☼ -

The game ended with the score fourteen to eight in Big Blue's favor.

Taylor clowned around. She loved to beat Calvert. She turned to see Francesca coming their way.

As she approached, the aristocrat extended her hand and with the air of a princess, inviting Taylor and Kate to eat with her after the team showered. "I'll be waiting for you in the dining hall. I have waited for years for the opportunity to talk to you two. Kate, did you know I'm good friends with Emily. You know Emily. She played on your team three years ago? She and I live about ten miles from where you live. At least that's what she told me. I'm from Ellicott City, aren't you from Linthicum?"

As Francesca walked away, Taylor and Kate looked in amazement at each other. Kate spoke first. "She and Emily McEvil are friends? Two-keg McEvil?"

Taylor smiled. "Kater, we need to give this girl big ups. She sounds like she could be part of our posse. Are you up for something to eat?"

The meal became secondary compared to the company. Francesca turned out to be a delightful human being. She was witty and down to earth. Taylor and Kate could hardly contain their laughter as they listened to Francesca's lacrosse stories. Underneath her aristocratic demeanor, she could be as coarse as a sailor.

Kate would definitely follow-up on Francesca's invitation to get together during the summer, and tour the hot spots in

Annapolis. Taylor was so taken she invited herself. "We can stay at Kate's place—oh you live near her, I forgot. We'll meet when?"

Taylor broke out her Macbeth. "When shall we three meet again, in thunder, lightning, or in rain?"

Francesca proved to be as quick verbally as well as on the field. She interrupted Taylor, and sealed their friendship with these words..."When the hurly-burly's done, when the battle's lost and won."

The ride home started a descent into the Valley and in the direction of the night sky. The darkening clouds looked like monstrous bruises, roiling behind the mountains, giving a hint of warning. Kate's part-time weather sense screamed alert, the conditions in the Shenandoah turned ugly in a jiffy. She curled into the corner of the seat and thought about the upcoming week. Turning to stare at the mountain shapes looming beyond the window, she shivered from the chill in the air, and the possibly of the journey ahead, a harsh test of the team's resolve; a test of character for which they could not study.

Within seven days they would face the Stone Gap Rattlers, a bitter rival in every way, a pre-season favorite to win the Middle Virginia Valley Conference title. Playing them at their home could be an intimidating prospect. Following Stone Gap, they trekked to North Carolina, playing two games in less than 24 hours. Three games in seven days, seven exceptional days. It was an excursion, which could make or break any team. Kate pondered the thought. How ordinary is this team, or how extra-ordinary?

Kate turned from the window toward the front of the van. The familiar sight of Taylor driving reassured her. When the vans neared Martinsburg West Virginia, the rain began to strike the van with gale-like force.

Near Front Royal, Coach Altman called out for a pit stop. Kate felt sure it was because of Gabrielle, her bladder came with a fifty-mile warranty. The rain had almost stopped, and the vans unloaded in a flurry of young women. The young male attendant at the Sunoco station thought he died and gone to heaven. About half a dozen girls went inside to buy drinks or snacks.

Taylor pumped gas and checked the tire pressure on both vans. While Taylor worked, Kate and Andi sat together on a bench. She looked at Andi. "Mini-mote, I think I could start a chain of women-operated service stations. Start with a few like Taylor, franchise it...."

"I have to pee."

"It's turning into a nice night, Andi."

"I still need to pee, Kater. I have things to do and don't want to waste time with my legs crossed."

"I have heard that a million times from you. I have things to do. By the way, is pee a profanity?"

"Of course not, you know I don't swear."

They waited patiently for the line to the woman's room to lessen. Kate tried to distract Andi, whose legs were really crossed. "You know we have a week from hell coming up. I wonder if the rookies are going to feel like traveling after they get back from North Carolina. Do you remember the first time we made the run?"

Andi nodded at Kate, but did not answer.

147

In response to the rapidly moving cold front, the stars now shone brilliantly in a near cloudless sky. The tree frogs were creating a high-pitched symphony of appreciation in the background. The song and the clearing night sky made it impossible for anyone to intrude on Kate's relaxed mood—or so she thought.

Andi turned toward her. "Did you notice anything strange in today's game?"

Kate jumped. Her revelry interrupted, she shrugged her shoulders to disguise her reaction. "Well I noticed Francesca dragging our butts up and down the field, but that wasn't strange—she's done it before."

"No I'm talking about our team. Did you notice Stacey didn't play one minute?"

Kate squeezed her eyes tight, trying to shut out the inevitable. She tried some of Andi's famous optimism. "Maybe she had an injury?"

Andi turned Kate's hopefulness back to skepticism. "I asked her about being injured, she told me no, and mind my own business. I think we might be in the middle of a lover's quarrel."

"What up, girlfriends?" Taylor walked up behind Andi.

"It's a beautiful night now, and the rest of the team is nearly loaded in the vans. Can't we enjoy the ride home? Did you pee, Andi?"

"Taken care of T-bomb, hey Kater, before we reach Crucible, I'll find out why Stacey didn't play."

"Never happen, Chiquita."

"I'll bet you five bucks I'll know the answer before we get home."

Andi stood confidently in front of Taylor and Kate, a good five inches shorter than both of them. Occasionally in the center of the field when the captains met, Kate and Taylor would deliberately stand together, blocking Andi's access to the huddle. She would have to move around them as they slowly moved to block her. Andi would not get mad, but she always got even.

"So it's a bet? Do you want some of this action too, Taylor? Kate's already in."

Taylor looked at Kate. She hesitated, but agreed to Andi's bet. Both of them knew Andi always kept something in reserve, something to give her an edge.

"Okay."

"Deal—By the way, did I tell you Stacey is sitting next to Penelope on this trip?"

"You are a scheming munchkin." Kate and Taylor knew Penelope could make anyone talk. They'd cracked themselves to her pale blue, cold, reptilian stare. Penelope could best be described as an authentic mountain woman. She could turn your blood icy with a glance and a few words. You found yourself babbling to her just to keep her from turning you into stone. Kate counted out her money. She tried to use as many pennies as she could.

Coach Altman shouted. "Let's get going"

Taylor gave up her drivers' seat and settled into her normal place, still burning about Andi. "That vertically challenged Smurf has taken me for the last time."

Kate tried to be philosophical. "We've said this for the last three years. I swear she's paying for her wedding trousseau with our money. "

When the vans finally arrived at the welcoming oaks of Spotswood, all departing players agreed that it had been a long day.

Black Jack

April 06

At seven o'clock on Sunday morning, Black Jack looked out her window. A perfect day coming, a perfect day to go to church, it looked cool and crisp with a dash of warmth. She took a deep breath and approached her phone. Last night she and Kate joked about needing to cleanse their souls of their evil deeds. Kate made Jackie promise, no matter what, she would call her early—so Kate could have time to dress for services. In one of those rare moments of stupidity, Jackie willingly volunteered to call Kate early, 'no matter what.'

Kate's phone buzzed. "Huhhh—dammit—loh,"

Jackie retreated under Kate's grunted greeting. She lied. "Hi, this is Andi, are you awake?"

Jackie guessed they were surely the youngest people in church today. The congregation of Mount Olive Creator Church looked as if they were on life support. They saw an ambulance parked in the back when they pulled in. "Let's sit near the rear so we can direct the paramedics."

They slid into a pew trying not to disturb anyone. "Careful, Kater, don't trip over any oxygen tanks."

The Minister came out swinging; his sermon invoked a fiery brand of boredom. The tufts of hair emanating from his ears became more fascinating as he droned on about the coming Armageddon, dust from his robe discharged at every emphatic gesture. Kate could not control her delight as she leaned over to point out the dust storm, and a new source of amusement. "The old guy on the end, sixth pew on the left, he's drooling and going to fall over any minute now."

They both watched intently as he tipped. This was more entertaining than watching dust particles in the light coming through the stained glass. The leaning man's bald head inclined into a ray of sunlight. Both agreed they were glad to be in church.

A magnificent old pipe organ began to blow its musical wind. The resulting sound energized and uplifted with A Mighty Fortress is Our God. Mount Olive's Creator Church's congregation rose as one. The music and words seemed to rejuvenate the geriatric members. Kate mumbled to no one. "This is my Grandmother's favorite."

Jackie knew what that meant. They'd gone to church together before.

Kate continued. "Losing her, damn cancer; it took a gentle, strong-willed woman from me. She was my friend, more like an anchor. I'm still not sure I forgive God. It will take a long time to absolve The Almighty for her loss."

Jackie waited. A once comedic sight of the sleeping man now took on a tragic overtone. Tears slowly trickled down Kate's face. She unconsciously stiffened, and sat taller as she released her resentment.

Jackie slipped around her shoulders—the touch of another human being gave warmth in the cold recess of pain. They sat together quietly, looking into the space surrounding them. Jackie would not ask why Kate cried and Kate would not say; which measured their friendship.

As they drove home, Jackie stretched out lazily. They were unusually quiet this time. Both lost in the scenery and the beauty of the mountains. Kate uncharacteristically thanked Jackie for 'Coming along with me to church.' The meaning behind those words meant volumes to her. Jackie defined her friends by exceptional sets of criteria. Things others might judge trifling were paramount. She knew Kate should never be embarrassed by any mention of her tears. What she respected about Kate involved knowing she would not be asked to, 'Not say anything.' When Kate trusted you, you were assured the trust was absolute. In Jackie's mind, guarantees were golden.

Later in her life Kate called Jackie and they talked about going to church. Kate told her she hated God at that time for what she believed she'd done, but that forgiving God was a rite of passage all living beings faced. She would deduce that handling the passage completed a sacrament, or karma, whatever you believed.

The repetitive nature of learning manifests itself in many ways. In the mind of a college senior one solution to the tedium is finding some harmless diversion. Sometimes what begins as innocent can become something more. Kate worked diligently on a sociology paper until she hit the wall of monotony.

The phone rang and its interrupting sound made her sigh in relief. She answered, "Hey, Kate here." Zack Tyler answered.

They talked about nothing and he asked about her hamstrings, but she sensed something else in his words. She thought she'd force the issue. "How's Traci?"

Thirty minutes later he paused to take a breath. In the torrent of information she remembered only one thing. Traci was history. When he resumed talking, his next statement became a question. "Kate, let's have a picnic. I'd like to get off campus. Would you like to come with me?"

She felt a chill, an involuntary reaction. She wondered if it came from excitement or apprehension. After all, Traci was a teammate and there might still be a chance Zack and she would get back together. "Sure, I'll have a loaded basket waiting. I'll bring the food."

Kate dug through her basement locker. She searched for a picnic basket her mother had given her. At the time Kate wondered what her mother was thinking, how many times did you go on picnics when you were in college?

When she found it she looked inside. Its emptiness made an impact. Something needed to be added. I better go to Chicken Hut.

She knew Zack loved fried chicken, what college boy didn't? She drove out of the parking lot with an unexpected thought in her mind. ...*What am I trying to get a man to do? No plans Kate, we are just having fun. Let's see how this goes and Traci might have something to say about this. There is nothing better than fried chicken to satisfy a man...well, there is one other thing.* With youth as her guide and disgust with her raging libido, she dismissed that concern. *Maybe I'll stop at the IGA and get a baguette and a chunk of Vermont cheddar...also a banana Moonpie.*

Her visit to the local IGA always fueled her imagination. Kate loved shopping in grocery stores that time forgot. She took the trip into the past with food and things her grandmother called sundries. She especially liked looking at handguns and

154

hunting knives, prominently on display next to their bakery. What a sensory overload, Berettas and Smith & Wesson were interspersed with a yummy odor of fresh-baked bread.

Something flashed in her periphery. She spoke out, "Coach?" She'd gotten a fleeting glance, and just then, the checkout girl asked, "Got any coupons?"
She turned and shook her head, then looked back. She saw no one there. She paid and looked at the entrance. Maybe Coach Von Mater had exited through the front door? Kate turned her head again. It couldn't be Coach. Kate dismissed the notion. Coach would have said hello, for sure. Besides, whoever she saw they were older and smaller than Georgia Von Mater.

Zack waited for Kate pulled in the parking lot. They drove to New Market and the picnic area at Battlefield Park. The Sunday sky looked crystal. They were both in the right mood for this kind of relaxation. The conversation stayed light. They discussed the state of the world in general.

Zack seemed to be amused by items in her picnic basket. "My favorites, how did you know?"

Kate picked at the cheese and fruit while he dug into the chicken. College men can eat remarkable amounts of food at one sitting. College athletes on the other hand can eat obscene amounts of food. Today, she nibbled, trying to be on her best behavior. She did not want to agitate her stomach with fried food and like most people who did not need to monitor their weight, she acted cautiously.

They packed up several hours later with full stomachs and relaxed minds. Zack reached for the basket and touched her hands. She felt another shiver. In her opinion nothing improper had happened. They were two friends enjoying each other's company.

- ☼ -

She had school work to finish this evening. Kate prepared a time-consuming demonstration lab. She had the information, now she needed to put together her ideas for the presentation. She booted her computer and thought this would be a good time to check her old e-mail. The first message originated from home, just a hello from her mother. The next message came from Francesca; Kate had forgotten her comment during the captain's introduction, the email reminded her of the event.

04/05 10:19:41 AM EST. Fran1@CC.edu (Francesca Falconer)
Subject: The war at Calvert
To: Kholl28@SpC.edu (Kate Holland), Tbomb@SpC.edu
(Taylor Braun)

Kate and Taylor. Yes I know your names!!! I wanted to tell you before the game I am your biggest fan. For four years, I wished I could play with you instead of against you. You two have chemistry. Kate beats you on one end and Taylor on the other. I think we will meet again. My coach tells me we are 'locks' to be selected for the division III Southern Senior All-Star team. Awesome!!! It will be played at Johns Hopkins—love the turf—it's so close to home, right Kate? Do not freak, but I get a stitch telling everyone how you two imitate me. I love it. Let's get together. Today though, I am going to kick your tails. Good luck and GOD SPEED!
Fran,

PS. I found your addresses from your college website.

////////////////////

They had dreaded Francesca as a player for four years. They turned their fear into a game of mockery to defuse the impact. Now Kate wished she'd spent some time getting to know this talented Calvert player, Fran, a name too mortal. She would always be 'Fron-cheska.'

April 07

Taylor promised Jen she would go with her to the Wellness Center in Crucible on this Monday, and that meant she volunteered Kate too. Jen helped out in the pediatric center as a lifeguard. She'd promised her girls and boys she would bring some players from Spotswood's team with her next time. She said they would teach them how to play lacrosse. Jen looked for situations where she could work with the underprivileged. Her energy for people in need was contagious.

Monday after practice the three Spotswood Stars headed to the Wellness Center. When they arrived, Taylor started complaining. She faced a deadline for a project, and her professor appeared less than receptive about extending the date.

The pressure made her cantankerous. "Y'all know we don't get a break when it comes to these kinds of things. The burden of performing in class is as hard as performing on the field. The same ol' professor who asks you to write y'all's 100 page papers in a week also asks, 'When is your team going to win a championship?' They make it sound like their status is on the line because we suck in Lacrosse."

Jen and Kate did what any friends would do in this situation. They treated her with total ridicule. "You are such a total baby. What about some cheese to go along with your whine?"

Taylor tried not to smile. Her friends' abuse was exactly what she needed. "I should have known better than to complain to you two. You both are as sympathetic as leeches on a bruise..." They laughed together in the darkness, putting some light on Taylor's depression.

"Y'all are right. Sympathy ne'er motivated fair maiden"

At the door they saw several children waiting anxiously for them, literally bouncing on their toes in anticipation. The look on their faces brightened everyone's mood.

An hour with these kids equaled ten hours of therapy. The faces and expressions of love from these special children pushed away any lack of enthusiasm. Work, stress; all became secondary to teaching their game to children who wanted so desperately to learn. Kate and Taylor were as patient and careful in their instructions as anyone could be. The results were often comedic, but only in a sense of having fun.

Taylor turned to Kate while her group, each one looking for attention and instruction, mobbed her. "Kater, I know we can get lost in our own troubles, but when y'all finally get to see what love looks like, it makes your spirit soar."

Kate holding a ball over the heads of an eager crowd finally glanced at Taylor. Both were surrounded by excited children. Kate dropped the ball. All of a sudden Kate tumbled to the ground, covered by children's bodies, all chasing after the ball. Next to her, in her own pile of love, Taylor lost all her concerns.

They rode home in silence. Each one content with the memory of their time well spent. Finally, Kate turned to Jen as they pulled into the parking lot. "Thanks Jen, I hope you call me again when you need someone to volunteer."

Jen smiled. "It's my pleasure. I don't want to sound…stupid, but you guys will be in my prayers."

Taylor frowned. "What do you say?"

"It's embarrassing, but I often give thanks to a generous God, for giving me friends like you two. You know I need a little help to get me through this life."

- ☼ -

Kate had a plastic container of dip and a bag of Mama Uma's Revenge chips for her buddy, Mooner. She'd had them ready for her next work-out. Kate took care not to get any dip on her hands. *I wonder if this stuff would make a good wood polish. I could sell this to the cleaning staff at the college.*

Mooner worked out in his accustomed spot. He swung his right leg with weights attached to it. He wasn't going to let a damaged knee keep him from his dream of playing football. He'd gotten an offer from a semi-pro league and seriously considered it.

"Hey, Kater, you brought me food."

"I promised you I would. How are things?"

"I'm still working on this knee. I've even gone to the Wellness Center to work it in their pool."

Thinking about her experience last night made Kate grin. "I visited there with Taylor and Jen. We had a blast."

"Did you run into Coach Von Mater?"

She wrinkled her brow. "What are you talking about?"

"You know, she goes there once a week for her chemo treatments or something."

The room began to get smaller. She fought a feeling of nausea. She could only remember the word 'chemo.'

"Are you okay, Kater? Damn, did you eat some dip?"

Kate began to summon her inner resolve. *Think of a peaceful place—think of a peaceful place.*

She turned toward Mooner and tried to ask him casually about Coach Von Mater...She heard someone screech, "You big donkey, what in the hell did you say?"

Mooner, a giant of a man, nearly fell from his seat. "Kate, I don't know. My Mom works there and she told me Coach Von Mater gets treatment for cancer."

Kate's face and mind turned stone cold, as she processed Mooner's comments. An odd thought crept into her mind. *What is God doing to me?"*

April 09

The following day she operated in a fog. The ride south to Stone Gap College would be lengthy, and the prospect of facing the hated Rattlers seemed daunting. While she packed, Kate tried to focus on the upcoming game. Her mind kept coming back to Coach—with cancer. She vowed to keep this information to herself. The news would disturb the team. Strange thoughts ran through her mind. *Shit happens in threes. First, we get Coach Burke and her indiscretion, then the visit to the Wellness Center and cancer. That's only two.*

She lugged her bags toward the Field House. The Stone Gap Rattlers might be a welcome relief.

Stone Gap

During the trip Kate nodded off in a fitful sleep, her thoughts as she drifted in and out of consciousness were of her grandmother. Negativity clouded her mind. It's a losing battle. If not Grandma, then it's Coach. Everyone I admire and respect going to....

"Kate, do you think Stone Gap has a very good team?" Cat made an attempt to engage Kate in conversation. For the last hour and some, the ride south on I-81 had been unusually quiet. Taylor, consumed with the upcoming game, had her bitch on. Jackie studied for an exam. This left Kate as the agent of van conversation. Caitlyn had switched vans when the other freshmen told her about the raucous stories and lively conversation in their van. She wanted some of the promised lively chatter.

"Kate!" Cat assumed Kate had not heard her. "Are they good?"

Kate seemed slow to process her question.

"Are they any good?" Cat repeated.

Jackie peeked over the top of her text-book; she'd been following this exchange between Cat and Kate. She took a shallow breath. I hope Kate remembers how fragile a freshman's ego can be. I'd better talk to Cat later about pulling on the tail of a tiger.

Kate leaned forward. Cat's ego was about to take a beating. "Cat, your native American heritage puts you closer to the game than any of us."

Cat unconsciously backed up in her seat. Kate leaned dangerously close to her.

"In the dream world of the Peacemaker, your direct ancestors played lacrosse long before this country became a nation. Can you summon the spirit each tribe felt when they played Baggataway or Tewaarathon? Feel the hunger for victory, or the blood lust to crush the enemy?"

Cat's eyes widened at the mention of her native heritage. "My great grandmother calls it Takitchawei, or 'bump hips.'"

Kate leaned even closer, her nose within two inches of Cat's. She spoke with more than a little menace in her voice. "Well, Cat, the Rattlers play 'bump hips' to destroy the other team, not to just win. Imagine Calvert's team—remember how rough? Well imagine a team like that with skill and speed. Now you have the Stone Gap Rattlers. I also believe that in late night ceremonies, they sacrifice injured players."

Cat wasn't sure whether to be insulted or to wet her pants. Her lips quivered.

Kate sensed her weakness, and realized she'd been a little harsh. In her mind she could only do one thing to do. Go for the kill, finish her off. "Just keep this in mind, Catbird, if you want to make it out alive...follow me, I'll show you what to do."

Taylor purred from the front seat. "Kater, y'all don't need to scare the crap out of the children."

The vans turned into metropolitan Big Stone Gap's main thoroughfare. "On your left you can see the Miner's Monument." Taylor tried her best to distract the rest of the team from Kate's chilling description of their opponent.

Marisol spoke up. "They have a monument dedicated to underage children?"

Every now and then it became clear Marisol's native language was not English.

The town of Big Stone Gap nestled in the Virginia portion of the Allegheny Mountains, between the borders of North Carolina, Tennessee, and Kentucky. The College of Stone Gap sits on the top of a ridge, seemingly gouged out of a mountaintop. Cool in the summer, and unthinkable in the winter, the wind often gale like added to the town's charm. However, the view from the lacrosse field looked spectacular.

The Rattlers were an annual impediment to Spotswood. They loomed in front of their team like the rattlesnakes they were. The Stars had taken many ugly beatings from this talented Rattler team. Losses weren't pretty, even in this wild and beautiful environment.

The Stars stepped out of the van just as the sun broke through the sky. The illuminated fields below and the view of the mountains were as Kate remembered, breathtaking. Stone Gap's field stayed in excellent condition, with the Bermuda grass level and well-manicured. You could tell this school had a substantial budget for their maintenance. Stone Gap was an old institution, but they displayed a modern perspective toward women's athletics.

Out beyond the fence surrounding the field, the tops of the Allegheny Range stretched north. The colors at this altitude seemed more vibrant and clearer. Kate stared. The chill in the air has probably numbed her brain. *This is the only place we play that makes our school look like it is on a plain.*

On the field, Kate saw Stacey warming up with the starters. She wandered over to Andi, the speaking Captain today. "Andi, ma petite chou, whazz-up?" Kate nodded toward Stacey.

Andi grumbled and answered Kate sharply, which rarely happened. "Stacey is starting over 'Donut' today."

"Instead of Courtney? Donut is clearly the better player. Next to Taylor, she picks up more ground balls than anyone. This is not the game to start experimenting with the line-up." Before she could utter another complaint, Coach Burke called the team together. She addressed the Stars cavalierly. "If you play your normal game we'll get beat. Be consistent, and do not let them beat us to ground balls."

Andi added a comment. It was out of character for her. "Let's try and not get hurt out there today."

Coach Burke turned to Taylor. "Captain, can you identify the players on the other team we should watch out for."

"Ask Kate," was her brusque answer.

Burke shrugged. "Okay, let's hear it, Kate."

"Number 6, Stasia—number 2, Tayo—number 9, Lindsay—number 14, Sudie, number 25, Jordan, and watch out for the goalie. She's been known to come out of the goal and lay a stick on you when the umpire's not looking."

Coach Altman, who rarely spoke, asked with a hint of amusement in her voice. "What's wrong with the remaining five?"

Taylor chimed in, "rookies."

Introductions were formal with a little touch of arrogance. Stasia, Tayo, and Sudie, the Rattler captains, stood close together. They chose not to mingle with the umpires and the players from Spotswood. No idle chitchat, just a face-to-face, these were the Rattlers. Kate wanted to dance around them singing and skipping. Trying to elicit some response from these Rattler captains would be a hoot. As she stood in the center of the field, Kate hoped this might be the year they put an end to the Stone Gap curse.

The game began with a high arching draw headed toward Kate. She jumped over her defender and snatched the ball out of the air. Kate took the ball down the sideline, looking for an opening to pass to Andi or Gabrielle. The Rattlers were triple teaming her, which meant someone, had to be open. "Where..." Kate could not find an opening. Kate found herself in a corner, so she ran through two defenders and behind the goal. Where is Andi? Finally, Kate saw Catbird. A quick pass and Cat managed an open shot on the goal. One to zip, the Stars had scored. A glimmer of hope seeped into the Stars.

It didn't last long. Stasia and Tayo were the lightning of the Rattlers' attack. They struck quickly and worked efficiently behind the goal. They were working on Stacey, exploiting her lack of experience. They scored two quick goals. Taylor tried to help Stacey, this opened up the left to slashing drives from Sudie. Ten minutes in, the score was now three to one in favor of the Rattlers.

The Stars offense seemed confused. Andi kept getting cut off, shooting wildly. Kate kept looking for the weakness in their defense—she couldn't find it. Focus, Kate, where is Gabrielle? Where is Traci?

After fifteen minutes, the game took on a familiar pattern. Stone gap won the draws, controlling the flow of the game. They also beat the Big Blue to ground balls. Kate knew they were in neck-deep.

A double team on Kate worked brilliantly. They'd literally taken Kate and Andi out of the offense. A small breakdown in the Rattler defense found Gabrielle in the middle. She turned her shoulder into two players. And they knocked her off-balance. She went down in a heap. Kate had witnessed this before, Gabrielle played every second of every game in pain from a congenital hip defect, and occasionally the hip slipped. When this happened she collapsed, unable to walk without limping. It sometimes took days for the muscles to relax and the hip to slide back into place.

Blake helped Gabrielle off the field as Black Jack took her place. Kate reached out and tapped Gabrielle on the butt when she walked by. "Take it easy, we need you for the 'big one.'"

Gabrielle turned to Kate and laughed through her pain. A private joke between teammates made her smile as she stretched out behind the bench.

Black Jack took the penalty shot for Gabrielle and scored. The Rattlers continued to pound inside trying to isolate Stacey. Ginni started to creep forward to cover her, and the Rattlers found the opening behind her. Andi looked at the sideline. She wanted the Coach to call timeout. No one looked back. She called to Kate. "We need to stop the bleeding, we need a timeout."

"Go ahead and call it, Shooter. Tell Burke we thought she'd asked for it."

Andi called time with five minutes left. She checked the scoreboard. "Stone Gap is up by three goals."

Coach Burke greeted them, angrily. "Anyone have any idea what's happening on the field? Who called for a timeout? Taylor, what's happening on the defensive end?"

"I don't know, ask someone else."

"Okay, you tell me what's happening, Andi?"

"Talk to Kate, maybe she has it figured out. All I know is they are double teaming me."

Tess Burke's simmering dislike for Kate overrode her competitive desire. On the lacrosse field, Kate had more knowledge than she did. While the team waited, Tess hesitated. The whistle blew and the Spotswood Stars trotted back out on the field. The matter still unresolved.

The last five minutes of the first half turned into a street brawl. The Stars were fighting mad and some of the frustrated members of the team were having at it. The checks were getting awfully close to the imaginary bubble around the head. Jen ran over Sudie in pursuit of the ball when the umpire rattled the pea in her whistle for what seemed an interminably long time. The Ump carded Jen and called the Captains over.

The steam from the nostrils of both side's Captains might have been more than breath mist in cold air. They all stood there glaring at each other like gladiators, ready to finish the fight. The vapor rising from their heads punctuated the silence. The umpire got directly to the point. "The next flagrant foul is going to cost you a player. Do you understand? Yes? In addition, the player who commits the foul will not be the one to go. It will be one of you Captains—got it?"

Sudie could not keep her mouth shut for long. "You can't do that." The older experienced umpire, glared into the eyes of everyone in the huddle. "Watch me, bitches."

The other umpire came over to the group and interrupted the standoff.

"Okay, Ladies, get this game going again."

No one wanted to be the first to move. "Move," the sharp retort from the umpire broke the spell. They all reluctantly trotted back to their teams.

The younger of the two umpires turned toward her cohort and expelled a whoosh of air in a sound of relief. "I'm glad you got there in time, it looked scary. You should have seen the looks in their eyes. They looked like wild animals, and I could have been a meat buffet."

The other umpire smiled at her friend. "With all the steam rising from their heads, you could tell a lot of thinking was going on. We better spank them real quick or the second half is going to become a brawl."

A Rattler slamming a stick into Kate's neck caused a flurry of pushing and shoving. This kind of behavior happened rarely in women's lacrosse. The veteran umpire separated the players while blowing her whistle. True to her word, she pointed toward Sudie, nowhere near the action. She took out her Red Card and waved it. Sudie's day ended. The score was five to two.

At half time they iced bruises and taped joints. Discussion of strategy didn't come up. Kate, however, had finally figured out what the Stone Gap defense used. They ran a complicated man-to-man with a hidden diamond-shaped zone in the center, no wonder she had trouble finding Black Jack or Traci.

On the defensive end Taylor now knew exactly what created the mess. They were covering ground normally in control of Courtney. This well-tuned defense had a monkey wrench jammed into its works by Coach Burke, and her determination to play Stacey.

The Stars were fighting themselves as well as the opponent. Kate slipped over to Gabrielle and asked her how she felt. "I'm OK, Kater, I wish I could get back on the field but until this spasm relaxes, I am no good. Watch your back out there. I told Black Jack to keep an eye on 35. She is trying to take your head off."

The whistle interrupted their chat.

Stone Gap had talent and the score began to climb in response to their ability. Kate could do nothing. She looked at the mountains, feeling helpless. This team stood like a peak they couldn't climb.

Stasia and Tayo scored again, now the score read eight to two. When Tayo scored the ninth Rattler goal, Kate sensed the moment when her team finally gave up, it happened with 15 minutes still on the clock. For all purposes, the game ended. With no hope, she began to think at last. Kate knew they could meet this team again if they qualified and won a first round game in the MVVC play-offs. She put her thoughts of Grandma, and Coach Von Mater away and started to analyze Stone Gap's team. She waited for a sign.

Andi scored the fourth goal for Spotswood as the clock ticked down to one minute. The score was ten to four. Kate's sign came with thirty seconds left.

The Rattlers pounded the ball into Spotswood territory and Stasia rammed home their eleventh goal as the whistle blew. Stasia began to celebrate, dancing like a deranged football player who'd scored a winning touchdown. Kate didn't watch. She looked at Penelope standing forlorn in the goal.

Kate hustled from her end and reached Penelope just as she turned toward the bench. Penelope had tears forming in her eyes. Kate grabbed her by the helmet and shook her. "Damn it. Goalies do not cry. Do you hear me? Goalies do not cry. I promise we will get even."

Kate walked Penelope off toward the bench. Penelope eyes cleared, Kate had vowed revenge, and Kate wouldn't renege on her promise.

The battered Stars packed up their belongings. First they would shower in the field house, and then get something to eat. The long trip home looked discouraging. A shower and some food in their bellies would brighten their outlook somewhat.

- ☼ -

Kate soaked. She thought she could stay there forever, relaxing in this steamy shower room and chatting mindlessly with her teammates. The Stone Gap facilities were marvelous. Marisol and Taylor both walked over and started showering, one on each side of Kate. Kate, lost in the warmth of the water, barely paid any attention to their conversation.

Out of the blue, Marisol asked Taylor if she'd overheard anything about Coach Burke being gay.

Kate snapped out of her lethargy. "Where did that come from?"

"I just wondered. Cat said she heard from someone who heard from someone else, Coach fooled around with a girl on our team."

"Y'all heard what, from whom?" Taylor gathered her thoughts by dancing around the original question.

"Allison told Cat." Marisol couldn't keep her source quiet.

Kate looked at Taylor. She hoped for an escape from this predicament. She saw nothing but a blank look. So she changed the subject.

"Hey! Could you two hard bodies pick a better spot to stand? Here I am in my full B-cup glory, between two amazons. Think how I look to the rest of the world."

Marisol smiled. "Thanks for noticing, Kater, but your ass is better than mine, and I think your B-cups are perky and cute."

Taylor rinsed off, "Time to go, girlfriends." Marisol shrugged as Kate followed. Kate knew they'd stuck their fingers in the leaking dam once more. Kate yelled at Marisol as she walked away. "By the way, my ass is definitely fabulous, thank you very much."

Van War

The first order of business after loading the van became food. Coach Burke checked a map and asked if anyone knew of a nearby place to eat. Taylor knew the area. "There are two towns near here, one is called Morris Butt, and the other is Cracker Neck. Towns with the names of butt and neck are unlikely to be able to keep Kosher. Of course we could always eat in Big Stone Gap proper. They have a Pizza Hut, and I'm always in the mood for pizza."

Kate looked around at the girls, this team seemed disheartened, but they were not destroyed. The vans began to buzz with gossip and chatter. Visions of pizza replaced the orange and black Rattler logo. Spotswood would live to play another game, and maybe, just maybe, they would get another chance to face the hated Rattlers. Kate prayed it would happen. On a brighter note, Coach Burke did not return with them. She'd gotten a ride home with a friend.

The Pizza Hut was jumping when they arrived. Like a western novel's gunslinger they entered through a swinging door. The people in the dining room all turned toward them. For a second the team felt alien among a strange crowd. Then the patrons shouted howdy's and greetings. The spontaneous welcome took them by surprise.

Spotswood's girls piled into their booths and ordered drinks. Andi dragged Kate to a booth near the back of the room while Taylor got the pizza. "Kater, things are not going to get any easier."

Kate and Andi were discussing the latest brush with the truth from Marisol. It created a spark in dry timber. "I agree. We are in deep doo-doo, miniscule one."

"What do you mean, we?"

Kate looked at Andi in mock surprise. "Why Andi, your Lilliputian mind made a microscopic joke. I almost laughed, and that would be a miracle after today's game. I don't think we'll be a happy group on the way home."

Andi looked at Kate with a crooked smile on her face. "I'll bet you five bucks I'll get the entire team to laugh before we reach Lexington."

Kate looked out at the tired and beleaguered team. "You're on short-cake."

After an impressive stint at the Pizza hut—they broke the local record for most pizzas consumed in an hour—the team piled into the vans and headed north. When they hit Interstate 81, they felt at home, only a four-hour ride to go. Marisol and Cat sat together, discussing what they'd done right or wrong against the Rattlers. Others half-heartedly listened in, stomachs full of pizza and feeling a little worn out by another loss.

Somewhere around Wytheville Virginia, Jackie looked out the window to her left. The other Spotswood van paralleled them as they cruised down the highway at 65 miles per hour. Jackie peered over at the other van, and then screeched deliriously—"VAN WAR!"

Andi revived a tradition from years past. As their van pulled next to Vanuno, Vandos drove by with all of the girls wearing pillowcases over their heads. Each pillowcase displayed a smiley face drawn in magic marker. The first volley in the van war occurred.

Vanuno plotted their revenge. Taylor sweet-talked a nervous Coach Altman as they readied their return pass. She eased the van near the other van, passing carefully on the open highway, until they were even. They held a blanket along the windows to shield them from the opposite van. When Daisy and Blake dropped the blanket, Vandos looked over to see nothing but legs sticking straight up in the air, making running motions. The legs kept moving as they pulled away.

The next pass by Vandos displayed all of the girls with their faces pressed against the right side windows. All nine of them were wearing bras on their heads.

Vanuno wasn't finished. They carefully orchestrated a game of tug-o-war as they hurried by. They hooked together their jerseys and formed two groups, one in front and one in back.

Vandos answered, in a preposterous reproduction of the van being rowed like an old Viking ship. The oars were, of course, lacrosse sticks.

By this time Coach Altman had a serious case of nerves. "This madness has to stop."

Kate called out. "I'll put an end to this—just pull alongside one more time. Turn your back, Blake."

When Vanuno passed, everyone on the other van was treated to a view of Kate's spectacular ass, pressed against the window, with a five-dollar bill stuck plastered between her cheeks. Kate had lost another bet.

Both vans pulled in near midnight. There were just a few cars waiting for them at the athletic complex parking lot. The empty parking spaces created an unnatural scene. Smoking exhausts were dead giveaways of waiting friends. The doors opened and bodies spilled out in slow torturous motions. Overhead, columns of argon lights created a peculiar brightness in the dark. The departing players walked between those minor suns, as if greenish light could supply a beacon of warmth. The illumination did little against the numbing cold of an early April night.

Coldness and darkness absorbed any sounds of shuffling feet or mumbled words. The silence of insects and birds told everyone to be in bed, somewhere warm and safe. Kate groaned slightly as she thought of the eight o'clock class awaiting her today. Just when she could not drag her body another step, the night got brighter. Zack waited with what looked like a cup of hot coffee. Kate couldn't determine who she was happier to see, him or the coffee. It didn't matter. They were both going to keep her warm tonight.

April 10

Kate's battered alarm rang at six-thirty; she turned to see if Zack still laid in her other bunk. Kate saw the neatly made-up bed and assumed that he'd left late in the night. She wondered if this budding romance would put an end to their friendship. She really enjoyed being around him. She also wondered if another wheel fell off the cart. First, Coach Van mater, the omnipresence of Burke, and now the possibility of creating a dust-up with Traci, things seemed like they were on a slippery slope for Big Blue's Stars.

The memories of being in Zack's embrace stayed fresh in her mind, this kind of afterglow made things look brighter. Even though she hadn't gotten a lot of sleep she felt less cranky this morning. Her impending class and hunger ended Kate's musing.

She acted very practical when it came to her hunger in the morning. She showered quickly and efficiently. She set her mind on a bagel and cream cheese from the dining hall, before going to her first class. The prospect of having to face professor Kasich on an empty stomach made her queasy.

As she left her room, she noticed someone had written a note on the message board tacked to the front of her door. Kate had been too foggy-eyed and distracted last night to notice anything, especially a message.

Kate, need to see you later, Jamal.

She guessed this wasn't about their Poker Club. Jackie's boyfriend occasionally played cards with Kate and a few other guys. If he'd come to her door after the game last night...she didn't want to think about what he had heard. This morning was not starting smoothly after all. She had an ominous feeling.

- ☼ -

Professor Kasich extolled the virtue of ice as a medical miracle when his mind shifted gears. "Do you remember Paul Bear Bryant?"

The class's eyes' glazed over.

"You mean you do not know the greatest living coach in football history? It amazes me how little you young people know. If I were to list my greatest coaches of all time, he would be the tip of the top."

The class reacted as if they were brain dead, hoping he would tire of his new topic quickly. They'd learned if you left him alone, J.E.B. Kasich's mind would seek a lower level.

Then the unthinkable happened. Maybe because of her lack of sleep, Kate raised her hand, tentatively at first; then she elevated her query to its fullest length. Her arms were very long.

177

"Professor Kasich, two things; Bear Bryant is dead, and does your list include any women coaches?"

The classroom seemed to become alive, eyes opened in anticipation. Kate could see Zack in her peripheral vision—He seemed to be waving.

Professor Kasich seemed to be mulling over an answer. While he thought, his face twisted into a shape you might make if you were sucking on a lemon. Kate spoke again. "May I reiterate; Bear Bryant is dead, muerto, morta, mortuus, morto, I saw it on an ESPN special years ago."

Kasich's face turned a warm shade of crimson.

She kept the conversation alive. "He's a big ol' fat football dude—famous for stupid hats."

Kasich's face reached beet red.

Before he could respond she asked again. "Professor, do you think there are any women worthy enough to be included on your list?"

Kasich did not operate well under pressure or when angry. In his decisive moment his reply proved that supposition. He blurted out before his brain became engaged. "The only good women coaches are probably lesbians, or perverts."

The absurdity of his statement struck everyone in the room at the same time. Once the first ripple of surprised amusement ran through the room, the following laughter became a tidal wave of released tension. They all seemed to see the entertainment in this boorish man.

"I meant perverts...or..."

Whatever he said, Professor Kasich got a response, a new wave of giggling throughout the room.

Kasich turned his frustration on the source of his embarrassment. He shouted over the laughter. "Holland, name me one woman I could respect enough to put on my list." The class, now silent, sat looking dumbfounded at this oaf.

"I'll name a woman I respect, whether you choose to respect her is entirely uncertain, but I'll give it a go."

Professor Kasich crossed his arms.

"Coach Georgia Von Mater."

In the blink of an eye professor Kasich's face changed and a smile creased his lips. The effect on the class was stupefying. It appeared someone had miraculously replaced a curmudgeon with a human being. "Well hmm... You know what, young Holland? I believe you are right. Georgia belongs near the top of my list. Thanks for reminding me."

When the class ended, Kate left the room in a hurry, walking quickly.

Zack caught up. He didn't mention last night. He seemed more interested in their last class. "Kate, that's the way you play cards. You suckered him in and then you threw down your aces. Did you see the old man's face when you mentioned Von Mater?"

Kate clapped her hand to her head and, with an exaggerated sigh of relief, vented her emotions. She talked rapidly, nervous tension escaping like steam from a kettle. "When I called Bear Bryant a football dude I thought I was cooked."

- ☼ -

On the way back to the dorm, a siren's call reached Kate and drew her toward Massanutten Hall for a cup of latte. She slid into a wooden booth, worn smooth by decades of students sliding their thighs and bottoms across its boards. She let her muscles relax for the first time since she'd left class. A thought popped into her mind. *Grandma would have loved what I said in class today.*

In a heartbeat Kate came perilously close to tears. She scolded herself. "Why am I so upset?"

She sat there, experiencing emotions and memories of her Grandmother's death, emotions which that were tucked into the recesses of her psyche. The revelation about Coach Von Mater and her growing lack of respect for Coach Burke were blended into her feelings. She studied her coffee. Just like this latte, the line between the coffee and the cream becomes muddier as the drink cools.

Shifting her attention to somewhere else, she looked for her center. At this moment, above the rim of cooling latte, the Massanutten Grill became her sole concern. She looked carefully around the room. The dark oak panels and bright neon sent distinct signals of warmth throughout the room. Most people were familiar and yet they were strangers. She observed them talking together. She noticed how relaxed everyone seemed.

This haven without motive, a sanctuary, created by the people who occupied it, warmed more than their bodies. This place exuded an atmosphere charged with the enthusiasm of young people on some mission. The search needed little definition. It could be a relationship, knowledge, or understanding. They were never there simply for coffee. Massanutten Grill, a site where a stranger could come and drink in companionship, without feeling out-of-place, should be a monument to learning.

She felt better and more in control. *This coffee works miracles. Maybe I can figure out a way to market it and make a ton of money. I'll call it Kampus Koffee. It'll sell to college grads looking for a wake-up call.* Kate had her mojo back.

Just as she started to leave, she saw Jamal. She called and he reacted with a smile. He plopped his tray of fries and gravy close to the edge of the table. He juggled his burger and drink while trying to slide into the booth. He obviously did a better job at balancing objects than he did with his diet.

Kate tried to make a joke. "I guess breakfast is over. Where's your chocolate food group?"

He reflexively reached into his pocket for a brownie he'd put there. "Here—in my pants." He blushed as he realized his unintentional double entendre.

"Darn, Kate, I wish I could say things like that on purpose." He stuffed a handful of fries into his mouth. "You got my note that I needed to talk to you? You know Jackie and I are going to get married, right?" Jamal was prone to state the obvious.

Kate waited patiently.

"Well Jackie is the smartest person I know, and when I discussed my problem with her she said one person could help us, you. Will you help an old poker buddy out?"

Kate's answered quickly and to the point. "That's what friends are for, but it might be helpful to know what the problem is." He let out an actual sigh.

"I don't know how you can do anything about what has happened, but Jackie said you are 'the Sensei', whatever that means."

Jamal launched into his situation. "I'm going to be two credits shy of graduating. My advisor gave me some bad advice.

He put me in an English course, that turned out to be way over my head, and one I didn't need. I finished with an incomplete because I didn't turn in my required reading list. Professor Williams didn't say a word, but he wielded a syllabus saying I had the following two weeks to make up the work. Kater, this happened in the middle of football season. I thought I would be able to make things up during the second semester break.

"Later, when I approached the professor, he told me no exceptions would be made, especially for my kind. Of course I got pissy. I reacted to the comment and accused Professor Williams of racism. Of course he said he meant football players...the whole thing got blown out of proportion and Williams denied the comment, my word against his.

"I'm going to have a hearing with Dean Roman and Professor Williams. All I want is a chance to make up the work. Jackie has been tutoring me and I know what to do. A friend of a friend told Jackie that Dean Roman and this professor are golfing buddies. So you know I'm going to get screwed, big time. The real problem is I already have a job lined up. It begins June first. If I have to go to a summer session, I'll lose the job and a head start on the money Jackie and I need to get married next July."

He swirled his fries gloomily one by one in the gravy, munching joylessly.

"When is the meeting?" Kate seemed business like.

"Friday at four."

She snatched a fry with a dollop of gravy from his plate, and plopped it into her mouth. "We're going to North Carolina on Friday at noon. I better get busy." Her matter-of-fact attitude surprised Jamal.

"What are you going to do?"

Kate gave him a little smile when she replied.

"I am going to give a shout out to my homey."

Just like when she played poker, Kate never revealed her hand too soon.

That evening, when Kate finished talking and had what she could for Jackie and Jamal; she spent extra time reading her textbook for Professor Kasich's class. She wanted to make sure he couldn't manufacture a reason to lower her grade. Kate thought about the time her grandfather gave her a poker lesson, then went on to win the stack of pennies he had given her. "That's not fair, Gramps."

She remembered to this day his words and his smile. "Life's not fair, Katie Kat. People who cry about something not being fair; those are people who won't make an effort to find a way to win."

Several years later, Kate sat at her Grandfather's feet playing poker with a dying man, a victim of asbestosis, a particularly hard way to end. As her Grandfather took in each precious breath with the aid of an oxygen tank, they played the game he loved—poker. They sat across from each other and they each arranged their stacks of pennies into rows. The game lasted for hours, and she proceeded to take every penny he had. The look on his face that day was how Kate always remembered him. He grinned with satisfaction. She knew he was proud of her.

Kate's Date

Kate paused in her frenzied dash to apply her make-up, and stared at the mirror. Jen and Casey watched her like cats focusing on a bug. They discussed her in the third person, someone not there. Jen spoke loudly, obviously to get attention.

"I hope she's not going to tart herself up by wearing that silver slip dress, it barely covers anything." Jen looked directly at Kate and knew very well what dress she wore.

"Remember the last time she wore the dress?" Casey responded, with a look of distain on her face.

"She showed it off at last year's homecoming dance. Her boyfriend at the time almost got into a fight when …"

Kate stuck two fingers in her mouth and let loose a loud whistle. "Aside from the slut factor, how do you like Kate's look tonight?"

She joined her friends in the third person conversation. "Do you think Kate's ass is too fat to wear this dress? How about Kate's makeup; too dark? Should we tell her to consider wearing silver pumps or a pair of Nike's?"

Jen studied Kate carefully, her hand propped under her chin in a pose of deep thought. "I think if you're going over to Zack's dorm, I'll be going with you until you are safely inside."

They rode together in Kate's car. When they arrived, Jen walked with Kate to the front door of the dorm. "Have a good time tonight and don't forget we have a long trip to make this weekend. Don't forget your black sweater, it might get cold. You don't have much cover up-top." Jen pointed coyly toward Kate's chest.

Kate wondered when her mother had enrolled at Spotswood and disguised herself as Jen. Somehow the good intentions of her friend touched her; she appreciated the thought behind her anxiety. "Zack told me to dress up tonight, that we were going first class. I wanted to look my best. You know, make a few heads turn. I also wanted to let these guys in the dorm know I'm a woman. They think I'm just one of the boys. Sam McIntire called me a man the other day."

"Well, Kater, I can tell you that the men in my dorm wouldn't have any trouble figuring out your gender."

"Thanks sistah, but no matter how long you hang around the doorway with me, you are not getting a good night kiss."

Jen exploded in mock outrage. "You are so full of—you tart—get going with your shameless wench behavior, which, by the way, is turning me on."

"No chance, girlfriend. You know which side I play on."

Before meeting Zack, Kate went to Jamal's room. She wanted to tell him she had done her best regarding his problem with graduation, and wish him luck in his meeting on Friday. She also knew the guys usually watched a baseball game in his room. Jamal had a big flat screen. Her motive for going to his room had nothing to do with his predicament, nothing so altruistic. Her male friend's perception of her needed changing. She knew they'd forgotten she was a woman. She had to test her hypothesis. "If I still have any femininity left..."

She stood at in the doorway, struck a pose and mustered her resolve. "Hello, boys, how are the Orioles doing tonight?"

No one looked up. They focused on the TV. Jamal looked up first and acknowledged her. "They're losing, Kate. When are the Birds going to get some decent pitching? ...Holy guacamole,

Kater, look at you, where in the heck have you been hiding that bod?"

Kate's dress molded to her, revealing every curve and every angle. From the stunned looks, her dress performed like a bug light to a flight of hungry mosquitoes. It had a low-cut front and a slit hem accentuated her sensual pose. She could tell from their reaction she had scored. The room erupted in a festival of leering followed by gross comments.

The boys were discovering a new Kate, the woman Kate. Ashur and Steve jumped up from the sofa. They bumped into each other and argued about who would give her their seat. Mooner acted like a security guard, fending off the rest of the guys.

Henry did little to disguise his lechery. "Kate you are 'da bomb,' if I had known you had a body like that, we could have been playing strip poker."

A roar from the television set made them refocus. They forgot her. She had established her point and felt good about it. She took a moment to give Jamal a whispered message, and left. Zack waited in his car and she wanted desperately to get his reaction to her dress.

Ten minutes later, Dave Retune and two other freshmen popped into the room. "Dudes, how about that ass on Holland, I used to think she was a little flat-chested, but what a set of knockers."

There was no response.

"I wouldn't mind a little piece of the bitch myself."

Things happened quickly after that. Dave found himself duct-taped to a chair while his friends sat cowering in a corner. Mooner solemnly added tape to his neatly combed hair.

One hour later Kate and Zack sat at a cozy table at the Sugar Tree Inn. He told her he wanted to go to a restaurant, which served food in an elegant style. "I'm trying to say y'all are a classy woman, Kate. You deserve food from a chef and not from under a sneeze bar. If it looks like I am trying to impress you, well I am."

Kate smiled. His effort to impress worked. There would be no impulsive kiss later on. It would be well thought out.

April 11

Vandos left Spotswood at 9:00 AM. Vanuno followed close behind. The trip to Greensboro would take at least five hours. The game with Alamance Creek began at 4:00 PM, and the experienced members of the team knew the game would be a relief at the end of their ride. After an hour's drive down I-81, the group began to get bored with the books or papers they were working on. Everyone labored with make-up work. Kate missed two classes today, classes she'd make up later.

Brooke looked uninterested in her textbook and decided to generate a conversation. She cast her conversational crumbs tentatively throughout the van. Jackie sat nearby. "Ginni told me she was going to have a summer get-together in New Jersey, and she would invite the team. She lives right on the ocean."

Jackie did not suffer fools gladly today. "We will verify this salient bit of information when we stop in Mt. Crawford for lunch, no doubt. Please make sure you have your information right. I wouldn't want to travel to New Jersey from New York without renewing my passport."

Brooke did not go away easily. "I just wanted a little conversation, Jackie, no reason for you to be so sarcastic, or northern."

From her back seat, Kate watched the incident unfold and considered the diverse emotional and psychological types who made up Spotswood's Stars. One consistent thread in each woman's character ran true, the 'not willing to walk away from a fight after your nose has been bloodied type.' Surely the dictionary could provide a better word, something more specific, but she could not think of it. She had seen some remarkable things accomplished by her Big Blue Star teammates in her four years.

A different mentality existed in lacrosse players personalities. She had seen commitment and mental toughness in other women's sports, but lacrosse players possessed a unique set of characteristics. They displayed the ability to continue while hurt, the ability to play in pain, the will. Again, these things were not unusual in an athlete, however, society rarely thought of these things prevalent in a woman's character.

People in this van were good examples of their diversity and their sameness. Kate seldom met a player who wouldn't run all day. They were lean, mean, running machines, whose elitism existed in their spirit.

To most, the stereotypical woman's lacrosse player came from an upper class private school, and acted like a princess.

Kate didn't belong to this perceived royalty; she'd graduated from a very public and diverse high school. Confrontations in the halls were an everyday occurrence. Kate tested her hypothesis.

Brooke would be the first person in her family to get a college degree. She attended Spotswood on an academic scholarship. Coach Altman was Jewish. Black Jackie, Marisol, and Caitlyn were certainly not white stereotypes. Taylor, well Taylor could be hard to define. The ideal country girl came to mind. She'd spent many an early morning milking cows. Jen was gay, and came from a blue-collar background. Behind them in the other van, a group composed of Italian, Czech, and Polish Americans also contradicted the stereotype. Maybe, just maybe, Daisy or Penelope would fit the mold. But one acted zany and the other could be a devil in disguise. Whatever their make-up, Kate knew she loved them all. A strong bond held them together.

Kate saw Brooke lean forward. She had restarted her argument with Jackie, in way over her head, she wouldn't give up. Jackie, on the other hand, teased Brooke like a cat plays with its food. The argument became symbolic more than informative. The two teammates were testing each other, finding the boundaries of their own chemistry. Thus the character of a team was molded.

In Kate's mind only one possible thing could disrupt their chemistry, the situation between Coach Burke and Stacey, and that seemed to have died down. Maybe later she and Traci might have a scuffle. It seemed that she had made some comments about getting back together with Zack, but right now Kate bet on her own chances. With her teammates in mind she imagined a possibility of Big Blue making it to the second round of the MVVC playoffs.

Near Lexington, Taylor took the wheel from Coach Altman. This meant the conversation level in the van needed to increase.

"Kater, tell me again what you ate for dinner on your date last night."

"What date?"

"You know what date, the one with your teammate's boyfriend."

It occurred to Kate that Taylor signaled her to stir up the troops. She took the hint. "Zack ate sautéed deer meat covered in peppers."

"How did the wine taste, home wrecker?"

Kate response was quick and sharp. "I didn't drink wine the night before a game. I drove."

"I'll bet you didn't."

"When I tell you I did not drink, I mean what I say, hayseed!" Kate's response stunned everyone.

Taylor shouted. "That would be the first time y'all said anything y'all meant, you overbearing bitch!"

Kate exploded, "Did I say something too complicated for your dumb farmer girl ass? Let me use smaller words. I...did...not...drink."

Marisol shouted. It must have unnerved her to hear Kate and Taylor at each other's throats. "Stop you two. We don't need this. We are a team."

For a minute, the van fell deadly silent. No one dared move or disturb the stillness. Finally, Jen spoke, and her words rang through the silence like a bell struck in an empty church. "You jackasses, those two planned this. It's their favorite game to play on freshmen."

Marisol and Cat both turned around and fired their pillows at Kate—direct hits. The laughter grew quickly. "You two are sick ..." Marisol looked embarrassed, but she eventually saw the fun in the joke. She tried to look angry but a smile kept popping out on her face.

Then Marisol pointed toward Brooke. "I thought I heard you whimpering in your seat." Brooke folded her arms and shrugged. Paige claimed she knew what was going on the whole time. Cat invoked the spirit of her grandmother to punish them both.

Their biggest laugh came from Coach Altman, when she said ... "Well, give me some warning next time, and pull over at the next gas station, I've got to change my underwear."

Carolina Hell

The vans arrived in Greensboro at about 2:50 PM. They checked into the Hotel near the coliseum and in 20 minutes they were back in the vans, dressed, and ready to go. There was hardly enough time to freshen up and go to the bathroom. The game began in forty-five minutes.

They arrived at Alamance Creek College thirty minutes before the game began. The Stars pulled their equipment from the back of the van. They lugged goalie pads and goalie helmets. Each player lugged a stick bag and carryall filled with extra shirts and other items. Water jugs and medical equipment were shared loads for the freshmen.

The clack and clatter of dragged equipment and spiked shoes on the asphalt walkway reminded Kate of stories of ancient Roman soldiers on the Apian Way.

"We are like invaders, carrying our lives on our backs." The Stars looked intimidating as they went about the business of preparing to battle.

The Regulators rarely beat the Stars, and were unlikely to do so today. Brooke was bemused by the appearance of the opponents. "Why are they wearing practice shorts instead of kilts?"

There was a world of difference in Spotswood's appearance as compared to Alamance. The Stars were in their blue away jerseys, with Spotswood emblazoned across the white lightning bolt on their chests. The gray plaid kilts, with black short compression pants underneath, were a striking contrast to the baggy long shorts and loose shirts worn by their opponents.

After a short warm-up, Andi gave a pep talk. She dredged up a speech from an old history paper. "During World War I, a unit of the British Army, called the Black Watch, went into combat with guns blazing and pipers screeching. When the battle ended, their enemies remarked on their bravery, they called them the 'Ladies from Hell.' Well today 'ladies', the Stars will show this Alamance team what part of hell we are from. It would be a mortal sin if a team dressed in shorts beats a team wearing a traditional uniform."

When the captains met in the center of the field, Andi stood between Taylor and Kate. They turned to face each other, sandwiching Andi in-between and four inches below them.

"Did you hear a short inspirational speech, Kate?"

"Sure did, Taylor, it sounded like a my-nute Rockne speech."

"Kah-nute." Andi corrected.

"God bless y'all, Andi."

- ☼ -

The Regulators stood toe to toe with Big Blue—for about five minutes. Then history, by the name of Kate, took over. For the past three years, Kate had turned the Regulator defense into a shambles. No matter whether they double-teamed, triple-teamed or zoned her side, she scored with impunity.

Few people knew what inspired her performance. Alamance's coach, Dean Clark, was a friend of her brother, Mack; they'd played together in high school, and in a summer league. Kate remembered meeting him, and at the age of twelve she developed a massive crush on the eighteen year old. Nothing could be as traumatic as a middle school crush.

Years later, when she prepared to choose a college, Dean became the newly hired head women's lacrosse coach at Alamance. He told Mack he wanted to build a team around Kate. She remembered how awkward it felt to turn him down, but her mind stayed set on Spotswood. He accepted her choice graciously, but made a light hearted comment to her, which he intended to be witty. He tousled her hair when he said, "Then I guess I'll have to make sure you don't score on Alamance."

Her first year against Dean's team, she scored four goals. Her sophomore year she scored six. When they met last year at Spotswood, he walked up to Kate before the game and apologized for making her angry. Kate scored seven goals. After that game, Andi asked her about her determined play. Kate explained she wanted to obliterate an old infatuation.

With the score six to nothing, Kate seemed hotter than ever, she'd scored five before the Regulators called time out. There were fifteen minutes left in the first half. Coach Burke began her substitutions. She looked down the bench at the faces of the women eager to join in the party. Her first call went to Jackie and Stacey. Jackie replaced Kate and Stacey replaced Taylor.

The rest of the first half Spotswood continued to score at will. The poor condition of the field mirrored the fortunes of the Regulators, bare in the center from use and abuse, and dusty in the middle. Balls hitting the ground were scooped up with streaming strands of dirt. When the players got ready to pass they created a tail of dust accompanying the ball. Alamance, as usual, found itself in a game which developed into a dusty, grimy, carnage.

The second half began with Stacey in the line-up along with the original starting unit. She took over Jen's spot. On the sideline, Allison threw her stick to the ground and sat down noisily on the bench.

Her angry performance caught Andi's attention. She sidled up to Kate and Taylor. "What's up? Allison hasn't played at all."

Taylor shrugged. "Hard to say, Shooter, maybe with the score so lop-sided, it would be a good idea to get her some playing time."

Spotswood continued its relentless attack, but from a spread out offense. This allowed the players room to attack the goal when the match-up favored them. Spreading out also meant Spotswood scored less often. The patient offense took chunks of time off the clock. The score reached fifteen to one in favor of the Stars. Kate, predictably, led the Stars in scoring. At twelve minutes, Andi and Kate took a break.

With five minutes left in the game, Kate and Andi returned. Everyone had played, except Allison. Kate caught a glimpse of her sulking on the end of the bench. She signaled, putting her hands in a t-shaped gesture, "Time out Ump."

Andi trotted over, "What's up homey?"

Kate nodded toward the sideline. "Allison, that's what's up, baby-girl."

When they approached the bench, Coach Burke steamed. "Why call time out? We need to end this game not drag it out."

Andi skillfully handled the coach. "Coach, I saw Ginni choking and I thought we needed to get the poor girl a drink. She could yak all over her uniform."

Burke turned her back, obviously angry, but seemed unwilling to scold Andi.

The team gathered around the water jug, trying to cut the dust in their throats. When the team returned to the field Allison had replaced Kate. Coach Burke didn't notice the switch. The game ended in a flurry of goals, at 19 to 2. A few minutes after the last handshake and the last bit of equipment stuffed into their bags, Alamance's coach walked over to congratulate Tess Burke.

While he talked to her, he spotted Kate. "Hey Katie, I'm glad you are graduating this year, you would have been a great Regulator. Say hello to Mack when you get home. Tell him we'll get together this summer."

Kate shook Dean's hand, then packed her gear and headed toward the field house. She bumped into Allison, who still fumed about her lack of playing time. Kate knew this seething resentment would come back and bite Coach Burke in the ass. She shrugged and muttered. "Oh well, she'd probably enjoy it."

They boarded the vans and went directly back to the hotel to shower and get ready to eat.

The Lady Stars became ravenous after a game, maybe even predatory. As Kate approached the van, she saw Andi standing at the back door displaying a five-dollar bill, stretched out between her hands. Kate defensively threw up her hands. "Hey, I didn't make a bet with you."

Andi smiled. "I won this five from Coach Altman. I made a bet you would—personally, outscore the Regulators and our bench—combined. It turned out to be close but I won by two."

Kate looked at Andi in amazement. "You are a multi-faceted character, short-cake."

"I'll treat for coffee tonight at 'Great Smokey Joe's Cafe.'" Andi was generous in victory.

The team dressed quickly, they were hungry and no one wanted to hold up their departure. They were going to the Golden Corral, not far from Interstate 40. The vans pulled in together; and the girls unloaded. The Lady Stars entered and stood in line, picking up their trays and utensils at the cash register. They waited patiently, tools at the ready, as they followed the chain divider into the dining area.

Tonight the assumption, of all-you-can-eat as a theory, would be severely tested. As usual, when they entered a place as a group, they drew attention to themselves. At first, the men in the room only stole surreptitious glances at the large group of attractive young women. Later everyone stared. The naturalness and jocularity, which the group expressed, seemed to gather attention. Their self-confidence and presence was electric, until they began to eat.

The restaurant patrons recoiled in alarm as the Big Blue Shooting Stars fell on the buffet. Mothers flinched, instinctively gathering their children out of harm's way. In the carnage, Taylor, Andi, and Kate sat together at one table, an island of quiet in the hectic clatter of plates and utensils.

One by one the girls paraded by. "They have soft serve ice cream and pound cake." Jackie loved ice cream.

"I need meat." Ginni looked determined to pile as many rib-eyes on her plate as possible.

"Taylor nudged her, "I'm not sure that is meat."

Jen called out to Marisol. "Marisol, your protein group must outweigh your salad group, remember?"

Andi, Kate, and Taylor were oblivious to the rest of the team. Most of the others noticed these three occasionally segregated themselves, forming a barrier. It wasn't elitist, or malicious, but a way of finding space.

As usual, Andi broke the silence. "I think we should hit the town tonight. I read that Kerri Smith is playing at Great Smokey Joe's Cafe, and I'm ready for a break from this team."

Taylor surgically de-boned a chicken breast, and meditated. "Y'all know they'll also be reading selected poems tonight, I'm a sucker for undiscovered Southern style angst."

Andi's generosity hadn't run dry. "I think we should ask someone to go with us, you know, pass on our tradition. I'll choose Jen. She's been busting her tail."

Taylor pointed her spoon filled with chocolate pudding in the direction of the table behind them, chunks flying. "I say we ask Catbird to come along. She has potential, and she'll be around for three more years."

Kate voiced her choice. "What about Gabrielle? She and Andi will be elected captains next year and it would be a good start for her to hit the town with the queen bee-aitches."

They laughed. They'd chosen to accept the nickname as a sign of respect.

- ☼ -

Later, at the hotel, some of the girls donned their swimsuits, preparing to spend the evening lounging around the pool. The Stars were not shy about showing off their athletic figures, and the crowd lounging poolside grew. The hotel lifeguard became more vigilant.

At poolside, drawing the most attention from the other patrons were Courtney, Ginni, Marisol and Brooke. Gabrielle paddled along the edge, and Paige and Traci swam laps. The voyeurs at the nearby bar focused in one direction, Marisol's.

Some players settled into their rooms, relaxing or watching television, some working on a project, or reading. The Spotswood Stars were in for the night, all except a select few.

Andi, Taylor, Jackie and Caitlyn, dressed appropriately, walked toward the lobby exit. Gabrielle declined the visit to Great Smokey Joe's Cafe. Her hip bothered her, and the walk would be too much, even if it was only a mile and a half. Jen expressed no interested. The pool seemed a better place to exercise her cramping muscles.

Coach Altman saw them as they neared the door. "You guys are a little dressed up to be headed to the pool. I hope you are not going to the bar?"

Kate answered quickly. "No Coach, we are going to a local coffee place near the University. We discovered this place two years ago. They'll have a band, and poetry readings. Hey, do you want to come along? Gabrielle and Jen backed out on us."

"Sounds like a place I used to go to when I played at Cornell. What the heck. Let me tell Coach Burke, and I'll meet you outside in ten. I need to put on some make-up."

"WTF!" Andi never used real profanity. She preferred to spell things out or use initials. "Kater, I have a feeling your invitation is going to mess up our evening."

Kate looked at Andi scornfully. "How about a five dollar bet?"

Andi thought for a minute, and replied, "You're on."

They met ten minutes later, and were on their way. The evening temperature was about 65 degrees, and the mile-and-a-half walk kept their temperature up. The conversation stayed casual and light. Coach Altman turned out to be okay. Kate mentally counted her money. It would be the first time in years

200

she'd won a bet with Andi. They passed Greensboro College and turned right on to Springgarden Street. A short walk, another right, and they were standing at their favorite coffee shop, Stir Crazy.

Coach Altman sounded delighted, almost giddy. She told them she felt like an undergrad. The cherry-red framed chalkboard and the local art lent a coffee-house atmosphere to the decor. Coach Altman commented about the black floor tiles, "They're just like the ones in Ithaca."

They sat near the front window and the small stage. Kate, wanted one thing, a great cup of coffee, and her hopes were buoyed when she spotted the coffee roaster nearby. "I'm going to have a Voltaire Latte, a double espresso with homemade hot chocolate, whipped cream, and a light dusting of cinnamon on top." Kate had a vision of an ideal drink, and this one sounded dreamy.

Taylor and Jackie ordered what Kate ordered. With whipped cream mustaches a-plenty, they spent an hour enjoying the ambiance and, listening to Kerri sing. Finally, to Taylor's delight the local poets read their work.

In the middle of a particularly intense reading, Coach Altman cornered Andi. "How did you know Kate would put on a shooting clinic today?"

Andi chuckled and gave a cryptic answer. "Kate extinguished an old flame today. The next coffee is on you, Coach Altman and I'm buying."

"I would appreciate it if you all would call me Ariel, tonight. It's a good Jewish name and I love it. Especially tonight, I'm turning 27 in three days and feeling old. Call me Coach Altman when it is appropriate."

Taylor held up a finger to her lips, frowning, deeply immersed in poetry. She was a sucker for iambic pentameter. "If all, y'all, don't keep quiet, I'm going to have to ask y'all to leave."

She made them smile and gained a few more moments of tranquility. During another obscure recital they started chatting again, this time about athletics and its value. Ariel owned a Master's degree and took the lead.

"Did you know girls are two times as likely to be inactive, in a neutral environment, as boys; and the U.S. Surgeon General said fourteen percent of girls 12 to 21 are sedentary and tend to stay that way."

Taylor jumped into the discussion. "Y'all, this is why we need to promote activity for young girls. They have to participate and stay in shape."

Jackie also thought participating in athletics improved your socialization skills, and general body control.

Kate voiced the last remark. "Athletics renew the brain for academics, it provides a break."

Andi tapped her watch. "Well, I hate to be the one to call a break, but this place closes at eleven-thirty, and we have to walk back."

On the way back to the hotel, Ariel made an obvious effort to walk with Kate. She seemed to have something on her mind. "Kate, I don't know when I'll get another opportunity like this, but I wanted to say a couple of things. I wanted to compliment you, to tell you that you play the most unselfish style of lacrosse I have ever seen. I watch what you do on offense to help me improve my defense. I see you move, and pull two defenders with you, to open the middle for Andi. You may not be as strong as Taylor or as athletic as Andi... "

"Whoa Coach, I can't stand all this love."

"Wait, there's a compliment coming. I've watched you do the little things to make the team better."

She paused. "I know some people don't see anything but the number of goals scored, but I wish there were five more like you. You are truly unselfish, and when you want to, you can light up the scoreboard. How Andi knew you'd become a scoring machine is a mystery."

Kate interrupted. "I'll give you some advice, Ariel; never make a bet with the mini-shark. I think I've only won once."

Ariel nodded, and added, "I also want to thank you for calling me before the Mount Shiloh game. Your concern for me regarding our team prayer, showed your depth of character. I didn't think anyone would bother to ask my opinion. I knew when I signed on to coach at a Christian college that my religion would take some lumps. You seem to put the welfare of others above self-promotion. I know you'll always be at the top of the food chain, whatever you choose to do. I think you would have been an excellent Jew."

They arrived at the hotel feeling light-hearted. When they entered, they saw Penelope sitting in a lobby chair, and by the look on her face, she bore some version of bad news. She started yapping immediately. "Dang you, the very people I needed to be here, when things went wrong." Her angry stare focused its unrelenting energy on them.

Coach Altman took a leap of faith. "What went wrong?"

Penelope extended her bony fingers. Between her index finger and her thumb, she held a plastic card, as if she were holding a dead animal. "Here is your room key, Coach. You dropped it on the way out. Martianne picked it up while slithering around the hotel and it got into Allison's hands when she ran into Martianne, stuck between a Pepsi Machine and an ice maker. So she helped Martianne around the machines, and in return she got Coach Altman's room key."

Penelope sputtered. "Allison was upset about her lack of playing time. She went looking for a captain, probably to vent, but you were gone."

The condemnation oozed out in her words. "Next she went to find you, Coach, but of course you were gone, frolicking."

Kate couldn't take any more. "Cut to the chase, goalie, what happened?"

Penelope measured Kate's eyes, and decided to get to the point. "Well, Allison decided to confront Coach Burke, she banged on her door and no one answered. Allison became frustrated. She was so angry she decided to use the key and wait in Coach Burke's room to confront her. She burst into the room and caught Coach Burke and Stacey having sex. I said s-e-x, sex"

Kate had enough. "We know how to spell, goalie, back up."

Penelope folded her arms in indignation, but moved a few steps away.

The thoughts flowing through their minds ran the gamut from disgust to self-blame. Taylor became angry at Coach Burke. Andi blamed herself. Cat acted disgusted. Jen wanted to kill Stacey, and Coach Altman obsessed about the key. One singular and strange thought popped into Kate's head. *God! I owe Andi another five dollars.*

Adversity

April 12

The sound of bumblebees buzzed in Kate's head. She turned, groping at the nightstand, looking for something to crunch, and found her wrist watch. She peered through the haze of her newly awakened eyes...Seven in the morning. Ughh! When Kate could focus, she looked around the room trying to sort out her surroundings. A screeching, buzzing noise annoyed her. It sounded like bumblebees. The bumblebees were not in her head. They were in the bathroom. Jen, ever concerned about her hair, fried herself with a hairdryer.

Kate remembered being in Greensboro and having another game today against the Quakers of Friends University. On a normal Saturday, she would have slept until eleven.

Today's game started at 1:00 PM., and the trip home would have the Stars arriving back at Spotswood after eight. There was some comfort in the fact they would be arriving late. There would be a period of clemency on Sunday before things would start to heat up. On Monday morning, the lacrosse team would be the talk of the school.

Gossip at Spotswood spread like the flu virus at a carnival kissing booth, by the end of the week everyone on campus would be infected by curiosity, and want to know what happened in North Carolina.

Kate dreaded today's breakfast. She'd talked to Catbird who'd overheard Allison calling her parents. The phone rang, and the voice on the other end announced breakfast at 7:30.

"Daisy, is this you?"

"Yep, it's me Kater. Coach told me to notify everyone. I think she is going to play this like nothing happened."

"Thanks for the heads-up."

She yelled at Jen, trying to drown out the hairdryer. "Jen, let's get some food. We do not want to miss the Academy Award performance and our bacon and egg breakfast."

Last night's sense of doom vanished temporarily with the stimulating odor of food. No one seemed to be outraged or in a particularly foul humor. The clatter of forks chasing food around their plates and the commotion of spoons striking bowls of fruit and cereal, gave the morning a natural feeling.

Kate sat with Taylor and Gabrielle near the end of a long table. They all were drinking orange juice and contemplating the gold filigree girdling the dining room. Taylor seemed to be particularly affable. "Kater, do y'all know why these rooms are always covered in wall-to-wall mirrors? And, did y'all know your watch has a cracked face?"

"Why, I believe the mirrors are there to enable humans to pick out any vampires in the room. Remember they have so little substance they don't cast a shadow or have a reflection."

Taylor slowly turned her head, looking carefully at the images of her teammates. "Why darlin', our coach won't cast much of a reflection either."

Taylor's sarcasm had a chilling effect on Kate. Everyone in this room harbored some resentment or indignation. When their emotion surfaced this team would get hurt. This team wouldn't heal until the uncertainty became certainty.

- ☼ -

Friends University was a twenty-minute ride toward the north. The Quakers of Friends University proved to be troublesome every year Spotswood played them in North Carolina. The Stars always played Alamance Creek first and the Quakers on the following day. This meant Quaker players could come to the Alamance game, scout, get ready, and be rested.

Kate's sense of how their team felt today eluded her. Most players were extremely quiet, not willing to open up. Allison rode in Vanuno. She'd switched with Daisy. The change in seating somehow effected the time-space continuum of their mini universe, Athletes were very much creatures of habit. A good option would be to sit back, and take in the ride.

The drive to FU took them through a lovely suburban area. Shopping malls and business parks looked new, and upscale. The homes were large with well-maintained, manicured lawns. Kate came to a decision this would be a great place to raise a family. In her present rancorous mind-set, she wondered if she could get off the van now and get started.

Halfway there some raindrops announced their intention. When the vans pulled on campus, the skies opened up. A steady rain fell, the kind farmers loved, a soaking rain, which wouldn't jeopardize a game. The only positive side of the situation occurred with the field. The grass, thick and close-cropped, seemed to soak up the water as if it were a sponge. Undoubtedly the game would be uncomfortable, but a wet field would not affect the outcome.

Kate, Andi, and Taylor met the Quakers at mid-field to discuss the ground rules. The umpires were new to Kate. She looked the field over and tried to watch the Quakers warming up. She saw nothing. It seemed immaterial and pointless. The

Stars were emotionally flat, and she could feel herself being drained. My feelings are as gray as the sky. No one wants to say it, but this team is the lowest I've ever seen it. Then we have the long trip home....

The game began at exactly 1:00 PM. Big Blue had nothing in reserve today. Andi finally ripped the nets after ten minutes of play. The score was four to one in the Quakers' favor. The rain still fell steadily as the half ended. Friends University now led eight to two.

The Stars huddled near the sideline. They stood motionless, without spirit, unable to do anything to avoid the downpour. No one spoke, resigned to their fate. In the center of that dispirited wet circle sat the only person who could turn them around, a leader in name only, Coach Burke at a crossroads. She started to speak. A lifetime of denial and persecution made her an emotional coward. So she stood there, absorbing the reprimand of the falling rain, embarrassed by the events of the previous night.

The five-minute break passed silently as they addressed their physical injuries. Kate watched a trainer wrapping an Ace bandage around Courtney's knee. She wondered if he had anything in his bag, which would cure their biggest wound. Kate found herself looking at the field across the way, staring at another field of play. A coed rugby tournament played on. They were laughing and running in the same rain, which punished Spotswood's team. She wanted to walk off this field and ask if she could join in their game. It looked like they were having fun.

When the final whistle blew, the Quakers celebrated the execution of their carefully worked out plan. They jumped with joy, and piled on each other in the center of the field, enjoying the rain. The festivity now anointed and relished in the elements. Within minutes, the rain stopped. The sun broke through in magnificent glory, and illuminated a Friends' University victory, fourteen to eight. It was suddenly a gorgeous day in North Carolina.

Loading their vans was a grueling job. The waterlogged equipment and uniforms were particularly nasty, and loading their van would be grueling. The mess would be with them for another six hours. Coach Burke informed them they'd stop in Roanoke for food. The message seemed to mean nothing. Unbelievably they weren't interested in eating. When the vans reached Roanoke, the combination of being back in Virginia and drying out lightened the mood and stirred their hunger. They stopped at a local Burger King, everyone crowding into a large area in the back, the only seats available.

Kate could sense some relaxation. She hoped things would work out and the team would come out stronger than before.

In an instant her hopes were ruined. "I am not sitting by any lesbians. They are an abomination, according to the bible." Traci's words exploded any positive thoughts. The tension came back quickly. Traci's declaration seemed to slowly grind time to a halt. It wasn't unexpected. They were, after all, in the Bible belt, and many of Spotswood's finest were conservative Christians.

She wondered why this remark bothered her. She searched for feelings of calmness to comfort her, time to sit quietly, and let things go. That's when she opened her mouth. "God is responsible for homosexuality."

The words slammed into the group like a brick through a pane of glass. Kate had everyone's attention. "You give credit to God for everything. Well, give her credit for gay people."

Most of the team figured if they stared blankly forward, they could pretend nothing had happened. Everyone's face stayed buried in their food, but the tension in the room felt almost unbearable. The open hostility of Traci and the hidden resentment of several others finally bubbled to the surface. The next few minutes would be critical for the members of this team. Either someone turned down the heat on their resentment, or the entire team would boil over into angry factions.

Kate continued, speaking to everyone, she avoided singling out Traci. "Without becoming involved in a holy war, let me remind you that whatever your religion, a basic tenet of all ideologies is faith. I'm asking you to believe in 'your God.'

"You should have faith, faith in a reason for making all manner of people. Have faith that all people are here for a reason. So, let's focus on what we know. We are a group, a team. We are, for the next months at least, still friends. If you can't show compassion and forgiveness to your friends, what kind of human being are you?"

Taylor stood up. "Y'all get the point? My outspoken friend here wants us to remember the Golden Rule. Someone once said, 'we have committed the Golden Rule to memory; let us now commit it to life.'"

Five seconds of silence, and then Marisol gave a response they were all relieved to hear. "Anyone want my fries? I am going to get sick if I eat another ounce of grease."

The conversations resumed, and the world returned to normal speed. They had withstood the first test threatening their team. Jen turned to Kate and in a quiet voice, spoke from her heart. "Kater, I love you, man." Jen's words were embarrassingly genuine.

Taylor whispered. "Jeez-Louise, Jen, that's what got us in trouble in the first place."

Gabrielle overheard Taylor's remark. She laughed and spit a chunk of hamburger out of her mouth. The girls around her laughed. The first sounds of amusement in nearly a day echoed in the room. Marisol, Gabrielle and Courtney were laughing enthusiastically. They were still a team in turmoil, but seeds were planted which would eventually flower into forgiveness.

The rest of the trip home passed normally. Next on the schedule had Spotswood's Big Blue Stars playing Fredericksburg at home. It marked their last home game of the season. It also was parents' and senior day. Honoring the seniors fell to the juniors on the team. The coach made appropriate comments.

Jackie and Andi sat together and decided not to leave anything to chance. They would organize the proceedings and write the Coach's speech. An hour later, the vans pulled into the parking lot and began to empty. Allison's parents were waiting.

April 13

Kate underestimated the insatiable appetite for gossip. Instead of a calm Sunday, the rumors were flying around campus by noon. She had her first inkling word leaked out about North Carolina, later that day. She ran into several members of the softball team at the field house, while Kate dropped off her practice clothes. April Shriller, the captain and catcher on the team, chatted in her normal boisterous fashion with several other softball players. She yelled at Kate. "Hey, Holland, I hear you went through a rough weekend in Greensboro."

April rarely ever spoke to her, just a cursory nod or greeting. She tried to ignore April, but found it impossible when she walked over stood close to Kate. "So, Holland, I hear things were tense, and you stood up for your friends."

Kate didn't process April's words, so she shrugged. April lowered her voice and spoke slowly as if this would help her understand her. "You know, gay friends. I hear you stood up for your gay teammates in a crowded restaurant."

Kate finally understood April. She flashed a small smile, remembering her sermon. "Oh, yeah, at Burger King, anyway, that's what friends are for."

April grunted an agreement, nodded and walked away with a comment: "Burger King—cool. Well, way to go, girlfriend. Good luck at your next game."

Kate wondered if she had entered a clandestine society. She mumbled. "I'll be damned if I'm going to learn any secret handshake."

She wondered if this might be a great day for her to see if Andi wanted to go to Wal-Mart. A trip to Wal-Mart with her was fun. The only problem she could foresee was Andi wanting to collect the bet they'd made in Greensboro. Andi never forgot a bet she'd won, and Andi always won.

While she waited Kate cleaned her room. Jackie stuck her head in the door and shouted over the vacuum cleaner. "I wanted to thank you for what you did for Jamal."

"What did I do?"

Jackie had a big grin on her face. "Your friend Dr. Browne, you know, the President of the College. He happened to drop in on Jamal's review on Friday. He made some suggestions and it appears Jamal will be given an opportunity to work out his problem and maybe even graduate on time."

Kate acted stoically. She sat there looking at Jackie as if she were listening to her talk about Physics, a subject Jackie was familiar with, it was her major.

"Why so frosty? You don't have to admit anything, Kater."

"Do not ask for favors or require thanks for the things you are willing to do."

Jackie looked confused. Kate glared at her. Conveniently, Andi entered the room. "Hey, what's up, girlfriends."

"Thank God," Jackie muttered.

April 14

Monday's classes were a reprieve. The classroom became a safe haven from the ongoing soap opera. Kate avoided casual friends. She ducked and dodged around trees and corridors like a felon. She became determined to protect her team.

Most people who knew her well did not bother her. They assumed they would get better information elsewhere. Besides, rumors are more interesting when you get them from people who have no first-hand knowledge. Gossip always sacrifices truth on the altar of a good story. The events in North Carolina were gutted, twisted and turned. In the small village of Spotswood College, in the coffee shop, and the common areas, the hot topic became the women's lacrosse team. Massanuttenmuffins were consumed in record numbers.

A connection, such as a friend of a friend, became an unimpeachable source. After a while, rumors became more interesting than the truth. Never mind the events would have to have occurred in a banquet hall to accommodate the growing numbers involved.

"Down in North Carolina they had one of them 'orgies.'"

"God will make them pay."

"They did it in the hotel pool."

"They were escorted by the Carolina State Police to the Virginia line."

Most people dismissed the orgy concept when they considered the players mentioned. The quickest dismissal came from Mooner. "No way Taylor or Kate is involved. The thought of that could make me puke."

His friends were impressed. Mooner, known as the man who won a hotdog-eating contest, and then finished it off with a milkshake and two beers, had a cast iron stomach.

The majority of the talk began to center on Tess Burke and a player. Good gossip nearly always contains a certain bit of truth. The identity of the player involved in this blasphemous affair remained the X factor. The guesses came fast and curious. They ranged from the ridiculous to the truth. Some names were just comedic. The most prevalent assumptions were Stacey, Jen, Allison and for purely circumstantial reasons, Kate. Kate had sealed her fate in the mix by her actions at Roanoke's Burger King. What she'd said in defense of her team became distorted into overt gay activity. 'Have it your way' took on a whole new meaning for wagging tongues.

The wildest rumor involved Kate, Taylor, Jackie and Coach Altman. Some said they were found frolicking in a lesbian coffee bar. Nudity, licentiousness, and caffeine created a true rainbow latte. The palates of the rumor mongers salivated.

One curious rumor maintained Zack Tyler and the coach were lovers, and the team covered it up in a vast conspiracy. The fact that Zack didn't accompany the team of the trip meant nothing. Martianne started the rumor. She was still unclear about what had happened.

In a college community the size of Spotswood, most people were uncomfortable discussing other people's sexual orientation. Academically, a philosophical discussion meant fun and excitement. In the real world however, the southern and mountain mentality prevailed. These were Spotswood people. The talk would soon become whispers and whatever the resolution, it would be decided on this campus and in the best interest of the college. Spotswood's Big Blue Stars must survive after all.

The people who really knew what happened in Greensboro carried on the most fascinating discussions. In the team room the atmosphere wasn't as toxic as people might have expected, since the players were trying to follow Kate's advice. However, the Golden Rule stretched a bit to accommodate a few laughs.

Kate sought an island of sanity in the training room. She noticed Gabrielle stretched out on a training table. Amber massaged her weary hamstrings. Several others were having their ankles taped as a precautionary measure. The business of being an athlete went on within the safety of the locker room.

"Careful how far up you rub Gabby's thighs, Amber."

"Shut up, Jackie."

"Did you guys hear the one about Alicia?" Penelope spoke, a rare moment of cordiality.

"Who is Alicia?" Paige sat up, immediately interested. She wanted to get every bit of information straight about the Greensboro trip. She hoped to write a book about her college experiences.

"Kate's sworn enemy in Professor Paciarelli's class. Nick Orwell told Alicia at breakfast that Kate turned out to be a lesbian. Alicia stood up and verbally attacked him. Then, when he said it was not a rumor, she dumped a dish of prunes in his lap, Alicia standing up for Kate, how surreal."

Marisol asked the un-obvious question. "You mean you know someone who actually eats those prunes at the breakfast bar? Now, that is truly bizarre."

"Did anyone hear about Zack and Traci breaking up? Something about his affair with an older woman...she might be a coach or something, maybe even a hotelsexual," Martianne's question left most of them scratching their heads.

Cat shook her head. "What in General Custer is a hotel sexual? Does she mean homosexual? I can't..."

Marisol tapped Cat on the shoulder and led her away from the others. "I heard Coach Burke has a job offer from a Florida college, something about starting a new program—and I got the Little Big Horn sarcasm, Cat."

"What school? So soon, where did you hear it? When would she leave?"

Taylor entered the locker room. Her presence stopped all gossip. Taylor made it plain she hated scandal. She got dressed, signaling a time to get serious. "I am running the drills today.

Coach Burke called me. She has a meeting this afternoon, and won't be able to make practice, and Coach Altman will be late."

Except for the clatter of spikes and sticks banging on the tile floor, no one spoke or made any noise. Idle conversation disappeared, only the noise of banging lockers and echoes from the shower area intruded.

Taylor alone disturbed the stillness. "Y'all, it's all I know, so don't bother me with any of y'all's questions."

No one in their right mind had entertained the idea of asking for more information, even the crazies in the room.

Practice was not very spirited and it had been hampered by a lack of numbers. Several players were not in attendance. Allison, Stacey, Andi and Kate were missing. Their absence cast a shadow over the team. Taylor knew why they weren't here. Kate and Andi were talking to the Athletic Director. She'd already suffered through her brief interview. A quote by Thoreau ran through her mind like a prayer. "Be true to your work, your word, and your friend." Taylor kept the team on her mind.

Monday night provided a blessed relief from the constant prodding questions of their friends. The Campus Players were presenting One Act Plays tonight. Would be sure to attract a large crowd, and turn their thoughts away from the lacrosse team.

Kate and Andi were in no mood to talk anyway. They'd endured a severe grilling by Spotswood's stellar Athletic Director. Things went south immediately after Andi reminded Tommy Lee Skocul she'd warned him several weeks ago about a problem.

They endured his insinuations and pretentious remarks. Everyone else took the blame. He shifted blame wherever he could. The irony in the situation nearly made them laugh, except the tears they fought back denied them that pleasure. Several things were made clear in the meeting. Tommy Lee confirmed that Stacey no longer is *a-goen to be on y'alls team*. She would receive some professional help at the college's expense, and would return when it was in her best interest. Coach Burke could not be disciplined for an allegation, where one person's word prevailed against another, and Allison would return next week after her parents calmed down.

T.L. Skocul ended the meeting with a cryptic solution. He spoke in a strange conspiratorial tone, "The end to this will come in time. *Things'ull gets better, right soon.*" Kate knew she wasn't going to get the Wisdom of Solomon, but she hadn't anticipated the wisdom of 'Bubba.' She knew one comment rang true. Things would start looking up. They were on the bottom now.

Later in the evening after the 'One Acts', Kate, Andi, Taylor, Zack, Blake and Eric met at Brannigan's pub. They only drank hot chocolate. Another infraction could bring down their house of cards. Kate brought up their next game. "We are going to be short players on Wednesday, and I don't mean like Andi. Our only substitutes are Jackie, Brooke, and—well, there are no others. If we run into a situation where someone needs extended rest we might be in trouble."

Andi thought ahead. "We can always bring Penelope out, and put Martianne in the goal. Penelope has world-class speed."

Blake sounded amazed. "Your goalie has speed? I thought all goalies were slow."

Andi smiled. "If you carried twenty pounds of equipment, it would slow you down too. I bet you five bucks she could out-sprint you for a hundred yards."

"No thanks."

The conversation turned toward more important matters. The Fredericksburg team had a bad record, and by all rights, Spotswood should beat them. Taylor had heard they were young and prone to making mistakes. If the Stars could keep their wits about them, they would wind up with third position in the MVVC tournament, and home field advantage for their first game.

Andi straightened up and leaned close. "You guys are not paying attention. Whether we win or lose Wednesday, we will wind up in the third slot. Our conference record would be 4 wins, 3 losses. Tappahannock is playing Lee on Thursday and would finish at 4 and 3. The best Fredericksburg or Jefferson and Henry could finish would be 3 and 4. So, since we beat Tappahannock, we get the third slot."

Kate turned to Blake. "Remind me to never let Andi join our poker club. Agreed?"

Blake nodded, "Agreed."

Kate called her parents to keep them posted on things. To Kate, her parents were her best sounding board. She would always pass her ideas by them. In a pinch or emotional distress, she wanted to talk to her mother. When she needed advice, she talked to her father—Money, father—Clothing, mother. This system worked for most college students, in one form or another. She tried not to let them know she needed them. The code of growing up required admitting nothing that would make you look like a child again.

Tonight she hoped to talk to both of them "Mom, are you guys going to be able to make Wednesday's game? I told you about Parents' Day, and the senior parents walking out on the field, didn't I?" The statement was a gentle plea for her parents to be there. She caught herself reverting to her little girl attitude, pretending not be disappointed, but making sure her voice conveyed the implication. She walked a fine line trying to separate herself from little girl to the woman she'd become.

Kate's father had retired during her sophomore year, and traveled to most of her games. He normally found a spot near the field and took pictures. With a high-powered lens and a sophisticated camera, his photographs were very good. He always made it. Kate's mother might not. She taught middle school and rarely missed any days.

Her mother said nothing would stop her from attending Kate's last home game.

The end of college days loomed large in Kate's mind. When she graduated, she planned on getting her Master's degree in counseling. She'd already applied to a graduate program. Her anxiety about the future became more ever-present. In times like this she would most need to talk to her mother. Talking to her mother relaxed her, and put her in a good mood to face the next hurdle, whatever it might be. She hung up with this thought: *Parents, they are a handful at times, but what would we do without them?*

April 15

The following day seemed almost normal for the Lady Stars. Practice was typical with the exception of two missing players. The team worked on passing drills and the transition game up to the restraining line. This year, the umpires were calling offside more vigilantly. Only seven players were allowed to cross this line on offense. The rule opened up the game, and kept coaches from packing the defensive or offensive ends with all their players.

The Stars always played a transition game and were rarely affected by the rule. Other teams attacked from behind. They set up behind the goal and passed to cutting players, a favorite of most men coaches. Every testosterone coach loved to dominate the game from the sideline. The beauty of the players determining the events on the field got lost on these coaches. Spotswood's team played a speed game. They needed to be in excellent shape, and they were.

April 16

Wednesday afternoon, Kate took her parents to the campus center. Afterward, they walked around the campus together while Kate informed them about the traditions and places making up her school. In her four years, she'd learned to love her college. She put a lot of herself in the image of Spotswood.

She endured more than most by choosing to be an athlete. Pain, tears, training, long hours on the road, these things were normal for people who represented their school for the pride of competition. This walk gave her an opportunity to show her pride in Spotswood. "This is where I took 'chem' classes, and I earned my first A. Our Library has the third largest collection of journals on the East Coast. We are online in every dorm room on campus."

The pride in her voice bubbled out. Her father put his arm around her. "Kiwi, you've become more than a student. You are part of this school.

The Quest

The Stars formed a circle for their warm-up routine. Kate, Andi, and Taylor led drills. Overhead, the sun peeked out from behind voluminous clouds. A beautiful cerulean sky framed the surrounding mountains. Some days the view seemed sharper, more precise.

Kate looked toward Mt. Shiloh. She noted its beauty. She mumbled. "God works in mysterious ways. She must be quite an artist—good day for a game, the ball will jump off the stick in this light and low humidity."

This was her last home game, a final time to step on Spotswood's field for a league game. If they were lucky, they would play one more time at this site. It would have to be in the MVVC tournament.

Today became special. Kate wanted to capture the moment; she smelled the air as if she were trying to identify scents from the past. The clean odor of the mountains and the surrounding trees dominated her senses; the smell of the power plant nearby lent an aroma of wood smoke to the area. She leaned over during a stretching drill to run her fingers through the closely cropped grass. How thick. The grass looked like emerald strips.

Fifty years from now she could stand at this spot and touch this earth, recall her youth and her athleticism, all with a handful of dirt. The field might change, the buildings disappear, but her sweat, her blood, her life force would always be a part of this place in the shadow of the Blue Ridge Mountains.

The emotions she felt were strong. Feelings pumped through her like a shot of adrenaline. She fought moment by moment, to keep under control.

The warm-up music began playing. She would say goodbye to many things today, some things as trivial as a country song, others as important as her athletic youth. After thirteen years of lacrosse, she finally reached the end of her athletic days.

Today, Andi assumed the speaking Captain role. She immediately turned to Kate and said, "We're in trouble, don't you recognize the umpires? This is a white or wheat situation. It's the first time we've gotten both of them at one time."

The kindest assessment some players made about Mindy, the largest umpire in the league, might be that she didn't sweat much for an overweight lady. For too many seasons, Mindy waddled through Spotswood games. If she actually disliked any team, it would be Big Blue. The other umpire, Reatha, hated them.

Kate and Taylor each gave an inward groan, except the sound escaped their lips. Both umpires turned toward the sound, "Well, ladies, are you ready for today's game?" The words seemed to crackle as they reached the Spotswood captain's ears, raising the hair on the nape of their necks. Taylor gave it her best shot, "Why yes'm, were as ready as piglets after teats." Kate swore Mindy's eyes contracted vertically like a goat's.

The ceremony introducing parents began. They made a quick retreat. The athletic department had rigged a portable sound system for today's game, giving the Stars a moment's respite from the usual hand-held bullhorn.

When the seniors' parents were introduced they were escorted on to the field and the senior's mothers were given a bouquet of yellow roses.

"Let's give a round of applause for our seniors and their parents; Lloyd and Cindy Holland, parents of Kate Holland—Otho and Alice Braun, parents of Taylor Braun—Prescott and Paula Preston, parents of Penelope Preston."

- ☼ -

From the beginning, the umpires interfered in the game. Every aggressive move Spotswood made drew a whistle. It seemed that when Spotswood came close to the center line they were deemed offside. On defense, the checks made by Spotswood defenders were called dangerous. After fifteen minutes the score was two to two, and Spotswood had three goals called back.

Their lack of substitutes worried Kate the most. The opposing team could run the defense ragged and only Brooke remained available to give someone a breather and defense and Brooke hated defense. With five minutes to go in the first half, bad luck struck like a lightning bolt. Gabrielle ran into a Fredericksburg player and fell, knocked off-balance. The umpire blew the whistle, calling a foul on Gabrielle. Kate held her breath as she watched her teammate struggle to get up.

The grimace on Gabrielle's face told Kate it had happened again, her hip popped out of joint. Zack and Blake sprinted out to the field to help her off. She would be out the rest of the game. Jackie replaced her.

Jackie provided a strong replacement, but now only Brooke provided help. The Falcons converted their penalty shot and went ahead by one goal.

With the timekeeper counting down from thirty seconds, Kate broke free from her defender. Jackie noticed Kate open near the goal and passed to her. Kate sprinted by the front of the goal and shot over her shoulder and behind her back, to the amazement of the goalie and the crowd. She scored, tying the game at the half.

The second half started with several running attacks from the Falcons. Spotswood showed signs of getting tired. These were athletes who could run all day, but the combination of injuries and accumulated bruises kept them from playing their best. The long van ride to North Carolina and stress from Burke's fiasco had also taken its toll. But, Big Blue would never quit. Andi heated up and she could be the difference. Andi bolted down the middle of the field, faked a pass to Kate, and dove in for a score. The Stars were ahead.

On the next draw, Caitlyn took the ball from her defender and attacked the middle, following Andi's lead. Just as the defense closed around her, she flipped a short pass out to Andi on her right. Andi was a blur as she scored again. Things were looking good, Kate thought. A few more goals and the Falcons will lose their enthusiasm and we'll bury them. This game is at the mercy of momentum.

The umpire placed the ball in between the two centers' crosses for the draw. The ball went backward in a high arc toward the Spotswood defense. Taylor sprinted after the ball. With her eyes focused on its flight, she slammed into Andi. Then the unbelievable happened; both Taylor and Andi dropped to the ground. Both lay still. They were stunned. The heart and soul of the team were helped off the field.

Coach Burke called timeout. Both Taylor and Andi were conscious, but when a player may have been unconscious even briefly, the trainers refuse to allow them to play. The trainers had total control. Both Taylor and Andi were now relegated to sitting on the bench with ice packs on the back of their necks.

Coach Burke tried to rally Spotswood. "I'm sure we can play with eleven players, but I'm concerned about Brooke replacing Andi at center."

Then in desperation, and for the first time this year, Coach Burke finally turned to Kate, "Kate, what about you—any thoughts?"

Kate didn't hesitate. She replied softly but forcefully. "Well, we figured if something happened...Andi mentioned we could put Martianne in goal, and you could bring Penelope out on the field. I played center in high school, and Brooke could move to third man and Courtney to wing. You could also move Marisol to offense and Jackie to my position—just a suggestion Coach."

"Let's go with that line-up. Thanks, Kate."

Coach Burke's gratitude surprised Kate.

Penelope slid out of her pads, and Paige walked Martianne out to the goal. Once Martianne comfortably settled in between the pipes, her insecurities disappeared. She rubbed her back on the left pipe, then on the right. She felt at home in a cage. If nothing else catastrophic happened, the Stars could still bring home a win.

Coach Burke called them together, they joined hands. "We are ahead by two. Let's show this team we won't quit."

The events of the past week, the underlying resentments, were all put aside. A team can forgive, and a team can forget, but only when they are a team. At this moment, the girls tried to communicate how much they would forgive. "VICTORY!"

The shouted response sent shivers through the crowd, and as she admitted later, through Assistant Coach Altman.

There were twenty-two minutes left in the game. The Stars were without time-outs, and without substitutes, although Gabrielle argued as she limped, about wanting back in the game. Their backs were up against the proverbial wall, they could fight on or quit.

Kate tried to think back to her high school days and the tricks she'd used to influence the draw. She needed every trick in her book.

The following minutes settled into a defensive struggle, with Spotswood having trouble getting to mid field. Kate found herself deeper and deeper on defensive. The Falcons used eight subs to rest their starters. It made it harder and harder for the Stars to keep up. With twelve minutes left, the Falcons scored on a brilliant corner shot.

The remaining twelve minutes of this contest became a slow crawl toward the inevitable. The Falcons scored again to close the gap to one goal. Their fresh legs were getting to the ground balls sooner, and beating their defenders. What gave Spotswood hope was Martianne in goal. She stopped two direct shots with reflexes like a blur. The Stars scored, and the Falcons answered back. One minute to go and Spotswood still led.

The umpire blew her whistle, indicating an infraction against Spotswood; this gave the ball to the Falcons at the twelve-meter mark. The Falcon player took a wicked shot at the upper corner. It looked like a sure goal until Martianne got her stick up to pick it out of the air. With thirty seconds left, they needed a good clear from the goalie. Martianne made a rookie mistake. As she hurried to throw the ball she stepped out of the crease, then back in, still in possession of the ball. The umpire blew her whistle, awarded the ball to the Falcons, and this time number 20 scored.

The whistle blew ending the game. They were going into overtime.

They would have a three-minute rest period before play began. Kate, the only captain left for Spotswood, met with the umpires and three captains from Fredericksburg. They would play two three-minute periods, a total of six minutes. They would switch goals at the end of three minutes. The team ahead after six minutes would win.

The umpire started OT with a draw and play began. The obviously worn out Stars still seemed ready to give their all. For six minutes, both teams trudged up and down the field, scoring two more goals each. When the umpire ended the OT, the score stayed even.

Kate was summoned out to the middle of the field again. Her teammates cheered her on.

Andi screamed from the sideline, "We have them where we want them Blue, they look like they're out of gas." Andi, ever the optimist, saw signs Spotswood's conditioning began to come into effect against the Fredericksburg team. Kate believed Andi might be right. Somehow, they'd exceeded a turning point, and they were the team left with energy.

The next overtime period involved sudden victory. The first team to score would win. Kate believed they were going to pull this one out. She steadied her feet as she prepared for the draw.

The umpire signaled draw by dropping her arm, and then blew the whistle. Kate flipped the ball right into Ginni's stick.

The umpire blew her whistle again, stopping the game. She awarded the ball to Fredericksburg. Kate was livid, but she controlled herself. The Falcons passed down the field to number 20 again, and Brooke ran into her at the eight-meter mark. The umpire stopped the game, and awarded the Falcons a penalty shot.

Number 20 from Fredericksburg stood face-to-face with Martianne. The rest of the players stood ready. She took one step, and fired a weak shot, which hit a stone lying in the crease. As fate would have it, the hard compressed rubber ball bounced off the rock like a knuckleball in baseball. It floated crazily over Martianne's stick.

The game ended, and Fredericksburg whooped and yelled as they ran out on the field. The Spotswood players immediately jogged out to their goalie, they surrounded her. The loss belonged to the team, a lesson learned from Coach Von Mater. After all, goalies have fragile egos.

The team lined up and shook hands with a raucous group of celebrating Fredericksburg players. Kate walked near the sideline and heard Coach Burke shouting at the umpires. "You two wanted to get home early and you took it away from us. There was no way we lost the draw." She got red-faced and angry. Kate edged near her, and just as Coach Burke paused, Kate spoke.

"Coach, you can blame this loss on me. When the umpire drew down her hand, I jumped. I didn't know she would blow the whistle a fraction of a second later. The other player waited, so I take the blame."

Coach Burke looked at Kate with a faraway stare. The umpires walked away. Her anger evaporated along with her interest. She seemed distant when she spoke to Kate.

"Tell Taylor and Andi I want to meet with you captains tomorrow at four—in my office."

In all of the furor and excitement, Kate forgot about her parents. She walked over to them feeling discouraged—before she could say a word, her mother hugged her. Over her mother's shoulder she saw her father standing there smiling.

He leaned in closer. "You were a monster out there today. If I were to pick one game to see, one game to measure the worth of my daughter's courage, I would pick this one. You honored the game today."

Maybe because of the flowers, or her mother's embrace, or maybe the pride she heard in her father's voice, Kate no longer held back her feelings—she began to cry. "Damn it," she sniffed. "They will think I'm crying because we lost."

Kate's pride would not allow her opponents the pleasure of her tears. Within seconds, she recovered. "Let's get something to eat, you buying, Pops?"

April 17

The training room had a bucket full of people this morning. Lacrosse players were wandering in and getting treatment. You could tell things were rough when the athletes came in early. Kate stopped by to get some rub for her hamstring. While she opened a jar of Atomic Bomb, she ran into Gabby getting treatment on her hip. Across the room, there were at least three other teammates getting some form of treatment. The battle with Fredericksburg had taken its toll.

The training room tolerated only a few topics of conversation, mostly your health and sex. Today, health became the prevalent topic of conversation. "How's the hip, Gabby?" Gabrielle winced as the trainer rotated her joint back to a normal position. "I'll be ready for L'Enfant on Friday. How about telling Coach I'll be late for practice today? I have a paper due and I'm presenting a verbal synopsis, it shouldn't take me more than thirty minutes, Okay?"

Kate slathered the gel on the back of her leg, dropping her running pants and working the ointment into her muscle. The warming effects began to penetrate her skin immediately. Kate loved the feel and the odor of balm, it smelled and felt like competition.

Kate looked over at the redness around Gabrielle's hip. "Gabby, take care in the upcoming games. We need you to play your best. The tournament is the one game I want to win. If we win, we get to continue in the play-offs. I need you out there in front of me."

Gabrielle reclined on the table and focused on the trainer working on her leg. She looked up, following Kate with her eyes as she walked away.

She lay still, quietly watching as Amber rotated her leg. The release of air as Gabrielle exhaled indicated how much pain she repressed when her leg flexed. They both made eye contact at the same time. Amber spoke, exhaling her words as if she'd been holding her breath. "Woo... what just happened? I heard Kate say she needed something from somebody. Holy cow, she must be mellowing in her old age." Amber went back to rotating Gabrielle's leg. She noticed a tear forming in Gabby's eye. It ran down her cheek.

"Am I hurting you?"

Gabrielle shook her head. "No."

The tears were thicker now. Amber knew Gabrielle was upset. Gabby covered her face with her arm.

"What's the problem?" Amber trained to mend bodies, but experience taught her healing started with a player's soul.

Gabby answered as if she were speaking to herself, her voice rock steady and even. "I'm going to miss seeing Kate when she graduates. She is something else, my friend. What gets to me is her saying she needs me to play my best. Does she think I would let her down? I would play on crutches if she needs me."

Gabrielle lay back. "Sorry, Amber, I think my hormones are working overtime." She folded her arms under her neck, her face a contradiction of determination and tears.

Amber continued her massage. She'd just finished writing a paper about team relationships. It occurred to her she'd witnessed her chapter two in action. She thought about what she'd written concerning bonds of friendship.

"Maybe I should rework the bonding part. If I had the guts I would call it love."

"What?"

"Nothing, Gabby. I'm talking to myself about a paper."

- ☼ -

It seemed like a good time to take a scenic route to class. Kate reveled in the feeling of hot balm penetrating her hamstring. She'd use any excuse to walk beneath the oak trees along Spotswood's Mall. These majestic trees seemed to put the events of college life in perspective. The oaks were enduring, what happened beneath their branches didn't matter, it seldom influenced their existence. Her mind wandered to what lay

233

ahead. Later, the three captains were going to go to the coach's office together. Misery loves company.

Taylor definitely wanted Kate with her if there might be some unpleasantness. They all agreed this meeting was unusual. Coach Burke rarely consulted with her captains. They'd lost three of their last four games, and it looked like the season would end with another loss. L'Enfant University a perennial division II program moved up next year to division I. They were ranked in the top five in most national polls. The perennial leaders in Spotswood's league, Lee University and Stone Gap, were ranked in the top twenty-five. Spotswood didn't make the list.

The prospect of Spotswood pulling an upset looked dim, especially with only two players on the bench. Taylor was resigned to their fate, knowing full well the best they can do is fight the good fight.

- ☼ -

Kate finished her exam in Professor Kasich's class with time to spare, the extra reading paid off, she believed she'd aced this test. She turned in her paper and headed toward Massanutten Hall for a sandwich.

Converging karma popped into Kate's mind when she sat down in a booth. Jackie and Jamal were cozy in a booth across the room, they didn't notice her. She stood up to join them when she saw someone approaching.

"Mind if I join you?" The familiar voice of Alicia, the girl who gave her fits in class, gave Kate a jolt, she reacted reflexively.

"Sure, I just sat down, I don't mind company." She flapped her sandwich, indicating the bench directly across from her.

Alicia sat down daintily. She neatly folded a napkin then placed a cup next to it. The amount of time it took her to place a cup and napkin fascinated Kate. Alicia's tidiness bordered on compulsive. Chapters from Kate's psychology texts were firing chemically through her brain, looking to form a hypothesis.

"What's that smell, Kate?" Alicia noticed the distinctive odor of the balm. Her nose literally wrinkled in response to the smell. Anyone who'd ever participated in organized sports would immediately recognize it.

"It is ointment, you know, like liniment, the stuff you use on sore muscles."

"I hope it's nothing serious. I saw you play your game yesterday, my first Spotswood sporting event. I am really impressed."

Kate took a leap of faith. She would try to be friendly. "Why thanks, Alicia, coming from you, that means a lot."

Alicia looked straight ahead, "Kate, could you do me a favor? I know we haven't been the best of friends, but I feel like I know you well enough to ask you something personal."

Kate moved into the realm of the surreal, Twilight Time territory. "Alicia, you can ask me anything."

"Do you know Morris Mooney very well?"

Kate blinked. This was heading in a strange direction. "Why yes, Mooner and I are good buddies. We get together regularly to play poker, I've gone camping with him, and we sometimes meet in the training room for rehab, why?"

Alicia did not have to say another word. Her body language spoke volumes. The obvious discomfort gave her away. Alicia harbored a crush on Kate's monster buddy, Mooner. She believed Mooner and Alicia created a match made in Dante's first level of hell. Kate laughed. This could be perfect. She pondered the circumstances—Mooner, twenty-inch neck, fifty-five inch chest, and thirty-four inch waist, weighing in at two hundred and forty pounds of hormones—Alicia, none of the above.

She mentally weighed her options. This might work. If Mooner hooks up with Alicia then I'm no better or worse off. Kate appraised the pairing in her mind, pretty, petite, polite, nasty and opinionated versus, handsome, huge, offensive, ill-mannered, and kind. Kate would pimp her friend in order to create a ripple in the cosmic balance of Spotswood College. "No need to say anything, Alicia, I'll talk to Moon...eh, Morris."

Kate watched Alicia daintily excuse herself and retreat to safer circumstances. Her mind conjured up some fiendish images. *If she hooks up with Mooner, she'll damn well recognize the smell of muscle balm.*

Coach's office

Taylor and Andi waited outside Burke's office, hoping Kate would be early. Going into this meeting, they wanted to make sure they presented a united front. Whatever the situation, it could not be good.

"Andi, I hope everyone realizes the hardship we go through as Captains. It is not all glory and honor. It is not about the adulation of your peers, or the power. Remember, Gray's Elegy Written in a Country Church Yard? 'The boast of heraldry, the pomp of power, and all that beauty, all that wealth e'er gave— Awaits alike th' inevitable hour: The paths of glory lead but to the grave.'"

"Taylor, I major Economics and minor in Health and Physical Education. Talk to me about muscles, diet, or the dollar floating against the euro, but please will you stop this literary..." Andi never crossed the line into profanity, although she often came close.

Kate arrived at the right time, smiling like she'd won the Lottery. "Hello, girls, guess what I just did? I just suffered through a pleasant conversation with Alicia. She wants to date Mooner, can you believe it?"

Andi reacted. "Are you shitting me?"

Andi clapped her hand over her mouth, trying to capture the escaped profanity; too late.

The words violated the air. Kate had finally made Andi swear. "As I live and breathe, Ms. Andrea Castaldo, I do believe you owe me five dollars. If you will recall the bet we made two years ago? I said I would make you swear before I graduate."

Andi took her loss with her typical graciousness. "Shit, puke, barf, damn, hell, and doo-doo. Two years down the drain. Kater, you are a demon, this is the first bet I've lost since my freshman year."

Taylor was so amused by the word doo-doo, she laughed so hard she started gasping for air. "Doo-doo, Andi?"

Kate grabbed Taylor's arm. "Let's go find out what's waiting for us." The prospect quickly drained their good humor.

They knocked and walked inside. Coach Burke wasn't there. What they saw painted a visual history of lacrosse at Spotswood College. Lining the walls were pictures and plaques. Every available surface had a trophy or memento. The memorabilia told the story of teams coming valiantly close but never reaching the pinnacle. This once homey office looked sterile. Even with pictures and souvenirs everywhere, it lacked humanity. Kate stared, fascinated. "Look at all this stuff. It's remarkable."

Taylor snorted. "Second place trophies, typical of a small college. The only chance Spotswood has is to catch lightning in a bottle. These awards measure how far each team progressed compared to other teams. Look at them; second Place, 1976 MVVC Tournament, second Place, 1982 MVVC Tournament, 1983, 1985, 1989, 1990, 1991, 1993, 1999, 2002...a covenant to unrequited championship hopes."

Kate seemed to be confused. "What are you saying? These trophies can't measure the heart and courage of Spotswood's teams. Trophy or not, win or lose, Spotswood puts a fighting team on the field. Look at this one."

They stared at a picture of the 1970 Lacrosse team. Hung inconspicuously in a thin wooden frame was a photo of sixteen young women, their camaraderie of over three decades, frozen in time. Written at the bottom in script Kate saw; 0-8 'The Unconquered.' Standing proudly in the back, a young Georgia Von Mater struck a familiar pose. Only Coach could love a team that never won a game.

Andi must have been reminiscing too. "I miss Von Mater. Things haven't been the same. When did this place become so sterile?"

Taylor had an answer. "When Coach Burke tried to erase some thirty years of tradition in less than a year. Her mission from the get-go had been to wipe out the team's past. Maybe her intentions were noble. Turn away from second place and look for first. But, humankind must have its past, no matter how good, or bad."

Taylor spent several moments looking at the team pictures on the wall. She seemed unusually absorbed by the photos. "When we are old, thirty or so, will some young thing stand here and look at our team? Will she smile at the goofy uniforms and wonder what has happened to those old women?"

The thought of being old disturbed them. They sat quietly, reflecting on a distant future while they waited for Coach Burke.

Kate's mind drifted. *I wish I had a fruity-flavored jellybean now.* For three years, Kate invented reasons to visit Coach Von Mater's office. It had a decor, which reminded her of a grandmother's parlor. A well-worn, overstuffed chair nestled in the corner, a small oriental carpet; plant stands overflowing with African Violets, a Tiffany lamp, these things contributed a sense of warmth.

The centerpiece, a large apothecary jar filled with jellybeans; red, blue, spiced, and fruity, set the tone. To Kate, these were the best tasting jellybeans ever. The moment she would dip her hand in she connected to the humanity of the Coach. The Coach's outside demeanor appeared reserved and cool, but she expressed her feelings through small gifts, or measured words of encouragement. The office exposed her warmth and her soul. Kate loved the tasty treats and her moments with Coach.

Kate noticed the change the first day she visited Coach Burke—it had begun with jellybeans. The chair was gone, and the jar replaced by a laptop. The desk looked sterile, except for a set of those annoying balls which strike each other and make a clacking noise, validating some law of physics. To Kate metal balls were no replacement for candy.

When Tess Burke entered, Kate noticed how small she looked. Burke's personality made her intimidating. She used her marginal social skills and her reticent personality as a weapon against the outside world. The small clique of players she liked fared no better than the ones she didn't.

Burke suffered in silence. Her existence could never overcome the stigma of being different, a social outcast from the beginning. As a child, she hid her aggression on the athletic field, but she remained alone, even on a team.

Burke took her seat and faced the girls behind the desk, creating another barrier. "I wanted to let you know the L'Enfant game will be my last."

The captains leaned forward. "When I accepted this job in August, I considered a division II job in Florida. I kept an application on file and stayed in contact with the university. They want to hire me—if I report there this Monday.

"I know we have a tournament game on Tuesday, but I have talked to the Athletic Director and Coach Altman, and we have worked something out."

Coach Burke maintained her stoic attitude. "We have not been the best of friends on the field, but I respect your ability. That's all I have to say."

Kate, Taylor, and Andi stood up mechanically. The meeting ended. Just before they exited, Kate turned around and walked back to Tess. She stood squarely in front of her. "I wish you the best at your new school. I hope you get to do things the way you want."

Outside the office Taylor raged. "The bee-aitch, how could she look us in the eye and tell us she left for a better job. I should go back in there and kick her deviant ass."

Taylor's voice reverberated off the walls. "I'm telling you, Kater, she never liked you from the beginning, for whatever the reason you were her biggest target. She put her personal feelings above the team."

Kate winced, sure Burke could hear Taylor. Andi reached her arm out and touched Taylor on the shoulder. The touch calmed her down.

Andi put her own spin on the situation. "I think she had everything in her favor, all the power on her side. She came in here with an attitude, and she would spank anyone to prove herself the boss. I also think she underestimated the girl she chose to whip. The spanking cost the team."

Taylor looked confused. "What the hell do you mean, Andi?"

"Let me roll out an analogy you'll understand—Coach never figured it out. Just like the Hindu saying, 'when elephants fight, it is the grass that suffers.'"

Taylor clapped her hands gleefully. "I'm awed by y'alls cogency, a teeny-weeny philosopher."

Kate was thinking about something else. "Andi, Taylor, did I cause the problem on our team?"

"Oh no, not likely girlfriend, y'all weren't surfing' Stacey's body when Allison walked into Burke's hotel room, old' Tess just couldn't keep her hormones under control. I guess she figured some mistakes are too much fun to only make once. She just hated you 'because you're not as buff as Andi and Me. You're too girly girl like."

"Well, I really did mean it when I wished her good luck."

- ☼ -

The team got the word at practice. Some players were upset at first. The freshmen in particular were not sure of what would happen next. Kate, Andi, and Taylor spent some time reassuring them things would work out. They reassured them that the team remained united, and prospects for next year were still good. When the last ego had been massaged, Taylor shook her head at the young player's reaction. "They don't know how lucky they are. We still have a chance to make playoffs, and they are going to get a new coach next year. Plus they will still have Andi to guide them."

There were no farther remarks or questions. The team settled into a practice rhythm. The shouts of encouragement, the idle chatter had a calming effect. Players seemed to accept this as another hurdle in a disastrous season. Slowly, naturally, the players gravitated to the center of the field where Andi,

Taylor, and Kate were plopped on the ground, resting their sticks by their side. Marisol tossed her stick on the pile. She sat down. Another stick promptly followed. Another stick and girl joined the group. The captains found they were surrounded by their teammates. The team waited for some sign.

Then Jackie and Ginni lit a little spark of conversation. They talked about nothing in particular, their sticks, and the condition of their spikes, even men. All the while the team waited.

Paige voiced a concern about the upcoming game. "What can we expect tomorrow? Is L'Enfant tough? Without any help, what happens when we get tired?"

Kate leaned back on her elbows; she stretched her legs and looked toward the sky, then spoke. "We will give the Engineers a battle, like we always do, but they are our most demanding test."

Taylor sprang to her feet. "I'll answer y'alls concerns with one quote."

The response was immediate, a loud groan followed by 'not again' from Marisol.

Andi stopped the groaning with a sharp ..."Let her talk, the truth will always be in there somewhere."

Taylor pursed her lips in a mock frown. "Y'all hurt my feelings', but anyway—one last time..."

A cheer went up.

Taylor wrinkled her nose. "Playing L'Enfant will be like wrestling with a gorilla. You don't quit when you are tired— you quit when the gorilla gets tired."

Cat asked Marisol. "What does she mean?"

Brooke looked worried. "Does it mean they're going to kick the stuffing out of us?"

Everyone expressed an opinion about Taylor's remark. The team forgot about Coach Burke leaving. They had bigger fish to fry. Still the freshman wanted to know the significance of Taylor's comment. Their lack of concentration during a drills frustrated Jackie. "Okay! Here is the answer, and may I say I am disappointed by your reasoning skills. Tomorrow we play L'Enfant until we have nothing left in us. Then we play on, until L'Enfant has nothing left—and when the gorilla gets tired we've got it where we want it."

Murmurs of, "Oh, I get it." Nods of agreement started to ripple through the team.

Paige laughed out loud and shouted out to everyone near her. "We fight them tooth and nail and they beat the crap out of us—then when their arms get tired from the beating, we whoop up on them! Give 'em hell, Big Blue!"

Kate turned to Andi. "I said at the beginning of the year this team might be special. I am starting to get the feeling this lunatic bunch isn't afraid of anything. Maybe...."

Kate's thought went uncompleted. She wondered if second place might not be a high enough goal.

Courageous in DC

April 18

Packed and ready to leave for a four o'clock game at
L'Enfant University, they would leave the parking lot at eleven
thirty. Standing beside Vanuno, Coach Burke looked impatient,
nervously checking her watch. All players arrived except one.
The ride to Washington D.C., and L'Enfant University took two
hours plus, along a busy Interstate 66. This game represented a
finale of sorts, and some people wanted the end to start as soon
as possible. Unfortunately, Kate still sat in professor Paciarelli's
classroom finishing an exam.

She eyed the clock and realized she could just make it. In
her senior year Kate learned how to take tests, by now she
could pass a multiple-choice test on any subject. Eliminate the
distracters, find the two answers which are similar, eliminate
the flawed sentence, look for an obvious mistake—select the
obviously correct answer. Kate finished in record time and
headed toward the professor's desk to turn in her paper.

Dr. Paciarelli quietly asked Kate if she had a game today.

"Yes, Ma'am, we are headed to D.C. We're playing L'Enfant.

"My Alma Mater" Dr. Paciarelli had a strange look on her
face.

"I didn't know you were an Engineer. If you want, I'll ask
the team to take it easy on them."

"Kate, all I am worried about is you getting the notes from
the lecture following this exam. Do you have someone who can
take good notes for you?"

Alicia's hand shot up. "Yes, she does, Dr. Paciarelli, I'll take care of getting Kate the notes. I'll even deliver them to her dorm."

Dr. Paciarelli looked confused. "You'll take notes for Kate?"

Ryan Malone whispered to no one in particular, "did they announce the apocalypse while I concentrated on this exam?"

- ☼ -

Kate sprinted toward the field house. She turned the corner just as Vandos pulled out of the driveway. Vanuno, however, waited with its door open. She tossed her bags into the van and jumped onboard. "Looks like you were going to leave without me."

Taylor made a snorting sound in response to Kate's remark. "Kater, it's highly unlikely this van would move until y'alls derriere got in its accustomed seat. Coach Burke might want to leave you behind, but we don't. We're fixin' to win this game. Let's get rolling, Coach Altman."

The chatter started. Kate immediately schooling the freshmen, "This is our final game with L'Enfant. The Engineers are moving up to division one. We play them alternating years at their place. The last time I played them I was a sophomore. They don't travel to Spotswood. Too good, I guess."

Kate combed her hair back into a ponytail and secured it with a rubber band. She talked with a ribbon between her teeth. "They certainly provided a learning experience. They are fast, they are accurate, and they play to win." Her mind wandered as she secured her hair with the bold blue ribbon. So did the thoughts of her teammates. Other things weighed on their minds. It didn't take long to surface.

Cat shouted toward the front. "Coach Altman, are you going to take over?"

The answer came out as evasive. "I will—would, love to have this team next year, but, I think our Athletic Director and Dr. Browne have worked something out. I can't tell you much more, but things will get better. I promise."

Kate's heart jumped at the mention of Dr. Browne. Her hopes soared at the mention of his name. If he were involved then the best interests of Spotswood lacrosse would be served.

Gabrielle's bladder reached its limit at The Plains. The vans pulled off the highway to route 626, looking for a place to stop. When they found a local gas station, they took a break. The difference in the two vans became immediately noticeable. The players in Vandos looked like they were traveling to a funeral, while the others were rowdy and full of good humor.

Penelope stormed over to Taylor and Kate and told them to send someone to the other van. "I'm riding with you guys, and do not give me an argument." No one considered protesting her demand. To his dismay, Blake served as the sacrificial lamb.

They pulled out of the gas station and continued east.

The blue and grey Spotswood vans merged on to I-66 east toward D.C., with Kate meditating in the back seat. As they drove by an outdoor ice cream stand, Kate mentally transformed her van into a time machine. She remembered other trips and other times along this road. She noted the exits and the towns as they sped by, advancing on D.C. The mountain scenery represented milestones toward destinations in her life.

They passed the Haymarket sign—where Kate always stopped for coffee and scones on her way home. Then she saw a sign for the Nissan Pavilion where she and Jackie, met Taylor and Jen for last summer's concert. Ahead, at Manassas, less than a month ago she saw a hit and run accident, and a man being apprehended by someone in a tuxedo. Then she saw Vienna, where she'd stopped with her parents at a marvelous Greek bakery.

As they neared D.C, she was inundated with sights. They crossed the Roosevelt Bridge and Kate saw the Kennedy Center, She stirred from her meditation. "Hey, I went to see the Phantom of the Opera there, on my sixteenth birthday. Then I took my Dad to see Miss Saigon on his fifty-fifth."

They approached the overwhelming sights of the city. They passed the Tidal Basin and Maine Avenue. The surrounding buildings were mountains of another variety, mountains of concrete and steel. They were a beautiful testament to the heart of their country. At the entrance of L'Enfant University, they were dazzled and appalled by the lush green fields hidden and surrounded by chain-link fence. Even if you had been there before, a sight like this amazed you.

Spotswood unloaded its gear and headed up toward the field, located on a hill overlooking the city center. Picturesque, and somewhat intimidating, they approached a gate leading to the field. A security guard at the entrance tipped his hat. Eventually they were inside the inner fence and felt more at ease. Now they had to face the daunting Engineers of L'Enfant.

At the field, Kate recognized two players from private schools she had played against in high school and in a summer league. They recognized her, nodding hello. She noticed they immediately turned to talk to their teammates. Kate knew they were discussing her. She'd played on an all-star team with them, and they were passing on the information.

She tried to find a way to make L'Enfant seem less formidable. "Anyone want to go to school behind a barbed wire fence?"

"No!"

They gathered in a circle and began their prayer. "Dear Lord, give us the will and blessing to have the strength to spank this gorilla. Amen."

"That's what my boyfriend likes." Paige chirped.

The laughter grew, becoming contagious. Andi glowered at Paige, and tried to gain back their focus. "Let's get it on."

The team answered with a shouted, "INTENSITY."

The Engineers stopped and watched, curious about the Spotswood team. L'Enfant seemed interested in the attitude displayed by this small group of players warming up on their field.

On the sideline, the coach of the Engineers looked concerned. She had heard a rumor Spotswood's team was in turmoil, and she hoped for an easy game today. If things went right they'd cruise by this team. L'Enfant faced a tough game on Tuesday with a top-ranked team.

Before the opening draw, the captains met to discuss ground rules. Grace and Susan, the umpires from the Tappahannock game were the umpires. They greeted her warmly. "Hey, we haven't done any of your games in a while. How's your season?"

Taylor exaggerated her southern accent. She said it made the northern girls overconfident. "Well, y'all know how it is. Y'all win some and we lose some."

After the meet and greet, they returned to their team and discussed the ground rules. They tried their best to make the others on the team feel at ease. Taylor mentioned their players were Northerners and Australians.

"How do you know they are from Australia?" Paige asked.

"Well, they didn't say 'gudday mate,' or ask if we wanted another shrimp on the Barbie, but their accents gave them away."

Paige smiled. "Like your accent Taylor?"

Taylor looked puzzled. "What accent?"

In the midst of this curious conversation, Traci lit an unintentional fire under her team. "I did the math. We don't have to win this game. It's meaningless concerning our standing in the MVVC."

Marisol didn't get it. "We don't need to win? Why play the game then? We might as well take our loss and go home."

Andi pushed Taylor aside. She boiled with confidence. "We are not losing this game today. The only thing we can lose today is our pride. So—let's win this one for the Gipper."

Andi beamed. "I always wanted to say that line."

The response was predictable. The girls discussed Andi's remark. "What the hell is a gipper?"

"I think it's a sushi fish?"

"I think you mean kipper?"

"Isn't gipper what the Aussies eat?"

Jackie shouted, "Let L'Enfant eat kippers, 'we bees' sushi eaters. Let's fire up this team with our wasabi."

Taylor touched Kate on the arm and leaned close. "This team is definitely not frightened."

"Do you think they're too stupid to be scared?"

"Y'all know stupid is as stupid does."

"Okay, Taylor, let's go get stupid."

The draw went to L'Enfant and they moved it quickly downfield. Their skill level made it clear there would be little extra body contact today. The passing game of the Engineers performed so well, Big Blue might not get close enough to check them. The first shot by L'Enfant came like a bullet toward the goal's upper right hand corner. Penelope's reacted quickly and accurately—she picked the ball out of the air. The crowd murmured in amazement.

Kate pumped her fist in the air and mouthed a word—"yes!"

She and Taylor had talked about those magical days when Penelope displayed super reflexes, when those days happened, she couldn't be beaten, and it just might be today.

Catbird took a long clearing pass up the sideline. She passed to Andi in the middle, who passed to Gabrielle cutting across the goal. Gabby's shot ricocheted off the goalie. Kate anticipated a miss and positioned herself near the goal. The ball bounced her way. The ball nestled in her crosse for a millisecond; she flicked it past the goalie into the net. The Engineers home crowd gasped. They were used to their team playing at top speed; they weren't always accustomed to another team running with them.

Just as the Spotswood Stars discovered in their game against Timonium, they could run with the big girls.

This game started fast and got faster. Spotswood ran with the Engineers, but they were not as skilled at making cutting passes. The Engineers pounded home two goals after attempting six shots. Penelope turned back three shots with spectacular moves. On their last missed shot an Engineer took her shot and tried to put it over Penelope's left ear, the only space available. She shot wide.

On Spotswood's offensive side, Kate pumped her fist in celebration again. L'Enfant developed a glitch in their offensive motor. Penelope's fine work in the goal made them tentative, looking for a perfect shot. They were aiming the ball, trying too hard to get by the wiry apparition guarding the nets for Spotswood.

Conversely, Kate would deliver a crushing blow to the confidence of the L'Enfant goalie. In a rare moment for this game, the ball glanced off a stick and hit the ground. Big Blue's forte, they dug and grunted for loose balls like a pissed off honey badger. Courtney picked it up, moving the defender aside with a deft hip flip.

The young players on Spotswood's team were being schooled every second they were on the field. They were playing up to the level of their opponent. Traci passed to Andi. A race for the goal began. Andi picked up a double team but still managed to get off a shot. Her ball nicked the pipe and ricocheted behind the goal at lightning speed. From the opposite corner, Kate flew toward the ball and snatched it up on a short hop. It happened fast.

Kate rolled the crease unguarded, one-on-one with the goalie. She saw the goalie set her feet. Kate faked. The Goalie moved. Kate dropped her stick low and shot between the girl's legs. The score was tied. Now Andi would get less attention and light up the scoreboard.

Lacrosse is a game of ebbs and flows. It didn't take too long for the Engineers all-American, Ali Silbert, to surface. Ali played skillfully and aggressively, the most ferocious player on the field, especially going after a ball in the air. Two more Engineer All-American players, Lorena Portillo, and Adrienne Stein also ramped up their game. L'Enfant's quality emerged.

But Big Blue had their stars too. Shot after shot on Spotswood's defense, Taylor began show her strength, and dominated the Engineer's best. L'Enfant players were now getting less open shots at the goal. Spotswood's quality came forward. Jen matched speeds with the all-Americans, and Penelope stood like a Spotswood oak in goal.

Near the half, it became clear that without Penelope, the score would be a lot to a little. After trading goals, the score was tied at three. Kate looked at the scoreboard clock. With five minutes left, they should call a timeout. The Stars did not have much in reserve. She looked at the Coach—no sign. Ali Silbert scored as the clock ran out. The Stars headed toward the water jug. They were dragging. There had been no substitutions. Coach Burke had been caught up in a fantasy.

Burke made changes at halftime. Martianne went in the goal, Penelope came out as a field player and Jackie started the half at Gabrielle's position. Brooke sat. She and Penelope were to relieve Courtney and Marisol ten minutes into play. No one questioned the move. They'd used it before and Kate had recommended it. Only a few wondered if a rookie goalie could hold up under the pressure.

The whistle blew ending what seemed like an instant to Kate. Jackie raised a cheer, "Let's win this one for sushi eaters."

The team responded, "INTENSITY!"

They went back on the field summoning every ounce of their reserve.

Along the sidelines, L'Enfant's fans were surprised their school of ten thousand found itself in a dog fight with a school one-hundredth its size.

The Engineers turned loose their guns at the beginning of the second half. Lorena Portillo and Ali Silbert fired shot after shot at the inexperienced Martianne. Meanwhile the offense of Spotswood performed as Kate expected. The center opened up for Andi, and they doubled Kate. Shooter caught on fire. She slipped through for three goals before the Engineers adjusted. When they doubled Andi, and doubled Kate, Gabrielle and Jackie popped in goals.

Even though the Engineers played ten substitutes, and Spotswood played three, neither team had an advantage at this point. With three minutes left, the score was fourteen to fourteen. In everyone's mind, this next draw was critical.

Kate moved over near Ali Silbert. If Ali wanted this draw, she'd need to go through Kate. The ball left the crosses of the centers in a high arc, headed toward Kate and Ali. Kate felt Ali's hip trying to move her over. She reacted by stepping inside of Ali's leg, effectively keeping her from jumping in the air. The ball sailed over both their heads into Ginni's crosse.
The crowd buzzed with anticipation and concern. This could be a huge upset. The final minutes ticked away in this, now, epic struggle. The Engineers closed off all passing lanes and survived two shots from Andi and Kate. Martianne did her best imitation of Penelope and stopped Ali Silbert cold—twice.

The clock unbelievably clicked on zero—overtime. Kate thought, *just what the doctor ordered*.

When the whistle blew to start the overtime period, the Stars came at the Engineers with a vengeance. After all, they knew how to do this overtime stuff. For six more minutes, they traded goals. The score now remained tied at sixteen.

Later, Kate replayed the last two minutes in her head, many, many, times. She saw her team attacking the center with crisp passes. Andi ran down the center, and the Engineer defense slid over to close her off. Kate saw the look in Andi's eyes. She read her thoughts. If Kate could cut across from the right, she would be wide open for a shot. Everything seemed to happen in slow motion. Then wham! Kate was pushed from behind. The action returned to full speed.

Kate slid through the grass; chin first, tits and elbows next, and finally her nose plowed into the turf. A defender stepped over her before she lifted her head. She pried a clot of dirt from her lips and looked up. Adrienne Stein, the third all-American, had intercepted the pass intended for her.

For an instant she paused, waiting for a whistle to stop the nightmare. It did not happen. Adrienne passed immediately up the field, before Kate could dig herself out of the dirt. Ali Silbert scored. L'Enfant won the final draw, and held on until Grace's whistle ended the game. The scoring ended at seventeen to sixteen and the Engineers were the winners. The Stars were victimized in overtime again.

No one celebrated on the field. The Engineers won and felt lucky. Each team lined up for the traditional handshake. As they passed each other in line, you could tell both sides had given its all, no one exhibited enough energy to rejoice or agonize. When Kate reached the end, she turned and stood face-to-face with Adrienne Stein. Adrienne grinned uncomfortably, shook her head and lowered her eyes. "I'm sorry I did what I did. I saw you'd picked up a step on me and my only choice was to foul you and hope the umpire wasn't looking. Are you okay?"

Kate stuck out her hand. "I'm fine. Don't sweat it. I would have done it to you if I had a chance. By the way, your field tastes like shit."

Adrienne grimaced. "I was sure the ump would call the foul. After, I felt a little ashamed. Lorena, she said she knows you, told me to talk to you, you'd understand."

"I know Lorena, and I understand."

That comment broke the ice. They both laughed and the battle became history. Adrienne still kept slipping in an apology. "I'm sorry I knocked you over."

"Forget about it. My old coach used to say, 'If the ump doesn't blow the whistle it didn't happen, so get back in the game.'"

"Smart. I just thought you might be angry about that play causing your team to lose."

"Old Coach had a saying for that, too. 'One player's error doesn't cost a team the game.' I just figure your hips are way bigger than mine." At that, Kate turned away. She had a limit to her benevolence. Adrienne smiled at Kate's back.

When the game began, Kate's objective was to earn the Engineers' respect. She would not know that later this game became part of their lore. Whenever the L'Enfant coach felt they were taking things too lightly, she would invoke the memory of Spotswood's Big Blue Stars.

Homecoming

The season ended with a loss. On the ride home, Jackie reminded the freshmen they'd played well, coming a long way from their beginning in March. "Our overall record is 9 wins and 6 losses, a better record than my first year, and our MVVC record is 4 and 3. We are far from losers. We still have the tournament on Tuesday, and the hope we can advance to the second round."

Marisol wanted to know what it meant. "Who won the League championship?"

The questions tumbled out. "Whom do we play in the tournament?"

"When do we turn in our uniforms?"

They asked the kinds of questions that let you know the season was over. Only the thin hope of advancing remained. Cat seemed dejected when she echoed the sentiments of most of the team. "All we have is one tournament game left."

Coach Altman raised her hand. 'Shush...I'm on the phone." Altman covered her other ear with her hand, and shouted, quieting the van. "Hey, I have the scoop on the tournament. Lee University beat Stone Gap for the League championship."

No one responded.

Ariel looked dumbfounded. "They have the first seed, because they are undefeated in the conference. Stone Gap is number two, and we are 'unbelievably' number three."

A murmur of disbelief ran through the group as Ariel delivered the litany. "Tappahannock beat Fredericksburg, and

Tappahannock has the same record in the conference as we do. We beat them, so we are third and they are fourth. Top three seeds get to play at home."

The group began to murmur, starting to process this information as good news. Marisol finally got it. "Wait...we play Fredericksburg on Tuesday at home. It looks like we finally got a break."

Jen however, added a note of pessimism into the conversation. "Right, all we have to do is beat Fredericksburg, a team that beat us. Then we probably would face Stone Gap—a team that beat us, so we can get a shot at Lee, a team...."

The whole van answered in unison..."A team that beat us. Hooray!"

Ariel Altman looked baffled. She shook her head as she called her husband. "We won, Honey. Break out the cigars and meet me at school. I want to get away from this lunatic bunch."

Everyone on the bus could hear his shouted response. "Won what?"

The vans emptied quickly and only a few players stayed behind to talk to Coach Burke. Kate said her good-bye previously, and saying it again would insincere. Once was enough. She started thinking ahead to tomorrow's practice. Coach Altman would take over, but she needed help. Whom did they get? For a scary moment she thought...what if they drafted J.E.B. Kasich? Could God be so unkind?

Jen and Penelope were in a heated conversation in the locker room. The conversation awkwardly stopped when Kate got near. "Whazz-up sistahs, what did I do wrong now?"

Jen shook her head negatively. "Nothing, Kater, we were just miserable on the way home. Burke's bus sucked. She depressed everyone. I can't wait until we all are in one bus."

"We have to win the first game before they break out a coach for tournaments, girlfriends."

Jen didn't seem encouraged. "Jackie says we are in trouble because of our tournament draw."

Andi popped her head into the group. "I heard you."

She had an impish grin. Something made her happy. "Coach Burke said it on the way home. I believe I have six witnesses she made a bet for five bucks on the next game. I said we would win by 5 goals. She put her money on Fredericksburg by two."

Kate whooped. "Andi, you are brilliant, a mini-nova."

April 19

Gosh, I'm anxious to get to practice. Kate crackled with nervous energy. This week had been extremely difficult with coursework and preparing for exams. It seemed her professors were piling on the projects. This added to her stress. In addition, today they'd find out whom they hired to help Coach Altman.

The field house looked different today. It must be her imagination, but it looked less sterile than it did when this season began.

Kate entered the team room feeling nostalgic. *This could be one of the last times I dress in this place.* She pulled on a pair of freshly laundered green shorts, and then picked up a sports bra. She smelled it to double-check its cleanliness. Immediately she considered her action. *That was stupid. I bury my nose in this underwear, what if it stunk like a skunk? I stuffed my face into it. I bet if I* *invented a pop-up tag 'kind of' like the ones on a Thanksgiving turkey...*her mind drifted.

The weather seemed warm enough to wear a thin cotton tee-shirt. She strapped on her ankle braces and laced on her cleats. Wearing the best footwear had been an obsession since middle school days. "The right shoe for the job."

Kate imagined her grandfather's words in her mind. For a second she struggled with the memory. She wanted to hear the words as they sounded in his voice. It became harder to do as the years passed by. She squeezed her eyes tight, trying to block out the room. *Why is this so important?* Kate couldn't find an answer, and she sensed her emotions slipping away from her. Another voice brought her back

"Kate, can you help me with this knee wrap?" Allison stood next to her. The upheaval with Burke could be classified as officially over. After Burke resigned, Allison's parents wanted her to go back to the team, but Kate could see she looked a little uncomfortable. The distraction of helping Allison helped Kate keep her emotions under control.

"I must be suffering from PMS."

"Why, Kater?"

"No reason, Ali, I'm just glad you're back on the team."

Kate grabbed her stick and they joined Marisol as she jogged toward the field. Marisol acted chatty and playful. As they approached, Kate saw Coach Altman standing near the bench. A partially obscured seated figure slumped forward. Kate could make out a woman wearing a jacket, although it felt warm today. Kate felt a tightening in her throat. It looked like..."Coach Von Mater."

Kate squeaked.

Marisol looked at her as if she were an alien. "Are you Okay? You look goofy."

As Kate got closer she noticed the Coach looked pale and drawn. Kate could tell Coach's illness took a heavy toll on her. Jackie and Jen saw Kate coming and followed her toward the bench. Kate's appearance gave the signal to gather. They must have been waiting for her. Andi and Taylor waited next to Coach Von Mater.

When she approached Coach, they locked eyes. Kate could see a look she'd never seen before, an unspoken message or plea. Kate reacted instinctively. "Coach, I knew they couldn't keep you away from this team, you were always a glutton for punishment."

Coach smiled, and some of the others chuckled nervously.

Kate made a sweeping gesture and an announcement. "For you freshmen, let me introduce the legendary Georgia Von Mater, the 'winningest' coach in Spotswood's history." Kate's voice reached a theatrical peak. The group pulled in tighter, surrounding the bench.

Kate looked into Coach's eyes, and continued. "Do not let her looks fool you. Just because she looks like your grandmother does not mean she won't come down hard on anyone who does not play her best. I'm guessing our job will be to give this legend her due. We are obligated to win the MVVC championship and nothing less."

Taylor spoke up. "Coach, should we start practice?" Coach Von Mater nodded.

"Let's go, Stars, out on the field for stretching exercises."

Then the quiet voice of Georgia Von Mater reached out to the captains. "Kate, Andi and Taylor, may I have a word with

261

you?" The sweet southern drawl remained as effective as ever, just not as strong.

Coach Altman nodded toward Georgia and barked out a command. "Jackie, Gabrielle, Penelope, you lead the exercises." While the others trotted out to the field, the captains waited. They dropped quietly down, legs crossed, at the Coach's feet, waiting. Von Mater seemed tentative. An extremely private person, she hesitated to share the most personal experiences of her life.

Georgia looked at the faces in front of her. In their eyes she saw strength and youth. She knew them and trusted them. As a devoutly religious woman, she knew God had given her these three young women when they were needed most. In her thirty-five years of coaching strong women, she'd never seen three women so solid, and they were on one team. These three were leaders. They were fighters. They were women of substance. "May I take a moment—a quick prayer, thanking God for his blessing?" The captains remained patient.

"Ladies, I believe you can tell from my appearance, I have an illness. I am currently engaged in a battle against cancer." Kate shuddered visibly, and sat upright, more rigid.

Georgia spoke on. "I believe with God's help and the attention of the finest doctors available, I will prevail. My doctors tell me my prognosis is stable but not guaranteed. As you know, nothing happens unless it is God's will. My doctors also advised me to seek the support of my family. I have always considered my teams to be family, so I happily volunteered my service when this team needed assistance. However, I need your help in dealing with certain things. I volunteered to aid Coach

Altman because she asked, she felt I might lend some experience to the situation, and frankly, I need the distraction. I believe a positive outcome will benefit my recovery."

She paused, her bearing improved as she began talking. "I have followed your progress from a distance, not wanting to interfere in Coach Burke's business, however I believe this team can play more effectively, and by doing so, put yourselves in a winning position."

Her next words rang like a bell. "Taylor, you will lead this team on the field, you will be my strength. Andi, you will be my resolve. When things look bleak you must gather our determination. Kate, you will be my courage. I expect you to be audacious, to summon the team to valor. When you three speak, the team will listen.

"Together, you will be me on the field. In alliance, we will be invincible. Please go out on the field today and convey my desires to your teammates, ask them if they are willing to pay the price."

"Yes ma'am."

Coach Von Mater raised her hand. The girls hesitated. "Before you three go, I want you to commit these verses to memory. I'm asking much of you and I believe a day will come when you will need help. So, Taylor, Matthew 11:28-20. Andi, Proverbs 3:5-6, and Kate, Second Timothy 1:7. I believe this will help get you through."

Andi, Kate and Taylor nodded in agreement and walked toward the team.

Georgia knew their strengths were immense. In her heart she knew that her life would be in good hands. She spoke aloud. A prayer well framed by the beauty of the Shenandoah. "Lord, you have given me much in my lifetime. Please, one last blessing. Watch over these girls."

Kate filtered the Coach's words into one thought. The Coach said if we win she becomes better. Those words ignited a fire within her. *We will not lose.*

Soon, the rest of the team knew the story of Coach's illness. She underwent extensive chemotherapy for breast cancer and battled hard to eliminate the cancer from her system. In the face of her deadly illness, Georgia Von Mater joined them. The bowed old woman, a shell of her physical self, would stand with them as Spotswood prepared to face Fredericksburg.

Coach Altman devised a strategy, and Kate, Taylor, and Andi carried out those instructions on the field. Throughout the day, players like Marisol, Catbird, and Brooke could feel the energy from the old woman. When practice ended, Kate walked back toward the field house. Cat walked along with her. "Kate, you told me stories of Von Mater, and I halfheartedly believed them, but today I felt—and I know you won't laugh. I felt the Creator's spirit. There is something in the old woman's soul making you feel the joy of the game. She almost wills you to love lacrosse. My ancestors would call her a Clan Mother.

"She is so much like my great-grandmother; her strength is—is..."

Cat got emotional. She paused. "The most native thing I have is a dream catcher I bought at the mall, and it most likely came from China, but today I feel like I could run forever, hunting elk or deer for my tribe."

Kate simply smiled and thought, *Coach Von Mater, still working her magic.*

In the face of adversity and conflict, college students never strayed far from their principles. Tonight would be a party night, like a weather condition, or force of nature, a fast-moving diversion centered on Spotswood College. The students agreed by some kind of instinctive collegiate telepathy that exams were imminent and the school year neared its end. It meant some friends would be missed until next school year, and seniors would become a passing memory. Too many emotions mixed with the stress of college academics could only mean one thing—party time.

Like lemmings running toward the sea, they headed to Atchison's barn for a year-ending jubilee.

Never let it be said a small Christian college did not know how to party.

At 9 PM, there were two hundred people crowded into the newly cleaned barn. No cow pies remained in sight. The party reached full swing at 9:10.

After an hour of revelry, Kate took a break in the eye of the party storm. Jumping, dancing celebrants surrounded her. Taylor found Kate and joined her. "Jackie took off her top. Thank god she wore a bra." They stood alone in a crowd talking casually through the noise.

Taylor leaned closer. "Zack Tyler told everyone he'd broken up with Traci. Traci told some friends she did the breaking and might have mentioned your name, something about not being able to live up to the goddess standard. I assume she meant you, although it might have been me."

Kate smiled, and nodded in affirmation. "Zack broke up with Traci a long time ago."

"Really, tell me all about it. Don't leave out and juicy parts."

Kate shrugged and changed the subject. "Taylor, you missed Marisol and Kelly over near the port-a-potty? Kelly told me she was cleared to play and would be back on Monday—Marisol yakked on Kelly's foot. First puke tonight, and in under an hour. Is that a record?"

Taylor and Kate stood still, contemplating the mayhem. Then two dancers knocked into Taylor, causing her to spill her drink down Kate's front.

"Hey!" Taylor turned toward the two. When she turned back, Kate disappeared, and then reappeared, dancing and swinging her shirt over her head. She and Jackie were now dancing together in a clumsy imitation of a primitive tribal dance, bumping their hips while they swung their blouses around their heads.

Taylor sighed in relief. It's a good thing they're both wearing... "Oh no—Kate!"

She thought about grabbing Kate and covering her up, but decided she needed a refill.

April 20

In the harsh light of Sunday morning, Kate and Jackie sat purposefully still in the last row of the Mt. Olive's Church of the Creator. They swore to each other last night they would attend services if they misbehaved at the party. Kate's head beat out a testament to her wickedness. Jackie tried not to move, any variation in her head position might start her spinning again.

"Kate, you were supposed to keep me from making a fool of myself."

Kate didn't argue. They both sat there blaming each other for the things they did last night. By the time the congregation started passing the offering plate, they were back to being friends again. On the way home, Kate's Tylenol kicked in and she started to feel more human. "Did you see Mooner and Alicia last night? They were slow dancing to everything and it looked like love to me."

Remembering the sight of huge Mooner and petite Alicia was enough to make them laugh. "For real, Kater, if they hook up you will have to get them a how-to manual." Jackie's mind dropped back into the gutter.

Kate looked at Jackie with a stern frown. "Jack, we just came from church, and now I have this gross image in my mind."

"Hello, you started it."

"No, Jack, who's the 'playah' waving her wet shirt around their head?"

"Who forgot to wear a..."

"Shut up, Jack."

The conversation continued at a middle school level for ten more minutes. At a pause in the blame game, Jackie asked Kate if she'd heard about Stacey coming back on Monday.

"Well, what do you know? We will be at full strength for the first time since the Sweet Water game."

Georgia Von Mater

April 21

At Monday's practice Coach Altman made them run until they eliminated all remaining contaminants through their pores. No one mentioned Saturday night. The sweat felt good and by now running was not a demanding activity. They could run for hours. After forty minutes, Coach Altman whistled them in, she signaled them to the water jug, and told them to take five. "Drink lots of water, girls. Let those kidneys do their job. Purify, distil, and filter away any nasty toxins."

Coach Von Mater stood off to the side, patiently waiting. When everyone settled down and caught their breath she spoke. "Tomorrow you have an opportunity to create your own destiny."

Her quiet voice seemed to penetrate their sweaty lethargy. Their heads turned toward her. "The next game we play is the MVVC tournament and the most important game of the season. If we do not win, we end our season. Win or lose, I believe you should be proud of what you have accomplished so far."

The effort to speak seemed to drain the color from Georgia Von Mater's face. Coach Altman brought a folding chair over and unobtrusively placed it next to her. Georgia sat down.

"Can anyone tell me why we lost the previous game against Fredericksburg?" Her voice had a quality which was spellbinding. Her soft southern accent fooled no one. You could hear the intensity in each measured word. The girls looked at each other, waiting for someone to speak first.

Paige spoke up. "We were getting bad calls from both umpires."

Coach Von Mater shook her head slightly. "The umpires were indeed not superior, but they called the game equally well for both teams."

Kate smiled at the Coach's style with words. She criticized the umpires but did not blame them.

Paige's comment opened the door for the others. The comments came rapid-fire.

"We were short on players and we got tired."

"They won on a lucky shot."

"Andi and Taylor got hurt in the second half."

"Coach Burke said Kate lost the game when she fouled on the draw in overtime." Traci's words were taunting, more like an accusation.

Penelope shouted at Traci, "Just like I told Coach Burke when she made the same comment—you are so full of it!"

Coach Von Mater interceded. "Penelope, in her indelicate way, is correct. I observed the umpire dropping her hand to start just before Kate moved. Then she blew the whistle. The more appropriate call would have been to re-draw. Perhaps Coach Burke did not notice it, because it is very hard to pay attention to everything."

Georgia Von Mater spoke calmly, but her words were being received passionately. "The Fredericksburg team is comprised of young and speedy players. The lack of substitutes made it difficult for us to play at full speed. We didn't take advance of their make-up, especially their inexperience, and we did not capitalize on the defining moment in the second half. Up by three goals, we would have broken their spirit if we had scored the next goal. I might also add the loss of Gabrielle was critical. The last ten minutes of regulation play determined who and when Fredericksburg won the game. Ten minutes—ten minutes to discover the heart of your team. Ten minutes of victory.

"Now—what happened on the positive side?"

They sat straighter, unconscious body language of a team listening closely.

Coach smiled. "The team responded to the loss of three important players, and nearly won. Kate used her mind and rallied the team. Martianne showed her goalie skills. Penelope showed her athleticism, and Jackie elevated her game. Neither a lucky shot; Kate's unfortunate movement nor Brooke's foul made the difference."

Coach paused. The clear pale blue sky provided a backdrop for the ribbons of clouds passing slowly by. Time waited for the Coach to speak.

"We lost on a combination of at least twenty events. Everything went in Fredericksburg's direction. I promise you with the conviction of an old Spotswood Star it will not happen tomorrow."

Her voice became the only sound on the field. "Let me ask three questions. The answers will determine our chances for victory. One, Taylor; tell us your plan for tomorrow?"

"Y'all, I am going to shut down number 20. She acted too smug in the first game, but she'll be quaking in her boots when I get done with her.

"Two, Andi, what is your?"

"I'm going to break their spirit before the first half ends."

"Three, Kate, why do you sometimes shoot so cavalierly behind your back?"

This wasn't the question Kate expected, Coach's question came of out-of-the-blue, but she thought about the question carefully. "I'm not trying to show off, but I want to make the goalie nervous, cautious, shake her up. I don't want her comfortable."

Coach Von Mater smiled; "One, two, three, a Spotswood victory." She sang the words like a children's nursery rhyme.

"Anyone else have anything to recall?"

Cat hesitantly raised her hand. "Yes, Ma'am, I remember how Fredericksburg celebrated, I didn't like it."

The Coach nodded. "A good point, let us all take a minute to remember the scene of the Fredericksburg players celebrating on our field, our good green grass, which we have fertilized with our sweat, and even our blood. It is time to take a moment to pray for an honorable game tomorrow."

They prayed but also contemplated how to stomp the crap out of the Fredericksburg Falcons.

April 22

Tuesday morning Kate listened to the local radio station. The Valley Sports Show reviewed tournaments today and they mentioned Spotswood Lacrosse. The two hosts talked about current sports: "*The Women's lacrosse team over at Spotswood College is facing an uphill battle today, Joe. They are playing a team they lost to just a week ago. Have you seen the Lady Stars play this year?*"

"*Pete, I always try to catch a game or two of the Lady Stars. They are a good-looking team, if you know what I mean?*"

"Who do you like in this game? I mean who will win, not who do you like to look at."

"I am taking Fredericksburg in a close one. I think Taylor Braun, a perennial all-MVVC choice, and the league's leading scorer, Andi Castaldo, make the team tough."

"What about Holland and Zary?"

"I told you I like to watch this team."

"Well folks, today at 4 o'clock, our own beautiful Stars take on the Falcons, stop by and enjoy the sight."

Kate snapped off the radio. "Awghhhh..." She made a sound out of frustration and hoped. Maybe someone will come to the game and be surprised at the quality of play instead of Marisol's tits. She hurried off for some breakfast, and then class

With her textbook open, Kate half-heartedly listened to the class discussion. A sense of peace made her mellow. "Young Holland, did you happen to listen to the Sports Show this morning?" A voice rudely interrupted her harmony.

Kate turned to face her annoyance. "Why, yes I did, Professor Kasich." Prepared for almost anything, he said something, which completely shocked her. "I believe those radio-jockeys don't know a thing about women's sports. I watched the Fredericksburg game and I saw some things they neglected to talk about; force of will being one."

The class redirected their attention to the surprising specter at the podium, an apparition occupying Professor Kasich's body.

Kasich continued, "Your team has been hounded by adversity, following a classic example in history—not unlike the Greek invasion of Persia in 400 BC. Cyrus the younger led them into disaster. Then they recovered and retreated

273

gloriously, led by Xenophon, who later wrote of this journey in his Anabasis. Class dismissed."

Kate left the room feeling light-headed. It would be a good thing to stay away from people today. Obviously the universe was tilting on its axis. She stopped at her locker and changed into shorts and a tee top, then went to the training room.

Order was restored when she saw Mooner stretched out on the trainer's table, still 'rehabbing' his knee from last football season. "Kater, come over next to me. I want to talk to you about Saturday night."

Kate rolled her eyes; this could be a diatribe about Alicia, or a rude remark about her...

Mooner interrupted her thought. "I want to thank you for hooking me up with Ali. We have so much in common it's scary."

Kate looked quizzically at Mooner. "To which Ali are you referring?"

Mooner looked sappy and puppy-like when he answered. "Alicia. Do you know we are both Democrats?"

"You are an animal, Mooner. I am going to warn Alicia about you when I see her in class."

Mooner jumped up from the table, his towel slipped embarrassingly low as he stood. "Kate please don't say anything, I really like this girl. Please, I can behave, honest."

Kate, with a disdainful look on her face, pointed at Mooner's lap. "Put your Junk away."

Mooner grabbed at his towel, while his face turned beet red.

"I think you'll make a great couple, Morris, as long as you don't show her your stuff." She felt smug as she turned toward her locker.

Mooner had no choice. He had to retaliate. "Hey, Kater, at the barn party—killer tits for a jock."

When the clock hit three, the team followed Taylor out to the field. They were unusually quiet as they lined up at the fence, entering the field at a slow jog. The few early fans applauded and yelled out words of encouragement. Kate stared up at the sky. There were just a few clouds in the bright blue background. It was another glorious day in the Shenandoah Valley.

The team got down to business and gathered in the center for the team prayer. After a hushed amen, the team shouted, "GO STARS!" During warm up Kate stood near midfield. She watched the Fredericksburg team. "Andi, there is something different today." Kate noticed the goalie warming up vigorously in the cage. "She's bigger than I remember. Oh, there's the other goalie, she has her left hand taped. File that away for later."

The Stars ran through their drills and the captains met in the center of the field. Kate recognized both umpires from last year. At tournament time, you usually get at least one good umpire. Kate remembered these two as a good pair. The conversation started as notably casual. The Fredericksburg players seemed at ease and confidant. Kate hoped this stayed the case for a few minutes.

Coach Altman stood nervously at the scorer's table talking to the timer and the official scorer. Coach Von Mater stood at the center of the team. She seemed to gain strength from the players surrounding her. "Today we begin a long campaign. We must take every step, one by one. No matter how hard this journey is we must never lose heart. Be proud of your teammates and what they have accomplished. Be even prouder to be part of what is to come."

The voice sounded soft and dewy, yet every woman in the huddle felt awash in an adrenaline flush. "Before we take the field—I want the first home to attack the edges, softening their zone for the wings, which will attack the middle. All others keep moving, probing for a weakness, when a weakness is found strike hard and strike often. Coach Altman's defense knows what to do."

The game plan was plotted that quickly.

Coach raised her hand for quiet even though no one spoke. "Also, I want Kate to tell us if there is anything new to report about this team?"

Kate answered slowly, self-consciously. "The goalie is new. She is not the goalie we played against last game."

"Excellent Kate, continue. Did you notice any weakness?"

"I noticed during warm-ups the coach worked hard on shots to her high side. She scooped up ground balls easily."

"Did you notice any other significant things?"

Kate let loose a torrent of words blocked since the season began. "The sky is bright, so in the first half it is in our favor. The grass is about a quarter-inch higher than normal, so get to ground balls quickly. I think the Falcons are overconfident. I expect them to start running hard early, trying to wear us out. Number 20 has a small limp, and number 15 looks like her stick will be illegal after she catches her first pass."

Coach Von mater chuckled. "How much money does the Fredericksburg coach have for the team's dinner?"

For a moment, everyone looked at Kate expectantly. Then they all laughed at once. The Fredericksburg players turned their heads toward the sound; a sign that things were going to be different today.

The whistle blew and the ball headed toward Gabrielle. The Stars were on the attack. Andi scored the first goal, and the goalie never saw the shot high over her weak side.

Kate won the next draw, she moved around the circle and her inexperienced defender stayed put. She passed to Gabby, but the defender knocked the ball loose. Kate anticipated the move and scooped the ball away, firing a pass on the run toward Andi. Andi shot—left shoulder high—goal!

The Fredericksburg Coach called time out with only two minutes off the clock.

With ten minutes remaining in the first half, the Stars held an eight-goal lead. Jackie replaced Kate, and Brooke replaced Jen, the Coach wisely planned on saving legs early in this game. Kate sat on the bench and turned toward the large crowd. She looked for her father. She saw him at the fence, with his ever-present camera. Kate smiled, gave a short wave with two fingers, a sign made between father and daughter when she thought they had the game in hand.

At the half, Daisy brought a small folding golf chair for Coach Von Mater, who eased herself on the seat with as much dignity as possible. Coach collected herself before speaking. "Anyone have any questions?"

The team seemed at ease, but still eager. Around the edges of the group, Coach Altman fine-tuned the defense by talking to players individually. Their man-to-man style stifled the struggling Falcon offense. Coach Altman asked for more effort from Allison and Stacey.

277

In the midst of their deliberations, Kelly sidled up to Kate. She whispered to her, "Kate, do you think I might get in the game today?"

Kate glanced instinctively at Kelly's leg, encased in a heavy metal and nylon brace. "You never know, stay ready. Coach likes to make sure everyone plays. She believes we'll eventually need all our players to win."

Kelly's face showed her concern, and Kate felt empathy for her. It had been nearly two months since she'd tasted the juice of competition. The umpire blew the whistle. The Stars were on the field first, ready to start.

Kate and Gabby were working well together today. Whenever the Falcons closed off a lane, they passed the ball to the open girl. The combination of their work in front of the goal made it easier for Andi to sprint down the middle. She was having a big game.

At the defensive end, Taylor lived up to her prediction. She stayed so tight on number 20 she frustrated her. Kate's observation about the limp also proved true. Taylor had this girl in her hip pocket. Frustration finally bubbled over when Taylor intercepted a pass intended for number 20. She tried to catch Taylor from behind but was not fast enough today. A defender cut in front of Taylor and allowed Number 20 to catch up. Angry about her poor play, she tried to check from behind, grazing Taylor's head. The umpire blew the whistle immediately.

Taylor ran her fingers through her braid, checking for blood. She flashed a look of disdain, about as bothered as if touched by a gnat. Kate turned to Gabrielle. "We have them, the players are losing their cool—this game is over." Of course, Kate felt comfortable predicting victory. The score was 12 to 3, with fifteen minutes to play.

Jackie subbed for Traci during the break. When Kate saw this, she held up her hand, a sign to the coach she wanted to come out of the game. Kelly would get her chance now. Coach Von Mater looked down the bench and saw Kelly on the edge of the bench, the last offensive substitute. Coach whispered, "Kelly, go in for Kate." Kelly reached the scorer's table before Von Mater finished her sentence.

As Kelly ran out on the field, she passed Kate on the run, touching her stick to Kate's in a lacrosse salute.

Kate sat on the bench with a smile. Marisol was next to her. She stared at Kate quizzically. "Kate Holland, I finally figured you out."

Kate frowned. Marisol stood her ground. "You're not going to scare me. Maybe earlier, but you—you are a humanitarian. I watched you maneuver the Coach into playing Kelly."

Kate rolled her eyes, turned away from Marisol and back to the game.
Marisol's remarks had a strange effect on her. For years she talked the game with Dad, they discussed the small things, which made the game so great. She determined her purpose early on. She would exalt the game and the team whenever she could. She felt you won by making the people around you better, and now her time was coming to a close. When the season started, Dad asked her if she would finally turn it loose this year. He smiled when he asked, but Kate knew what he wanted.

Jackie sprinted past the bench covered by two Falcon defenders. Kate jumped to her feet, yelling. "Pass to Kelly behind you." The play continued down the field. Kate sat back on the bench. In her mind you played lacrosse because you loved the game.

The whistle blew—game over, Spotswood won by ten goals. Kate led the players on a charge toward Penelope. They congratulated their goalie, pounding on her helmet.

Coach Von Mater called the team together at the far end of the field. "I want to thank you for playing with élan today."

Taylor put her hand over Brooke's mouth. She whispered, "It means with spirit, not a guy's name."

Brooke looked back and mouthed, "Okay. I knew that."

The next announcement was received with little emotion. "We will play the winner of the Stone Gap versus Clifton Forge game. Check later, I will post the result outside Coach Altman's office. For you freshmen, the tournament is always held at the field of last year's MVVC winner, so it will be at Lee University. I also want to thank Coach Altman for giving me the opportunity to assist her with the team. Coach Altman, your thoughts?"

"I want to tell you all I am so proud of the way you beat a team that beat you earlier. I'll leave it at that. Coach Von Mater has advised me it's best to celebrate when we get to the end of the journey.

"I also want to thank the Coach for teaching me more in a week than I..." She caught herself and changed the subject. "Anyone have any comments?"

Kate spoke up, "Four hundred dollars."

"Pardon?"

"Four hundred dollars."

Ariel looked confused. "Yes, what do you mean?"

"Coach Von Mater wanted to know how much money the Fredericksburg coach had for dinner. She has four hundred dollars. I asked her, and she told me." They erupted in laughter.

The Falcon team walked past as the Stars laughed. There was no rolling around, jumping and screaming. The Stars scored a final point.

Tea and Jellybeans

The girls lingered in the locker room, holding on to the glow of victory as long as they could. Winning became a drug, but a drug which goes through the system very quickly. Another event to conquer lay ahead, dampening the rush and images of victory. Then adrenaline dissipated and the reality of pain and bruises replaced it. The heat of the shower cleansed their bodies and eased the ache of a hundred accumulated blows.

The Spotswood Stars relaxed together. They were enveloped in each other's comfort. The small comfort of discussing the game with your teammates had to be savored. Like warm bread, it was mouth-watering for only a short time. Things that took place were discussed—just in case some lore, some history would be uncovered. This formed the magic of a team. The combined validation of life's moments. There were very few who dressed and left. They basked in their 'esprit de corps, as fine a perfume as you could find.'

Kate soaked, using the spray to find the muscles still craving warmth and relaxation. After ten minutes she still found spots to lather, and places needing healing warmth. She looked up from her hypnotic state and noticed Marisol and Taylor standing on either side of her. "For Pete's sake, can't you two find another place to stand? Why do you insist on standing next to me, how about Jen or Andi instead of you two?"

Taylor looked at Marisol and shrugged her shoulders. "Maybe we could wear tee-shirts? We could put on mustaches and no one would know who we were. Maybe even fake beards."

Kate smiled at her companion's lack of sympathy "And, I would be standing next to two women with mustaches, beards and big boobs. Duh! You know if Jen or Stacey stood beside me, I would be pretty busty."
Taylor thought for a second. "Yes, and you would be in danger of losing your virginity."

Kate theatrically turned her shower off. "I must bid you adieu. These comments and images are making me uncomfortable. Especially the image of you guys in beards and mustaches, you'd be the ones fighting off the advances from Jen and Stacey." She grabbed her towel and walked toward her locker. Marisol continued to rub soap over her body. She looked puzzled.

Taylor anticipated her question. "No."

Marisol looked at Taylor. "How do you know what I wanted going to ask?"

"I think I've spent too much time in the shower with you. Kate hasn't saved anything. It was a joke. Y'all think she's a goalie?"

Jen, Jackie and Gabrielle met in a small group around the trainer's table. Kate could hear them talking about the game. It seemed heartwarming to hear them talk about how they faked this way or dodged that way, checking and shooting—the tale of victory in the locker room, a much sweeter conversation than the silent analysis of a loss.

Kate shook her head, and felt strangely isolated. She stared at the future and realized the crew near the trainer's table would be back next year, in this same place at a different time, discussing another game, reminiscing about ringing the church bell signifying a victory.

She closed her eyes and tried to envision this year's team photo. What would Coach Von Mater write at the bottom of their picture? On her way past Coach Altman's office she paused only slightly to look at the scribbled note posted in Coach Von Mater's hand... 'We play Stone Gap.'

Years later, someone would ask Kate what she thought when she saw the memo which most likely would end her college career. Kate knew exactly what passed through her mind. It became her mantra as she prepared for the game and what followed later in her life. Kate remembered walking home and getting to the top step of her dorm and turning back toward the athletic complex, the lights of the building outlining its shape in the twilight as it sat beneath the familiar Blue Ridge Mountains. She had one thought in mind. *Dad's gonna get his wish on Friday. I am finally going to turn it loose.*"

April 23

Professor Paciarelli seemed unusually interested in the lacrosse team this morning. "Kate, will your team beat Stone Gap?"

Kate's answer sounded cryptic. "We are going to turn it loose on them, Doc."

The use of the diminutive familiarity, and the out-of-character response, broke the class up.

Dr. Paciarelli could not resist smiling. "Well Kate, I hope Stone Gap will be able to handle the disappointment, after all, my husband reminds me it is a Rattler tradition to beat Spotswood on the way to the championship."

Ryan raised his hand. "Dr. Paciarelli, is your husband a Stone Gap fan?"

The look on Dr. Paciarelli's face answered the question. "Ryan, there are no Stone Gap fans, only dogmatists. For the last ten years, at our summer family reunion, I have been forced to place a wager with my husband on the outcome of the Spotswood versus Stone Gap game. I have yet to win. What started out as a friendly bet became a quixotic quest. Every year I look for inside information from a member of the team. Every year I hear, 'Well...Dr. Paciarelli, they are tough and I think we have a good chance, blah, blah, blah."

Dr. Paciarelli's rare moment of rancor intrigued the group. "My husband's sister is a Stone Gap coach. Each subsequent year I have to listen to the braying... ah, boasting of my sister-in-law about destroying the Stars. You might expect a civilized conversation, among college graduates, but no. I think I'll never be able to discuss the arts until this curse is lifted."

She turned toward Kate, her eyes sparkling. "This is the first time I have ever heard a student respond with such an enigmatic and confidence inspiring statement."

She spread her arms in a mock gesture, emulating a plea. "Should I trust Ms. Holland and my instincts, and possibly increase my bet this year? She stood arms apart, looking for someone to answer her rhetorical question.

Penelope raised her hand. "Dr. Paciarelli, Kate promised me we'd get revenge on this team. I think it will take a miracle. But I've never known Kate to go back on her word. If I were you I'd double down."

Dr. Paciarelli made her choice. "I am going to come to the game Friday, at Lee University—that is right isn't it? I shall ask my husband to take me to the game. The noteworthy part of this tableau is how much I am disinterested in sports."

April 24

The game with Stone Gap had taken on a life of its own at Spotswood's campus. The distraction from studying, the sheer impossibility of their quest, and the underdog status of the Stars, made them the hot topic.

Marisol chatted excitedly about the interest from people on campus. Even people who'd previously shown no interest in the team would approach her with one question, "Can you beat the Rattlers?"

The others had similar stories.

"The good-looking guy in my literature class came up to me today and he started talking about the game."

"My Physiology professor even talked about the game."

Daisy threw a downer into the conversation. "The baseball team got eliminated earlier today."

"Aww...I was hoping they'd win."

Thursday evening, they assembled for tea and cookies in the field house. Coach Von Mater worked on constructing a gentler answer to creating team chemistry. They waxed philosophically as they sipped tea and conversed, the stress of the game forgotten. They were hardly athletes now, just young college women.

Coach Altman watched their interaction with a clinical eye. Andi mingled, Taylor, Gabrielle and Jackie, talked to anyone who wandered their way. Penelope glowered and the freshmen were packed solidly together, as if they could gain strength from their closeness. They were all affable and enjoying the rare chance to socialize away from sports.

The team looked like the Young Women's Social League; they chatted and discussed current events, and talked about societal issues. Only Stacey, Traci, and Martianne seemed ill at ease. The bleachers were pulled down on one side, and a long table covered with a lace tablecloth, held two silver urns with punch and tea. The cookies and an apothecary jar full of jellybeans were the center of attention. Coach had asked them to dress up and they did, some were even without their customary running shoes.

Coach Altman looked around the room. Then an odd sensation came over her, as if she were being watched. She glanced back over her shoulder. Sitting a few feet above the others in the bleachers lurked Kate. Jackie and Jen sat directly below her, somehow attached. Kate studied the room. Trying to learn what? Coach Altman wondered. If she ascribed animal characteristics to humans, would Kate be an eagle? Watching, looking for...?

It reminded Ariel of her conversation with her husband last night. He'd brought up the subject of the captains and their impact on the others.

"Andi... Taylor... Kate, who is the best athlete,"

"That's a hard choice. I would probably say Andi."

286

"What about Taylor?"

Ariel did not hesitate. "Taylor dominates the field, she is a presence."

"What about this mysterious Kate you talk about?"

The phone interrupted them. Last night's unfinished question went unanswered.

Ariel looked carefully at Kate, sitting in the midst of her friends. They are around her but she appears to be alone. *What about Kate?* Her husband would have thought her crazy if he'd asked the question, "Who is the best player?" Ariel knew her answer—an answer she truly believed. *Look at her, long red hair, those long crossed legs...and the confidence of a tiger.*

Kate sat above the group, her legs crossed in a long form-fitting skirt, with a high side slit. She swung her top leg rhythmically. Marisol, carrying a cup of tea, slid unceremoniously next to Kate, trying to manage her mini-skirt and not reveal too much. Catbird, however, just hiked up her skirt and climbed the bleachers to join them. When she found her spot, she roughly used her hips to push Brooke aside. They looked around the room without talking.

Near a bountiful jar of jellybeans, Georgia Von Mater sat in a rocking chair, surrounded by her team. Her face glowed. She never felt better. Her body told her otherwise, but her spirit soared as she felt the energy of her beloved girls. She regretted leaving them earlier; her fear of intimacy came from her desire to protect them from the news of her cancer. Once again, in the presence of life's adversity she took a moment to pray. *Thank you, Jesus, for the bounty you've seen fit to bestow on your lowly servant.*

She felt a surge of vigor. *Look at them. I can see their concern for me. I wish I could tell them there is nothing to fear. I wish they understood what they have given me is more valuable than any award or wealth. No matter what, I love them all.* She did not begrudge their youth and their strength. She would give what knowledge and energy she had left to them. They were the ones with the long journey ahead.

High above the room, Kate noticed Courtney and Allison talking to Coach Von Mater. "Go ahead girls, suck up some wisdom." She spoke out loud. Marisol, Cat, and Jen were near enough to hear.

"Hey, Kater, what do you think Allison is going to learn." Jen loved teasing Kate.

"My guess— probably some compassion, or forgiveness."
Marisol sounded impressed "Esoteric, Kater."

Cat studied the group below them. "I saw Coach Von Mater... it looked like she might be praying, she does it a lot. I wonder why?"

Kate answered quietly, "She's talking to an old friend."

They all turned toward the smiling face of Georgia Von Mater below, as she basked in the exuberance of her girls.

It's Radio Stupid

April 25

"Good Morning Valley sports fans. This is Pete Medved and Joe Gravis, reviewing the upcoming local sports situation. Let's start with the only team still in contention for a championship, the women's lacrosse team. What about it, Joe?"

"Well I am going to travel to Lee University this afternoon to watch the Stars take on the Rattlers from Stone Gap."

"You missed last Tuesday's game when you predicted the Stars would fall to the Falcons, how about a prediction today?"

"Hey I have to shop at the mall and I don't want any Spotswood fans putting little stars all over my car."

"Joe, your reputation as a prognosticator precedes you; we know you will give us the straight scoop."

"OK, here it is fans. The Big Blue Stars are going to get stomped. The Rattlers beat them by six goals just two weeks ago to the day. I am going on record that the difference will be even bigger this time."

"Joe, you are a regular...whatchallit...Notre-dame-us. You predict 'em...end of story."

"Thanks, Pete. Now y'all stay tuned because after a commercial, Duey Hill is coming on with the stock prices. I hear beef and sheep are doing well. Let's all listen up to the following words from Jim Bob's tractor and pump repair shop. He's got a whopper of a sale going on."

- ☼ -

Taylor yanked the radio off her nightstand and threw it across the room. The precision and velocity of her throw caused plastic splinters to scatter everywhere. "'Gul-durned' red-necked, radio geeks."

In an instant she hopped into her car and drove toward I-81, on her way to give those jerks at the radio station a piece of her mind. She dialed her cell phone, trying to call the station, but the lines were all busy. In less than fifteen minutes, Taylor pulled into the small station parking lot. While she maneuvered her car into a space, she noticed her boyfriend, Eric, sitting on one of the retaining walls outside the station.

"Eric, what are y'all doing here?"

Eric flashed a grin on his face. "Your roommate called and told me you were coming. I knew I could beat you here."

Taylor fumed. "Eric you can't stop me, I am going to give those rednecks a piece of my mind."

"Honey, I've already talked to the program director, she's waiting for you. You are going to be a guest on the show with Joe and Pete."

Kate met Jackie and Gabrielle at breakfast. Jackie asked, "Hey do you see the tall good-looking guy over in the corner, how about if we eat with him?" It was Zack.

Kate always thought of him as good-looking, but circumstances and timing limited her to fascination. They'd developed a friendship, which grew stronger in their senior year. They had one night of passion they never spoke of, the night she'd come home from Stone Gap. Their passion turned into compassion and Kate regretted acting impulsively. She liked him—a lot, but regretted him being attached to Traci

290

when they turned to each other. After that, things advanced slowly and carefully.

Zack told her wanted things to grow between them, but the timing thing never worked out right. Even now, having just broken his long-standing relationship with Traci, Kate worried that a rebound romance would be temporary. She didn't want to lose him. For an instant, she remembered his abdominal muscles and warming her hands at the Lee game.

"Kater, you are blushing." Gabrielle had a wicked smile.

They joined Zack, and began to talk about the Sports Show. Jackie hopped on her soapbox. "I heard those jackasses ten minutes ago. I cannot believe those idiots. What jerks, two pin heads making us sound so pathetic. After he predicted we would bomb-out, they proceeded to compare our team to their team, position by position. Then they said we were more suited for a beauty pageant than a lacrosse game. What dicks."

Jackie wouldn't quit about Joe and Pete. She and Gabrielle were in an animated conversation about idiots on the radio. Kate tried to participate in the conversation, but she could see Zack staring at her. She listened but didn't pay attention. It seemed to her he has something on his mind.

She thought about Gabrielle's remark and his abdominals. His eyes stayed on her. She unconsciously licked her lips.

Zack sucked the air out of the ongoing conversation. "Kate, are you ready to start dating seriously?"

Jackie and Gabrielle turned toward Kate, waiting along for an answer. Kate felt a shiver working its way into her stomach. Making a joke could relieve her, but ignoring Zack would not satisfy him. She knew him too well.

She timidly asked. "Why do you want to know?"

"Well, I guess you know what I want."

"And that means?"

"Don't be shy, Kate, it means I've had a crush on you for a long time, and if you are not averse to going out with me, I would like a chance, before it's too late. I'm not going to let you get away without making a play."

A slight smile wrinkled Kate's face. He had touched something in her with his straight-forward plea. She grabbed a pat of butter and painted her bagel. It helped her collect her thoughts. *You're no coward Holland. Go with your gut.*

The silence got uncomfortable. Gabrielle turned peeling an orange into an art form. Jackie raised her eyebrows.

Zack didn't give up. "I think my query deserves an answer, don't you?"

Gabrielle's impatience bubbled out. She wanted to hear an answer. "I agree with Zack, do not keep us hanging, Kate. Jackie, Zack and I want to know what your intentions are."

Even though her mind buzzed, Kate heard the radio in the background...

Marisol had an uneasy feeling about driving with Cat and Brooke in her car. She turned off the highway on to the road leading to Reddish Knob. Her father had given her the car at the semester break with explicit instructions. Unfortunately, he did not cover this particular circumstance in his directions. As long as she maintained good grades, she could drive for necessities, or for emergencies. The trip to Reddish Knob didn't qualify as a necessity. Cat claimed this mission fell under the emergency category.

- ☼ -

Two days ago Cat called home to let her parents know when the tournament would begin. They told her they would come on Friday. She was thrilled, her parents had only been able to make it to one game this year, and she missed them. They passed the phone around. Cat talked to her sister and brother. Then her father said great-grandmother asked to speak to her.

Her grandmother's voice sounded clear over the phone. "Catbird, I invoked a dream last night. I saw you and your new clan take the strength of the eagle. The Great Spirit smiled. I wanted to tell you this. Your clan has a strong presence. Follow the footsteps of the warrior. There is something you must do."

She'd kind of chuckled at the old woman's prophecy and request—then. Cat knew how serious Granny could be. Maybe there might be something to it. After the phone conversation, she worked up her courage and spoke to Taylor. She found out where she could find what Granny said she needed. She would find her destiny at the IGA in Crucible.

She'd organized this early morning trip, hoping they would be back in time for their classes. The bus left for Lee University later that day, and they were cutting it close.

Marisol had the wheels, and Brooke acted as their guide. They couldn't turn her down, especially after she'd told them her great-grandmother, who was very much into her Native heritage, sent them on this medicine quest.

"Your great granny is ill?" Brooke misunderstood again.

"Brooke, we have to find an eagle feather, and then somehow attach it to our team. When we do, we will have the strength and the skill of the animal. I just do not know how we can use one feather for 16 players."

Brooke thought about what Cat said. "Okay, Catbird. If you get the feather, I think I know how to use it. All we need is Coach Altman's help."

They endured a meeting with Ronnie Joe, the checker at the IGA. He nearly toppled over trying to check out Marisol's boobs, and Cat's legs, but he knew where they could buy a feather. "And for fine lookin' gals like you, it'll be pretty cheap."

They drove toward Reddish Knob, one of the high points in the Shenandoah Mountains. They were going to meet Big Bob Skokie. The dust from the road sprayed out from behind the car. Marisol listened to every ping as her tires sent small stones scurrying to the roadside. "I feel like we are headed into 'nowheresville.' If I see a road sign saying Deliverance, we are hauling our asses out of here."

Cat checked the directions. "Keep driving, Paleface."

Brooke chimed in from the back seat. "Could we at least listen to the radio?"

- ☼ -

Pete and Joe took a break. They relaxed during a commercial set. They were winding down their show. Pete noticed Taylor on her way to the sound booth. Taylor watched him look her over from head to toe, with a lengthy delay at her chest.

He winked. "What's up, darling?"

"Your producer, Nelly, said she wanted me to finish up your show."

"Boy howdy, that'll be a treat. Come on over and sit. No need to be nervous. We'll just chat."

Taylor stayed calm and ready, her athleticism kicked in, she crossed her legs and her skirt hiked up. She had their complete attention.

"Welcome back, sports fans, Joe and I have a special guest in our studio this hour, Taylor Braun she just dropped in to say howdy. Isn't that right Taylor?"

"That's right, Pete, howdy. If y'all will let me, I'm fixin' to talk about the Spotswood lacrosse team."

"Well, Joe, do we have time for this pretty young thang?"

"Sure do Pete, and for those people out there who don't know valley sports, Taylor Braun is an all-conference basketball player and all-conference lacrosse player for the Stars over at Spotswood."

"Don't forget those years at Buffalo Gap high school when Taylor earned all-everything in basketball, and track. How'd you get started in lacrosse, Taylor?"

"Long story Pete, but once I did, I found my true love."

"Met a boy, eh?"

"Yes, I did, but maybe I should have waited. You two are sure the pick of the litter, if I don't know my livestock."

"Hey there, Taylor Braun, we forgot y'all are a farm girl."

"So tell us about your team, you and Andi Castaldo are the big guns, right?

"We have several players that are essential to our team. I think you all have checked out Kate Holland, yes? Well she and Penelope Preston are our secret weapons. Oh, I also want to shout out to Gabrielle, Jen and Ginni."

"I like the Holland girl."

"Well I bet you do, Pete, you know how to pick 'em, similar to your misogynistic partner over there. By the way, does your wife know about Kate being your favorite?"

"I... ah. Hey, Taylor, at the top of the hour Joe predicted the Rattlers are going to beat your team pretty badly today. Let's take a break for commercial messages. We'll be right back. Be sure to stop over at the Rockingham Fair grounds this week, Marvin Sheffield has his new line of John Deere's on display. We'll be back in one minute."

Joe looked annoyed, "What does massage-oh-nist, mean, Taylor?"

"Y'all know what a massage therapist is. Well this is even more specialized. They concentrate on women athletes."

"Oh, I see, well I do appreciate the women athletes. Cheerleaders especially, it's a tougher sport than most people realize."

Pete still burned about the reference to his wife. Every local knew how she dominated Pete, and Taylor mentioning her would create problems. "Let's end this with a couple of questions, Taylor. Then Joe and I have to take some calls."

"Welcome back folks, we are talking to Taylor Braun, the all-conference lacrosse player from Spotswood College. The Stars are in for a tough one this afternoon. They are playing Stone Gap at four. The winner gets to move on to the next level. Who's going to win Taylor, any predictions?"

"Pete, I don't have the cache Joe has, he's the one who knows the future. Joe is the pundit. With his spurious advice, all the good ol' boys are sure to make a killin'."

"Thanks Taylor, I tell it like it is. Let me ask you if things go as expected, who's going to win the championship game, Lee or Stone Gap?"

"Can't say, fur-sure boys, but I'll bet the farm your ostentatious show will provide the imperceptive answer."

"Well thanks for dropping by, Taylor. We hope no one gets hurt. We are sorry we have to forecast a loss for the Stars, but we have faith in Joe's predictions."

"No problem guys, you know what Shakespeare says...He wears his faith but as the fashion of his hat."

"We will be back in two minutes to take your phone calls—Thanks to Taylor Braun for stopping by. What a nice gal."

Pete looked agitated. The interview with Taylor did not go as he expected. Nelly, the producer, stuck her head in the room, and signaled with her fingers. Pete looked at the phone lines. They were all lit. "Welcome back, sports fans. We'll be taking calls from listeners this next half-hour."

"Howdy, caller, what can we do you for?"

"Hey, Joe and Pete, this is Ernie down at Ernie's Shell."

"Hey, Ernie, we haven't heard from you in a while, what's the topic?"

"I have two passions in life, Pete, sports and crossword puzzles. I just think you two pin heads ought to review the tape of this show. Young Taylor just carved you two new anal orifices. She called you everything but blind. Don't bet any money on Stone Gap beating Spotswood. If Spotswood's team is as slick as Taylor, they'll be hard to beat...you butterbeans."

- ☼ -

Marisol nearly doubled over with laughter when she heard Taylor give Pete his due. She slowed down. They'd made their purchase and were headed back to school. The radio still basted a commercial from the Pete and Joe Show. "Did you hear Taylor?"

Brooke hic-cupped little bursts of laugher, she lost control. Cat sat in front with her precious eagle feather firmly clutched in her hands. She smiled broadly thinking about the two radio hosts... "Butterbeans, whatever it meant it sounded funny."

The dining hall buzzed like a poked hornet's nest. Jay Davies, Spotswood's gadget man, had plugged his portable radio into the room's audio system. Half the school listened to Taylor take on Pete and Joe. The other half would hear about it before the day ended. When Taylor's interview concluded, Jackie nudged Kate. "Are you going to make us wait all day for our answer?"

Kate turned to Zack and smiled affectionately. She knew what was in her heart. "I'd date a man who laughed at the word ostentatious when Taylor lit into Pete and Joe, I'd date a man who has the courage to ask me, especially if I really like him, and incidentally, the word averse gives me shivers. If it isn't already obvious, let me explain that I have developed strong feelings for you. I think I'm more than ready to give you a try. Sorry I waited so long."

Gabrielle winked at Jackie.

- ☼ -

While Brooke and Cat argued about the eagle feather and how to use it, Marisol brought them back to reality. "Catbird, no matter how you intend to honor your grandmother's vision, you are not going to be able to do anything today. We have to be in class in twenty minutes, and afterward we travel to Doe Hill for the game. Whatever we do, it is going to have to wait."

"You're right, unfortunately." Cat looked at the feather she held carefully in her hands, she stared at the magnificent structure as if it were made of gold. It was once a living part of the eagle, a talisman of the animal's spirit. Only her great-grandmother could have stirred Cat's emotions this way.

"I have what Granny said we needed, but it might be too late. I hope something or someone else will get us through today."

Playoff

Lee University's stadium sported a fresh coat of paint for the playoff games. Patriot Field looked in pretty good shape in spite of a long season of wear and tear. Colorful temporary banners and signs were draped around the fence separating the stands from the field, with advertising from farming equipment to Coca-Cola. Lee's stadium rested neatly in the outskirts of the town of Doe Hill. The meandering Bull pasture River bubbled one hundred yards south of the stadium. As a perfect frame for this idyllic scene, Mount Jackson loomed in the background.

At the far eastern end, flags flapped in the breeze. The slap—snap—slap of flags called attention to the schools they symbolized. The largest flag was the Middle Virginia and Valley Conference championship banner, the centerpiece of the display, along with last year's champion, the green and white of Lee University. Next to it flew the black and orange of Stone Gap.

The blue and gray of Spotswood and the crimson and corn of Tappahannock flapped desperately from the end stanchions. Kate looked at the flags. *How symbolic, I bet they needed to dust off the Spotswood flag. We are out where they think we belong.*

Spotswood's players waited patiently. Minutes ago the first game of the semi-finals had just ended in a victory for Lee University. They'd beaten a tough Tappahannock team by a score of 15 to 10. As the teams gathered their equipment and the

Tappahannock and Lee fans departed from the stadium, the Spotswood players began to feel nervous.

Just before they were ready to enter, Coach called them together. She spoke softly to a silent group of women. "We have made this trip before, and have returned home without victory. I would like to return tomorrow for the championship game. Only one thing stands in our way. We must conquer our own team, not the Stone Gap Rattlers. We control our destiny."

She paused, lengthening her delay dramatically. Coach Von Mater looked out at the expectant faces. She searched for the right words. "Everyone on this team has a job. Go out on the field and do your best until the final whistle blows. I am confident it will be enough to carry the day. I want you to attack—attack—attack, then the center and wings will follow. The defense will bend, but it will hold. The attack must carry the day."

The Stars entered the field passing the smiling, joking, players of Lee. Taylor led the team, Andi and Kate brought up the rear. Kate focused on the sounds of her teammates, the usual clatter of cleats, bags, sticks, and gear. As they passed, Kate locked eyes with Deanna, talking happily with her Lee teammates. Dee smiled and nodded, nothing more. She would understand. This is game time, and neither would be in the mood to socialize. Kate wondered how Lee University regarded Spotswood's chances today. She knew the answer. Lee will prepare to play Stone Gap.

Spotswood followed their routines, starting with Coach Von Mater leading the team in prayer. The girls punctuated the breezy silence with a strong emphatic; AMEN—"BEAT 'EM BIG BLUE STARS!"

They quickly organized into their stretching exercises. Coach Altman walked around the outside of their circle and pulled a strand of hair from each player. No one cared.

Across the way, the Rattlers confidently took the field and were going through their pre-game warm-up. The two teams were conscious of each other, like two boxers circling the ring; they avoided contact until necessary. A ball rolled loose from the Stone Gap side, and stopped near Ginni and Marisol. Marisol started to retrieve the ball, but Ginni gripped her arm before she could move. A player from the Rattlers crossed warily over the line and picked up the ball. The Stars ignored her. No words were spoken, but the terms of this contest were defined in the exchange.

Spotswood began their passing drill. Taylor chose that moment to let the rest of the team, and the world, know her intentions today. She bellowed out a deafening rebel yell, a tongue-rolling screech that turned everyone's head. The sound reverberated in the natural quiet of Doe Hill. The Stars reserve broke, they began to shout and yell. The Rattlers stayed quiet, watching the Spotswood team's sudden exuberance. Taylor's yell gained momentum. Jen, Courtney and Stacey reached down into their genetic past, and mimicked the unique rebel war cry.

Coach Von Mater turned to Ariel Altman. She winked and nodded her approval. "Sometimes, Ariel, the emotion of the game is won before the first draw."

Ariel had a fleeting surge of self-esteem. She felt proud, proud the Coach had included her in the small society of coaching. Then she paused, wondering. *I wish I'd brought along my IPod, I should be texting all these things to my home computer. This 'old woman' is a master at motivation.*

- ☼ -

Kate, Taylor, and Andi met the Stone Gap captains at mid-field. Kate spoke out loud, "Déjà Vu."

Stasia, Tayo, and Sudie, the Rattler captains, were flanked by the same umpires who refereed their last game. Kate thought; *No one is going to commit any fouls today. The flag will be in the air before a player takes a wrong step.*

The younger umpire spoke first. "Who's speaking today?"

Taylor answered. "I am, Ma'am."

"I will talk today." Sudie answered firmly.

"Call the coin in the air, Stone Gap."

"Tails!"

The instructions to the teams were as Kate expected, the umpires reminded both teams they would call this game closely. Everyone shook hands and returned to their teams. Kate waited to shake Stasia's hand.

When she did, Kate looked directly into her eyes, holding on to her hand, "Don't forget to watch my goalie dance when this game is over."

Stasia looked at Kate as if she'd lost her mind. "Go to hell, Holland."

Kate loosened her grip. "If that's where we play, I'll meet you there." Kate noticed a small smile on Stasia's face. Her Rattler enemy had gotten the invitation.

The draw arched high in the air toward Sudie, she set her feet, and 'swish,' the rustling sound of cloth passed her as Kate snatched the ball from her stick. From the first second, Kate gambled and guessed correctly, she left her position and sprinted over toward the center. The next two minutes showed the composure of both teams. The only sound from the field was chatter between players, setting up the offense, and the response from the defenders.

"Watch 26—watch 26."

"Slide Jordan—watch 26."

"Left."

"Gabby, look at Cat."

"Zone-zone-slide."

"Who's got 26?"

"Sudie, pick-up, pick-up."

The ball reached Gabby behind the goal. Gabby passed, firing a strike to Kate on the left side.

"Double!!"

"Cutter!"

Kate sliced through a double team and turned her shoulder slightly to slip behind her defender. Her angle at the goal gave her a look at an opening about the size of a cereal box. She shot the ball squarely into the only space available. "GOAL!"

The fans erupted. Kate reacted, stunned by the sound of the crowd. They'd been silent until this moment. As the umpire signaled with both arms a goal scored, Kate looked into the stands. There were more people than Kate had ever seen at a Spotswood game. The response of the crowd stirred her blood.

The Rattlers were determined at the draw. Two defenders locked in Kate but Taylor picked up the ball. Taylor seemed formidable, and she seemed to grow as the game progressed.

"Cut—cut—cut."

"Watch 26."

"Break right—28—28 in space."

The Rattlers were overplaying Andi, and relying on a sliding double team to contain Kate. They were using the old tactic they'd used in the first game. Kate knew the only way to break this defense engage the wings, Paige and Catbird, getting them to attack. These two young players would lead the offense.

Kate knew what she should do. She took a short pass from Traci and, dove into the heart of the double team and the zone. She fired her shot as she elevated over the combined sticks of a triple team. The ball headed for the corner of the right pipe. It slipped into the net, rippling the cords.

"GOAL!"

The Stone Gap coach called for a time out, Kate had attacked their strength.

When the teams came back on the field, they lined up for the draw. The ball went to the Rattlers. Stasia, anxious to score as soon as the ball touched her stick flew toward the goal. Ginni stayed put and turned her away, Courtney helped, and the ball was checked loose.

Stasia looked surprised. She must have remembered how easily she knifed through the Stars in their last game. This time she faced the skill of Courtney and Ginni rather than the inexperienced Stacey. Taylor scooped it up and passed to Jen who turned her speed up the field. An attack from the right opened up. The defense of Stone Gap leaned left, in Kate's direction. They began their chatter.

"Cover 28, cover 28."

"Slide on 26—who has 26?"

"Right—slide right."

"Cutter, cutter, cut-her off!"

Andi sliced through and took a clean pass. She slammed home a goal. The goalie banged the cage and shouted in frustration. "Put a stick on someone." After seven incredible minutes, the Stars led 3 to 0.

In the next eight minutes Stone Gap shot four times, they were controlling the mid-field area, and getting all of the breaks. Penelope did her job. She stopped all but one shot. Kate saw a pivotal moment. If Spotswood could score the next goal, the Rattlers would believe Spotswood is for real and begin to doubt their own invincibility.

As the teams lined up for the next draw, Kate slid over to the middle. She focused on the ball as it nestled between Andi and Stasia's sticks. Then she heard a sound, a sound penetrating her mind like the screech of the dead mockingbird. "Get me the ball—get me the ball."

Coach Von Mater spoke from the sideline. The Rattler fans and the cheers of Big Blue supporters should have drowned her voice out. Yet, it sliced through Kate's mind like an arrow through air. The arrow struck its target. "Get me the ball—make it happen."

The ball came out, a line drive headed for the middle of the circle, barely high enough to be legal. Kate reached full speed and shouldered her way past two Rattler players. She caught the ball then did a rapid pirouette around a flat-footed defender, who got caught lunging forward. Kate faced the goalie with no one in front of her, and heard no whistle, no foul call.

Kate knew the best shot would be over the goalie's shoulder, weak-side. So far all of their goals had gone in that direction. All she need do was cradle the ball so the goalie wouldn't know when she shot. The ball would come out of her crosse in a blur disguised by elbows, arms and stick. She shot where they believed the goalie was strongest, between her padded legs...GOAL!

The Spotswood fans went wild. They sensed something they only dared hope. For the first time, they turned to each other. "We can win this game." Just before the first half ended, Stone Gap scored on a nifty play from Stasia to Tayo. The Rattlers were fighting for their team's life.

Big Blue stood along the sideline, cups filled. They toweled down and gathered their resources. In amongst her teammates, Kate separated her mind. She looked at the crowd and could feel herself drawing energy from them.

Andi jumped into the middle of the huddle. "Anyone want to win this game today?" Then another defining moment happened, a moment showing the character of the team, a moment invoking the fire from the L'Enfant game. Someone shouted. "Let's win this one for all the sushi eaters!"

The second-half draw went to Stasia, and the Rattlers. She scooped up the ball on the first hop, quickly passing down the field. Kate watched from the mid-field line as Blue's defense ground the Rattlers speedy attack to a slow crawl. She watched Taylor leading the point of the defense. In lacrosse, the most effective defense takes away the things an offense does well. Big Blue ran as a coordinated unit today, moving in synchronization with each other. It was beautiful to watch.

During the next five minutes both teams seemed to move into a higher gear. One team would answer the other team's effort. A game like this made fans from both sides cheer and groan. Penelope would stop a shot, the Spotswood fans would hold their breath, then cheer. The Rattler fans were cheering and groaning. One thing the Stone Gap fans knew with certainty, their team was unexpectedly behind.

Gabby scored, answering a Stone Gap's score. The Stars were still ahead. Before the draw, Jackie subbed for Kate and Allison for Jen. As they slammed down on the bench, catching their breath, Jen turned to Kate.

"Good look, Kater."

"No! Good look from you."

"No! Good look from you!"

The noise from the Rattler fans interrupted their playfulness. Stasia had put a lightning bolt into the upper corner. The score was 6 to 4. Coach Von Mater stood up slowly, "Time out."

The Stars walked purposefully over to their coach. She raised a finger for silence even though no one made a sound. "There are twenty minutes left on the clock, look beyond the moment, and use your heads. Think out each situation. You know and I know we are the better team today. If we remain focused, we will triumph. Our victory will come from our determination."

The two minutes were up and Coach quietly returned to her chair. Kate glanced at her. This game is giving her strength, she thought. Then Kate as she often did, spoke the thought in her mind. "We are going to win."

Coach Von Mater turned to Kate and smiled. "Thanks for taking the suspense out of the game for me, Katherine, but we still need to play it out."

The team laughed; an inexplicable reaction from a team, which had suffered so much adversity. At this moment, they believed.

"Kate, go back in at first home—Jackie, take Gabrielle's place—Brooke you are in for Courtney. Kelly, be ready to replace Traci." Coach thought ahead. This game would be won at the last-minute, and she wanted to have everyone on the field ready to give their all.

During the next ten minutes, each team scored twice. Andi lived up to her nickname and her reputation. 'Shooter' drove recklessly through the outside defenders into the eight-meter area. Once inside nothing could stop her. She scored two more goals. Even though Andi was a force, the Rattler's were unable to concentrate on her, and when only one defender covered Andi, she shot and made them pay. Andi proved her nickname, Shooter.

Spotswood held the lead at 8 to 6, with ten minutes to play, a lacrosse eternity. The fans in the stands started watching the clock at the ten-minute mark. The tension in the stands fueled the players, and the game found a higher level. Coach stood alongside Stacey. She put her arm around her, giving directions. "Now when Stone Gap scores...."

The Rattlers scored and were within one goal of tying this game up. Stacey entered the game for the first time, with eight minutes to play. She looked like a deer caught in the headlights as she moved into position. The umpire bent over to tie her shoe. Time stood still. While they waited, Kate moved over to talk to Stacey. "Scared, Stacey?"

Stacey expelled her breath she'd been holding it. "Shitless, Kate, shitless."

"Well, I'm afraid too."

"What. Why?"

"I'm afraid that when you get this draw, you will pass the ball to Andi, and forget about me."

"God, I hope it doesn't come my way."

"Coach knows what she's doing. Remember—don't forget to look my way."

Stacey had a tenth of a second to gather her thoughts. As Coach predicted the ball headed right at her. Only Courtney and a Rattler defender were between Stacey and the ball. She stayed low as Courtney and the other team's player left their feet, jumping for the ball. They collided and the ball rolled loose on the ground. It spun for what seemed an eternity, until Stacey's mind unlocked and she sprinted after it, bending low. *Keep your ass down—keep your ass down.* Stacey repeated in her mind.

She scooped up the ball and turned up field. When she took her first look, all she saw were Kate's long arms waving, her red ponytail flashing like a beacon, she threw the ball as hard as she could toward Kate's stick. The relief she felt turned into joy when she saw Kate's ponytail disappear into a mass of Rattler defenders, a few seconds later she heard the crowd erupt... GOAL!

Stacey jumped up and down, waving her arms, as Kate started back up the field, Gabby and Jackie were 'high-fiving' her, when Stacey noticed Kate stop and point a finger in her direction.

Brooke, Traci, Allison, and Kelly stood shoulder to shoulder along the sideline. They were watching the clock. They were so nervous they were bouncing on the balls of their feet, periodically turning to each other and chattering with joy. "We can win, we can win."

Jackie stood next to Coach Von Mater, ready at a moment's notice to get back in the game.

"SCORE!" The Stone Gap fans yelled in delight when Stasia fired in her fourth goal.

The following draw went to Stone Gap. At this critical moment they pounded the ball into Big Blue's end of the field. At this moment everyone expected the tide had turned.

Traci became the unofficial leader of the players on the sideline. She turned to them, and yelled, "Two goal lead, with two minutes to go." Every Spotswood fan stood, the Stone Gap fans were cheering for the Rattlers to score. The tension was thick, everywhere but on the field.

Traci saw it first. She nudged Allison, just as Taylor intercepted a pass. Kate sprinted forward, hoping Taylor would see she'd slipped free. Taylor must have been looking for the red ponytail. She immediately threw the ball across the field to Kate, who spun and turned up field. From seemingly nowhere Sudie ran directly into Kate's body from behind. A lesser athlete might have fallen forward, but Kate's body responded, she caught herself, precariously balanced on one foot just as the other defender slammed into her. Kate went down in a heap.

The Umpire's whistle blew immediately. She reached for her yellow card. Kate laid prone, flat on the ground clutching her leg. The entire Stars' team heard Kate's voice.

"Not now—not now—not nowww!" Zack reached her first. He looked at her face and saw tears as she moaned in pain. "Where, Kate?"

Kate could barely sit still. She pointed at her ankle. "It's blown Zack."

"Hold on Kate, hold on." He looked into her eyes, she settled down to a low moan just as Blake and a trainer from Stone Gap joined them. They tried to relax her leg and get her through the pain. After five minutes, they helped her off the field. The fans from both sides stood and applauded.

The umpire shouted, "Spotswood ball, get a substitute in here Coach." Coach Von Mater did not say a word. She tapped Jackie. Kate and Jackie passed on the way. Jackie stopped. "Hang in there, Kater."

Kate sobbed in pain, but she spoke to Jackie through her clenched teeth. "Get the ball back to Penelope. She'll know what to do."

Jackie looked up at the clock and studied the position of the defenders, as the umpire handed her the ball. There was one minute and forty seconds left in this game. When the whistle blew, Jackie instantly sprinted back toward the Spotswood end. It caught the defense by surprise. Jackie sprinted by Ginni, and flipped the ball to her own goalie.

Penelope stood in the center of the goal. The clock in her mind started ticking. She had ten seconds to clear the ball. The defense surrounded her. She sprinted out of the cage, catching the Rattlers by surprise. The defense attacked her. She threw the ball to Ginni, who returned it. Fifteen seconds ticked off the clock. Penelope stood still counting down. The Stone Gap defenders were frantic.

When they attacked her she dropped the ball into the net. She entered the crease while the defense stood helpless. At the count of nine she sprinted out of the goal, circling it. Each time she did this, she used twenty more seconds. The defense swarmed all over her. When it looked like they would overwhelm her she passed up field to Taylor. The defense spun around. When Taylor reached the twelve-meter mark the clock counted down to zero, and the umpire blew her whistle. The game ended.

The Spotswood crowd erupted. Several Stone Gap players threw their sticks down in disgust, sat down with their hands covering their face. Sudie and Tayo stood upright, but they were in tears. The Spotswood players ran out on the field, jumping in a big pile to celebrate. All except Penelope, she stood in front of the goal and danced a little jig, then threw the ball up the field toward the Stone Gap end. Then, without hesitating, she sprinted directly over to where the trainers were working on Kate.

When she got to Kate, she saw her tear-streaked face. Zack had wrapped her ankle. A large bag of ice balanced on it. He talked to Blake about how they would transport her home.

Penelope leaned down. "Kate, we did it. I know you didn't get a chance to see it, but this is for you." Penelope danced a clumsy, noisy, equipment-laden dance whirling and spinning like a top.

Kate began to laugh, the sound of laughter through hiccupping, blubbering sobs, meant one thing, victory.

The team began their congratulatory walk, shaking hands with their opponents. Kate remained seated at the sideline while her team mixed with the Stone Gap team. Stasia broke away from the line and walked toward Kate.

"Are you alright?" Stasia looked into Kate's face.

Kate tried to stand. She wanted to talk to this player on her feet, not sitting like a wounded duck.

"Stay down, damn—it!" Zack firmly held her leg. He wrapped her ankle and put a new baggie of ice in an Ace bandage. "Your ankle is nearly the size of a softball."

Stasia knelt beside her. "Will you be able to play? If we can't do it, I want your team to beat Lee, and I think you are the one player they can't stop."

Kate smiled bravely, fighting to recover her composure. "I'll be ready, but I think you are overestimating me."

Stasia shook her head. "I don't know what everyone one else thinks, but our coach told us the only way your team could beat us would be if Spotswood turned 28 loose. We built our defense around stopping you, and—well, we didn't. You played a heck of a game today."

Stasia stood next to her and they chatted about things in general. Then she mentioned Penelope's dance. "I watched your goalie. I know what her dance meant. I'm sorry I acted like a hotdog last game, it was a onetime thing, and the second I did it, I regretted it. But I think you got even."

Kate shook her head. "It wasn't about you, it was about my goalie."

Stasia understood. She would do anything for a teammate too.

They engaged in small talk, neither one seemed willing to end this moment of goodwill. Stasia wanted to know where Kate came from.

"I'm from Maryland, near Annapolis, how about you Stasia?"

"Long Island, Mattituck."

They'd played against each other for four years. As competitors, they'd formed a bond. In the brief time they'd spoken, each one realized they could have been friends in other circumstances. In the real world, a reasonable distance separated them, but in the certainty of their lives, the distance could have been another galaxy away. Both of them were holding on to the moment, aware they might never meet again.

Kate's dad reached her. She saw the concern on her father's face; he stood over her, trying not to look worried. "Are you Okay?"

Kate shrugged and nodded. Her Dad seemed satisfied for the time being, he tried to distract her with chatter about the game. "What a game. You were fantastic. You finally beat Stone Gap—did you hear Andi broke her finger?"

Gut Check

Kate wanted to ride home with her father. She was unusually quiet as she acknowledged the congratulatory comments from her friends and teammates. Finally she pulled on his arm. "Dad, get me out of here, I see Coach Von Mater, and Coach Altman waiting at the bus. Can you take me back to school now?"

She handed her stick bag to him and zippered up her team bag. When she stood up, she faced Coach Billings from Lee University.

"Congratulations, Holland, I watched you slice through the Rattlers like a hot knife through butter. You played an outstanding game."

Kate smiled and shook hands with the coach. "Thanks, I got lucky today."

Coach Billings smiled shrewdly at her. "How's the ankle? Do you think you'll be ready for our game?"

Kate slung the strap of her team bag over her shoulder. "Yes ma'am, I'll show up if you do."

They both laughed. Kate waited until the coach walked ahead before she turned to her father. "Can you carry this for me? My ankle feels like it is going to explode. We need to get to my dorm. Zack Tyler is going to meet me there."

- ☼ -

Andi groaned, in pain. She waited patiently for the team to load their things on to the bus. She'd taken a stick to the hand just as Kate went down. The pain she felt spread immediately

317

through her arm. She knew it what a break felt like, and this had to be bad. Instead of her own pain she remembered the sight of Kate on the ground, and the effect on the team. She immediately went to work, talking, cajoling, and encouraging the others. Someone needed to pick up the rest of the players.

She remembered Coach Von Mater saying she was to show determination when things looked bad. Kate screaming uncharacteristically was a jolt to them, and not only the rookies. Even now, Ginni stood outside of the bus with tears in her eyes.

Andi acted quickly, "Ginni, if Kate sees you crying, she will be here in a heartbeat to slap you silly. Remember when she attacked Penelope for crying?"

"You're right. I don't want her mad at me. Don't worry, I won't cry."

Andi motioned to Blake. She needed to tape her fingers together. When Blake saw her hand he told her it might be broken, and needed to be X-rayed. While her hand throbbed she thought of how well the team had held together. One moment, one game—it felt glorious. She was glad she'd been there.

A lightning strike of misfortune, in one eventful minute, dealt the Spotswood Stars a catastrophic blow. In sixty seconds, three things happened to shatter the Stars hope for tomorrow. The sequence of events unfolded so quickly most people were unaware. First, Kate's ankle buckled, and then Andi had been struck on the hand by a Stone Gap defender who chased after the ball. The third, unseen event was the reaction of Coach Von Mater. She began the day feeling weak but determined. The stress of the game caused her to nearly black out. Coach Altman fortunately stood at her side, supporting her. Neither coach saw the dramatic final seconds of their victory.

As they prepared to leave, Coach Altman was relieved they'd worked up a contingency plan. She remembered talking to the Athletic Director, and she particularly remembered his attitude. "I guess we should plan to travel tomorrow, but I think it's more likely your 'gals' will be turning in their uniforms."

Her concern for Coach Von Mater was uppermost in her mind, but she relished seeing what the AD's face would look like when she gave him the news. "Maybe we'll announce it to him by ringing the church bell."

The Stars' bus pulled out of the parking lot toward home. They had made it to the championship game. No matter what happened tomorrow, they'd won today. They'd taken this team farther than any Spotswood lacrosse team had gone before. A few weeks ago, the team teetered on the verge of a collapse. Today, Ginni shouted from the back of the bus, "We are going to ring the bell."

When the team returned to campus, the players separated, most of them headed to dinner, the timing was perfect. The news of their victory would be spread in the dining hall. Some headed directly to the training room. Food could wait. The abrasions and bruises needed attention. Taylor led a group up the stairs of the bell tower. They announced the victory to every corner of the campus.

~ ☼ ~

Andi sat in the cold whiteness of the emergency room. The antiseptic solitude of the hospital unsettled her; she'd just left the warm exuberance of her friends and teammates, to sit, waiting in a plastic row of chairs. She thumbed through a Boater's World magazine while she waited for the results of her X-ray. She wondered why doctors thought putting their old magazines in the waiting room constituted a tax write-off. Andi was clever when it came to money. After an hour's wait, Andi entered the doctor's office. She began to get nervous as she waited for the news.

The doctor smiled, and delivered the verdict. "You are lucky. The break is an incomplete fracture, what we call a greenstick break. We can immobilize the finger and give you some pain medicine. The best thing is to keep it still. Your own body heals this fracture best. You do not want to aggravate the area. How did this happen?" Andi paused for a second. "I hurt it fooling around in the dorm."

The doctor looked at Andi's shoes. Andi had changed her clothes by slipping on a skirt and sweatshirt; however, she still wore her cleats. "If you injure this hand again, you run the risk of damaging nerves, muscles—you need to protect your hand."

Andi thanked the doctor. "I'll do my best, Doc."

- ☼ -

Kate's father helped her up the stairs. He was arguing about the swelling not being a good sign when Zack walked into the room. "We'll take care of her, Mr. Holland. I promise if she's hurt too badly, I'll make the decision. She won't be allowed to play tomorrow night."

The comment caused a double verbal explosion.

"The hell I'm not playing tomorrow."

"Play tomorrow—no way—she's not...!"

Zack could see where Kate got her temper. He turned to Kate. He needed to let her know he was in charge. "If your ankle is still swollen in the morning, you will not play, period—end of story, and I will make the call."

Their exchange seemed to ease Mr. Holland's concerns. "I'll be staying at the Crucible Inn. You call me if you need anything."

He leaned over and gave Kate a kiss and a pat on the head. "I love you, Kiwi. I don't want you to wind up with any permanent damage. It's only a game. I'll call Mom, and let her know. She'll probably come down tonight."

He left the room and Kate's body sagged. "What can you do to fix me?"

Zack found himself in a difficult position. Finally, Kate gave him a chance romantically, and he faced the possibility of keeping her away from the game tomorrow. The words, conflict of interest, ran through his mind. He knew that at this moment, Kate wanted to play in tomorrow's game more than anything.

He would play it by the book. "Kate, if your ankle is swollen tomorrow morning, you can't play. If it's not swollen, and you play, I will pull you from the game if I see you limp. Do you understand?"

Kate looked at him. Tears were forming in her eyes. "I need to play. If I'm not in the game, something might happen to Coach."

He looked puzzled. "Are you crazy? You are not responsible for Coach Von Mater's health?"

Kate looked at him, she turned her eyes toward him and he felt defenseless. "Help me find a way, Zack, please."

- ☼ -

The phone rang in Jamal's room. He listened, nodding at the receiver. "We'll be there."

Jamal hurried down the hall. He searched for the boys in the poker club. Mooner, Steve, Henry and Sam piled in to Sam's Jeep and they drove to Wilson dorm. They'd learned Kate needed their help. None of them asked why.

On the way, Steve asked, "What are we doing? Kate's in trouble, right? Someone need an ass whippin?"

Jamal filled them in, "Tyler called, and told me Kate's injury is serious. The only way she might be able to play in the game tomorrow is if she gets treatment every two hours, for the next twenty hours. We will have to take turns through the night. Anyone want out?"

Zack organized the group into two-man teams. Mooner teamed up with Sam, Steve and Henry agreed they would take the late shift. He and Jamal would start. "We are going to give it the RICE treatment... Rest, Ice, Compression, Elevation. Sam, you check with Miss Olive, and see if we can borrow a galvanized trashcan, a small one. Make sure it's clean, and don't forget to tell her it is for Kate.

"Mooner, take the jeep and get as much ice as you can from the ice machine in the field house. Use those big plastic garbage bags. You know where to go, Steve. See if you can find a wedge-shaped cushion, we'll need it to elevate her leg when we're not icing it."

Kate listened in awe at the efficiency of her men. She'd never seen them move so quickly. They were all used to being on a team, and they responded smoothly.

"Okay, Kate, you need to change into shorts and sweatshirt. Jamal we need about a half-dozen pairs of long socks. Try the football team room."

Zack smiled at Kate. "Alright, who do you want to help you get undressed, Henry or me?"

Kate sat gingerly on the edge of the tub; Casey and Candy were helping her shower. Her suitemates could not get over the size of her ankle. "Gosh, Kate that is the ugliest looking bruise I've ever seen. It's all swollen, doesn't it hurt?"

Kate nodded. "It hurts like a bitch, but I'm not letting it stop me."

Candy glanced into Kate's side of the suite. The group of guys in Kate's room dazzled her. "Kate, when you get finished with them, could you throw the leftovers into our side?" Kate's smile indicated her spirit was winning the battle with pain.

She relaxed as the warm water-soaked the dirt off her body. "Did you know they were going to flip a coin to see who got to undress me, and help me shower?"

Casey did not sound amused. "What would you have done if we hadn't come along?"

Kate could not resist. "Why, we would all have stripped down and I would use one guy under each arm to support me."

Candy thought it a delightful solution. "If I had your body, Kate, I would do it, too."

Casey grunted in disgust. Her roommates were going to hell in a hand-basket.

Georgia Von Mater felt beyond tired. The chemicals fighting the cancer in her body seemed to take all of her strength tonight. The doctors warned her she would undergo these periods. She would experience bouts of fever, chills, and nausea at various times. These things were symptoms she could fight, but the fatigue and the depression, which accompanied it, were the hardest to overcome.

She perked up when she heard the phone...It would be Ariel. "Coach, how are you?"

"Bless you, I'm fine Ariel, I rested, and I'm feeling better."

"I'm glad you let me drive you home. My husband thought you were very pale. Are you feeling stronger?"

"The chemicals I take only make my body weak. They cannot affect my spirit. Can you believe what happened today? These girls are extraordinary. I believe this is a special team, and I assure you, they do not come along very often.

"We have a million things to talk about." They chatted for an hour, reviewing things the team needed to do tomorrow. They both agreed Lee would try to take away their offense by focusing on Andi and Kate.

Georgia believed the rest of the offense would meet the test. "This team is capable of scoring. Kate will show them the way, and Andi will get it done. All we need is a defense to hold Bailey and Delong."

Ariel sounded excited by the challenge. "I think we can hold them, we are a far different team than the one they played at the beginning of the season. All we need is to believe. This team has come a long way, through some bad times."

When Coach Von Mater hung up the phone she could feel her strength returning. These girls were her family. She'd once foolishly shut them out. The lure of self-pity and denial took her away from the things she needed most. She expended a moment of strength to offer a prayer, thanking God for the rewards he'd given her. The more she became involved in her team, the more she could cope with tomorrow.

"Tomorrow's game, tomorrow's challenge," Georgia looked forward. She sat back in her rocking chair, her mind filled with schemes and thoughts of how they would attack Lee University. Her eyes wandered to a framed quote, a gift from her first team thirty years ago. She called them The Unconquered, a team with indomitable spirit, even though they'd lost every game. She had waited thirty years before seeing their like again. As she rocked, she read the quote from a Sanskrit proverb, etched in a plaque her first team presented to her.

Look to this day.
For this life, the very life of life.
In its brief course lie all the realities and verities of existence;
The bliss of growth, the splendor of action,
The glory of power, the splendor of beauty.
For yesterday is but a dream and tomorrow is only a vision.
But today, well lived makes every yesterday a dream of happiness
And every tomorrow a vision of hope.
Look well, therefore, to this day.

Andi showed Blake her taped fingers, she felt confident she could play. "I'll shoot left-handed. My top hand will be the broken one. That's been my secret for years, I'm actually left-handed, but I was taught to play right-handed. This will be a big surprise for Lee tomorrow."

Blake smiled at Andi's confidence. "I guess Kate must be going to play on one leg then. The two of you are something.

Maybe we could break Taylor's nose. Do you want to make a bet on the game?"

Blake teased Andi, hoping to get her mind off her hand.

Andi shook her head. "I need to look in Kater's eyes before I make any bets."

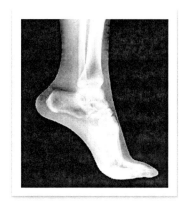

Pain

Kate cried. Mooner swore he'd sit on her lap unless she kept her foot in the bucket of ice and water. "Kater, you keep it in there for ten minutes, and then I'll elevate your leg."

Kate sobbed, and bit her lower lip. She knew Mooner would do what he said. She tried to think of something else, trying to block the pain from the freezing ice.

Ten minutes later, Mooner slipped his arms around her back and under her legs. He picked her up effortlessly. She seemed like a toy in his massive arms. "Gosh, Kater, you are as light as a feather."

Kate was glad it was Mooner who'd picked her up. A few more words like that and she would begin to blubber again. He placed her on the bed. He looked at her ankle, inspecting it. "Put this wedge under your leg. The swelling is coming down, and this is only your third treatment. I'll wake you up in two hours. You're a fast healer, girl."

She sighed heavily, closed her eyes, and remarkably fell asleep.

Mooner pulled his chair close, and fixed the blanket slipping away from Kate's leg. He looked around the room. The clock read 11:00 PM, the soft light from the bed lamp and the clock's cracked face made it hard to read.

He leaned closer to the light and flipped through a text-book. He had been sitting next to Kate for over an hour. When he could, he studied for an Invertebrate Anatomy test. At this time of the night he lost interest rapidly. Zack and Jamal were crashing in the suite next door. Henry had made another run to get ice.

The room sounded funereal, quiet, so he took a minute to look at Kate. She dazzled him. Until he'd met Alicia, Kate was the ultimate in women. At one time he had a crush on her, but that came before Ali. He smiled, thinking of Alicia, they were perfect together, and he owed his relationship to Kate.

Kate led the way; women were not objects or creatures of mystery, they were flesh and blood. Maybe they cried easier, maybe they were moody, but he'd learned that when things got rough, no shortage of guts and determination inhabited his feminine friends. He stared at Kate, relaxed in sleep. "She's like a butterfly, when the light catches her—so delicate...but a delicate killer butterfly."

- ☼ -

Zack sat motionless on Kate's bed. He waited until the last moment to wake her. They'd iced her ankle two more times since eleven, each time he marveled at the pain Kate endured. At four in the morning and he thought her ankle looked normal after six hours of rest. She truly did heal fast. He thought he would give her some Ibuprofen and then she could sleep until noon. He would come back and tape her ankle, afterward he would distance himself from her and watch to see if she limped, if she did, she would not be allowed to play.

He worried she would resent him if he made that decision, but for her sake and for his own sense of ethics, it could not be done any other way.

"Kate." He whispered, leaning near her ear. The nearer he got, the more he noticed her face, she slept, rumpled from hours of stress, and pain-filled therapy. She wore no makeup, yet he thought, what a beauty, what a gorgeous face.

"Zack!"

He jerked upright at the sound of his name, startled. "Whoa, Mooner, you scared the shit out of me."

Mooner stood behind him, smiling. "Don't get too close to her, if you are going to wake her up. She's liable to break your nose with a right hook."

Zack nodded. "Thanks Moon Man."

"Do you need any help?"

"No, I've got it covered, thanks."

He whispered to her, "Kate."

She opened her eyes and mumbled something unintelligible. He thought it sounded like a profanity.

"Kate, I am going to wrap your ankle, and give you some Ibuprofen. No more ice."

Kate sighed, and nodded with her eyes closed. When he finished wrapping her ankle, he gave her two tablets, and a sip of water. "Your ankle looks pretty good. We'll see if it holds up later today."

He covered her up and started to lean back.

"Zack?" Kate whispered, her voice subdued by sleep.

He leaned closer. "Yes?"

She stretched to put her arms around his neck and pulled him toward her. He was surprised by the strength in her arms, then stunned when she kissed him, brushing her lips against his. He felt even more astonished when she spoke..."Thanks, I love you... and the guys."

Zack switched off the light and returned to the couch. He was suddenly wide-awake. He could not get the taste of her out of his mind. He forced himself to close his eyes and attempt sleep. He thought. *We love you too. Someday I'll convince you to say it again—just to me.*

Andi awoke at six. She'd rested surprisingly well after taking the painkillers prescribed by her doctor. Her finger was still taped snugly, and she wanted to get started with the day. If she could have a big game, the Stars would give the Patriots a tough time. Andi had some news she needed to pass on to Taylor. It might be the break they needed.

Yesterday, when she finally returned to her room she saw her phone message light blinking. She settled in her favorite overstuffed chair, punched the play button, and closed her eyes as she listened. There were several messages from her family, worried about her finger, one from her study partner and a message which made her sit up straight and lean forward. Donna Hilburn, her high school friend called.

Donna played defense for the Tappahannock Clippers. The Clippers lost to Lee University just before the Spotswood versus Stone Gap game. "Andi, I have some good news for you, call me when you get in, call 804-955-5555."

Donna was a no-nonsense girl and when Andi called they spent thirty seconds on small talk. Then Donna got to the point. "Andi, I covered Mo Bailey in our game. She scored three goals before I found out she was hurting. I got a peek under her kilt. She's wrapped up like a mummy. It's her quad, I think."

Andi bluntly asked, "How did she score three?"

"They used her as a stationary target at the eight-meter line. They work the ball around to keep her from running."

"What did you do to shut her down?"

"Well, eventually I finally figured it out, I told Lois, and she stuck to her like glue, and made her work."

Andi was curious. "How did they beat you?"

"Delong, she shot the lights out. We couldn't stop her."

"Thanks for the help, I'll see you at home this summer, maybe you can help me celebrate."

"I said she is hurt, she's not dead."

Andi took a minute to talk about home and their summer plans. When she hung up, she shook her head and muttering to herself. "Today's game will be won by the team that can take the pain."

- ☼ -

Fourteen pairs of eyes watched the half-dollar as it tumbled through the sunlight. There was a hopeful call of "Heads!"

Lee University had won the first of many skirmishes.

Coach Billing's instructions to the Patriots were a warning as well as encouraging. "We are not going to fall into the trap of underestimating this team. They have the league's leading scorer on their team, Andi Castaldo, number 26, but the engine driving the offense is 28, Holland. I looked it up. She leads the league in combined points—goals and assists. Shut her down at all costs. Stone Gap tried and they failed. You all know what happened."

The coach paused. "The Stars have regained their heart. Across our field is the smartest coach I've ever met, but no one is unbeatable. We can beat her. We can beat the Stars. We must beat them with our minds and our skill. Keep working the ball around the perimeter. Mo is still gimpy, so, Deanna, you've got to keep driving into the middle. Watch Taylor Braun, she is tougher than owl shit."

The team laughed. They were confident. It was easy to believe they would beat this Spotswood team. They'd done it before. History was on their side.

Hanna, the defensive captain had something to add. "Don't get your panties twisted, girls. I will make 28 wish she were home playing with her dolls. All you have to do is score some goals. The defense will shut them down, and Castaldo will be lucky to score more than one."

Deanna had heard Hanna's rap before. She was glad this would be the last time she would have to put up with her crude, foul ways. During the warm-up drill, she was surprised when Hanna came up to her. "Dee, I know you and pony-tail are buddies. When you see her later, I want you to give her my regards."

Deanna looked shocked. Hanna continued. "I rode her hard for four years."

"Kate and I have been friends for a long, long, time. You can't intimidate her, so you've wasted four years." She turned away and trotted over to the sideline to stretch out.

While she stretched, Dee thought about her friend across the field. They had been teammates and sometime opponents since they were eight years old. The Spotswood team worried her, but she felt confident that they'd win. Kate is on the other side again, always an unknown variable in any equation. Kate has a hunger to win way down in her heart. There are days when she feeds her hunger. Not today—not today, sistah!

- ☼ -

While the Stars were warming up, Cat approached Andi. "Could I talk to the team? I have something I need to share."

"You can have thirty seconds, right after Kate talks."

The stadium clock showed five minutes until game time when Coach Von Mater called them together. "This day two things will be proven, the sun rises, and it will set. Nothing happens on this field today, which will provide proof of your measure as women. You have met your goals. What you do now is an honor. If you want to claim this honor, you will have to show courage. A woman of courage is a woman of faith.

"One among us knows the way to win this game. One of you will show the way, and one of us...will become the way. This is a team with one leader, and that leader is within each of you."

Coach Altman stepped into the center of the huddle with Coach Von Mater. "Shut down Mo Bailey, Ginni, this is your job. Taylor and Jen, you are going to ride Delong until she breaks. If someone can give us some goals, we will be in this game at the end. Don't worry about tomorrow, worry about each second. Do your best in every second."

Taylor spoke next. "Y'all know twenty years from now we will be a picture on the wall in Coach's office. We won't be disappointed in the things we do, do. The things we don't do today will disappoint us."

Andi poked Taylor. "Do-do, don't-do, come on T-Bomb get it together."

The team chuckled. Andi held up her hand for silence. "Play this game for fun, the more fun we have the less they will have."

Kate stepped forward. She had a feeling like a clenched fist in her stomach. She spoke in a calm but compelling manner. "Don't step out on this field unless you are ready to give it your all. Deny pain and fatigue. If you can't, then get the hell out of my way."

The players nodded in agreement and began to chatter, getting ready for a cheer. Andi raised her hand again and asked for silence. "Catbird wants to say something."

Cat winced at the nickname. It was permanent now. "My great-grandma, a Native American medicine woman, dreamed a vision. She told me we would soar like eagles today, if we wore its feather. I checked, and we couldn't get enough feathers for everyone, so we, umm, Marisol, Brooke, and I, found one eagle feather. Do not ask how we got it, but Marisol better stay away from Reddish Knob forever. She might have—sort of—made a promise to a certain Mr. Big Bob Skokie which involved costumes and raw meat."

A shudder of sympathy traveled through the team.

"The feather is attached to this leather bag. The bag has a strand of hair from all of us, compliments of Coach Altman, and her quirky superstition."

Coach Altman looked embarrassed. "I twist them together to signify unity."

Cat held out the small leather bag with the feather attached. Taylor took the bag, put it in her crosse, and held it in the air. The team reached skyward with their sticks, touching the bag. They pressed tightly into a huddle. They shouted. "TOGETHER! FOREVER! SISTERS!"

Off to the side Andi tightened the tape on her fingers, one strip turned sticky side out, to help her grip. She thought back to the last time they'd played this team, and the horrible weather conditions they endured. She looked at the sky. This is a beautiful day to play a lacrosse game.

In the moment before the whistle, both teams tried to gather their thoughts. Across the way, Maureen Bailey touched the ace bandage around her thigh. Mo hoped Taylor did not find out she was hurting. If she or the big girl on defense knew she couldn't plant her feet, well she could be in for a rough day.

Deanna looked out across the field, she could not resist. She searched the Spotswood huddle until she found Kate. She was surprised to see Kate staring at her. She nodded, and Kate returned the nod—nothing more, one nod. She knew the game was on.

Kate tried not to smile when she saw Dee's face. Taylor noticed her slight smile. "Find your friend?"

Kate nodded. "I love playing with her or against her. She's the best. Watch yourself out there today, girlfriend. She'll come at you like a freight train. Oh, one little hint, when she's in a tight spot she usually goes left. Most players stay to their right hand, Dee doesn't."

As she tightened the straps on her gloves, Kate thought about Coach Altman's assessment of her friend. "Ride her till she breaks."

Kate knew what it would take to break Dee... nothing, because it could not be done.

Déjà Friggin' Vu

The draw sailed over Deanna's head. Taylor muscled her way to it. Spotswood went on the attack. The chatter started immediately. It was more controlled, more studied, more focused. The Patriots and Stars were in no need of false bravado.

"Slide! Watch 26!"

"Zone—zone—zone."

"Cutter!"

"Double 28—double!"

Kate made her first cut toward the ball. Gabby passed to her. She switched hands and turned toward Hanna. She lunged right, Hanna flinched right, and Kate sailed by on the left. She ripped the net in the upper corner. Kate heard Hanna's, "Bloody hell!"

The large crowd sounded stunned. The Stars had scored first. They had heard about the Star's ability to jump out ahead, but it didn't seem possible against their team.

Andi ran over to Kate. "Way to go, Kater." She lowered her voice. "How's the ankle?"

Kate's face looked gray. "Shush! Hurts like a bitch, 'ma petite choux.'"

Andi chuckled. "Well you got their attention."

The Patriots tried to attack the Stars at the perimeter. The defenders of Big Blue denied them at every point. Finally, Deanna attacked the middle. Taylor and Jen met her. No matter what they tried Dee found an opening. After the early scores both defenses settled down. Eight minutes into the game the score was one to one.

Women's lacrosse is a scoring game. Finally, the teams broke loose. Lee attacked again. "Keep your eye on the ball," Taylor shouted to Jen.

"Left—slide left. Back—back—back—right." Penelope called the direction of the ball out to her defenders.

"Watch 10."

"Cutter! Here comes the wing."

"Slide—Slide—Slide!"

Taylor stepped into a passing lane and picked off an errant pass. She flipped the ball to Marisol on the right-wing. Marisol ran down the sideline looking for Catbird or Traci. She saw Hanna creeping toward the middle, leaving Kate open for an instant. She fired a bullet to Kate. Kate threw a perfect pass to Andi. Andi did not miss. Big Blue surged ahead.

Kate had beaten Hanna twice. She could hear her yelling to the other defenders. "Give me some help on the left."

The grumbling sound from the defense was music to Kate's ears. She whispered. "If I frustrate Hanna, maybe the defense will crumble."

One Stars' defender stuck like glue to Mo Bailey. Ginni used Andi's tip about Bailey's leg problem, and someone played her close. Mo worked for every pass. Every step she took she had to push through Ginni, who leaned as much of her body on Mo as she could get away with. When Mo finally worked her way open, the Spotswood defenders closed fast. Without her normal speed, she turned away from the goal, and had to be satisfied with passing or taking a long shot. Mo looked like she was getting frustrated.

It was evident to everyone that Lee University was not as organized as usual. Although, it looked like their normal defense was in place, Hanna covered Kate and a loosely disguised zone covered the middle. When Andi touched the ball, part of the zone dissolved and two defenders would cover her. So far, Hanna was sticking with Kate, but she was getting jumpy. She was inching her way toward the middle when Andi attacked.

The crowd noise seemed far away, Kate only heard the pounding of cleats. The intensity of the play on the field narrowed concentration to a point where sounds were distilled. Grunts and heavy breathing blended into the slap of shoes digging into the field. A stick being checked cracked like a whip, a huffing sound, steady breathing from your opponent, all noises your mind processed. Then the voices of the players exploded all around.

"Pass."

"Slide, watch 26—CUTTER!"

"Double. Double."

"Cat—CUT LEFT!"

Andi attacked the middle. She switched easily to her left hand and ducked under a defender. Hanna sprinted toward the center, trying to get a stick on Andi's crosse. Just as she reached out to check Andi, Hanna saw the short flick of Andi's stick and the ball headed back where Kate waited.

The crowd erupted— "GOAL!"

Hanna slammed her stick on the ground. It bounced crazily, "Bloody Bitch, she got me again."

The minutes ticked by with the Stars holding a two-goal lead. When the umpires called a penalty on the Patriots, Kate

339

trotted up the field to get into position. The pain from her ankle was intense. She glanced toward the bench. Damn it! Zack is watching me like a hawk. Kate cleared her mind, trying to sublimate the pain. Think of the mountains. Think of the blue sky. Focus on the ball. Someone called her name, interrupting Kate's meditation.

"Kate. Who's covering you?" Jackie came out on the field to replace her.

Kate almost lost her cool, "10, watch her stick, she likes to put it up your ass."

She trotted off the field to the bench and avoided passing near Coach Von Mater. She plopped down on the bench in a huff next to Catbird. Zack kneeled beside her in an instant. He slapped a bag of ice on her ankle, and propped up her leg. "You limped."

Kate looked like she'd been shot. "What? Are you crazy? I freaking limped? I've been up and down this field for twenty minutes, have you seen me limp?"

Zack looked into Kate's eyes, into the heart of a woman warrior. He did not back down. "I told Coach I wanted you off for the next five minutes. Kate, I swear you limped. Tell me the truth, how does your ankle feel?"

Kate tried to control her emotions. She knew she must get back on the field. "I feel fine, I feel phenomenal, awesome, and do I look like I'm having a bad hair day?"

A glimmer of a smile on his face, "Okay, Kate, maybe I'll tell Coach she can put you back in the second half."

- ☼ -

Across the field, Dee also watched Kate leave. She felt a moment of relief. *Glad to see you go, girlfriend.* She kept an eye on her. She noticed something, something different. It was imperceptible, a small movement most people might not have noticed. Dee tried to let her intuition work. *She's hurting, I think Kate's still injured.*

Dee felt excited. If Kate were hurt, this would free up Hanna in the middle. Deanna had watched the red ponytail too many times not to know something was up. I've got to keep an eye on this.

While she readied herself for the draw, she looked over at Mo. Mo was dragging her leg. *If she were healthy, we would be ahead by now.*

The ball flipped up in the air, Dee anticipated the spot and caught the ball. She turned downfield. The clock still showed nine minutes left in the first half.

Taylor saw Delong heading her way. She took a quick look at Bailey and decided she wouldn't be a factor. Taylor made her move. She cut across the field intending to drive her away from the goal. Taylor knew about this player, Kate warned her not to underestimate Delong's skills, and she was coming her way.

Two green and white uniforms blurred in front of Taylor, setting a pick, she pushed through the pick and found herself nose to nose with Delong. Taylor reached forward, trying to dislodge the ball from her stick. The blur of Delong dodged, switching hands, and was now running toward Taylor's right side. Taylor was trapped in front of the pick. Delong dived around and moved past her.

Dee's shot so violently Penelope did not have time to react, the ball skipped by her into the goal. Taylor jumped straight up in the air in frustration. She felt like the cartoon coyote dusted by the road runner. "Meep! Meep!" Taylor chirped.

She gave the devil its due. Kate warned her, but nothing prepared you for the first lightning move. She promised to be ready next time. *We'll see what happens when you bring y'alls train through here again.*

Hanna looked re-energized. She no longer needed to follow Ponytail all over the field. She turned her aggressiveness loose. She moved out front, roaming the field looking for a confrontation. Spotswood attacked the middle again. The Stars' voices rang out.

"Cut—Andi."

"Traci, look left."

"Black Jack, Black Jack, Black Jack!"

Hanna watched 26 run past the goal, calling a play. The girl ran behind the goal and, another player, the black chick, cut toward the goal. Just as Andi let go of the ball, Hanna cut in front and the girl slammed into Hanna. She barely flinched, as she intercepted and then flipped the ball out to the wing. Before the Star could get to her feet, the Patriots were halfway toward the goal.

Hanna noticed Castaldo so far out of the play she was stuck on the other end. A blocking foul happened and the action stopped. Andi Castaldo now stood right by her side. She had moved over toward her. Hanna chose to stir the soup. "Cheerio, sweetie, don't try to come our way again. We have too many manly women to lose to your team." She grinned while she flexed her muscles in a body builder's pose.

Andi turned around. "I'll bet you five bucks our lesbians will beat your lesbians." Hanna blinked, and Andi disappeared in a flash.

Hanna shouted, "You're on, 26. I'll bet you five."

The half ended just as Lee scored a goal, putting them up by one. Mo Bailey worked herself free and took advantage of the extra step. Penelope got caught flat-footed. The whistle blew and the patriots walked off the field feeling order restored to the universe. In thirty minutes, the inevitable would happen and Lee would be champion again.

Hanna hummed a tune as she grabbed her water. Dee waited, watching for a sign to relax. She took a long pull from her squeeze bottle. She looked toward the Spotswood bench. *Where is Kate? Is she really hurt?* She finally located her. Kate stood apart from her team, spinning her stick like it was a baton. She was skipping and dancing in place. *Damn! She's not hurt. She just got ten minutes of rest.* Dee suddenly felt uneasy.

- ☼ -

Coach Von Mater stood quietly aside. She informed Ariel she didn't feel well. "Ariel, I think you should take them through this second half."

Without batting an eye Coach Altman gathered the team, and began to issue the instructions, which she hoped would guide them through this conflict. "We are doing the job on every end of the field. Our defense is out playing their offense. What's missing?"

The players stopped drinking, trying to come up with an answer.

Kate spoke. "Nothing is missing. All we need is the ball. Whoever has the ball wins. We are going to get the ball. Andi told me she bet Hanna Christens, the big defender, five bucks we would win."

The Stars erupted in a loud whoop. The fans on the sidelines knew Spotswood still had some fight left.

Just then, one of those anomalies in the Valley weather happened. Through a clear blue sky a gentle rain began to fall. You could hear the sizzle of the falling drops before you felt them. Then a cool wash touched their faces. Kate glanced out toward Mount Jackson, she saw a rainbow. She nudged Cat, standing next to her. "Look, Catbird, I think the Great Spirit came to see you play." Cat smiled, she focused on the game. Kate's words were a calming wind.

"I want the same team on the field that started the game." Coach Altman turned to Zack, "Can she play?" Everyone on the sideline knew who she referred to. Zack hesitated. He'd told Kate the only way she could get back in the game was to do a dance to show him she was sound. Kate astounded him by dancing and twirling her stick.

"Is she all right?" Coach Altman repeated firmly.

"She can play, but I don't think she is ever right."

The Stars trotted on the field and Kate returned to the bench for her gloves. She walked by Zack. "Thanks, Tyler."

He avoided her eyes. He was angry with himself, and he couldn't be sure Kate's green eyes had not melted his resolve. She reached up and caressed his cheek. "I know you want the best for me, but for the next thirty minutes, unless I scream, or I'm gushing blood, let this senior captain end her career where she should—on the field." Kate wasn't very good at hiding her feelings. She reached up and kissed him, cupping her hands on his face with her leather gloves.

Traci saw it. Everyone saw her kiss Zack.

Across the field, Hanna watched. The gentle rain stopped as quickly as it started. "Bugger, she's back."

A one-goal lead suddenly seemed small.

The Stars followed Kate's lead. Gabrielle watched Kate attack the middle, going directly at Hanna. When Hanna moved, Kate moved. Paige muscled her way past a defender and threw the ball to Gabby. She scored.

The fans were yelling and chanting. "STARS, GO BLUE! STARS, GO BIG BLUE!"

The Patriots won the next draw, and worked the perimeter with patience. Dee found an opening, an opening a mortal wouldn't try, but she wormed her way through and shot in another goal. For the next fifteen minutes, the two teams threw impossible shots and heroic defenses at each other. Gabby got hot. Mo Bailey ran smoothly again, this game was classic.

Lloyd and Cindy Holland were sitting next to Andi's parents, watching the roller-coaster ride on the field. They and the rest of the people in the stands began to realize they were watching a classic.

Lee University called time out with two minutes remaining in the game. The score was tied and Lee had possession of the ball.

You could hear Lee's coach on the sidelines. "Let's get the last shot. Make it count. I will expect there will be some time left after we score, so we must get the draw, or play tough defense. Do you understand?"

The Patriots were well aware of what they must do. They were ready to end this game. Everyone in the huddle and the stands knew where the ball should go. The coach confirmed their thoughts. "I want Dee to work the center, Maddie and Nicole, set a block on number 25, Braun, just like you did in the first half. Can you bring us home, Dee?"

Deanna was rehearsing the movements in her mind, barely aware of the Coach. "Uh—no sweat Coach. I'll get it done."

- ☼ -

The Patriots moved the ball steadily. They worked the edges until Dee broke free at midfield. She took the pass and turned down the middle. Taylor saw Delong headed her way. She took a quick look over her shoulder, there was Mo Bailey, and she cover...her mind instantly replayed this scenario.

Then she yelped, "Déjà friggin vu. Here comes the train again."

Dee sliced toward the middle. Taylor waited. She felt the hair on her arm raise when two players cut in front of her. Dee was flying. Taylor stayed behind the pick, and remembered Kate's warning. At the last second she guessed left. Dee switched hands. She broke to the left around the pick. Taylor was standing flat-footed and absolutely still. Dee slammed straight into her.

The ball came loose. Taylor and Dee collided—a face plant, they hit the ground. The ball popped loose, and players from both teams scrambled after the elusive ball. The sound of the umpire's whistle penetrated the confusion. The players looked up, trying to find the reason for the whistle. The umpire stood with her right hand behind her head. She then turned and pointed up field.

"Offensive foul—charge, possession—Spotswood."

Taylor picked herself up and dusted the dirt off her kilt. She felt places on her body still throbbing, and her eyes were fuzzy, but this passed quickly, forgotten when the umpire placed the ball firmly in her crosse.

346

Her first glance was up field. Kate looked coated with Hanna. In a fraction of a second she found the uncovered player, Jen, wide open along the sideline. When the whistle blew, Taylor fired the ball over to Jen. Jen took off down the sideline, with less than a minute on the clock, the timer walked out on the field to count out the remaining sixty seconds for the umpire. The falling shadows of the sun cast an ominous pall on the field. This late in the day the lowering sun was shining brightly over the Patriots goal.

Jen looked to pass, she saw Catbird open at midfield. She passed to the only open player. Cat remembered how Kate attacked the middle, so she took off for the center. Cat dodged through two players and broke open. Hanna planted herself in front of her. She saw Kate in the corner of her eye, backing up slowly. She passed to her. Now, Hanna was between Kate and the goal.

Cat saw the events in slow motion it was like a dream. She was dreaming she played for her tribe and her clan on a great plain. She would wake up when the Creator's face began to form in the clouds. Reality took over. She knew exactly what would happen—it was coming. As Kate sprinted toward the goal, Cat ran too. As Kate got close, the entire Lee defense shifted her way. Cat waited.

Kate passed behind her back.

The ball settled in Cat's stick. She switched hands. The grass rippled as she flew toward the goal. Her feet felt like they were skimming along the ground. The sound of the crowd and the yelling voices became a whisper, and then faded. Hanna, trapped between two evils, chose Cat. Cat knew Hanna waited a fraction too long to decide. What had Kate told her? Find the emptiness.

There it was, in the upper right-hand corner of the goal, where the pipes met. It glowed from the reddish hue of the sun's light. It was a target no larger than a grapefruit. Hanna barreled full tilt toward her. Cat knew exactly what to do. Follow the path. Her body crackled with electricity, all of her neurons firing; at this moment she felt nothing, she heard nothing, she was one with the game. She threw her right hand forward and screamed. "This is for you, Granny."

Catbird shot toward the sun.

Banquet

Life is about priorities, and priorities change. What always remained important were teammates, family, and the bonds which stayed with you all of your life. This evening Kate would receive an engraved plaque, inscribed with her four-year accomplishments. She remembered how she couldn't wait for this day to come. Now the day was here, and it almost meant nothing to her. Where there should have been joy in her heart, there was a big hole.

Kate's parents had made the trip for tonight's banquet. She needed them for this final chapter. She'd followed her spirit and gave everything to her sport. She was done.

She looked around the room, verbalizing her thoughts. "I'm a beginnings person. Maybe I should enjoy endings too, because it's one step closer to another start." Kate's mother touched her arm in mid-sentence, making her jump.

"Honey, your father and I are going to sit with the Castaldo's. Dad's going to take pictures."

"I know. The freshmen asked me to ask if they could have their picture taken with me—how embarrassing."

One by one the young Spotswood Stars surrounded Kate. "Kater, I'm going to miss you sooooo—much. It won't be the same without you."

Marisol's eyes began to well up. Next to her Catbird was strangely quiet. She tucked in under Kate's arm, almost like she was hanging on. Brooke and Martianne squeezed in from behind. Kelly shyly stepped in front. They held the pose for the camera.

Catbird whispered to Kate. "I think we are going to get a tattoo on our ass. What do you think we should get?"

Kate sighed, "How about little sisters of war?"

"That's better than my suggestion; Kater's Girls."

Kate lost her composure just as her father snapped the picture. They were laughing so hard it took five minutes to take another. Kate's father was glad to hear her laugh, it had been a while.

Cat tugged at her. "Kater, could you come with me for a minute? I want to introduce you to someone special." Cat was unexpectedly serious.

"Boyfriend, Cat?"

"Duh...puh-leezze! As if I'd let you near my boyfriend."

They walked over to the table where Cat's parents were sitting. Then, she focused on a tiny, no, fragile, old woman. The old woman she'd met at Timonium. Before anyone could speak, Cat's sister introduced herself. "Cat says you are a 'shaman'. She also said you are a giant. I think you are tall, but not so tall."

Cat nudged her sister aside with a well-aimed hip. Then, with a great deal of formality and purpose, she formally introduced Kate to the old woman who sat with her chin resting on her hands. She looked amused.

"Kate, this is my great-grandmother, she has been asking to meet you."

Kate reached out to shake the proffered hand of the frail old woman. Her grip was surprisingly strong. Kate noticed a marvelous twinkle in the woman's eyes, as if she knew a joke, but was keeping it to herself.

"We've met before, many times. I want to tell you something, something only a clan mother can say. I have seen you play three times in the dream of the little sisters."

Kate was confused, what dream? The old woman's voice had a lyrical quality.

"You need to know your name. I heard it in the dream, and I see it in your eyes; 'Eagle Woman.' I would also like to tell you the Creator is pleased by the way you play his game."

Kate had an instantaneous connection to this old woman, and although her comments were strange, Kate understood. "Thank you, I know you'll enjoy watching Catbird the next three years. She's going to be a star."

"She will follow her own destiny, but she will still follow the path of the Eagle."

Cat jumped into the conversation. "Granny, you are starting to scare Kate, she's not used to you like I am."

The old woman cackled, "Piffle! The Eagle Warrior understands. By the way, I love your outfit. I saw something like it at Nordstrom's—Maggy London?"

"Thanks, my mom got it for me. It's going to double as a work outfit."

"Lovely, I wish I could pull something like that off. It's just not my color."

Out of the corner of her eye Kate saw her mother trying to get her attention. "Time to go, my mother is calling. It was great meeting you all. Enjoy the evening."

Kate walked away, charmed by the encounter. She noticed several people looking at her dress. She began a mental dialogue, describing her outfit to an imaginary audience. *Kate is wearing a sleeveless light blue dress, with a daring scalloped neckline and a side slit, tastefully revealing. It has a matching single-button jacket, which she wears alluringly open—a subtle glimpse of cleavage to casually catch a man's eye, an outfit for those hard to land job interviews.*

Obviously, her mother has chosen well. "Hmmm..."Her mind wandered again. *If I could design a convertible dress fastened by Velcro, perfect for job interviews, and when you were done, rip—zip—casual sportswear. I could make a fortune...*

The room filled with chatting parents and students. It was a pleasant gathering, parents and student-athletes mingled, with no other aim than to receive recognition for their efforts in behalf of their college.

The speaker approached the podium. "Ladies, gentlemen, will y'all please settle in and get you some dessert, and a cup of coffee. We will be starting in a few minutes."

As was their custom, the lacrosse team sat together. The activities began with a prayer. After the prayer, Tom Lee Skocul introduced the first team to receive their awards.

The lacrosse team continued a running commentary amongst themselves. They were tastefully noisy, and on occasion, would laugh at anything resembling a joke. The tempo of the banquet took a decided upswing when Coach Malone approached the dais. The baseball team had gone far this season, and Coach Malone gave his boys their due. Famous for his mangled thoughts, he usually made a speech come out funnier than he intended. "I told my team at the start of the season we are a veteran team, and if we did not succeed we would run the risk of failing."

Kate was the first to giggle. Coach Malone took it as encouragement. He dedicated himself to delivering a profound speech. "Billy Blewett was the reason this team turned around

360 degrees. He is a rare athlete, not only is he ambidextrous, he can throw with either hand."

At the head table, Dr. Browne faked a sneeze to stifle a laugh.

While the front table cleared and preparations were made for the next team, Tom Lee Skocul took the podium. Taylor switched seats and sat next to Kate. She still smiled, thinking about Malone, but she also thought about something else. "Kate, I can't believe we lost our last game. I know if you and Andi...we would have beaten them."

"T-bomb, we traveled through a fantastic season. We went farther than anyone expected and beyond any other Spotswood lacrosse team. Things were tough. For the entire regular season, a coach with her own agenda tried to tear this team apart. This team faced all kinds of internal distractions, yet we persevered. I love them all—we finished our journey...but it cost us dearly. In our winning we lost"

"I hear that sister."

Coach Altman approached the podium. It was the lacrosse team's turn. "I would like to thank the parents and fans that supported us this year. I want to thank the staff, the statisticians, the trainers, and the laundry staff." The first nervous giggle went through the room.

"I want to thank Olive, who provided us with food on those long get-away days, or early mornings. I especially want to thank Coach Von Mater, who taught me so much in a short time..."

A hush came over the room... "She is truly a legend. It is rare in a lifetime to meet a person who exceeds their reputation.

Coach Von Mater meets all criteria, as a human being, as a coach, as a representative of Spotswood College."

Everyone rose, they stood and applauded a woman who gave a full measure of herself to her work—and to the women she loved.

Ariel relaxed slightly. "I've gotten through the hard part. Let's talk about the team. I prepared for this by asking my husband to look up the definition of team, he provided this: A group organized to work together. I told him the definition was not adequate. It did not describe the Spotswood women's lacrosse team. Something was missing, because I witnessed other things. I saw compassion. I saw tolerance. I saw love, and above all, I saw the spirit of determination. We played in the cold, in the rain, the wind, the snow, and under a cloud of adversity. With all that, this team never quit.

"We won and we lost, and in the end, what we accomplished was enough. We hope we brought honor to this institution."

The lacrosse team stood and applauded, the reaction spread around the room.

"I would like to have the first year players come forward, Caitlyn Birdsong, Martianne Bouralis, Marisol Flores, Brooke Gipson, and Kelly Watson." The coach handed out varsity letters

"Next, we have the second year players, who will receive a framed certificate. Stacey Carter, Paige Mullen, Allison Scaglioti, Courtney Zuck."

They formed their line along the front of the head table joining the others.

"Next, the third year players, Andi Castaldo, Traci Kubek, Jackie Patton, Jen King, Ginni Wojtowicz, and Gabrielle Zary. These players will receive a Spotswood watch."

Ariel shook hands with each player, "Finally our three seniors; Taylor Braun, Penelope Preston, and Kate Holland. Each will receive a plaque."

Coach Altman beamed as she said; "I would like to announce that Taylor and Andi both were selected as All-MVVC first team, and Taylor and Kate were selected to the South division III, Senior all-star team.

"Finally, as a team, we donated $350 to the American Cancer Society, thanks to the Spring Fling. Thank you all, this was a season to remember. As a great lady once told me, a team like this rarely comes around. Thank you. Dr. Browne the podium is yours."

The last fifteen minutes of the evening would be turned over to Dr. Browne for his closing comments. Kate focused on her parents across the room. She knew what lay ahead. She saw the pride in her parents' faces. She also thought about her friends. She knew Taylor and Jen would always be in touch, and of course, Andi. The rest she may never see again. She looked over at Zack Tyler, he just told her he'd accepted a teaching assistant's job at The University of Maryland, "And isn't that near where you live?"

Things were ready to begin again, but first they would listen to Dr. Browne.

Dr. Browne gathered himself. He was a powerful speaker, and the people who'd heard him before settled in comfortably. They knew his words would measure the evening's events.

"Thank you, parents, for attending this evening, I marvel each time I see you at the different venues, supporting the student-athletes of Spotswood College. The hours of travel and dedication show the effort reflected in the character of your sons and daughters.

"I would like to begin by honoring an old friend, Coach Georgia Von Mater, our retired field hockey and lacrosse coach. As Coach Altman was so correct to point out, she is the paragon of Spotswood College personnel. This wonderful woman, at great sacrifice to her well-being, came to our rescue when Spotswood called upon her one more time. As most know, on May 5th, two days after the championship game, and Coach Von Mater's birthday, she lost her battle with cancer..."

Kate began to sob quietly. Her teammates moved closer to her. Her eyes were flooded with tears and Dr. Browne's words were lost to her. She cried for her friend, her mentor whom she loved. Her tears celebrated the memory of a wonderful human being. Arms from all directions linked together, surrounding her. They sheltered Kate, blocked her from the eyes of the others. They sheltered each other, as they'd done on the field.

A comment from President Browne seemed to knife through the air. "... I salute you Georgia Von Mater, as your legion of women do by their behavior. They learned at the foot of a master. You were first class, a role model for the ages—you simply did it right.

"As your old friend Dr. Kasich said so powerfully at your memorial service: 'There must be a great game looming in heaven and God is gathering a team—the odds now favor the righteous. The finest coach who ever lived will surely lead God's side."

Kate felt lost as Dr. Browne talked on. "... The playing field does not exist simply as recreation, or a place to enjoy your favorite pastime. I would be hard pressed to force myself to raise resources to make this fine institution better, if that was all it was about. We stand for excellence—in academics, in athletics, in our music program, and in anything in which we involve ourselves. Nevertheless—there is no place on campus where leadership and excellence is better demonstrated than on our playing fields? It is not just about sports, for I see your grades. I often send you notes, congratulating you. I am astonished by your ability to excel in the classroom as well as on the field.

"Because you play sports, you will be a better person. Because you play sports, you will be a better employee. It follows you will be a better citizen, a better family person. Why? It is because you know what it is to take responsibility for your team and for your school. You have balance, a holistic education, whether you are first team all-conference, a substitute off the bench, or a member of the support staff. I am sure there were times when you were bruised and battered, dirt streaking down your face, when you wondered why you were doing this. I tip my cap to you."

Dr. Browne paused. He took a drink of water, and returned his eyes to the group. "I would like to end with a personal reminiscence. Some of you know I have been a fan of one particular team. I am confessing my bias, and ask your forgiveness. I followed my heart. They do not know it, but the women's lacrosse team brought tears to my eyes.

"I was attending a conference at L'Enfant University in Washington, D.C. It was a gathering of prestigious academics, college presidents and the illuminati in our field. During a break, I wandered out the back door. It led to the athletic fields. While I was chatting with my colleagues, I spotted the blue and gray of the Spotswood lacrosse team.

"In the company of the L'Enfant president, I watched for 30 minutes as a tired and battered few went into overtime against a great university. We had to leave, but I watched from the window as we lost. I can tell you my heart went out to you. Later, Hub Hill, the president of L'Enfant approached me. He is a great sports fan. He was all a-buzz about our team. I wanted so much to call you and tell you how on that day you won the hearts of many.

"Far away from home you stood against a stronger foe and took them to their limit. With very few people to witness your valor—what gave you such courage? I believe it was the Spotswood spirit, a spirit that values the best in humanity. With only the honor of your school as your goal, your team stood the test. I will never forget what happened that day.

"I also will never forget, just eight days later, the joyous day at Lee University, when this band of twenty-one courageous women beat the perennial victors of Lee University, and gained the MVVC championship. Who can forget the last-minute goal by young Caitlyn Birdsong winning us a championship? I thank you all for the moments you gave the fans of Spotswood College. Moreover, for every man and for every woman in all sports, who have stood on the playing field to honor our school, I thank you. Good night, and have a safe trip home."

- ☼ -

Kate and Taylor met after the banquet to discuss their summer plans, and the North-South game in July. Taylor seemed delighted when Kate's parents asked her to come up a week early to take in the sights around Annapolis. They started walking without speaking, walking several yards before Taylor spoke. "You brought her a championship, Kater."

"T, as long as I live I'll never meet a finer human being. Coach Altman said that when she visited her in the hospital, Coach told her..."

Kate fought to regain her composure. Her words caught in her throat. She felt shamed by her inability to speak calmly.

"She, she... she'd finished her job, left a legacy—and was happier now than ever."

They turned the corner toward Howard Hall. Kate's voice choked. "How many tears do I have left?" Taylor eyes were wet too, but she held on for her friend's sake. "She'll always be with us, Kater. I'm as sure as ever there is life after death, Coach Von mater would never lie to us, and she believed in it. I never questioned her on the field, and I sure as hell don't believe she isn't somewhere in this universe. She is too fine—to end as nothing."

As they walked slowly along the tree-lined path, each battled to control their emotions. They walked toward the dorm, both women now quiet. The cool evening and the bright stars overhead lent an aura of serenity to their stroll. With the mountains looming in the background, Kate recalled something the coach said. "What did your verse mean, Taylor?"

"Oh, you mean what Coach told us to commit to memory? Y'all know the old woman. She pegged me good. My verse from the bible was, 'I will give you rest.' I know Andi made hers into a sign. 'I will direct your steps.' What was yours, Kater?"

"I have not given you a spirit of fear."

Taylor seemed a million miles away, she abruptly returned to her latest obsession. It was hard for Taylor to stay melancholy or forgive failure. "We should have beaten that Yankee team."

Taylor was still burning about the NCAA tournament game they'd lost. "I should have known a team called Union City would use Yankee tricks to defeat us. We could have won, if you and Andi were able to play. Plus we were forced to play them on Yankee soil, New Jersey—who knew?"

"Taylor, we lost by eight goals. They beat us like a drum."

"I have to admit it, Kate, they were good."

Taylor's mind shifted gears. "That reminds me, Dr. Browne was eloquent tonight. I thought of Henry the Fifth."

"Pray tell how winning a championship dredged up Will Shakespeare."

"I love that y'all always get what I'm talkin' about. I imagined his speech at the battle of Agincourt only like Coach would have said it."

"Like how, T?"

Taylor raised her head skyward. "She would have said; this story shall the good woman teach her daughter; from this day to the ending of the world, but y'all in it shall be remembered. We few, we happy few, y'alls little sisters of war; for she today that sheds her sweat and tears with us shall be as one, sisters that fought b'longst the Bull Pasture River."

Kate was stunned by the analogy and the truth of Taylor's parody of Henry the Fifth. The lump in Kate's throat grew again. "That's wonderful, T, but what does b'longst mean?"

"Y'all know I made that up. It sounds cooler than by or along, more like Willy might have said."

"Willy said y'alls little sisters of war?"

"Something akin to that; hey, Kater, get this. After the game, I'm walking off to meet Eric, when this old lady stops me. She said she was on Coach Von Mater's first team, you know, the picture on the wall in her office."

"Cool!"

"We talked a bit, and then she said the 'durndest' thing. She asked me what the best thing about winning the championship was. I started to think, and all I could come up with was—the looks on everyone's faces, how happy we were. So then she looks at me and says, 'I thought so. I know your team went through some tough times this year. Our team had problems too. We never won a game. In the end we gained sisterhood.' Kater, old people are spooky at times."

"You are spooky, Taylor."

"Life's a game, Kater. 'Such as we are made of, such we be.' We were champions for a day."

Kate smiled, and then sighed. "Wasn't Dr. Browne's speech great?"

"It would have been a better story if we'd whooped up on L'Enfant."

"You missed the point Taylor."

"Did not."

"Chill, did too...White or wheat?"

"What?"

"White or wheat, remember? Even when they're out of wheat, don't let it stop you from making the right choice."

Taylor smiled. Kate's words meant a great deal to her, Kate would always be part of the Shenandoah Valley tradition. She remembered Andi's question, a long month ago, after the

Clifton Forge game, when Kate bounced one off the goalie's mask. "Why not score the goal?" Taylor knew the answer. Kate could have scored, but her nature was to protect her teammate.

She summoned one more Shakespearean quote for her friend. "Thank God thou art the best o' th' cut-throats."

They sat quietly on the steps of Wilson Hall, afraid that entering would complete the journey. There was really no drama in their passage. It was an expedition of accomplishment marked by an extraordinary normality. No fireworks, some tragedy, a grand revelation here and there. At the end they were better prepared for their next beginning.

Kate finally spoke. "I'm going to get my degree and the odds of waiting tables at the Truck n' Wash diner is another day slimmer."

Present Day Epilogue

Hall of Fame

....I can't believe I'm here. It has been more than a decade since I walked under the oaks of Spotswood. Too many hurtful memories, but still... There was only one thing that could bring me back, my promise.

Well, I suppose it wasn't so much a promise at the time. I remember the bet. Ten years ago at a reunion game, Andi sidled up to me and made her bet. 'Kater, I bet I'm going to be selected on the All Sports Ultimate Team.' That was Andi. We were both out of shape and puffing up and down the field, but Andi had a way. She could suck me into her vortex, just with her smile.

I remember what I'd said; I'd remembered it almost every day for ten years. I knew she didn't need the money, so our five-buck bets just wouldn't cut it. I tried to figure what a Financial Advisor with her own apartment in New York City would want. I knew just the thing. She'd take my dignity. "Bull crap,

Andi, if they pick you, I'll stand up on the dais and introduce you personally. I'll sing your diminutive praise to the oaks of Spotswood."

- ☼ -

The college reserved as many motel rooms as it could for the alumni on the occasion of its 150th year, and Hall of Fame induction. When Taylor contacted the alumni committee, they were happy to let me present a new member of the All Sports Ultimate Team. The best thing about being a presenter was I was given a place close to campus. I have a sense of peace knowing Virginia and the Shenandoah were out there. Of course my window faced the local Pick and Pay.

I feel pretty weird unpacking, putting my clothes away in the homespun dressers under a poor copy of a Renoir painting. The sounds of other reunion people echoed through the spotless, white-painted walls. I was lost in a real Chamomile tea moment.

Nothing had changed and nothing stayed the same. This was once my home, now I was a visitor in a place taken over by women and men who were living the best times of their lives...too bad they were too young to realize it.

Bang! Bang! Bang! Three hammer like blows on the door and the fake Renoir tilted.

"Kater, open the dad-gum door. Your roommate needs to potty."

Taylor was not the type to wait. "Good gravy, Taylor, how long has it been?"

"Y'all know it was twenty minutes. In case you wonder, I parked the car and called Eric. I told him we were all here safely. To save you the trouble I asked him to call Zack. I didn't want you to get all blubbery about leaving your kids. I was afraid little Madilyn would cry for her mommy and you'd cancel. That little Ginger Devil has a powerful hold on you."

"I wish I could have stayed."

"Kate, are you alright, are y'all having a Yankee flashback?"

I shrugged and watched Taylor unconsciously rub her pregnant belly. Two children later and she still looked trim and fit. Even with the next one due in a month she looked like she could kick ass out on the field. She sized up our room in an instant, moved my bag and took the bed closest to the bathroom.

"Here are your car keys, Kate, just leave them out in plain sight, just in case this critter tries to get here early."

One thing for sure, she'd drive herself to the hospital. Taylor always drove.

"I'm fine, Taylor, no Yankee flashbacks, I was just thinking about our 'Little Sisters of War', and how they will have changed."

"Y'all are making my brain hurt, Kater. Let's call Catbird and tell her we're here. She's going to send someone to pick us up. She said parking was going to be a bitch, and to let her send us a driver instead. I can't wait to see this year's team. The college has an alumni tent before the game and they are fixin' to feed us. Y'all know how hungry I get when I'm knocked up."

- ☼ -

When the van pulled up outside the portico, Taylor nudged me. I knew exactly what she meant. It was déjà vu. We'd been teammates and then neighbors for nearly fourteen years. One nudge was worth a thousand words. We were closer than ever,

Kater and T-bomb. She was one teammate I'd never lost track of.

When the van driver stepped out, I recognized her from the lacrosse website. It was Nelly Kelly, Cat's assistant coach. I saw Taylor sizing her up just like she'd done a million times, two jocks meeting for the first time. Of course one of them would drop a calf if she had to run up and down a lacrosse field.

"Hi, you must be Taylor and Kate. Coach Birdsong-Jones asked me to pick you up. I'm Nelly Kelly, her assistant."

"Nice to meet you, I'm Kate and this pregnant load is Taylor."

We slid into the van and immediately took our seats. Taylor got behind the wheel. Nelly must have thought we were an odd pair. She was all of twenty-two, and still had hope.

"Umm... Coach Birdsong said I was not to let you drive. She said you'd try and she'd kill me if you did."

Taylor had a look, but she graciously, or as graciously as she could when she was annoyed and pregnant, moved to the passenger side.

"I recognized you two from Coach Birdsong's pictures. She has a blown up team photo of your team, legendary team, excuse me. Coach always prefaces her comments about your time with that expression. It's nice to meet the captains of a 'legendary team.'"

"Don't blow smoke up our asses, Nelly. I don't know about Taylor, but I'm long past needing strokes to my athletic past. Catbird must have warned you."

Nelly grimaced. "Actually, Caitlyn told me if I survived the ride with you two, she'd renew my contract for next year. So, tell me, four Spotswood Hall of Fame players on one team, were you guys good or what?"

- ☼ -

We sat down at the table reserved for Women's lacrosse. This was the first time I'd seen the new field house, it was big, but colder looking than the old place. In a minute they started coming...

The first old Star to arrive was Catbird. "God, Kater, T-bomb, you guys haven't changed one bit since I last saw you."

"Catbird, you glorious liar, give me a hug."

In ten minutes we were all there, at least all of those who could make it. There it was again, I felt the emotion swelling in my throat, pushing behind my excitement. I looked at Taylor. She was offering her swollen belly to Paige, who was moaning about her inability to get pregnant. There was no question she'd start talking about her attempts, graphically going into detail.

Taylor was pretending to care, what a saint. Just a quick glance at her and I felt better. "Kate and I have five children between us, six in another month, any other two Little Sisters able to top it?" Taylor turned any moment into a contest.

We began to do what we did best when we were together years ago. We ate and talked. Then Jackie brought out an old roster and a schedule, fifteen women crowded around, looking at the faded names....

....The program was a catalyst, a group of thirty-something year olds pulled our chairs together and we talked about the year, and how it began. There were stories about everything, each Little Sister of War trying to tell her version of an unusual season.

Nelly Kelly escorted in two players from this year's team; "Coach, how about introducing us to the 'legendary-team?'"

Cat beamed. "Ladies, let me introduce you to my next year's captains, Cassidy and Carmen, I call them my 'C cups.'"

"Ladies, meet Taylor and Kate, two of our captains from my legendary team. The only one missing is Andi...."

We started talking lacrosse. The girls actually seemed interested and the rest of the sisters were hard to silence. It was in a rare quiet moment when Carmen asked to no one in particular if they thought next year's team had any hope, considering the season they were finishing up. She said the fateful words... "All we have left is the tournament."

Everyone started talking at once. It sounded like a meeting in the Tower of Babel. We had to tell them our story...Cat started talking about her beginning, and how it was prophesied we all were on a special journey.
Taylor stood up as gracefully as she could. "Oh happy dagger. This is thy sheath; there rust, and let me die."

The girls let out a chorus of hoots. "Oh my God, I'd forgotten Taylor's proclivity for tedious quotes from the Bard."

"In civility thou seem'st so empty'—any-hoo—it's not important."

I'd floated in and out of the conversation for the better part of the last hour and a half. Finally, the C cups were out on the field. I was amazed how much of the Little Sisters' story revolved around me. Taylor had told me as much on one of our Saturday night get-together, me with my coffee and she with her virgin Bloody Mary. Neither one of us had a desire to sit around with cocktails. We'd both stopped drinking alcohol sometime after we turned twenty-one. Somehow the thrill lost its luster when we could legally do it.

Listening to everyone's remarks, I figured a pivotal point in all our lives needs a fulcrum. No matter how much I disliked the idea, I guess I'd take the heat. So far, no one had gotten to the real trouble ahead. They seemed to be waiting, dancing around my emotions.

They were right. Tonight would be the test. My speech tonight honoring Andi would make or break me. I'd call on the spirit of the Little Sisters one more time at tonight's banquet. I saw Taylor nodding. It was time to watch the C cups in action. "I'm getting nervous Taylor, how many hours until I have to give my speech?"

"Maybe four or five, don't worry, you'll be fine. Andi asked you to do this for a reason."

"Don't get me started. My stomach feels like it's going to flip. Four hours seems too short."

"Why don't you think in terms of basketball hours? You know how the last five minutes of a basketball game takes twenty minutes."

Taylor had lied. The hours flew by in an instant. The dinner consisted of some imitation chicken stuffed with rice. After the meal the speeches began. I nervously looked out at the darkening crystal sky over the Blue Ridge... My mind went back again to the season. I had to take a drink of water. My heart-felt like it wanted to climb out of my throat. All of the speakers said things that sounded profound. Then, my moment came. I heard applause and everyone around me stood up. I heard my name.

My turn to speak about Andi...Taylor, sitting in the aisle, with her eyes locked on me, willed me courage. I had to begin.

No more waiting, I looked out and saw Catbird and Marisol, Paige and Jackie. The Little Sisters were there, like they always were. Kelly, Brooke, Gabby, Jen, Courtney, Martianne and Ginni, the ones who could be here were.

I cleared my head with a short prayer and began. The words on my tongue were brought up from the depths of my heart.

"Good evening, I'm here to present another member of the All Time Sports Team. I've listened respectfully to the previous honorees and I am in awe of the achievements they've reached on the fields, courts, diamonds, as well as their following years of service. I have the honor of speaking for an athlete who excelled, a woman whose deeds on the lacrosse field will be hard to duplicate. An athlete who was taken from us too soon, lost in a plane crash. Andi excelled in life as well as on the field. Many of you know how rapidly she rose in her chosen occupation of finances. It is safe to say she made millions for her clients.

"How like her to use her vacation time to help children. On a fateful Christian mission, while delivering aid in South America, her plane crashed. Ten good souls were extinguished. One, a soul like no other, left us before she had a chance to give the world the fullness of her miraculous abilities.

"Here at Spotswood we lost our shooting star."

A collective and audible sigh came from the Little Sisters when Kate mentioned Andi's nickname.

"She was taken from us and I must tell you that standing here is the hardest thing I have ever done."

Tears welled up. When her eyes began to mist she stood straighter. She had given her word to her friend. She had lost their last bet. "We are all sisters and brothers on the earth. We are bound together by the past and the road that lies before us. The light of Andi Castaldo, the exploits of her athleticism, is a beacon for everyone. Andi's spirit helps the coming passage through the darkness.

"This tribute is for you Andi, the best of the Little Sisters of War. Your body may be at rest, but your heart will run forever.

"The game of lacrosse is a gift from the Creator. In the centuries the game has been played, there are a few who were given gifts beyond all others. Andi Castaldo owned the gift...she plays on in our memory, the tallest Star."

- ☼ -

Later on, Taylor and Kate walked along the sidewalk, still lined by the oaks of Spotswood. They walked toward the dorms. They walked toward old memories.

"You were better than good, girlfriend. I never saw you break once."

"Thanks, T. I wish Andi could have been here to hear it. She'd be betting how long I'd go before I made a mistake."

"Y'all were fine. You said some powerful things. I never imagined I'd hear words like that from either of us."

"Life's like that. I never thought I'd say, 'Don't wipe your waffle on the kitty, but my little Madeline changed that assumption."

"She's the spitting image of you, Kater."

Kate took a deep breath of night air, and thought about what they had accomplished since their days of youth. But tonight, in the presence of the brooding mountains of the Shenandoah Valley, everything seemed insignificant.

She knew the pain she felt tonight about Andi's loss would also continue to dull with time. Kate called on the memory of her grandmother, and Coach Von Mater, and knew the pain would always remain. Healing never stopped but it diminished. Kate would always be joined together with them, and her teammates, all Spotswood Stars.

It was good to know this part of her passage finally came to a close. Then again, until the day she died, there would always be the specter of a cold winter blast of southern wind coming up the valley. Of the things she knew for sure, these thoughts never left her.

"T, I'm glad we were together in this story and what I know for sure is that the final chapters will be better each coming year."

Taylor reached over to touch her arm. "Kater, listen."

High above the Blue Ridge Mountains the evening mist parted. The moonlight illuminated the campus below, nestled in the comforting arms of the Shenandoah Valley. While two friends chatted about their future and walked beneath the canopy of oak, the great-grandson of the 'Dead Mockingbird' of Wilson Hall began a nighttime song. His sound ran through the brick canyons of the campus, echoing among the buildings. He sang with the joy of a bird who knew he commanded the center of this small universe. In the mystery of the surrounding ridges, the song sounded like... "Well played. Well played. Well played—Little Sisters!"

End

WOMEN'S LACROSSE: ROSTER/SCHEDULE

Spotswood College
100 Oak St.
Crucible, Virginia 22800

Spotswood College...   Stars Roster

No.	Name	Position/Year	Hometown/ HS
1	Kelly Watson	Off / Fr.	Marlton, NJ/Cherokee
4	Brooke Gipson	Def / Fr.	Cullowhee, NC/St. Paul's
6	Paige Mullen	Off / So	Boiling Springs, PA/ Riley
8	Stacey Carter	Def / So.	Emporia, VA/Jefferson
9	Traci Kubek	Off / Jr.	Arnold, MD/Magothy
10	Allison Scaglioti	Def / So.	Seaford, DE/Seaford
13	Marisol Flores	Mid / Fr.	Gundy, VA/Lee
15	Gabrielle Zary	Off / Jr.	Columbia, MD/Centennial
21	Jacq Patton	Off / Jr.	Glen Head, NY/Northern
22	Jen King	Def / Jr.	Ayett, VA/First Colonial
23	Courtney Zuck	Mid / So.	Reston, VA/Bishop
24	Catrina Birdsong	Off / Fr.	Wye Mills, MD/ Queens
25	*Taylor Braun	Def / Sr.	Mt. Solon, VA/Buffalo Gap
26	*Andrea Castaldo	Off / Jr.	Annapolis, MD/St. Anne's
28	*Kate Holland	Off / Sr.	Severn, MD/Friendship
30	Ginni Wojtowicz	Def / Jr.	Steelmantown, NJ/Ocean City
33	Penelope Preston	Goal / Sr.	Lutherville, MD/Heritage

88 Martianne Bouralis Goal / Fr. Los Olivos, CA/A.J. Dunn

* Indicates Captain

Head coach: Tess Burke. Asst. coach: Ariel Altman

Women's Lacrosse Schedule

MARCH

05	Wed.	Lee University* (Patriots)
08	Sat.	Timonium University (Racers)
11	Tue.	Sweet Water College (Foxes)
13	Thu.	Mount Shiloh College (Eagles)
18	Tue.	J and H University * (Colonials)
20	Thu.	Skyline University (Hornets)
24	Mon.	Tappahannock College * (Clippers)
26	Wed.	Appomattox College (Tribe)

APRIL

02	Wed.	Clifton Forge College* (Bulldogs)
05	Sat.	Calvert College (Cardinal)
08	Tue.	Stone Gap College* (Rattlers)
11	Fri.	Alamance Creek College * (Regulators)
12	Sat.	Friends University (Quakers)

16	Wed.	Fredricksburg College* (Falcons)
18	Fri.	L'Enfant University (Engineers)
22	Tue.	MVVC Tournament
25-26	Fri/Sat.	MVVC Tournament

MAY

| 03 | Sat. | NCAA Tournament |

Home games in bold / * Denotes Middle Virginia Valley Conference game

Team Prospects: Coach Burke begins her first year in the MVVC. She led the Stars to a 6 and 12 record in her inaugural field hockey season. The Lady

Stars are an experienced team, bringing back 9 starters and look to improve over last year's 8 – 8 record. Led by Andi Castaldo on offense and Taylor Braun on defense, the Spotswood Team will have high expectations. Four year starter Kate Holland and Junior Jen King add experience. Newcomers Kelly Watson, Brooke Gipson, Catrina Birdsong, and Marisol Flores, will contribute. Senior, Penelope Preston handles goal.

CPSIA information can be obtained at www.ICGtesting.com
Printed in the USA
LVOW072028030113

314253LV00023B/584/P